SCARLET SORROW

A TRIED AND TRUE NOVEL

BOOK ONE

CHARLI RAHE

TRIED AND TRUE PUBLISHING

First paperback edition January 2023
First hardcover edition January 2023

Cover Art by Miblart
Chapter Art by Etheric Designs
Edited by Genevieve Lerner

ISBN (ebook) 978-1-958055-00-7

ISBN (paperback) 978-1-958055-01-4

ISBN (hardcover) 978-1-958055-02-1

✾ Created with Vellum

I wouldn't have published if it weren't for the K&Q crew. My sister was first to sketch the MCs and discuss the vision of Tidings with me. To all my first readers who spent their time deep diving into my imagination, I am so grateful to you. A special thanks to the McGowens for letting me pepper them with questions; I hope to pass it on one day. When I think of books, I think of my Saltmates who always attend conventions with me and share my love of spicy books. To my kids, I will always write children into my books and multiple pregnancies as often as possible because of you.

Finally, for my husband, who will undoubtedly be embarrassed when his family reads the series.

I love you.

NOTE FROM THE AUTHOR

Scarlet's fantastical story follows a woman's journey through her magical heritage in which she encounters several dark scenarios. It is not intended for readers under 18 years of age and includes adult content.

While I'd prefer you to experience it as you go, your mental health matters. Please refer to www.charlirahe.com for a detailed list of possible triggers.

TIDINGS

ELIVAGAR

ANGUHLAN

LITR

REGN

ROT

VAR

LYCANS

NATT

BJORN

CRATMODE

VETR

SVELL

GLITR

KALLA

MINTAUR

SNJAR

KALDR

JOTNAR

GONS

STRAUMR

MOSSUR

TOWN CENTER

TOKER

TIO

HVALL

JARN

VALKYRIES

LLA

PROLOGUE

W ren's giggling turned into a squeal as Lark and Hawk burst through the bushes.

"Faster!" Sparrow shouted; her smile almost as bright as Wren's.

Sparrow's ankle caught Wren's, and they both yelped as they tumbled over the sunburnt leaves, tangling in their long brunette hair and heavy dresses until they rolled to a stop on the gentle slope. They breathed heavily, trying to catch their breath while laughing.

"Caught!" Hawk shouted as he sprung into their line of sight.

Sparrow raised her arms, wriggling her fingers so Hawk would pull her up. He lifted her in one swift movement so she was caught in his arm before she could run away. Her laughing tapered off as she ran her fingertips through his dark hair and leaned in for a kiss.

When Hawk shut his eyes to claim his prize, she jerked free and ran towards the castle looming in the distance. Hawk feigned a groan but couldn't hide his smile as he turned to catch her once again.

Lark gave Wren a slow grin as she reached a hand up so he could help her. Instead, he plopped down beside her, so their heads touched as they gazed at the darkening sky. Lark threaded his strong fingers through hers and she fought off a blush.

Any girl would kill to be in her position.

"Do you think your father will take Hawk to the Dagr palace soon to betroth them before she is with child?"

The leaves crunched as he angled his head to look at her. Wren made a face and shifted to meet his eyes.

"They are not doing *that* yet." She wrinkled her nose.

Lark chuckled and shifted on his side. Wren preferred not to have his intense grey gaze capture hers. It was hard to break that gaze until he let you loose. There wasn't a girl in Mabon who didn't have a crush on Lark Haust. As her Hawk's best friend, he was always around, and Wren liked to think herself accustomed to his good looks and calm manner.

"We are fifteen-year-old future Guardians. My sister has fallen for the illustrious Regn, and so our parents have carted her off. What do you think

Hawk and Sparrow do once he catches her out of our line of sight?" Lark teased.

Wren's fair skin reddened, and she glanced away from his full, soft-looking lips. "Kiss?" She didn't mean to make it sound like a question. "Who are you doing *that* with then if we're at that age?"

He shrugged as he spun a golden leaf between his fingers. "No one. I plan to wait until marriage."

Wren scowled at him and shoved his chest with her free hand, and he chuckled.

"You are making fun of me."

"I am not. I have not so much as kissed a girl. The timing never seems right, and who would I do it with? A Natt?" He scoffed and watched the leaf's lazy descent to her mauve taffeta dress.

She narrowed her dark eyes at him. "Everyone knows the Natts are *the* most beautiful women. Their tempers are their downfall, but worth it for their beauty...so I have heard."

"A little temper is good, shows spirit—but all the looks in Tidings do not make up for being heartless. *That* is the Natt downfall."

slid into her hair. Wren's hands reached for balance and landed on his chest as his lips parted hers. She could feel his heart racing where her fingers rested. His tongue slid into her mouth, and she slid her own to meet it.

His weight urged her to the ground. She swallowed a soft, mortifying moan. Lark's fingers curled in her hair as their lips met in deep kisses. Then his body was on her—he was a half foot taller than she was already and she felt small beneath him.

Wren thought her own heart would beat clear out of her chest. It was exhilarating and her body felt more alive and aware of itself than ever...yet foggy and confused.

Lark was panting. His kisses involved his entire body and Wren did what she swore she wouldn't do. Her breaths came quick through parted lips as he kissed over her throat. Leaves crunched and her dress rustled when he settled between her legs.

The line between friends and lovers blurred as he kissed along her neckline. Wren's own hands held fast to his silken hair, bringing his mouth back up to hers. She slid her hands down his flexing back to untuck his shirt and run her fingers over his skin.

His back arched as she lightly scratched it, and he breathed roughly in her ear. "By the Mother, Wren." He groaned and Wren felt a sensation deep inside her she'd never felt before but recognized as *need*.

Lark stiffened and his weight seemed to increase on top of her so she was soaking in the scent of sun crisped leaves and damp soil.

"Lark?" Wren asked, concerned that he'd stopped moving altogether and was looking away from her. "Are you hurt?"

He flung himself off her and curled in on himself, groaning. "Go, Wren. *Please*," he rasped. "Get my father, tell him where I am." He made a rough noise in his throat as she scrambled to her feet.

"I am sorry, Lark. Did I hurt you?" She reached for his back.

"Go!" he shouted, and Wren staggered back.

He'd never spoken like that to her before.

She picked up her skirts and ran as fast as her legs would carry her back to the Haust castle where she found her mother and father getting ready to call them in for dinner.

Flint steadied her shoulders and looked over her ragged appearance. "Wren, darling, did you lose a fight with a Leshy?" he teased.

She fought back tears. She didn't know why she should cry.

"I hurt Lark. He is asking for his father. He is on the other side of the hill, at the valley before the creek," she said, fisting her hands in her skirt.

Flint's silver hair caught the fading sun as he looked in the direction Wren had showed. "Do not worry, darling. He will be okay. Go inside and freshen up."

She nodded as her mother looped her arm through hers and they went inside, skirting the dining hall. Pearl brought her into one of the spare room's private bathrooms and dampened a towel before wiping it over Wren's reddened face.

"You and Lark? You were...kissing?" she asked with twinkling emerald eyes.

"We are friends, Mother. We have never kissed before and will never kiss again. He *yelled* at me," Wren told her, taking the towel from her hand and looking to the mirror.

Her face was red, lips swollen, and hair tangled and full of leaves. Odin's eye! Her father had seen her in such a state!

"An easy fix, darling," Pearl said, as she called to the air with a twirl of her finger to remove the leaves and then a bit of heat to curl her waves. "Get a little carried away with that kiss?" she asked, and Wren's face reddened.

"We did not mean to. I want to go home to Thrimilci far from this castle and Mabon. I cannot face him again today. I feel like a fool," Wren pouted.

"I do not expect we will see Lark for some time, my darling. Come. I will take you home and we will draw a bath. I imagine your brother will wander home when Sparrow must return home herself." She shook her head ruefully but smiled as she took her to the portal room.

Beltane in Ostara was Wren's favorite celebration. Better than the Midsummer Festival or even Yuletide. Sparrow and she had taken turns braiding floral crowns for one another, and now they giggled as they set them on one another's heads. Sparrow was in a buttercup yellow caftan while Wren had chosen an uncharacteristic white; she hoped it didn't wash her out with her fair skin.

It had been six months since her first kiss with Lark, and at sixteen years old, she reckoned it was time for another.

Lark and Hawk were going to meet them at the festival, so Wren had readied with the Dagrs. Sparrow's older sister Sea was being courted by Lark's older brother Peak. At only a year older, Sea seemed wiser by far. She had cut off her long dark curls and chosen the more feminine, softer look some Guardian women chose in Ostara as opposed to Sparrow and Wren's wild waves.

"Robin is back. Secretly married to a Regn, no less, with a toddling baby boy," Sparrow said, skipping along the glittering crushed stones.

"Do not gossip about others. You never know if you will find yourself in such a position," Sea chastised, and Sparrow's cheeks reddened.

"*Never*. I am the Maiden Fair," Wren said, twirling so her white dress fanned out around her, and older women smiled at her careless youth.

Sparrow giggled and even Sea cracked a smile of her full mouth. "Where is Hawk? It has been ages."

Wren knit her brows. "Who cares when there are all these new people about? I have never been to the Beltane festival alone before. I bet my parents are lurking behind the maypole!" She sprung with a growl at Sparrow, who playfully shoved her.

"Sweet Wren. I almost pity whoever steals your heart. I do not think you could ever give it twice. You are too romantic," Sea said wistfully.

"I see nothing wrong with that. I plan to only give it once myself." Lark appeared behind Sparrow and Sea, and Wren folded her arms over her chest with a sniff.

She and Lark had never spoken about that day in the woods. He never hinted at what went wrong and they were back to being friends. The only difference now was that he never touched her, not even to hold her hand as he had so many times before. She didn't miss the kissing, but she missed his companionship.

Sparrow immediately drifted to Hawk who held out a bright red flower he called a Middle Mist that Robin's new eighteen-year-old husband had stolen from his grandfather's private greenhouse for him just so he could give to Sparrow. She practically swooned.

That was when Wren glanced to Lark so they could share an exasperated look and found his dreamy grey eyes were staring fixedly at Sea who appeared to share his interest. Lark's eyes flared to an unnatural silver.

"Lark Haust," he said, introducing himself. "You must be Sea Dagr. My brother's description of you hardly does you justice. He has been detained, but please allow me to escort you until he arrives." Lark offered her his arm and Sea visibly shook herself before taking it.

Sparrow and Hawk looked from them to Wren and gave her apologetic smiles. Her brow furrowed. She could not discern why she felt so uncomfortable. Hurt, even.

"I believe I saw Robin down by the wand cart. I will catch up later," Wren told them.

"Stay, Wren. We can all have fun together," Hawk insisted, Sparrow nodding emphatically along.

She shook her head as she watched Lark and Sea strolling along together as if they'd been doing it for years. "I will never meet a husband for myself if I am always hanging out with you and your scoundrel friends. Let me be. I will see you later."

Wren stomped from the maypole and passed the wand cart. She hadn't seen Robin, but knew she had to sort out her unspeakable emotions before she could spend time with the lot of *them*.

After an hour of crushing flowers under her shoes, she reached an archway where purple and white flowers hung in strands above the path. She couldn't hear the music or the sounds of merriment from the festival. She had spent little time in Ostara; her parents weren't good friends with the Var like they were with the Haust and Dagr.

"Now I am lost. Brilliant," Wren growled, plopping down in the center of the path.

She heard giggling before a pudgy boy exploded from the shrubbery and tackled her backwards. She yelped as her toddling assailant tried to rub strawberry ice cream off his face and onto her white dress.

"You little snot!" she scolded.

"Jackal!" a man's shout rumbled forth as the boy was lifted off her.

"My dress! That little heathen sullied my dress."

Wren got to her feet as the floppy-haired boy kicked a grown man in the stomach, forcing him to drop him, and took off running. His little feet were a blur along the path.

The man straightened and Wren took a step back and dropped her glare. Taller than Lark and exceptionally broad, he had soft, powder blue eyes and corn silk hair that complemented his tan complexion.

"I am sorry. My brother... my mother dotes on him. He is spoiled rotten, as you now know." His voice was deep, guttural even, coming from his broad chest.

"Yes, well, perhaps next time he is around the general public you should leash him," Wren said, holding her skirts out to see if the boy had gotten strawberry anywhere other than her short sleeves.

"Allow me, please. It is the least I can do," the big man said as he approached.

Wren held her head high until he cupped her face in a big sturdy hand and rubbed a spot on her cheek with his thumb. She watched him out of the corner of his eye until he smiled brilliantly white teeth at her, forcing her to drop her eyes. He licked his thumb and aimed for her cheek again.

"What?" She yanked her chin away as he chuckled.

"I wanted to see what you looked like *if* you smiled. My apologies." He held his hands up in surrender.

"I smile often, thank you very much. Would you be so kind as to point the way back to the festival?" Wren asked.

He bent down, picked up her crown of flowers, and laid it back on her head. "You are not from Ostara. Even if you knew your way around, your hair is too dark, as are your eyes, and your skin too fair. I would say you are a Natt or a Geol, but I know their families and you are neither."

"You are easy enough. Blonde, tan, and roughly the size of a house; you are native here."

He chuckled again, infuriating Wren. "You have been to Beltane, yes? Why not spend your time doing something you have not done before? Ostara has the most beautiful gardens in all of Tidings. I know all the best ones." His blue eyes glittered when he looked at her.

Had any man's eyes glittered when directed at hers before? Wren pondered.

"I thought for a moment you were going to suggest something unsavory. I have been to Beltane and this year's is especially droll." She looked to her soiled sleeve. "Perhaps a pond or a stream first so I can wash my dress before the stain sets?"

His eyes widened, but he recovered and took her hand in his to lead her farther down the path. His callouses were more pronounced than Lark's. She asked him how old he was.

"Eighteen. Nineteen this year, and by next they will induct me into Valla U," he said. He looked much older than that, even for a Guardian.

They came to a hidden spring that flowed into a deep looking pond and Wren removed her dress. The man made a noise in his throat like he was choking and she shifted her head his way.

"You are going to undress right here in the open?" he asked, looking up to the clouds.

Wren's cheeks heated. She was a late bloomer and while she realized the last year had changed her so she had a woman's body, she had a hard time believing any man saw her as a woman when she still felt like a little girl.

"No one told you to look," she said haughtily as she let the thick belt fall to the moss-covered stones and unzipped the sides of her dress.

"Are you going to swim?" he asked. She noticed his eyes dart over to her while her arms were over her head trying to free herself of the dress.

Her voice came muffled. "I did not plan on it. Did you want to?"

Her dress was tugged gently free and she began to feel very vulnerable standing in her undergarments while the man held her dress and was fully clothed. He folded the dress, placed it next to the fallen belt and began disrobing himself.

"We can clean it later. I would like to swim." he told her.

Wren twisted her hands together, keenly aware that she was a girl by any standards, but her new blond friend was a grown man. Sculpted muscle covered his body that she had a hard time looking away from.

And then he was barefoot, and he hooked his thumbs in his undergarments and tugged them off.

Her face blushed furiously, and she wondered why she hadn't gone into the water sooner. He smiled up at her.

"The water is always just right in Ostara," he promised.

Such a bright smile on his chiseled face made him look like a younger man. She smiled back, and then he dove in.

She dipped a toe in, and he leapt up, grabbing her ankle, and pulled her under.

Wren spluttered as she surfaced, slapping the water at the great buffoon. "Are you purposely trying to drown me or is that an excuse to kiss me while I am being resuscitated?"

He floated closer until Wren's back was against the stone edge of the pond, the spring trickling next to her. "I do not need an excuse to kiss you, do I? A beautiful woman wandering around without an escort...stripping in the woods with a stranger." His lips pursed as if he was suppressing a smile and Wren realized he was teasing her.

"You are just as much a hellion as your brother. At least he makes no pretense of it. I—"

The man darted forward and pressed himself to Wren, claiming her mouth with his own. At first, she pushed against his hard chest, but then that feeling was back. That foreign *need*.

"Slow down," he whispered against her lips as she attempted to climb him.

Wren tried to do as he said and to meet his moves with her own, but she was far too eager to wait. She was afraid whatever she'd done to Lark would happen again to this man and she'd be the only maiden in Valla U.

He pulled away and Wren went after him until he stilled her with his hands.

"How old are you?" he asked, and she rolled her eyes.

"Sixteen," she told him and puckered her lips for another kiss.

He chuckled and she drew back to frown at him. "I am getting the sneaking suspicion that you have never done this before."

She swallowed and folded her arms. "No one is doing anything but talking."

"Very true," he said, smiling and running his hand over his handsome face. "Do you want to touch me, girl?"

Wren's cheeks heated. If he only knew how badly she wanted to.

"I only ask because I do not wish to take advantage. Sixteen is young."

She narrowed her eyes. "How old were you?"

"I am a man, it is different," he said dropping his voice.

"Hogwash. It is the same." Wren turned to dig her fingers into the moss at the edge of the pond and her toes found a crack between the stones to climb out.

Men all had double standards. Even Hawk was treating her differently. It was absolutely infuriating.

He floated over to the edge as she sat, content to scrub her dress clean and then leave him there and find her own way back.

"Come back in the water." His tone had dropped again but was no longer condescending.

Wren raised her head and noticed him noticing her. Her undergarments were soaked through. She nodded in understanding and then agreement, and gently placed her dress on the stone

He gripped her hips to help her in. Only...he held on, and instead of kissing her right away, he slowly began to remove her last articles of clothing.

CHAPTER 1

TIME AND TIME WAIT FOR NO MAN

The joke of a graduation ceremony had nearly wrapped up. I rose from my metal folding chair and crossed the gymnasium floor to accept my diploma from the dean on stage. I gave my family on the bleachers the obligatory smile and wave while stifling a yawn.

I didn't want to be bored *and* rude.

One or the other would do.

The university didn't bust out the big guns for mid-year graduations. Ours was deadly dull.

There were only twenty of us on the cold metal chairs that stuck to my thighs when I stood. We were just the students who didn't get all their credits to graduate last spring, and the overachievers, i.e., my cousin and me. Tawny had decorated my cap for me. It distracted her from the shoe drop I was still sulking over.

My life was supposed to be a coming-of-age story.

I'd mapped it out myself.

What it was was a *going* of age.

As in, *there go my hopes and dreams.*

The dean was speaking and while I was looking at him, I was not listening. Years of nonstop studying had *finally* paid off. My mom had pushed me to take Advanced Placement classes during high school, as well as extra courses during summer. While my friends had finished eighth grade to spend days lounging around the beach and maybe dating their first boyfriends, I was spending my first of many summers in classes so I could graduate high school early, only to push through college at an equally breakneck speed and get my bachelor's degree in English. Heavy on creative writing.

Scarlett Tio, author.

Gone.

There I was, a college graduate, creative writing major, and I did not know what I was going to do with myself. My only consolation prize for allowing my mother to push me was that my cousin was pushed right along with me. She also was my best friend. Tawny sat three seats to my left. My aunt and uncle were with my mother in the stands with Tawny's younger brother.

It's funny how in hindsight, our parents making us take all the extra classes made sense. They'd been been planning for us to move for years, but we'd only found out a few weeks ago. Graduate school...on their home island.

It pushed Tawny's teenage angst to the edge. After my initial blowup fueled by complete disbelief that my mom would uproot us and go to god only knew where, I'd been giving her the silent treatment. Seemed more adult-like to do.

I didn't care where we were going, or what we were going to do there. I had a life, here, friends...granted, I rarely saw them or went out because of my workload. Well, I *could* have friends if it wasn't for how busy I was all the time. After being the youngest people at our senior prom and barely old enough to have our driver's licenses when starting college, I felt entitled to a break.

Friendships, *gone.* Well, acquaintances were gone.

Our family had all but confessed that they'd been buying time until Tawny's little brother, Gypsum, had graduated from high school so we could return. He had been pushed too, but not nearly as hard. He'd graduated a week earlier—another midyear graduation, another yawn fest.

We were moving to Tidings.

Never heard of it.

I'd Googled the graduate school called Valla University and found one result that was under construction when I clicked on it. Tawny and I had thought about getting jobs and moving in together instead of going to wherever this Tidings place was, but life without our family was inconceivable. Where they were *was* home. We hadn't even stayed in dorm rooms while in college because our parents were emphatic about us sticking together, not to mention that our campus was literally down the street from our house.

Tawny leaned forward and gave me a wink of one of her wide hazel eyes. A fashion merchandising major, she was my go-to girl for all things clothing. There was quite the gaggle of Tawny worshippers since we entered college. She had lost her baby fat and was now a beautiful woman with long, wavy, dark brown locks with matching thick shapely brows and a fair heart-shaped face. She had never played sports with me, not being the "joining" type, but she never missed a game.

Just like that, the ceremony was over.

Another thing going, going, *gone*.

I wouldn't be throwing my cap in the air; the idea of only a handful of caps being thrown seemed completely ridiculous. I wouldn't be cheering for myself either, not like in the movies when the entire class did it together outside on a sunny spring day. It was two weeks before Christmas, and it was freezing out.

I stood up and turned towards Tawny. Some of the other over-achievers were hugging. I sidled past them and hoped no one singled me out.

Tawny caught me in a hug. She was nearly my height in her super-high heels.

"*Woo hoo!* Congrats!" she said in feigned celebration, her wide mouth spreading into a sardonic grin.

I twirled my finger in the air, fighting the sigh of defeat.

Any chance of shenanigans living on our own, figuring adulting out together, *gone*.

We could've found an apartment in Chicago and started our own lives, but neither of us were comfortable with the idea of our parents moving so far away. We'd always been together. Maybe I just wasn't ready to leave the nest and they had a graduate school I could take classes at closer to my interests.

Our families were making their way to us from the bleachers. It was a pitiful turnout, maybe thirty family members combined. I took my cap off and ran my fingers through my long caramel waves.

My mom smiled warmly as she made her way towards me. Long hair was the only feature we shared; she looked like my aunt's sister but in fact it was Tawny's dad who was her twin brother. Both women were dark of hair and eyes, not like me at all.

My uncle was the only man in my life. He was radiating happiness that was infecting everyone around him, and even *I* couldn't help but smile. My uncle had already gone grey, but there were still hints of dark brown mixed into his hair. My grandfather had gone prematurely grey, too, they'd told me. It suited him.

Hawk was what you'd call a silver fox.

He taught world history at our high school. Whenever I'd walked past his class, girls were always in a tizzy over him, but my uncle was oblivious. He couldn't comprehend girls having a "hot for teacher" thing for him. It was hilarious to me but infuriating for Tawny, which only increased my amusement.

He grabbed us both with a lean muscled arm and squeezed us to him. "I'm proud of you."

We both received kisses on our cheeks.

My mom moved in for a hug. She was teary-eyed as she handed me a bouquet with a big foil balloon bobbing above it. Tawny received an identical gift from Sparrow. I eased up on my mom for the moment.

She still hadn't let go of me. My mom was slightly shorter than I was, average height. She looked impeccable in her chic sweater dress. My mother wasn't one for much makeup. "A smile is the best makeup a girl can wear," she'd repeat from a line she heard elsewhere.

Sparrow saved me, giving me a hug and pulling my hair behind me, fidgeting with it. She looked a bit more controlled than my mom. She must have finished her crying before reaching us.

"You look beautiful, sweetheart. Are you hungry? We made reservations at Gale Street Inn in an hour." Sparrow smiled. It wasn't her usual smile that'd always been radiant and sassy like herself, but bittersweet.

"That'd be great, I'm starved." I hadn't eaten all day.

Truth be told, even though I hated the stupid little ceremony, it *was* a big deal. I was leaving behind my childhood—and with the move, everything I'd *ever* known, and nothing would ever be the same. It was such a monumental event in a person's life...and then it was over.

Gone.

My aunt and uncle looked like a pair out of a fashion magazine. Regular people didn't look like them, especially parents of teenagers. They didn't look a day past thirty.

My aunt managed an art gallery; all my mom's paintings were there. My mom's card said she was a website designer, but she was really an emotionally involved artist. She'd get all dark and brooding in her little painting shed (I would too since there isn't anything there aside from a space heater and a fan), come inside the house, and tell me, "Creativity is intelligence having fun."

That'd last a few days and then she'd return to her usual self. My mom was all round corners, soft...except her center. It was cold hard steel; no one could sway her once she'd decided on something.

I felt a crashing wave of embarrassment wash over me for having been difficult over the move. I should've cut my mom some slack. God only knew how she kept it together, because the one thing that hadn't changed was that my dad was *gone*.

Always had been.

"Congrats, ladies."

Gypsum was a heartbreaker with those big brown eyes of his and unassuming charm. He was okay with the move, not ecstatic, but not putting up a fight either. He was like that though, a go-with-the-flow kind of guy. Our tension easer, he had that effect between us and our moms, breaking the strain of finality the move had smothered over us.

He was seventeen and looked like he was twenty at the very least. Just good genes.

Gypsum had been an immediate hit with the girls at our high school. Baseball superstar, he was a state all-star every year. His long black hair was uncommon for boys, but he played it off well with his olive skin tone and dark winged eyebrows. It didn't hurt that he was apparently going to skip that whole awkward stage that most of us took forever to grow out of.

"Come here, chief. You sure clean up well."

I grabbed my would-be brother and gave him a side squeeze. It surprised me every time to realize he was taller than I was, as tall as Hawk.

He was wearing cologne. I wanted him to smell like dirt, sunshine, and the wind like he used to. My wild little chief. I ached for things to stay the same. I knew it was the move and finishing college that was prompting my sudden nostalgia.

"Scarlett's blood sugar is dropping. She's hugging everyone!" Gypsum teased in feigned panic.

I shoved him away and he chuckled before sliding his arm back around my shoulders. I was a hugger. We all were.

Tawny and I took off our black robes and folded them into our purses. We held our caps in our hands and walked arm in arm as Hawk ushered us out of the gymnasium.

Just like that, we were *gone*.

Goodbye, college. Hello, Tidings.

My mom slid into her old white hatchback. I turned the heat on even though it always made me sleepy.

My mom seemed happy, but there was an underlying uneasiness. It was hard for me to break out of my angst and cheer her up when I was irritated about the move. I debated shoving the blah-blue graduation gown under my heels as my mom drove.

You would think that at nineteen years old, I'd be all out of angst, but I'd been somehow stunted by not having experienced most of what I should've by the time I reached my twenties.

"I'm so proud of you, Scarlett. I know you don't want to talk about the move, but maybe we should since it's happening tomorrow." She was so hesitant, and I could tell she was bone-deep sad, even if she was proud.

"You're moving us out of the country to somewhere I've never even *heard* of. You know they aren't even online? I couldn't even get an address to give to my friends." She didn't give me a look reminding me that Tawny and Gyps were my only friends. "I'll be at the university full time, so I won't even care." I cared.

It hurt that I hadn't been included in planning all this. I was supposed to be an adult.

I didn't want to look at my mom who was trying to watch my face as she drove. It annoyed me beyond reason.

"You're going to like this new place. Tawny, Gypsum, Hawk, and Sparrow will live with us, *and* you and Tawny will bunk together at the university. We'll be less than five minutes away for visits. It'll be good, you're going to meet interesting people." She hesitated.

If by interesting people she meant that we'd be transported back to the dark ages where people didn't even have Wi-Fi or toothbrushes, then yeah, they'd be interesting alright.

"I doubt it." I scoffed. "Is the *village* so small there's not enough houses to go around?"

I crossed my arms over my plum sweater dress she'd helped me pick out, I had added a black belt to match my black wedge ankle boots.

Guilt always got the best of me; I couldn't help it. I enjoyed making other people happy.

"Not that I won't love bunking with Tawny," I muttered.

Until then, "I don't care" or "Whatever" were my typical responses.

"Scar, there's so much you don't know about this move. Where we're going, it's my home. We have family there you've never met. I've wanted to tell you about it for so long, but we couldn't go back until now. You, Tawny, and Gypsum weren't ready; now you are. It's beautiful, the place you'll call home is enormous. There'll be plenty of space for all of us."

She *was* excited. Positively glowing while she spoke, but still hesitant. I knew my mother; we didn't keep secrets from one another. She gave me a smile as she glanced my way and squeezed my leg. "You'll have email so your friends can contact you."

My mood lifted a touch. Only a mother could be deluded into thinking I had friends. "Did you sell the rest of the furniture?"

She'd been selling off odds and ends on online apps until last month and it became a free-for-all. She said the new place was furnished and there wouldn't be room for it. If the new place wasn't bad enough, then all new things would make it worse. Nothing from home would be there. My empty stomach knotted with nervousness.

"The Goodwill truck will come by before we set off to take what is left tomorrow. It's going to be a busy morning."

"Perfect."

I turned towards the passenger window, not wanting to glimpse my mom. It'd been tense for weeks. The one thing that made me not *hate* that we were going was the knowledge that I would finally see where my parents came from.

Parents.

Bile rose into my throat.

"Mom?" I turned towards her, gauging her reaction. "Is my dad there?"

Her face paled and she squeezed the steering wheel until her knuckles went white. She was struggling with something. "I haven't spoken to him since we moved. Why? Do you want to meet him?" It was her turn to watch my face react at the stoplight.

I never felt incomplete with my Uncle Hawk around, and I'd always thought the man who could leave my mother while pregnant and marry another woman was not someone I wanted in my life.

Naturally, I shrugged.

"You know, I've told you, he married someone else before you were born. Well, I know he has at least one son now who'd be your half-brother. I didn't tell you before because you didn't seem interested in knowing him."

It spilled out of her mouth like it had been pushing against her lips to escape.

My head swam. I had a brother. I *might* have a sister. I could see why my mom wouldn't tell me about my dad if I wasn't interested in hearing about him, but a brother was another case entirely.

I felt better. It made sense why she'd been so weird and why she thought I'd like it.

My mom pulled into the lot and found a parking spot in the back. Hawk was already parked a few spots down.

She unbuckled her seatbelt and faced me. "Scar, there will be a sundry of things in Tidings that will surprise you. I can only do my best to control the rate at which the surprises come. I thought about this, as you might imagine, and I think it's best for me to explain as it comes. Trying to explain beforehand might lead you to having me committed." She laughed as if that softened the bombshells she was dropping on me.

Sundry?

My mom rushed out of the car, leaving me stunned. Her perfume hung heavy after her. Roses and jasmine. Just like my mother herself: strong and sweet, glamorous and feminine. She opened the trunk and grabbed something out of it.

"Scar, you coming or what?"

Tawny gave me a flat look, knowing I'd likely folded under my mother's guilt. I was a sap. We were supposed to hold our "we hate the idea of moving" stance firm.

I got out and everyone walked towards the restaurant that boasted

Chicago's finest ribs. We were escorted to the second dining room where they'd pushed tables together to accommodate our group.

I was still shocked, but trying to focus to what was going on around me.

Tawny was nudging me with a menu. "Hello...?"
No one was paying attention to us looking over the menus and settling in.

I hung my coat on the back of my chair and whispered to Tawny, "Not now.

How do you feel about a slumber party?"
Tawny leaned in conspiratorially. "I think that's the plan. You and I share an inflatable mattress at our house, very fancy. Besides, Chuck invited me to his house later for a celebratory party." She was making fun of me, making shifty eyes and trying not to smile.
"You're such a fanny pack. *Fine.* But we need to talk and I don't want to get grounded for winter break."
"No problem. I'll handle it." She winked using her mouth dramatically.

My mom pulled gifts out from under her chair; they must have been what she had in the trunk. She had two large white gift boxes with smaller boxes on top, wrapped together with big glittery silver bows.
Hawk, Sparrow, and Wren beamed. Sparrow had a smaller white gift bow with a blue bow that she passed to Gypsum. I couldn't help feeling a brief flutter about getting a present; a good surprise would be welcomed.
"If you're trying to buy our forgiveness, these'd better be good."

Tawny was smiling while she said it, but there was a hint of truth in it. My mom passed them out.

"Thanks, Mom." I ran my fingers along the box trying not to be too obvious.

Anticipation was a drug.

I gripped one side of the ribbon and pulled until the bow came apart and I opened the big box.

Satisfaction? Also a drug.

I gasped. In the box is the most beautiful dress I'd ever seen in person. I only pulled it partway out of the box, not wanting it to touch the floor, or the table that hadn't been cleared.

The dress was made of layers of sheer aqua chiffon. The back was heavily beaded in silver and gold, tracing along a sheer panel. It had an empire waist, and the swirling beaded pattern went below the breast. Even its short sleeves were heavily beaded. It was exquisite; I couldn't wear the dress and *not* feel like a goddess.

I opened the smaller box, not taking a second to savor the moment. Patience was not one of my virtues. It was an aqua mask painted in the same pattern as the beads in gold and silver on the mask, with two jeweled flowers the size of plums along the right side of it.

I snapped out of my reverie. Tawny was positively glowing. She was in the same euphoric trance I was in. I glanced at her box and spotted a glittering midnight blue dress with a matching mask.

Gypsum had opened his box with much skepticism; in it was a sheet of paper with a picture printed on it.

"*Uh*, thanks, I guess. Cool printed picture of a sword." He looked a bit disappointed after Tawny and I had gushed our thanks.

Hawk cleared his throat. "It's a called a seax. A single-edged, fourteen-inch-long blade. There're centuries-old gold and silver hammered into the blade. And we couldn't very well bring a long sword into a restaurant, could we? It's a gift.

It used to be my father's. He'd want you to have it."

We rarely spoke about our grandfather. He'd died nearly two decades ago, right after I'd been born. Hawk's eyes brightened when he was speaking of the seax; I did not know my studious uncle was such a weapons aficionado.

"These dresses are beautiful, really. I don't want to sound ungrateful, but where are we supposed to wear them?"

I really appreciated the dresses, but it was feeling like a sore reminder that we didn't have social lives.

"We wanted it to be a surprise. We know it's been incredibly hard on you guys with the move and school and all. *But*, the days before school starts are a time of celebration in Tidings. There are always two big celebrations. One is a masquerade during Yuletide. The other is just before you start school, which is a large banquet that everyone is invited to. Those are your dresses for the masquerade." Sparrow's dark eyes were glinting, darting from Tawny to me.

Finally, something I could *really* get excited about.

"Why didn't I get a costume?" Gypsum asked, starting to get a wee bit pouty.

"Your first masquerade will be your first year at the university, and that's when you'll get your invite. There's a gathering where we'll be living, the kids will be there and some of the local adults. Everyone is invited to the feast before Valla U starts, so you'll be coming to that with us."

Hawk was a man I'd always known, but when he spoke about going back and the celebrations, the air seemed to crackle around him he was so full of energy—he seemed like a different person.

Tawny looked around at the parents. "One of the other graduates invited us over to a get-together at his house tonight. I was hoping Scar and I could stop over for a little bit. It's only a few blocks from home."

Tawny spat it all out before anyone could object, giving her best *please Daddy?* face. Hawk would do anything for her, it was Sparrow who she'd have to convince. My mom would get swept along; she rarely kept me from doing things Sparrow would let Tawny do. Basically, I had three parents.

One look at Sparrow's indulgent expression and I knew we were going out.

I checked my teeth in the passenger mirror, hoping the spinach from dinner wasn't in them.

My cheeks were flushed; I was riding high after the dress and the promise of celebrations when we reach our new home. I took out my Stila Sugar Plum lip gloss.

I was tired of being upset. I felt like the move could be a good thing. A clean slate.

My mom looked tired, which wasn't surprising—all those emotions were exhausting. "Just remember not to come back too late, we have a long day tomorrow."

"I know, we won't. I think Tawny wants to blow off some steam. I want to celebrate a little more. It feels weird to not be a student anymore, like, suddenly

I'm an adult."

My mom laughed, and it was a warm feminine sound even though it was at my expense. "I think *that* might take a bit more growing up, but you've taken a big step today. Are you feeling better? You're talking to me again, and nicely."

"I am sorry. I had made plans in my head and none of them are going to happen. A different adventure, right?" I flexed my fingers and ran them along my thighs, mentally erasing my previous frustrations.

Mom was trying to glimpse my face, probably trying to detect if I meant what I was saying.

"We're going to drive to Colt State Park in Rhode Island. There's a way to get to Tidings from there. I'm glad we've reconciled...*but* before this whole thing is over, you might find yourself more angry, or frustrated...upset. I don't know. But I love you. If I could change the way things have happened, I would. I did what I thought was right at the time and just...please remember that I love you." She was rambling, and I thought I could see tears threatening to overflow in her eyes.

I reached for her hand. I'd been such a sugar foot. Of course I knew she loved me. Some days it felt like I was all she loved in the world. It put a lot pressure on a girl.

"I'll focus on Valla U and you on your art. I have Tawny there. It'll be just like here."

She wiped her eyes with a quick hand. "I hope you still feel that way when we get there."

Sparrow waved to my mom as she walked through the yard to the house.

I'd borrowed clothes from Tawny and get ready there before we headed out. I followed Tawny upstairs, digesting everything my mom had said.

I carefully closed the door behind me so we can start getting ready to head back out, it was already late. "Tawny…"

She was already elbow deep in a box of clothes.

I hated the little reminders that we were leaving even if I wasn't upset about moving anymore. Tawny's once colorful room was stripped, walls bare, bed dismantled, dresser sold off. A sad-looking inflatable mattress sat in the middle of the room unmade, her comforter and pillows tossed on top of it.

Our last night in Chicago; we were going to make it count.

"Do you have something for me to wear? I didn't want to waste time at my house, it's depressing seeing the culmination of my worldly possessions in two sad boxes. I see they sold off your furniture."

Not even a mirror to do our makeup in.

I plopped down on the mattress and stretched my long legs. If I shut my eyes, I would sleep.. I laid back, my golden hair fanning out like a halo. I wanted to tell

Tawny how weird my mom was being, but short of "my mom says she loves me no matter what forever and always," what could I say? It wasn't really what she said, but how she said it.

What did she mean by doing what was right and not hurting me intentionally? I would not tell Tawny; she wouldn't be able to decipher my mom's guarded words any better than I could.

"Sure, dig in." A lazy smile played on her lips as she pointed to boxes she was digging through.

I sighed and scooted to the edge of the bed and dug through it alongside her. She was still wearing her clothes from our graduation. A silky blush and black bow shirt and a black leather flounce skirt, totally chic. I could never in a million years wear leather. I didn't think I had the right attitude for it. But Tawny looked like she'd just stepped off a Vogue photo shoot.

I'd never been jealous of Tawny; if she had something I'd wanted too, I'd be glad she got to have it. The cattiness that some girls developed in high school was a stage we'd never gone through. We were our own clique. Even though we were friendly, girls didn't really like us. It probably had to do with that whole being-comfortable-in-our-own-skin thing. If I was *really* being honest with myself, I knew it was because most of their crushes had, at some point, been crushing on Tawny.

She dug out two long-sleeve shirts in plum and teal. I grabbed the teal one as she handed me a denim skirt. It went well with my black boots and black chevron tights.

Tawny thought it'd be fun to do each other's makeup instead of using the vanity. It felt like we were little again, playing with our moms' cosmetics. It felt good to do something a little silly after the long day.

I trusted Tawny not to make me look like a clown; we knew what looked good on one another. Tawny knew just how to apply shadow to flatter my almond eyes because hers were just a little wider and under slightly thicker brows. It was about the only thing we had that made us look related. That, and our long wavy hair. I finished applying gloss to her wide mouth, and with a brushstroke along her slightly upturned nose, finished applying a little bronzer.

We strode past the inflatable beds Hawk, Sparrow, and Gypsum were huddled on in what once was the master bedroom. They were watching a movie on a laptop, killing time before bed.

"Thanks again for letting us go. We won't be back too late. Love you." Tawny kissed her mom and dad goodnight then tousled Gypsum's hair.

I leaned down and gave them all hugs. The benefit of being the cousin was that I could give Gypsum hugs without him mocking me...most of the time. He was barely two years younger than us, but it still didn't feel right bringing him to a house party.

"Be back soon."

I pulled down the hem of my skirt, self-conscious of how short Tawny's skirt was on me before we slipped on our coats and headed out the front door.

CHAPTER 2

 We rounded the back of the house where party was being held and headed into the basement. The kid who invited us held a bag of red cups and a jar full of singles. He admired Tawny appreciatively as I hung up our coats.

"Hey, Chuck. How's it going? We'll take two, thanks," Tawny purred.

"Sure thing, pretty lady. Party's just getting started." Chuck gave Tawny an impish smile and his eyes met mine. "Scar, Chris is here. He asked about you."

I groaned internally and my cheeks heated. My one big mistake had spread through our high school like wildfire, and I'd never lived it down. Thankfully, I had graduated early so I didn't have to see those people long after prom. My stomach twisted like a boy scout was using my intestines to practice knots.

His one-armed hug lasted a second too long. Tawny smiled and walked into the larger room of the basement. We spotted the keg in a partially rehabbed closet and started that way.

Music was beating through the speakers in the room to our left with multicolored laser lights pulsing through the dark. Flashes between people dancing shone with the strobe lights, and a state-of-the-art stereo system was hooked up to a laptop. We bypassed it to get beers.

The two keg tenders had big grins as we approached, cups raised, and my heart started beating in my ears.

Chris.

My big mistake was manning the keg with another guy with dark hair and a goatee who would've looked more at home at a bar instead of a basement kegger.

Chris was Chuck's cousin; I should've known he'd be there. His college was probably out for winter break, so he'd be lurking around the neighborhood for the next couple weeks. Moving out of the country seemed like a great idea right about now.

Goatee Guy smirked at Tawny, and she smirked back, but kept her eye on me. "*Wow.* You've grown up, sugar lips."

Sugar lips.

I resisted the urge to cover my mouth with a hand. I had finally filled out and my lips fit my face. Some guys liked full lips on a girl, but in high school they'd tease you about anything.

"Chris," I said without inflection.

I'd seen him at parties over the last few years since my fateful prom night, but we didn't have conversations. He had dated random girls since graduating and was now much too cool for an overachiever like me. I never had time to date anymore, that was a fact. Back in high school, we'd played sports so we were always passing on the field or in the gym—we were friends. When Chris had asked me to prom, I felt like I hit it big.

I took my cup after Goatee Guy filled it, turning my back to Chris. Tawny sipped from her cup and took a measure of the crowd.

Chris looked like a frat boy extraordinaire in his navy polo that showed the light blue shirt underneath and distressed jeans. His chestnut hair was tousled, his lips in that permanent smirk. *And* what was that sweatband about on his forearm?

"Thanks," I muttered before I walked with Tawny towards the dancing room, I could feel his eyes on me as I walked away.

"Save me a dance, sugar lips."

Determined to have fun, I ignored him.

The music was Billboard's top one hundred. Despite the catchy tunes, Tawny and I passed by the dancers and into the adjoining room where two tables were set up: one was a beer pong table and the other was a card table with folding chairs. We grabbed some seats and joined the game of Cards Against Humanity at the card table. We had little experience with drinking games, but seeing as it was our last night in Chicago, we were making exceptions.

Three hours later and approximately six red solo cups full apiece, we made our way on to the dance floor. Tawny's beer goggles were Coke bottle thick, and Goatee Guy had followed her into the gyrating throng. He was a bit more Tawny's type and from the way she was swaying her hips, he knew it.

The music washed over us, getting into our skin. There was an overt tension in the crowd comprised of one part sensuous rhythm, two parts liquid courage. Chris found me on the dance floor, and I made a beeline for the opposite side. He was an excellent dancer. I knew from personal experience, but I couldn't handle his familiar hands on me.

Chris was persistent as ever and he pulled me back onto the dance floor with that smirk of his. His dreamy, sky-blue eyes glittered as his hands rested on my hips, mine on his shoulders. His leg slid between mine and I rolled my body. One dance wouldn't kill me; maybe he'd leave me in peace after it was over.

Caught up in the seductive music, losing track of the time, I turned around and pressed my back into Chris's torso. I closed my eyes. My brain put up a sign that said, *Sorry we're closed,* and let my body take over.

It was hot and my skin was aware of every touch. Hormones were not my friend. Every pore was calling out for attention.

Chris had been our football captain his senior year, and since I'd played sports, I was always in the gym or on the field. We had been friends, or at least I thought we were. Falling back into old habits was easy. He'd never showed me much interest until my senior year when I had turned sixteen.

It did feel better to be friends again rather than avoiding him.

"Wanna go someplace quiet?" he asked.

I nodded gratefully. It didn't look like I was getting Tawny away anytime soon, and from the way she and Goatee Guy were grinding so close, there should've been sparks.

He led me into the larger room connected to the keg closet. He smiled at me again and pulled me in, shutting the door behind us.

A couple oversized couches and a flat screen were all that occupied it. I was surprised none of the happy couples in the game room/make-out room hadn't scoped it out.

We sat down on the couch and I sunk in. Lethargy swept over me and I realized I'd had a few cups too many. My mom would not approve. I vaguely wondered if Tawny was as drunk. I breathed deeply in the cooler room, willing my body to behave itself.

"You look so good. It's been a while."

Something in his tone made my red flags fly.

I scoffed. "As if you noticed."

He was pawing at me before I could lift my head, tongue thrust into my mouth before I could decide if I even wanted to be kissed. He tasted like the beer we'd been drinking all night. The smell of it assaulted my nostrils as he exhaled, and yet, something stirred in me. I felt charged, alive. Chris's too-eager hands were everywhere. My sluggish mind finally decided it wasn't the best idea and to get out.

I lifted my arms to push him away and his drunken body weight pressed me down until my back was against the couch cushion. I'd stopped kissing him back, but he was too intoxicated to notice.

"Slow down."

I was trying to hold his hands still. A streak of panic spiked through me. Chris's method of seduction was pushing with zero finesse. I promised myself the next time I would be madly in love the boy or wait until I was married.

"Chris," I said, pleading for him to listen.

His fingers were under my skirt and he groped clumsily at my underwear.

"Get off her, douche," Tawny said from beside the couch.

She grabbed my arm and pulled me sideways so I fell to the floor and out from under Chris.

"You're such a cockblock, Tawny," he slurred.

Chris used to be a nice guy. Not so much when he'd been drinking. Tawny pulled back her fist, but I caught her arm before she could punch him and dragged her out of the room.

"You should've let me punch him."

I stumbled but caught my balance. The world had picked up speed, spinning faster than normal.

"It wouldn't change anything. I would've handled it tonight, but thanks for helping me out. You're fiddlesticking awesome."

Tawny scoffed. I wanted her to slip in the snow.

My mom and I had always had an open dialogue about boys, but there wasn't anything to tell. She didn't know about Chris; I'd come home from prom and went straight to the shower. She had thought I was hungover, but I wouldn't let her check on me. I didn't want to be touched. Other than my family, I still didn't like to be touched.

"Don't you dare beat yourself up about this." Tawny threw her arm over me. "Did you at least enjoy it?"

"I wish he took it slower," I confessed.

Her long dark tresses were disheveled and there wasn't even a trace a gloss on her wide smirking mouth.

"What did *you* do?" I asked, giving her the stink eye, and she guffawed.

Laugh and the world laughed with you, weep and you wept alone. I wouldn't let Chris put me in a funk.

"I played a little baseball."

"Did he *slide* into home?" I teased.

"How do you make baseball sound so disgusting? But, *no*, he may or may not have rounded a few bases." She looked at me slyly.

I ran my fingers through my long hair and rubbed under my eyes in case my makeup was running. I straightened my skirt over my long legs. A wash of relief flooded over me; I was glad Tawny didn't take it further with Goatee Guy. She'd been more physical lately. A crimson winter rose in full bloom, sweet fragrance enticing. I'd always been more reserved than her. If I was being honest, I'd say I was terrified of spending my life alone like my mother. I'd say, if I had been in the same situation, I wouldn't be strong enough to do what she'd had to do.

I knew my mother still loved my father, and he broke her heart irreparably. I was much more careful with mine—at least I aspired to be. Girls with daddy issues went one of two ways, in my experience: 1) Compensated by dating boys by the bucketful, or 2) Clammed up, allowed no trust.

I was the latter. The only men I trusted were Hawk and Gypsum, and I didn't feel bad about that in the least. Guys like Chris proved my point time and time again.

We quietly snuck inside, afraid to wake anyone up. Tawny passed me a pair of magenta sweatpants and an oversized t-shirt that read Northeastern Illinois University from our college. I dug through a box and found a pair of brown fuzzy socks.

Crawling under the goose down comforter, I tucked an arm under my borrowed pillow. "My mom is being weird. Even weirder than she has been. I think they're hiding something. My gut's telling me there's a closet full of skeletons about to break through the door. I don't know what it could be."

"Scar, the definition of anxiety is panicking because there's something you think you won't be able to handle. Do you think that there's anything that your mom, my parents, or I wouldn't help you get through?"

The inflatable bed bounced as Tawny got in and I shook my head.

In the dark she must have sensed it. "Don't worry. This is exciting, it's a *good* thing. I know you think of Chicago as your home, but you can't tell me you ever really felt like you *belonged*. But you're right, there have been too many secrets. The good news is our questions are about to be answered."

"What if we only have more questions? I think that's what has been eating at me." A beam of moonlight rested over Tawny's face as I watched her.

"I'm too drunk to be having deep conversations." She poked my nose with an index finger and rolled over.

She was asleep in seconds. It left me alone with my nagging questions, and a sluggish mind unable to break any of them down. Resigned, I fell asleep too.

I was walking through carnage. I felt her, heard her, but I couldn't see her. She told me I could fix this. I tried not to look at the bodies, the battleground alongside a castle. Not everyone was dead. Frozen angry faces stared up at angry faces on the castle. I couldn't tell if the faces were human. They all looked like monsters to me. The wind was whipping at me. I looked up at the sky, even the sky was angry. Black clouds, lightening without rain. She was all around me. "You are night."

I stood in the middle of a circle, people around the edges. A man lay in the center, blood pooling around his body. Light and gushing wind blasted from my body—my hair, my hands all shot straight up. My mouth opened in a silent scream.

My heart was pounding, I didn't jackknife out of bed like in the movies. I lay there, hands on my borrowed NEIU T-shirt over my heart, its beats pulsing against my palms.

Tawny stirred; eyes still closed. "Nightmare?"

My breath slowed to a normal pace. My heart felt more like a human's rather than a rabid squirrel's. "Yes. I still can't see her."

I'd been having the same nightmare for as long as I could remember. It never changed, except that now I recognized myself in the dream. When I was little, I didn't realize I was the woman even though I'd always *been* her. My mom knew about the dreams; she'd always held me and told me I was safe, that there was nothing that needed fixing.

I wanted to believe her, but I knew something was wrong. Either with me or whatever needed fixing. But like all nightmares, when I woke up, it faded into the recesses of my mind.

I sat up, finger combing my hair that had tangled while sleeping. I felt disgusting. With the late-night party and nightmare, my stomach was a gurgling wreck.

"I'm gonna hop in the shower. I can't get my head on straight."

I didn't have any toiletries, but I needed to wash away the nightmare, not to mention last night's booze breath.

There was no curtain on the shower, so I ran a bath. I soaked my whole body in water so hot I could barely stand it. I purged of all my icky feelings, the weight lifting off my shoulders, which was good since now I had to deal with the move.

The not-so-dreaded-anymore move.

Tawny wasn't in her room after my bath. There was a pile of clothes my mother must have brought over in the otherwise completely empty room. Now *that* was depressing: Tawny's bedroom from *forever* completely and totally empty.

I piled my wet hair on top of my head, pulled on the blush-colored crewneck fitted sweater and leggings, sucked it up, and headed downstairs.

Everyone was running around; the Goodwill truck had just pulled up and their helpers were dragging the last of the large items onto the lift. I looked out the front door and saw my Uncle Hawk completing the sale of his and my mom's cars. Our rental car already sat at the curb. Little panicky butterflies beat their wings in my stomach.

In the kitchen, my mom, Sparrow, Gypsum, and Tawny were leaning against the counters eating breakfast off paper plates. Sparrow and my mom had similar styles. Both had dark hair center-parted, so long it reached their elbows. Tawny's hair was wet too, piled on top of her head like mine. She looked worse for wear, but comfortable in her grey and black notched baseball tee and black leggings.

"We've got eggs and bacon. Last batch before Goodwill takes off with our pots and pans." Gypsum joked.

I was pretty sure Gypsum was a model in a past life and it somehow trickled into this one.

No seventeen-year-old boy should be so confident. He had that indescribable quality, like he was invincible, and life was a glorious adventure that he was looking forward to experiencing. Optimistic. Gypsum was *optimistic*, what was with that? His look was effortless in his brown popover hoodie and slim-cut jeans, the slouchy beanie on his head. His long midnight hair shone glossier than mine on my best day.

"Morning, chief. Surprised you didn't eat it all."

My would-be brother smiled his dimpled grin. I wished I had his carefree attitude.

"Rough night?" My mom's big brown eyes looked me over as she ate.

"Nightmare. Nothing new."

If I hadn't been hoping they wouldn't question me about our party, I would've noted the fleeting glance my mom gave Sparrow.

Hawk walked into the kitchen. He always looked handsome. In passing, I wondered if he knew my dad.

"Good morning, girls. Did you have fun last night? Is everyone ready?" Dark, intelligent eyes gave us a once-over.

I hoped I looked as unabashed as Tawny. "It was great, Daddy. As ready as we're gonna be."

"Yup, Pops, ready," Gyps said between bites.

Our moms were nodding but looking a little distressed.

"What's next?" I chirped in.

I tossed my paper plate and plastic utensils in the garbage bag and tied it up. That was it. That was the last bit of *us* in the house.

"Gyps, run that out back would you, please?" Sparrow rubbed her hands together.

"I guess that's that, we're ready to go." My mom gave Sparrow's hand a squeeze and grabbed her coat and purse on the way out.

Sparrow put an arm around Gypsum and followed. Tawny and Hawk talked about the lengthy drive as their footsteps faded out the door. I lingered just a moment longer.

I stood in my cousins' empty house, having trouble believing that we were leaving. Walking around the rooms, I took all the memories with me. I stored them in my mental lockbox; it hurt a little. Squeezing my eyes shut, I accepted things were about to change, but I would make sure they were for the better. I stepped over the threshold and into the bright white of the day.

CHAPTER 3

Gypsum was nudging me. He had ruined a perfectly wonderful dream where Chris was a gentleman, and I was his willing participant in a bedroom scene fit for a fairytale. *Ugh*, he was saying something. What'd be nice was if he *wasn't*.

"Scar, move it. We're here."

"Where?" My eyes were trying to focus—they did *not* want to open.

I must have fallen asleep in an awkward position because my neck was incredibly sore. My eyes finally focused, and I was blocking Gyps and Tawny from getting out of the car.

"I don't know, I woke up when the car stopped. Everyone jumped out and then we woke you up. Come on, hustle." Gypsum nudged me again.

"I'm moving." My legs were stiff, and I groaned as I moved.

I slipped out the car door and did a few groggy stretches. I heard Tawny gasp and I popped up from touching my toes a little too fast and my head swam.

The floor was mirrored tiles, and it reflected the light from the ceiling. There were thousands of little blue lights in the cavernous room. That was why I didn't know where we were—it mimicked the night sky all around us. The effect was dazzling.

"I'll unload the car and bring it to the cache house." Hawk helped take out our few boxes and we jumped back in the car to grab our personal items.

We were so absorbed by the beauty of the room, groggy from just waking up, we at first didn't notice the woman who'd come up behind us. Her bright blue, floor-length dress was clasped by gold belts under her breasts and above them, the blue matched her intense eyes. Her chin-length hair was midnight black; a gold chain dangled a sun on the center of her forehead.

Her red lips formed a thin smile. "Welcome. I'm here to show you to your rooms. Would you like time to rest before your meal or would you like to eat first?" Her words were simple and somewhat clipped, all business.

"We'll eat after we freshen up, thank you," Sparrow said with a small smile.

Hawk gave her a quick kiss on her cheek and got back into the SUV. I gaped as a bright white light swallowed the SUV and Hawk disappeared. Huge double doors closed behind him, and I noticed they were mirrored with spokes radiating from a gold center circle with white ovals around each one. It looked like a blazing sun.

Gypsum's jaw dropped, "What in the world is that?"

"Portal doors. We are in the portal room—this is the only door to the portal in the palace. If you will please follow me."

Tawny gaped at me as I mouthed the word *"Palace?"*

The blue-clad woman turned in her very practical gold slippers and headed out another door at the opposite side of the room. The portal room wasn't as big as I initially thought: all the mirrors made it look enormous, but it was only a big empty room...except for a magical door.

Truth be told, I wrote off the magic door as bright sunlight reflecting off the snow, and since the room was dimly-lit in faux blue starlight, my brain accepted the reasoning.

When we walked out of the room, we were in a hallway. The woman glided to her right and continued down a second hall. We didn't follow —we were captivated by the dawn.

I breathed deep; it was the freshest breath of air I'd ever taken.

Along the entire left half of the hall were five-foot-wide arched, glassless windows at least three feet high; twisting mosaic glasswork wound up intersecting pillars in white, blue, and gold. But it was what was beyond the windows that really drew our attention. The sun was coming up over what looked like a desert.

The sky looked like it was on fire, burning red where it met the Earth. If this was even Earth. Directly below was a white city.

We were in a palace, a palace on top of a mountain. On the side of the mountain was a city, white with mosaic ramparts along the connecting walls, on glassless windows and blue roofs. It looked like there were shimmering white stoned roads, and greenery, probably cacti, behind mosaic plastered fences. I could hear the roar of water somewhere close, but I couldn't see it.

My mother had tears in her eyes. I'd never seen her so weepy before. "It's just as I remembered. As beautiful as a dream."

Sparrow stood to her other side clasping her hand. The two of them standing there like that struck a chord in me. It was like they'd never been happier than they were in this moment, as if they've just let out a collective breath they didn't know they had been holding.

I'd found my steel center and promised myself that no matter what I found out, I'd remember this moment and go to it during times of doubt. I *wanted* to be that happy forever. Surrounded by the people I loved, in the most beautiful place in the world. I thought it must be what heaven was like.

I rested my head on my mom's. Tawny tucked under Sparrow's arm and when Gyps tried to step in next to his mom, he was accosted with kisses.

If the woman was in a rush, she tolerated our glimpse into forever after well. My mom was the first one to pull away from the window and shifted towards her, and the woman turned around as if nothing had happened and continued down the hall.

When the woman said it was a palace, she wasn't joking; it *was* a palace.

Every single inch of the high arched ceilings was covered in geometrical pieces of mosaic in blue, gold, and white swirling and mandala patterns. I tried to wrap my head around how long it would take to complete something like it, but I couldn't. It was impossibly elegant.

We walked past others that appeared to be staff. Blue and white seemed to be the dress code for them, the women in flowing folds of dresses crossing at the back cinched by gold bands like our guide's. Men wore white pants tucked into brown suede boots that came to midway up their calves, and blue sleeveless linen tunics tucked into their pants with wide brown leather belts. They moved about as if it was part of a dance. Most had two bracelets and a necklace on, even the men.

After a few twists and turns while following the woman, and going up an enchanting staircase, we reached the level our bedrooms were on.

She stopped in front of an intricately carved door. "Tawny, this is your room, the next door down is yours, Scarlett. You have an adjoining bathroom. I shall return in an hour to help you find the breakfast table."

"I'll take my old room. Is it prepared?" My mom seemed to want to head out on her own.

"Hawk's old room is good for us too." Our guide nodded at Sparrow as if she expected it.

"They are both ready, and Gypsum's room is on the next floor." Gyps looked a little uncomfortable being on his own.

Our parents gave us a wave and headed down the hall. "See you girls at breakfast." My mom's eyes still looked watery, but now they looked like happy tears.

The guide stood with us a second longer. "Feel free to explore this wing, if you so choose. To find your own way to breakfast, go down two floors and head to the center, and there is an informal dining area there. Good day, ladies."

She gave us her thin smile and strode off, bright blue dress trailing behind her, Gypsum in tow.

Tawny stood at her door and I at mine. We smiled broadly and opened the doors.

It was like entering a Moroccan palace, but I was certain we were nowhere near Morocco. A royal blue and gold jacquard loveseat and matching chaise lounge were in the seating area directly in front of me. There was an octagonal table and an end table around the seats, resting atop a large blue and beige fringed rug. On both sides of the couches were doors; one was obviously a closet and the other led to the shared bathroom.

Through a gaping archway, intricate woodwork was displayed on the headboard of a huge canopy bed. Its bedspread matched the gold and royal blue of the couches. It was a bed fit for a queen—or five queens, it was enormous. I could roll over ten times and only *then* would I reach the edge. It was nothing like my old twin bed back home.

Back home. It felt like a punch to the gut. It was home now.

At the opposite wall were heavy jacquard drapes. I set my purse down on the chaise at the foot of the bed and pushed back the curtains. A beautiful little nook was nestled behind them. It had stained glass arched windows that went to the ceiling, ending at intricately carved knobs, and jacquard window seats circled around the nook. I peered out the window and finally saw the source of the rushing water noise. A waterfall dropped off directly behind it.

"There's a fiddlesticking waterfall!" Tawny yelled from her room.

I couldn't even see the bottom of the falls.

She came rushing in. "Your room is just as fabulous! Can you believe these fiddlesticking rooms? *AH!*"

Her squeal started me laughing.

"Are you secretly a princess?" I asked it jokingly, but Tawny's eyes widened in an *Aha!* moment. "Dude, we're not princesses. It was a joke."

I checked my cell phone...no service. I had a hard time imagining a cell tower there, or even a cell phone store. Something started nagging at me I couldn't put my finger on.

Tawny let her hair down and threw herself across my bed.

"Why not? Maybe that's why they've been so hush-hush. We're royalty, but they wanted us to grow up humble, so we had to live far away." She smiled brightly and rolled onto her back, finger combing her hair.

I took her lead and let down my hair too.

I plopped down beside her. "So, is Hawk the king? Or is grandma the queen? I just want to know what my number is in the line of succession."

Tawny shrugged and gazed about the white-walled room.

"What was with that door?" She slapped her hands palm down on the bed. "And the way people dress around here? I feel downright frumpy, and I'm never frumpy. They're all so elegant, kind of Middle Eastern, or Grecian...it's gorgeous.." I nodded.

I'd noticed as well. Any minute a sultan was going to come into the room and wonder what we were doing in his boudoir.

"Seeing this place makes me glad we didn't bring our old furniture or all our clothes. I wonder when they'll take us shopping. At least we have our dresses for the masquerade already," I said gleefully.

I couldn't wait to wear mine.

"I bet they were waiting until we finished school. My dad told me he went to the university when he was our age."

I rolled off the bed and onto my feet. "We should probably get ready. Do you want to wait until that woman comes back or head out on our own?"

"*Meh*. Let's see when we're done. If she's back, we'll go with her. If not, we explore."

After a nineteen-hour drive, I knew that if I lay down, I wouldn't get back up for hours. I arched an eyebrow at her. Her devilish grin made me a coconspirator.

"Not a single outlet." I walked around the opulent room with a straightener in my hand.

"I can't even find a light switch," Tawny said pointedly.

The sun had risen so we didn't *need* a light switch, but it was the principle.

"Something is screwy here—there aren't even candle holders. My phone has no service, I hadn't seen any televisions, or computers. It's the literal Dark Ages here." I sat down on the sapphire chaise and groaned in exasperation.

"We'll get ready without it for now, but there must be some explanation. Maybe they rehabbed this room and the contractor forgot to put in outlets?"

Tawny was grasping at straws. If there was one thing I knew about people, it was that with enough time, they could logically explain anything to their satisfaction.

"I don't think so, there's those metal plates where the switches should be. We'll ask at breakfast. We're due a ton of answers, how to turn on a light is the least of them."

I dug through my purse and pulled out my compact. I looked tired, my eyes were bloodshot, and my face was puffy. This was *not* how I wanted to meet my grandmother. Tawny had reached the same conclusion: we both looked like crap.

Someone knocked on Tawny's door, and we both ran into her room to see who it was. It couldn't be time for breakfast already.

Tawny swung open the bedroom door to reveal Hawk. He carried in a box of her things and another man carried in one behind him. They placed them next to an identical chaise to the one I had, except this one was silver and navy blue.

"How are you girls settling in? Someone will be by shortly with your boxes,

Scarlett."

"Thanks, we're good. It's amazing here. It's where you grew up?"

I couldn't pass up the opportunity to ask questions without my mom lurking nearby. I didn't think Hawk would tell me anything he thought would bother her anyway.

"Yes, and so did your mother. Although, that was very many years ago." Hawk got a faraway look on his handsome face, dark intelligent eyes staring past me.

"As in *here*? In this palace?" Hawk absently nodded.

"OH! How do you turn on the lights?" Tawny blurted.

I thought she startled Hawk; his stance changed faster than I could blink and then he gave out a loud guffaw. He pressed his hand to the metal plate by the door, and the lights came to life. I observed him and it looked like he sighed deeply with something long held back.

His eyes passed over me slowly and then Tawny, like he was searching our expressions. "The entire room is energized now, so all your electronics should work. Just remember to turn them off before you leave the room. You do not have to unplug anything here. See you girls at breakfast."

Hawk's figure retreated from the room before I could bombard him with more questions.

I heard Tawny squeal from the bathroom. "Cordless straighteners!" She stood in the doorway doing her hair.

Our escort wound up waiting fifteen minutes for us.

The bathroom was just as elaborate as the bedrooms. A huge

bathtub sat in the middle of the room, all done in pearl and iridescent tiles. It had two split sides so one person could sit facing the other in two separate baths. Two low tiled walls hid a huge shower. Water sprayed from every direction. There was even a waterfall of sorts at the entrance that fell across the low wall so no one could see you if you were showering past it. It was all controlled by some buttons outside the wall —ingenious, I thought. The opposite side was wall-to-wall mirror with double sinks trimmed in swirling champagne and silver tiles. It was modern compared to the rest of the palace.

I combed and curled my long light brown hair just enough to give it a beachy wave. I felt underdressed compared to everyone I'd seen so I put on a white maxi halter dress—it was as close as I was going to get to the local attire. Tawny's beautiful hair was also down, and she wore black plunging back maxi dress. I'd taken extra careful care with my makeup so my unique turquoise eyes were bright, and my lips pouty and pink. Tawny looked just as radiant with her red lip stain and long dark lashes.

If our guide thought we looked appropriately attired, she kept it to herself. The stoic escort led us down a couple flights of stairs and around some turns until we finally reached a dining area.

If this was the *informal* dining hall, I wondered if the formal one was made of solid gold. A high-domed ceiling curved with white beams trimmed in gold. It started out dark blue at the walls and faded to white at the peak of the dome, with elegant birds painted in the segments between the beams. The walls were predominantly white but had smaller subtler mosaic patterns in teals and blues.

The maharaja was going to ride in on an elephant at any second.

In the center of the room was a rectangular table that sat sixteen made of a delicately carved, light-colored wood, painted in golds and silvers. The chairs were the same type of wood and upholstered in heavy gold and silver embroidery on white fabric. Lanterns hung from the walls in copper, blues, and gold in with intricate metalwork framing the glass.

My mom sat to the right of the head of the table, and I noticed her eyes were red rimmed and puffy as if she'd been crying, but she looked happy. Hawk sat to the left and gave us a tight smile, as if he too was withholding powerful emotions. Sparrow sat next to him and Gypsum next to her. Tawny took the seat by her brother, and I by my mother. Before we could start exchanging pleasantries or figure out why everyone had been crying, the double doors in the back of the room opened.

A voluptuous woman who appeared to be in her fifties strode confidently into the room. It couldn't possibly be my grandmother, she was far too young. Her presence commanded attention, and her posture was that of a woman who knew her self-worth. Coppery brown curls brushed her shoulders, and she wore a floor-length dress in the same emerald green of her big, catlike eyes. Folds of fabric swished as she glided elegantly into the room. I felt like I should curtsey.

A few feet away from the table, she raised her arms, and Hawk and my mother flew into them. Everyone at the table was standing, even myself, even though I didn't remember moving. It left no doubt that this gorgeous woman was indeed my grandmother Pearl. I stood waiting to be summoned, wanting to run to her and seek her approval. But I was rooted. I couldn't process what they were saying as they embraced, and I just stood there dumbfounded.

Tawny drew my attention; she had glistening tears on her cheeks, and I realized I was crying too. I was overwhelmed with the joy my mother so obviously felt towards this woman. Gypsum's dark eyes were darting between the group hugging and his mom, trying to figure out what to do next.

My mom and Hawk fell to Pearl's sides and held out their arms, introducing us. Sparrow had reached Pearl and was whispering to her. Pearl drank us in and smiled, using a kerchief to wipe her happy tears away.

I went to my mother's side. Pearl and Sparrow had finished hugging and everyone's full attention was on us.

"Mother, this is Scarlett."

I was surprised they hadn't introduced us all at once, but I supposed she wanted to hug us each. Satin and lace clad arms enveloped me before I could say anything.

"My darling! I have seen your pictures for years." She tucked me under an arm and held out her free one for Tawny.

"Tawny, what a beautiful woman you have become. Gypsum, my grandson! I have never had the pleasure. Much like my husband, so handsome! The Mother has blessed this day."

She hugged us for quite a while, I hugged back and happy crying. I didn't think she wanted to let us go, and it felt good to be wanted and so loved.

I swore I recognized her scent; it was floral and musky at the same time. It didn't remind me of anyone else, but it was ridiculous to think that I could remember her smell from when I was just a baby. I inhaled it deeply before letting her go and returning to my seat next to my mother. She was smiling as brightly as I'd ever seen her.

The palace staff served a family-style breakfast, bringing in every type of early morning dish under the sun. We filled our bellies and told our grandmother about college and our old house until we finished our meal, then sat back to digest—and not just the food.

As things wound down, staff cleared the table and brought out tea. I knew tension was rippling through the room. I started shifting in my chair, thinking maybe I ate too much. That was entirely possible. More food than I'd ever seen had passed over the table.

I couldn't take my eyes off Pearl—she was enchanting. Her every movement was graceful. My mother had her same mannerisms. They didn't look alike though; my mother and Hawk must have looked like their father. They stood and we traded seats to be closer to Pearl.

"My darlings, it is good to have you back and to meet you Gypsum. Such a handsome young man. I know you have been besieged by new information, but I am afraid there is still much more to come. We realize you have had a long night; however, some truths are best heard from us.

Context matters." She took her time meeting at each of our gazes, a brilliant smile on her tanned face.

My mom held my hand, and Tawny held Sparrow's. Pearl held one of Gypsum's in both of hers.

"It is best to start from the beginning, yes?"

She patted Gypsum's hand and took a sip of her tea. "Thrimilci, this island, is one of five. There is also Elivagar, Mabon, Ostara, and Valla. You will learn all about them with time. Combined, they are Tidings. Tidings is inhabited by tribes and Guardians. I am a Guardian, as are Sparrow and Hawk. Wren will be soon enough, and with training, so will the three of you." Pearl made sure we were absorbing what she told us.

"Guardians can *call,* which means they have passed the challenges of Valla University. Right now, Tawny and Scarlett, you are considered tyros. Gypsum, you are a neophyte at the academy until the year you turn twenty and then you are inducted to Valla University. Darlings, what I am getting at is that everyone who lives here is a caretaker of nature. This is better shown than explained."

She smoothly glided across the room in a swirl of satin and lace to a large terracotta pot. She raised her hand, and from it light and water streamed. Out from the pot, a green sprout emerged, which wound up towards Pearl's hand and then divided into several curling stems. It covered the wall behind her, the tiny tendrils clinging to the mosaic tiles, and with a burst, blue morning glories blossomed right before our eyes.

Tawny and I jumped with the sudden burst of blue, Gypsum white knuckled the edge of the table. Pearl sashayed back and sat. She picked up one of Gypsum's hands and rubbed the top of it.

"Sorry, darling. I did not mean to surprise you. We can call nature's elements. Wind, water, light, lightning...Hawk explained to me he did this for you. Did you not realize what was happening?"

Sparrow and Wren simultaneously shot stink-eyes at Hawk, who gave a shrug. "The girls needed to do their hair." His dark eyes twinkled.

I knew he thought we were amusing, but did he think it was funny that we didn't question it?

Probably. Modern technology explained everything away for us.

Sparrow laughed at our perplexed expressions. "Pearl, nowadays there are rooms you can enter and speak a single command to get the lights to turn on, to light your fireplace for you, pretty much anything. I doubt the girls gave it a second thought."

How right she was. Tawny was dumbfounded. "I thought it was a fancy handprint recognition plate!"

"I knew that was a magic door! So do we know how to do that too?" Gypsum was pointing to the blue flowers that covered a good fourth of the wall.

The four of them relaxed at this, as if the hardest part was over so it seemed.

Hawk answered. "You'll need training. That's what the university is for, where Tawny and Scar are going this coming year. You can learn other things though, like how to use the seax I gave you. We have quite the trainer, I hear."

Hawk smiled over at Pearl, and I got the sense that they were learning each other again after all these years. Pearl gave a nod to Gypsum, a silent agreement to have someone train him. Gypsum couldn't possibly be more excited.

"You are at a disadvantage, most can *call* at an early age, so there will be much catching up to do. The university is not what the name implies—the true name is Valla University for Guardian Mastery. The year you turn twenty you are eligible to train. They teach you how to *call* energies, about the native tribes, and battle training, as well as the usual college curriculums of arithmetic, languages, et cetera. Hawk will supply his expertise in American history. We have never had such an expert; it will open a lot of doors for tyros who would like to venture out of Tidings." She smiled fondly at Hawk.

"I just want to sum this up while we're all here and save myself the headache later. So, we can summon energies..." I blinked at Pearl.

"*Call,* darling,"

I nodded. "*Call*...so those plates in our room, Hawk *called* something like electricity into the room?"

Hawk was like...a warlock? A wizard?

"It is a bit more complicated than that, but yes. We shall have someone help you girls get your rooms charged every day so it will not be a problem"

My mom was looking better by the minute. I didn't realize how much weight she'd been carrying around on her shoulders.

"We're going to this university that will teach us how to do that, and teach us how to battle? Battle what?"

Battle? I was a city girl! What would I be battling? The only thing I battled in Chicago was the summer months' humidity.

More answers, more questions. I knew it.

"Battle training is mandatory for the university. There are three types of physical training: weapons training, hand-to-hand combat, and strategy. You two will be at a disadvantage, having been raised outside of Tidings. You have received no previous training, so I can offer a sort of tutoring when not in classes. Gypsum will be ready when it is his time for the university, Sparrow and I will see to that," Hawk said, reassuring me.

"So...we're magic?" Gypsum asked warily. As if we were playing an elaborate prank on him.

Pearl pursed her lips and her gaze fell upon Hawk. "Magic is a term we do not use. We have gifts, and we *call* on them," she said with a kind smile.

"You are human, you just have a little extra gift. You do heal faster, and age slower. Once you are experienced, you will *call* to make yourself faster and stronger. You will understand once you start your training," Hawk declared, running his hand along his silver stubbled chin.

"None of this explains *whom* we'll have to fight."

The nagging in my stomach was back. I hated not having all the details.

The moment I said it, I felt insensitive. I didn't know why what I said was wrong, but there was a lot of fidgeting and watery eyes. I wanted to take it back, erase it.

"On our island there are three native tribes: the Wemic, Faunelle, and Merfolk. We occasionally have issue with the Merfolk, but we try to keep the peace. That is *this* island, you understand. Every island has different tribes. At times, we have problems with these tribes and fights have occurred. These tribesmen have skills of their own, so it makes sense to be prepared. Anywhere you have criminal types, there will be battles. We are not devoid of those characters ourselves, although we are all advocates for harmony, as our purpose in life is peace and balance."

What Pearl said resonated with me. It made sense, and I could see how it fit so well with my mom and the rest of the family.

"As Guardians, we are sent out to help nature maintain balance. We send our Guardians all over, try to encourage growth. Many are proven tried and true and go on out into the world and continue their education. Some even decide their efforts are most effective on the outside and stay there, coming back only for Yuletide and our Midsummer festivals." The vacant expression on our faces must have let her know we weren't following.

"Therefore, we decided to wait until you arrived to explain. It is very difficult to put it all into words at once without enough of a foundation of information. Do you have any questions? Maybe that will be easier."

Pearl had all the patience of a grandmother, but none of the looks. I guessed that whole aging slowly gift really worked.

Gypsum jumped all over the chance to ask a question. "How come you've never visited? It sounds like you've been getting letters from our parents, but they don't have so much as a single snapshot of you." Good question.

I was proud of my would-be brother for getting straight to the point. That little soon-to-be-a-man brain, figuring out the problem and fixing it.

I *felt* approval. I thought I was picking it up from Pearl.

"I think it is time for a story. Nineteen years ago, we were celebrating the induction of the new students at Yuletide. All the families were gathered at Valla University, watching the inducting ceremony of the new tyros, when a widespread attack was launched. Right there at the university. We don't typically bring weapons to the ceremonies so most only had *calling*. It was enough to stop the rogues, but not enough to stop the attack before several fatalities. The greater families are always near the stage, and the attackers sprang up from behind it and killed several family members, including our father."

"Greater families implies lesser." Tawny said pointedly.

Hawk drank from his goblet. His eyes had frosted over, completely unreadable.

"Greater families help govern. Lesser families aid in smaller ways." He took a deep breath and continued. "I was only twenty-three; Scarlett, you were only a few months old. We all sat there at the front when the Red Kings attacked. The university was closed, and all communication between the islands was completely cut off except for the Valla town portal, but only a few families even had access to that. The Red Kings are from Elivagar, so there was a great deal of finger pointing and blame. Wren took Scarlett and we took Tawny to the Chicago. We believed we were safer there; we could not risk contact if someone was looking for you. We sent them letters every week, so they knew how we fared."

I gaped. All these years, I'd had no idea. Not even the faintest glimmer.

"It was especially hard when Gypsum was born," Pearl said. "It was hard the entire time, but knowing that a member of our family was born outside of Tidings and that years would pass before we would meet was almost too much." Gypsum's eyes were glistening when I glanced to him.

"The university reopened two years ago. We made contact and planned for your return. There was no explanation for the assault. It was believed for quite some time that it was to cover up a few specific assassinations. So, we divided." Pearl continued.

"We kept our distance for everyone's safety. We believe the worst of the threat is behind us and so we could all return." Hawk ran his hand over his silver hair and didn't look to be comfortable with his assessment.

I *felt* appreciation.

We survived an attack that killed my grandfather, and we ran in fear for our lives. They divided us and sent us away. The nagging in my stomach didn't give way completely.

We were all silent for a few moments, absorbing another round of new information. Funny thing was, the whole *calling* energies bit didn't surprise me. It was a lot to deal with, but I'd explained away suspicious things in my past It felt like I found a flashlight in the dark. Sure tons was still hidden but I had the right tools to find the answer. Or even knew enough to ask the question. I was done for the day. I needed rest.

My body was weary and my brain was crammed with answers I'd only been partially prepared for. Selfishly, I'd completely overlooked the fact that my mother and Hawk were there when their father was killed in front of them. Not by some disaster, but by another person. I wanted to ask what happened to the Red Kings—surely they couldn't defeat them all, if they were so fearsome but it felt horribly inappropriate to ask and I'd already put my foot in my mouth once.

"I think that might be enough for today, yes?"

The three of us nodded at Pearl. Her eyes were dry; I suspected she was all cried out about her husband long ago.

"Excellent. On a lighter subject, today is the first day of Yuletide. Tonight is the masquerade in Valla. Gypsum, there is a celebration on the island for people not invited to the masquerade. By the by, mistletoes do require kisses here just like where you are from. Plan your paths accordingly." Pearl's emerald cat eyes twinkled.

The idea of celebrating with us all for the first time must have lifted her spirits, and she was smiling again. "I should warn you: your parents are familiar that the drinking age begins at your eighteenth year. Not your birthday, mind you, but the year you turn eighteen, which means for the three of you it is entirely within our customs. I would suggest taking it easy since you are not accustomed to our drinks and have not imbibed in excess—I am assuming of course." She gave us a wickedly mischievous smile.

She checked a clock on the wall. "You should get some rest, mull over the new information. We shall offer more answers tomorrow. Tonight we feast and dance, for several reasons. I have arranged for someone to come to your rooms to help you prepare and lead you back for our trip to Valla. A late lunch will be brought to your room." She got up and kissed each one of us on the top of our heads and walked out through the double doors, her dress trailing behind her on the tiles.

I pushed my chair back and stood, Tawny with me.

"We'll join you girls."

Our mothers led the way out of the room, and it was only then that I noticed they were both wearing the Grecian-styled dresses.

My mother was in plum, and Sparrow in wine colors. They looked magnificent; this place was really their home. I wondered if I'd ever fit in. Gypsum sat with Hawk, probably going into more detail of the night's event for Gyps. *Or* more details about everything. I thought they'd given us the gist at breakfast but didn't want to scare us with a ton of new stuff. We'd been through so much in the last twenty-four hours already.

One question nagged at me: why would we have been in danger?

Our mothers chatted us up about the bedrooms, making small talk. The four of us walked, arms linked up, to our rooms. We passed more glassless windows, through which we could see the waterfall and the rainbow its mist created. It spanned as far as the eye could see. We'd been transported through time into a fairytale.

I stopped at the wall of windows. "It's breathtaking."

My mom placed her slim elbows down on the windowsill, while Tawny and Sparrow shared their own window. "I get why you brought us back."

I could see now that the waterfall emptied into a river that appeared to meet into an ocean.

"The Merfolk live that way. We'll show you around the island eventually; we have all the time in the world now. We've finally come home."

My mom ushered me along to my room and followed in after. Tawny and Sparrow came in just after her.

I changed into a tank top and pajama pants; it was taking all my effort to stay awake sitting on the massive bed. Tawny changed and lay on her stomach next to me, while our moms sat propped up by the pillows at the headboard.

"How are you girls doing?"

Sparrow's wine-colored dress spilled over the side of the bed, her dark eyes red and tired. My mom looked exhausted too. It was more than physically, I knew, considering everything we found out today.

"Tired. It was a lot to take in. I'm sorry, Mom, about what happened."

I couldn't meet her eyes. The burden she had to bear alone was unimaginable. It made me hate my father—that he could marry someone else, that he wasn't there for her when she needed him the most.

She waved dismissively, but she swallowed hard. "It was a long time ago. You two hearing it for the first time though, you're alright?"

"Yeah, we're good, I think." Tawny looked at me and I nodded.

"If you want us to elaborate on anything, just let us know. We weren't sure if you were comfortable asking the grandma you just met more questions."

"Is there something to the names? Our names?" No one could deny that "Hawk" and "Gypsum" weren't-run-of-the-mill names.

My mother smiled. "On winter solstice, the council announces the theme for that year. The children are usually named according to the theme, although you may choose not to. Each child gets his or her own *Ausa Vatni,* or baptismal of sorts, where their parents announce their name. For example, this year's theme is elements, so you can expect a great deal of 'Coppers' and 'Cobalts' at the university in nineteen years."

"I think it's a safe bet that color was the theme for our year." I flashed Tawny a sarcastic smile.

"Baptismal?" Tawny asked.

As far as we knew, we weren't a part of any religion.

"It's more spiritual than religious. We worship the land. Mother Nature if you need a name," Sparrow offered.

"Hippies," Tawny snorted.

Sparrow leveled her eyes at Tawny, but let it go. If Pearl was a hippie, then I was three-headed dragon. *Sugarfoot!* Were there really dragons? I added that one to the list of questions. Double sugarfoot! They said *Merfolk,* didn't they?

Mom and Sparrow glanced at each other and Sparrow cleared her throat. "I know we've been through *that* talk before, but here is differ-ent. It's a lot freer and easier here. We just want to let you know before you head to the masquerade, in case you should see something."

Tawny and I made faces at them, my compounding list temporarily forgotten.

"I don't want you to get the wrong idea: people don't get divorced here. They marry young, have children young, and are very peaceful. *But* there is a lot of love to go around. People are...very affectionate, even in public."

My mom was smiling. She didn't look older than early thirties, but when she smiled, especially when saying something horrendously awkward like she was now, she could be in her twenties.

"What we're trying to get at is that young people don't put much emotion into being physical. Marriages are usually arranged while you're at the university, and you marry when you're finished. Before you are engaged, many younger people are more physical than they are outside of Tidings, that's all." Sparrow huffed out a breath, looking irri-tated with herself that she couldn't just spit it out.

"Kids like to fool around. *Check.*"

Tawny was delighting in her mom's awkwardness. I wanted to curl under a rock and die.

"I just don't want you gawking or getting swept up in some boy." Sparrow got off the bed, her long dark hair swinging around her back.

I pulled a pillow over my face so she couldn't hear me laughing or or see me blushing. Tawny shoved me with a foot and my mom and Sparrow laughed. "You two better get some sleep. These feasts tend to go until the wee hours of the morning." My mom kissed the top of my head and exited the room with Sparrow.

"Mom?" I called at the last second.

"Yes, Scarlett?" Her wide mouth spread into a smile at the carved wooden door.

"Are there really Merfolk? Like mermaids?" I asked a with a grin.

"What do you think?" she said as she closed the door.

That was a big yes.

Tawny and I crawled under the royal blue satin comforter of the massive bed and fell asleep dreaming of exotic mermaid islands.

CHAPTER 4

Vaguely, I heard someone knocking. The bed was way too comfortable. The knocking continued. I was pretty sure if I yelled *"Come in!"* they would, but that'd be rude.

I stretched my long limbs. Rubbing my face, I noticed my nails needed a serious manicure. I swore I'd had one before graduation. I gave Tawny a shove, she moaned and pulled a fluffy pillow over her head.

"Five more minutes."

"The hairdressers are here. Get up. I'm going to let them in."

I lumbered over to the beautifully carved door that seemed a million miles away and swung it open. Three women were standing there in white flowing dresses with gold, empire waist belts and draped sleeves that come from their backs and attached to their forearms by gold bands. Two blondes and a busty brunette sauntered in with rolling cases behind them.

"Hi, I'm Scarlett, please come in."

Tawny made an appearance, sitting down on the chaise lounge.

"Hi. Tawny. Pleased to meet you." She yawned drowsily.

I *felt* interest and skepticism.

"I am Cricket, this is my sister Katydid, and"—the blonde named Cricket pointed to the brunette—"this is Bronze. We are here to help you get ready for the masquerade, and any service you may need, we are here to provide. Do you wish to shower first?"

I hadn't been to very many salons, but if Cricket and her troop were working at a salon in Chicago, I'd be willing to bet it'd be on the Magnificent Mile. These women were professionals. I was a little intimidated by them.

"Yes. Sorry we're not ready for you."

I hated when people had to wait for me, but I was pretty sure it made me more uncomfortable than they even cared.

"Dibs on the bath!" Tawny strode off towards the modern bathroom.

"Is there any prep I need to do to make your job easier?" I asked, trying to make up for wasting their time.

"Yes, please do not shave."

"Anything?"

"Not a hair."

"*Um*, okay."

I went into the bathroom after Tawny and found a robe waiting for me. One side of the double tub was half-filled.

"Hey, they said not to waste time shaving." I widened my eyes in not-so-mock terror.

"*Man*, I could really use a beauty day. This is just the ticket. I wonder what the hairstyles are like here."

"Judging from what we've seen, I'd say pretty much the same as always for us. I feel like a scumbag for making them wait like this."

Tawny murmured her agreement as I walked into the waterfall shower. It was amazing.

Ten minutes later, they had us sitting in the chairs in front of the bathroom mirror, drilling us on how we usually wore our hair, what color makeup we liked to wear, what colors our dresses were, and more. After the interrogation, Bronze the busty brunette started incinerating our body hair.

She opened the robes we were wearing and slowly zapped the hairs out of existence. I nearly jumped out of my seat. She said she could *call* the tiniest most precise light that would be just as effective as the laser treatments we had back home.

Awesome. More of that, please.

While my body hair was disappearing, Katydid was using gale force winds to blow my hair dry. It all took about ten minutes. Cricket had done the same for Tawny and was now using air to lift her hair and heat to give it a wave. It was even more amazing than Pearl growing those blue morning glories.

Bronze then started doing our makeup. Since my masquerade dress was aqua, she went with a light gold blending into a dark aqua, highlighting my cheekbones and brow so much they shimmered. My eyelashes looked inches long when she was done curling and separating them, and she finished my look with a light pink lip gloss. That's when they gave me a much-needed manicure in light pink to match my lips.

Katydid helped me into my dress afterwards and finished my hair. I saw Tawny before I got to see myself. She had never looked more beautiful. They had given her a shimmering midnight blue smoky eye and nude lip gloss; her cheeks had a rosy blush and she had shimmering cheekbones. Her dress had a plunging neckline, its pleated skirt fit snuggly over her hips. In fact, it fit snug everywhere. Her fair skin highlighted in the dark dress, it looked creamy and soft to the touch.

"If I was a guy, I'd do you."

That was just about the best compliment I could give her judging by the way she beamed a smile at me. No blushing there, she knew she looked hot.

"You aren't so bad yourself." She waggled her eyebrows at me, and I quirked one of mine up with a lopsided smile and strode over in my gold, neck-breaking high heels.

We stood in the bathroom while the beauticians/magicians must have been *calling* air to clean up, because things were flying here and there. I faced the mirror, Tawny standing next to me. For a second, I tried to look around for myself. Like I wasn't the golden-brown haired woman staring back. I didn't even recognize myself. Those women were *good*. I wondered if they would take a tip—then I wondered if they even dealt in dollars.

They had accentuated my every attribute, my hair swept up very loose and romantic looking with big curls cascading down one side. The aqua colored dress my mother gave me had an empire waist with a beaded mock belt under my breasts. As I admired the intricate work, the dress billowed out, the folds of light fabric swirling out from my waist. I wondered what I did in a past life to deserve this; I felt like an enchantress.

Cricket, Katydid, and Bronze sat us back down and put our masks on, hiding the near invisible elastic of the masks in our hair.

"Thank you, so much. You guys are seriously amazing."

I kind of felt like an idiot by the way I gushed, but they really did an awesome job.

"We are happy to have helped. We can lead you to the dining area if you like.

Your family is ready and waiting."

Cricket was so professional, but something about her made me think she was honored to be doing it. Maybe my grandmother made her feel honored; I was certain it wasn't me or Tawny.

Tawny, who was currently checking out her behind in the mirror.

"Yeah, seriously. This is probably the best I've looked in my life. I'm going to have to get your numbers."

I felt their confusion immediately, then chimed in, "I'm sure Pearl knows how to get ahold of you ladies. We'd love for you to lead us to everyone, if you don't mind."

Cricket dismissed my worries with a gesture and the three filed out into the hall. We followed their procession without a word, just taking in the atmosphere which had subtly changed. There was a charge to the air, an excitement simmering. Some of the staff around the palace were dressed in equally amazing dresses, but none had their masks on as they hurried to finish whatever needed to be done before heading to the extravaganza.

We headed into the "informal" dining room, the ladies waving goodbye to us as they kept right on moving. The incandescent lighting was dim, but it was bright enough to see our moms, Hawk, and Pearl standing together talking in full regalia.

I knew after seeing my own reflection that they would also be dressed to the nines, but I wasn't sure *nines* summed up just how wonderful they looked. It could have been that I'd hardly ever seen them outside of jeans except for work, but they looked like royalty. Like they belonged in this magnificent palace. They looked as magical as I imagined they would, and better.

My mother had on a royal purple floor-length dress with a small train, which gathered above one thigh at a long gold leaf. Sparrow's olive green dress flowed to the floor, and big gold sequin rectangles crossing her torso pulled it snug against her middle.

Hawk had on a black satin suit jacket, a white under tunic, and a black lace ascot. His pants were also black and tucked into black boots that went up to his mid-calf. He was the only one wearing a mask: it was black and white and horned, and the sides came down to his jawline exposing only his mouth and chin. The black and white combination complemented his silver hair. I was stunned by my uncle's appearance; he looked dangerous. I'd never thought of him as a dangerous man in all my life. The dresses were amazing, granted, but my uncle looked like he was from another time.

I *felt* sadness, happiness, and excitement all at once.

Tawny's mouth had dropped; undoubtedly, she'd never seen her dad look like that. Parents should look noticeably older than their kids, otherwise was just weird.

Pearl's curvy shape was accentuated by the wide sash of her dusky blue dress. Folds of graceful chiffon floated around her. And *she* was supposed to be my grandmother. I hoped I would look that good when I was a grandma.

"Are we ready?" As giddy as a grandma could possibly be, I could *feel* her happiness.

Her family together again, as they should be.

She was hugging everyone, trying not to muss our outfits. She slid a dusky blue half-mask on with copper jeweled flowers. My mom slid hers down: it was purple with gold paisley painted on it, a large jewel in the spot that rested over the forehead like an amethyst eye. Sparrow's was also a half-mask of solid gold lace; it barely covered her face, but it was ridiculously intricate. I hoped I looked half as beautiful as I knew they did.

Hawk cleared his throat, probably to bring us all to attention. We'd been distracted while taking one another in. My mom didn't have to say anything; she squeezed my hand as she walked to me and turned to Hawk and gave a nod. I *felt* love, unabashed unconditional love. It warmed me to my core, and I tried not to let the water works run.

"Yes, we're ready." Hawk grabbed Sparrow's hand and offered the other to Tawny.

She looked much too big to be holding her dad's hand, but she didn't hesitate. Pearl walked out the double doors and back into the halls, us in her wake. Back through the mosaic filled walls of her sprawling palace, I was beginning to get the idea that gold and royal blue were kind of their *thing* around here. She led us through a door and I immediately recognized the blue faux starlight. We were back in the portal room.

"I want to explain how this works before we enter the masquerade, in case we become separated." Pearl gestured towards the door with an elegant arm. "It will take you to any other portal door if you only think of your destination as you open it. You only need an idea of where you wish to go," she explained.

"Why would we get separated?" Tawny asked out curiously, pushing a long loose strand of hair away from her mask.

"Just a precaution, but it's quite the party. There will be a lot of kids your age and you'd hardly want to stick with your old fart parents all night," Sparrow joked.

Pearl's eyes widened at the word *fart;* it was pretty funny, her calling herself a fart in her evening gown.

I stifled a giggle.

Tawny let out a loud guffaw. "I see your point. Cool, we'll be good."

"And don't forget about the drinking, girls. Here, you're adults. Most of the other women your age are already in arranged marriages and a bit more experienced than you two. I'm not trying to intimidate you, just prepare you. You're good girls, have fun, but keep those things in mind."

Hawk had his feet planted in his shiny leather boots. He meant business in a loving way.

I couldn't help but feel like he thought we would make ourselves look silly at some point, or do something stupid. I hoped we didn't.

We both nodded, somewhat dumbfounded at the repeated warnings. We'd never given them serious cause to be worried about us. We really were good girls, in every sense of the term.

I *felt* eagerness rippling from Tawny; if I didn't know any better I'd say she was planning to do the exact opposite of what her dad just warned her *not* to do. *But*, I did know her better, and maybe she wasn't *planning* to but she probably would anyway.

Pearl opened the door to the portal and the bright light blazed. She stepped through, her shape winking out the moment she reached it. Tawny and I made eye contact and sidled over to one another as Hawk and Sparrow glided through.

My mom came up behind us. "Have fun girls, you'll do great."

She stepped back so we had space to walk through the doorway together. I *felt* anxiety rolling off my mom like smoke, a suffocating black smoke that made my stomach knot like a rock.

What in the world was going on with that?

I looked behind me and she gave a brave face, but I was seeing right through it.

She was fall-down-fainting nervous about something, and I had no clue what. Oblivious, Tawny grabbed my hand and walked through.

It was another portal room. A long, yellowed stone wall full of arched wooden doors stretched behind us with women in gorgeous dresses and men in fitted pants and waistcoats and other period pieces of clothing, just like Hawk. It should have been illegal for so many beautiful people to gather in one place.

My mom came in right on our heels since we hadn't taken a single step–we were still holding hands directly in front of the door.

"Follow your grandmother."

I could see Pearl, Hawk, and Sparrow just ahead, nodding at other partygoers.

I started towards them, letting go of Tawny's hand, and the three of us made our way over.

There were so many different masks. People really got into it. I felt pretty good about my mask, the metallic aqua and jeweled flowers fit right in with what the girls my age were wearing. I also immediately decided that my dress was demure. Women wore dresses that were barely opaque. Others had strategically placed lace or sequins, or at least I thought they were sequins. I was starting to get the impression that these people didn't do imitation, and they very well could have been real gemstones covering the sheer dresses. I felt like I was surrounded by movie stars on a red carpet, complete sensory overload.

I vaguely felt myself guided along all the perfumed swirling dresses and around the elaborate masks. Men were predominantly in blacks, whites, golds, and silvers. Leather pants were a big hit, and aside from the men who looked on the other side of fifty, they were all insanely fit. I couldn't tear my eyes off them. The masks gave them an element of erotic mystery that was so foreign to me, I caught myself gawking; I was helpless to my own curiosity. There was a tall, dark-skinned man, probably gorgeous under his gold half-mask that had dark feathered wings stretching at least a foot above his head. A young, fair-skinned man dressed in all white, with white laced antlers attached to his half-mask above a soft pouty mouth, was getting a drink. I was suddenly happy my mother had picked out my outfit; there was no way I would've known what to wear.

Tawny was gawking just as much as I was, except she had the biggest, most ridiculous grin on her face. She was going to gorge herself on decadence. My slight influence over her would be temporarily out of order.

We followed Hawk, Sparrow, Pearl, and my mother into a cavernous room. Huge, tiered chandeliers hung from the high ceiling, and tiny mirrored pieces were nestled into the stone walls, reflecting the light from the chandeliers like starlight.

And I was back to feeling like I was a princess. The whole day had been something out of a fairytale. How my mom could've ever thought we wouldn't love this place was beyond me. I didn't know why we hadn't come sooner.

I sighed and tried to focus; my uncle was asking me something, but the ethereal music flowing through the room had me transfixed. I wanted to dance, I wanted to explore, I wanted to wander!

"Do you want to try some wassail? It's the traditional drink here, a kind of alcoholic punch. Just make sure you eat afterwards; it tends to be a bit strong." Hawk gave us a wink and I nodded, perhaps a little too enthusiastically.

I couldn't believe I'd be legally drinking with my mom at nineteen. I was on the fast-track to adulthood. Our parents had always trusted us implicitly, but this was letting us into their grown-up club.

Hawk brought over crystal goblets for us. The punch was warm with bits of fruit floating in it. It smelled delicious. Tawny beamed at me and raised her eyebrows.

"We haven't seen any of our friends for quite some time," said Hawk, "so we will see you girls around? Is that all right?"

Sparrow seemed nervous, but nothing like the waves of anxiety crashing into me from my mother. I kept mentally stamping them out with my own excitement, but it was suffocating.

"Of course. Do you want to meet at the portal at a designated time?"

I couldn't wait to break out on our own. Not that I didn't want to spend time with my newfound grandmother, but I learned better by observing.

"We could meet you back at Grandma Pearl's?" Tawny chirped in with a sly smile.

"Use your best judgement. I won't embarrass you with a kiss right now. I love you, and we'll see you in the morning." My mom squeezed my hand.

"Your extended family is here. I'm not sure what they have on to identify them, but they know you're here," Hawk said.

I *felt* a spike of nervousness.

We stood smiling, with the need to giggle excitedly creeping up in my belly after they left, having spotted people they knew.

I didn't even notice that Pearl hadn't moved; she was watching us. "You girls are more beautiful than a dream. Have fun tonight. I am so thankful you are finally here. It means so much to us. *All* of us." She hugged us both for the umpteenth time and sashayed away, dusky blue fabric swishing behind her.

"Pinch me," Tawny said. "I think I've died and gone to heaven. On second thought, don't pinch me. I don't want to wake up."

"It's surreal. It's like a small society of amazingly good-looking people. It shouldn't be legal." I took a sip of my wassail. "Wow, this stuff is dangerous."

"Mm-hmm. Better keep count of how many refills we get."

"Right." I nodded, watching a man in a crescent moon mask that was at least three feet long.

Some of the masks were creepy.

"What if we're fairies or something?" Tawny chuckled into her goblet.

I was going to have to count how many she had as well.

"Fairies are only a foot tall and look to be made of twigs and grass.

You ladies are *much* more lovely. My name is Ash, I do not believe I have ever had the pleasure."

A man wearing a black, brown, and gold fox mask with unnervingly tall ears had come up behind us. Even though the mask covered most of his face, I could tell he was the most handsome man I'd ever seen, much less spoken to. His skin was a creamy caramel, his big shining eyes a light, bright green. He had on black leather pants tucked into black boots with a gold crescent moon buckle, and a black satin jerkin with a gold ascot. His ornate bracers of black and gold caught the light as he extended a hand to each of us, kissing ours in turn.

"Sorry, we didn't know fairies were a real people."

I put that on the list of the millions of questions I still had for my mom. I blushed tomato red when he kissed my hand; his lips lingering sent my stomach whirling.

"I'm Scarlett, and this is my cousin, Tawny. Pleased to meet you." He released my hand leaving me just a little disappointed.

"It's our first day here...as in Valla, Thrimilci...with the Guardians. We're from Chicago."

Tawny's filter had broken and her thoughts were verbalized.

She didn't seem as taken with Ash as I was, even though he had the look that she normally went for. With his leather pants and short crew cut, it wouldn't hurt if he had some tattoos and possibly a motorcycle. Except I hadn't seen a single gas-powered vehicle since we arrived. I'd bet my grandma's palace they didn't have a single fuel *anything* here; it seemed against the whole Guardians of nature bit.

He simply smiled at Tawny's outburst. "Then I welcome you to Tidings. We have many new arrivals tonight. As this is the beginning of the new year, this is the new tyros' first Yuletide masquerade."

I couldn't get a feel for his emotions while he had a mask on. Being unable to read people's faces while we interacted with them was going to be difficult without having met any of them before. I still *felt* excitement mingled with disappointment wafting my way, but whether it was from Ash or not, I couldn't be certain. There were so many people milling about it could be coming from anywhere. If the disappointment was Ash's, I hoped it wasn't from our ignorance, or me.

"Yes, we were told that much. It's very beautiful, I've never seen anything like it. How will we be able to know who is a new tyro? "

Maybe he could point us towards others our own age.

His self-assured stance and beautiful face were intimidating. I figured he had to be in his mid-twenties, and he was tall, over six feet. Tawny was mostly paying attention, but her eyes were flitting around to all the gorgeous man meat in her periphery.

"I, myself, am a first year."

My heart stopped when he gave us a killer smile with his well-sculpted lips. Tawny couldn't resist his smile either, and gave him her best one in return.

"I would be happy to introduce you to a few fellow first years." He gave us each an elbow and we slid our arms through his.

It was then that I noticed a tall, black leather clad man leaning against a glittering pillar. There were so many people around that he wouldn't have drawn my eye, except that he was the only one perfectly still, staring directly at me. He didn't seem to care that I had caught him. He was gigantic, well over six feet, and muscular—if his arms were any indication. His exposed arms had black bracers on them, muscles roped around them, and he crossed them over his broad chest. Everything was leather on leather, even his antlered half-mask. He had glossy black hair in waves that fell past his strong bronze jaw and disappeared over his shoulders.

Ash was leading us away from the shadow man, and I remembered to breathe. I was being drawn *toward* him; walking away felt impossibly wrong. Ash must have noticed my distraction. I *felt* irritation, it made me glance up at Ash breaking the spell the shadow man had cast. His face was impassive. I checked for the man, but he was gone. My heart returned to its usual *THUMP thump* and we were led away.

We walked past the band playing the ethereal music. I didn't recognize a single instrument besides drum. They had started playing louder, and people were partnering up on the dance floor. I saw Sparrow, her long, dark hair loose over her halter dress, being swept onto the dance floor by Hawk, looking dapper. After decades, they were still so in love.

I searched for my mom through the masses but couldn't see her. I hoped she'd found someone to dance with besides Hawk. It dawned on me that my father could be here. I started searching the faces in the crowd in earnest, and soon realized how foolish the idea was. Not only had I never seen him, but everyone was wearing a mask. There was no way I'd recognize him without anyone helping me. I had to find my mom and ask her outright.

Ash tugged us along until we entered an adjoining room. He slid his arm out from Tawny's, pushed back feather-light red curtains that enclosed the room, and held them aside for her to pass.

Wall-to-wall draped fabric in oranges, reds and yellows surrounded the room. Pillows lined the walls and the low tables. People lounged about, splayed on the colorful pillows. Most still had their masks on, but I could tell they were the younger crowd. Ash explained that the room was specially set up for university tyros to socialize and escape their parents and provosts.

Ash led us in, and I could smell the flavored tobacco and saw the water pipes sitting on low tables, watched people passing hoses around, sucking out the flavors. I was surprised. I guessed I imagined them all as a bunch of tree huggers, planting flowers, singing kumbaya. These people had an air of wealth to them and seemed carefree. I tried to fit in the attack by the Red Kings my grandmother had told us about, but when I saw these nonchalant attitudes and aristocratic lifestyles, I couldn't put the pieces together. I knew there was much the story that they hadn't told me, but I couldn't justify it so far.

Some of the masked eyes lifted to ours as we passed through, but I was sure they were wondering who Ash was with, instead of who we were as individuals. It was clear that Ash was popular in that circle.

Tawny and I were catching some dirty looks from the glamorous gals leisurely sitting around the tables. Ash still had his arm hooked in mine while Tawny walked a step behind us, midnight blue glittering in the low lights. I felt a little weird, like he'd claimed me and was showing me off to the crowd. But that was ridiculous, he was way out of my league. I'd only seen men as good-looking as he was in calendars.

"This is Scarlett and Tawny. First years from the myopics." Ash gestured towards the piles of cushions nestled in the far back, around a table four girls and two guys sat around.

Myopics?

I wasn't going to ask with this group of people I'd never met staring at me like I was dirt under their feet. Myopic must have been a negative term. I frowned internally at Ash. Why bother being friendly if he was only going to insult us?

The man in all white with the lace antlers I'd seen when we arrived was sitting between a hazel-eyed brunette in a red, off-the-shoulder dress, and a bosomy blonde in turquoise. The blonde's mask was one of the most beautiful I'd seen all night: it was a gold, lacework butterfly half-mask. One half had an oversized wing, the other had a black wing painted over the gold mask, her green eyes sparkling through it.

It was rivaled only by the other blonde at the table whose mask was a light blue garden of beadwork, beaded flowers extending elegantly a few inches over the top of the mask. Her dress was tiered with ivory lace and light blue taffeta, the blue matching her eyes perfectly. The third man had a dark green half-mask made to look scaly, with gold fangs and gold rope trim. He had brown hair and eyes so blue they looked purple, and his dark green satin doublet was paired with a gold ascot and black leather pants. These guys liked their leather.

I wasn't complaining, but I thought only rockstars wore that type of stuff.

"Ladies, this is Novaculite, Quartzite, Indigo, Sage, and Sterling. The passed-out blonde is Jonquil." He gestured to the brunette, the bosomy blonde, the slight blonde, then the man in white and the snake-masked man.

I hadn't even noticed the blonde resting on cushions off the side of the table. She had short blonde hair, the sides shaved. Her skintight black dress left little to the imagination. Her mask had slid off at some point, and she was just as beautiful as the rest of them.

"Nova and Quartz are second years, but the rest of us will be first years." Ash gestured to the cushions for us to sit.

I sat next to Sterling in his green snake mask and Ash quickly slid next to me. His thigh overlapped mine; his touch warmed me, and I bit my lip trying not to blush. My aqua dress fanned out beneath me, and I tucked my legs under it. Tawny sat on the other side of Ash looking somewhat irritated not to be sitting next to me. To her right was the slim, blonde Indigo.

Indigo was the only girl at the table showing us any interest. Her open smile was a comfort from the disregard of the brunette Nova and the bosomy, blonde Quartz. "Nice to meet you." Indigo shook our hands, leaning over the table, as the other two rolled their eyes. "Sage is my brother." She pointed to the guy in white. "We're not twins or anything, like Nova and Quartz. I'm adopted."

She laughed warmly; she must explain that a lot. She passed Tawny the hose of the water pipe.

"It's blueberry," she whispered as she passed it to Tawny. "You don't have to inhale."

I liked Indigo immediately. I was still unsure about Ash; he seemed like one of those guys who got away with being rude because he was so good-looking.

"Where are you from?" Sage asked, not looking at anyone in particular.

His voice breezed out from his pouty mouth like silk.

"Chicago. You know a lot about the world outside of Tidings?" Tawny had put up her defenses as she pretended to take drags of the water pipe and passed it to Ash.

Nova snorted, tossing her long dark hair. "Not that it matters, but we are extensively trained and taught in all subjects. We *could* have all the same technology you have, but we choose to put nature's interests before our own." No friends made there.

Indigo saved us. "We have a technology room in Valla, with computers and cell phones and all that. We typically don't need any of it while we do our work. We're allowed to go to anywhere else there's a portal to see movies, or shop. Not that you'd want to wear the clothes here, but it's fun to shop."

Tawny nodded in agreement. I was glad we wouldn't be cut off from our world completely. I couldn't believe I didn't ask any of that already.

The passed-out blonde stirred. "*Ugh*, why *are* you talking so loudly?"

She sat up and opened her wide blue eyes, in sharp contrast to her bright red lips, which curled into a vulpine smile. "Who invited the myopics?"

Quartz tittered annoyingly. "Ash brought them over."

That seemed to wake her up. "Oh. How *hospitable* of you," she said, her sarcastic tone making me want to roll my eyes.

Ash narrowed his eyes and gave a tight smile. "Surprised to see you awake, Jonquil, maybe you should have another?"

He placed one hand on my thigh and leaned over the table to shove a plate of brown chopped mushrooms across to her. They must have been a drug, but since I'd never so much as taken a puff of pot, I couldn't be sure. I blushed at the familiarity Ash showed me.

It was Jonquil's turn to blush—well, it could have been blushing, or turning red with rage. "Play with your toy, Ash." She gave me a snarl of a smile, rose with catlike grace, and left the room.

After Jonquil left, things simmered down. Tawny even warmed up talking to Ash and Indigo. They told us Sterling, Novaculite, and Quartzite were siblings and cousins with Sage and Indigo. Ash had a younger sister who wasn't going to start at the university until next year that was betrothed to Sterling. Ash lived on Valla, the three siblings in Mabon, and Indigo and her brother lived in Ostara. I tried to keep up with all the information they fed me—I wanted to know what they were talking about eventually—but I could feel some of it seeping away.

We had our own punch bowl of wassail that Ash kept getting us rounds of drinks from, and I could feel a warm buzz under my skin. Ash had started running his fingers along my thigh, and I tried desperately not to squirm. I wasn't blind. He and the saucy blonde Jonquil were on the outs, but normally a couple. I didn't want to get in the middle.

Hated before I could even get to know anyone was not what I wanted. Ash kept smiling down at me, and it was hard not to smile back. Tawny looked to be having a good time, but I could tell she wanted to find a man of her own, the wassail giving her liquid courage to go exploring.

The only other table at the back of the room had a loud group, even though there were only four people sitting there. They kept laughing boisterously, two girls hanging on one of the guys. The guy had a short crew cut like Ash's, but blond. He had tanned skin and was athletically built. And of course, he was wearing black leather pants and a black tunic under a silver waistcoat, and ascot with a Batman half-mask. He was doing most of the talking, keeping the ladies laughing. The other man had a similar outfit, but with a deep blue waistcoat and ascot and a half-mask that was a sharp-horned dragon mask.

What was surprising was that the women both appeared to be sharing Batman. They had no need to either; they were both exquisitely beautiful. The girl on the left of Batman had long raven hair, porcelain skin, cobalt almond eyes, and a body to die for—which was obvious since her maroon dress only had sequins where it counted. The one to his right was mocha-skinned with dark hair and dark eyes, giving her an exotic look. Her black dress was only slightly less revealing than the other girl's.

Ash caught me looking over at the group and sighed. "My cousin," he said, nodding towards the mocha-skinned girl. He shook his head.

"I take it you don't approve? They seem happy." I wasn't defending them, just making an observation.

His eyes flashed and his hand stopped stroking my thigh, but he recovered. I couldn't figure him out. I was so flattered to be receiving his attention, and *yes*, he was extremely good-looking; I didn't want to scare him off.

"Never mind them." He started the stroking again.

Tawny leaned back from her spot to get a better look.

"Come on over, the more the merrier," Batman shouted over to her with a smug smile.

I hated men who knew they were good-looking, I could read Tawny's face. We were going over to the rowdy table.

"We should go introduce ourselves," Tawny said, but it was a demand.

Ash didn't seem to want to let me out of his sight and I became nervous that she'd leave me alone with the two witches and the guy I couldn't figure out if I liked or not. I didn't know if I could withstand his advances if he chose to push it. I didn't even know if I *didn't* want him to push it.

Ash looked to the entrance and sighed. A man passed by, and I caught a shock of white hair before he disappeared.

"Excuse me, I shall be back." Ash stood and exited the draped room abruptly after giving my thigh a squeeze.

Indigo smiled as we stood after him. There was no way we were staying with these other people.

"You must come back and visit again. It is so refreshing to meet new people." She nodded towards Nova and Quartz, and I stifled a laugh.

"We will," I whispered into her ear. Indigo smiled and kissed my cheek.

She whispered back, "I feel like I've met you before, it's the strangest feeling."

She gave Tawny a kiss and sat back down at the table with Sage, Sterling, and the twin girls. Their ability to ignore us completely for almost an hour was quite the skill. I hoped the university was big enough that we'd never have to interact with them again.

We walked over to Batman's table. Belatedly, I realized I'd not kept track of my drinks. Tawny was no steadier than me on her feet. The man in the blue dragon mask grabbed her elbow to balance her as she sat down next to him, across from Batman and his two ladies. I sat on the other side of blue dragon man.

Batman flipped up his mask. "Like it?" He held up the mask, then set it on the low table. "Pop culture, I love it. Can't get enough of it. I can quote almost any

American movie. It's my talent."

I almost shook my head when he winked. Batman was a beautiful man. Ridiculously so, and he knew it. He oozed confidence and sex appeal.

"I love movies." Batman was speaking my language.

"I've noticed most of the people here don't have an accent, why is that?"

I didn't know where the question came from, it was much more of a

Tawny question.

Batman and the babes chuckled. "We know a lot of languages, but we've settled on speaking English. Most of us, when we leave, stay in the U.S. We bring back the culture and it seeps in."

He had one arm around the mocha goddess and the other around Snow White. They thought everything he said was amazing. I checked on Tawny, surprised she hadn't had a bout of verbal diarrhea. Blue dragon mask had an arm around her shoulder and was leaning into her ear speaking in whispers. The sugarfoot-eating grin on her face told me she didn't need saving. He could've been Batman's twin, the only difference being a less-severe jaw and his blonde hair was a little longer.

So they were both gorgeous; it was starting to get ridiculous.

"I'm Jett. This is Amethyst and Cerise—everyone calls her Cherry." Jett gestured to the mocha goddess then to Snow White.

Cerise smiled broadly and shook my hand. "It's so nice to meet a girl without a man on her hands. You're not with Ash, are you?"

The way she said it made me blink at her. Was she coming on to me? I glanced back to Ash's table. Indigo and Sterling had left the girls with Sage; they sneered at Cerise—or Cherry, as she liked to be called—and went back to their hushed conversation. Amethyst inclined her head to me. There was something about her despite the giggling that suggested a certain pedigree.

They didn't offer blue dragon mask's name. He was occupied with Tawny. She flipped her hair and I knew she was totally into him as she laughed a little too loudly.

"I'm Scarlett, that's Tawny. We're new here," I said shyly, trying not to make a fool of myself.

The room was spinning.

Jett leaned forward, his light green-blue eyes dancing. "Pleasure to meet you both. I look forward to getting to know you better."

His voice was deep and held a hint of amusement. My guess was that it usually did and had nothing to do with me. I blinked at him. *He* wasn't coming on to me, but there was something in his tone I couldn't put my finger on that made me uncomfortable.

"*Um*, yeah. Me too," I stammered.

Tawny leaned past blue dragon mask guy, interrupting, "We're going to go dance and he's going to show me around."

She gave me a wink, and blue dragon mask had pulled his mask back down over his face and led her away. I smiled at her and gave a little wave. I was glad that she was having fun and had apparently made a studly friend.

The two beauties and Jett studied me as they talked about Valla University. Apparently, the mocha goddess was the Overseer's daughter, which would explain the posh attitude. The Overseer was also called the Prime and ran everything—the university, the Guardians—and she was his only daughter.

Jett was watching me with too much interest for me to be comfortable. I rose to my feet unsteadily, and Jett moved as if to help me. I gave him a small smile and he stood and hopped over the table. He was tall, over six feet, and powerfully built. I craned my neck back to look at him. He stood inches away from me and searched my eyes.

What did they feed these people?

He lifted my mask to my hairline and let his fingers trail down my face. His smile was bright and beautiful, and my pulse raced with the intimacy of his touch and total confusion.

"You're even more breathtaking in person," he whispered and pulled me into a tight embrace, smelling like sunshine and a woody amber musk.

What does one say to that? I hadn't been hit on much in my life, and unless I was reading him totally wrong, he looked at me like he'd just discovered Santa was real and coming twice this year, but not like I was his new toy.

"I'm going to pee," I said stupidly, and winced as he laughed loud and rich while releasing me.

"We'll see you around," Jett said, returning to his ladies who were giving me contemplative looks, but not a hint of jealousy.

I walked in my too-high gold heels from the water pipe room and headed down a random hall. I had no idea where I was going, but I really did have to use the ladies' room. There were little nooks where the doors were and endless stone halls, but I couldn't appreciate the beauty of it with everything going through my head.

I found myself in a long stone hallway—that looked like all the others—and heard a familiar voice arguing in hushed tones, and then a much deeper one. I stopped moving. I would've felt bad for eavesdropping, but I was drunk. I'd left my manners in the bottom of the wassail bowl.

"I do not know if it is safe for you. If she...if my uncle...I could not stand to lose you again, Little Bird." The guttural voice was tight, and then I heard the rustle of fabric.

"I can't hide any longer. It's not fair to Scarlett, not to know who she *is*. It'll be alright. You'll have to stay away. I can't risk them finding out yet. Wait until she's safe. I'll have to wait too."

"I do not know how long I can stay away. I thought you were dead, all these long years. That *they* were dead," the guttural voice said, and then he punched something hard. "Meet me at the pond. If not tonight, then soon. I will wait every night in the hope that you may come."

A sob was strangled by the sounds of kissing. "By the Mother, Tree. I have missed you. You don't know what it was like waiting each day wondering if you would find me. Hoping you would find us. Lark *died* so we could run. Ridge died so Sparrow and Tawny could survive."

I freaked out. "Mom!" I threw my hands over my mouth as soon as it came out.

"Scar?" My mom, her face flushed, came rushing out of a doorway nook.

I just stared back at her. A man came out of the nook, tall, blonde, and tan. His powder blue eyes took me in. He was the tallest man I'd ever seen and had the frame of a man who had a lot of muscle on him. I couldn't tell, though; he was head-to-toe black satin, and had a plain black half-mask pushed on top of his short blonde flat-top.

I could tell he wanted to say something, ask something, but my mom intervened, saying, " We'll discuss this later." I wasn't sure who she was talking to, but I chose that moment to run off.

My mom didn't bother calling after me; she knew it'd be pointless. I was trying not to cry and failing miserably. I couldn't tell exactly why I was crying, but I guessed it was the shock of seeing my mother with whom I was sure was my dad, or if not, then her lover, along with all the events of the day. Who were Lark and Ridge? I'd heard the pain in my mother's voice when she'd said Lark's name, as if it squeezed out involuntarily with an exhale.

More than I could handle, simple.

The bathroom was abandoned, thank goodness, because I already felt like a complete idiot going through a mini crisis in front of perfect strangers. I wondered where Tawny was—probably dancing the night away with blue dragon mask. I was happy for her.

In the stall, I dried my face after my bouts of crying and slid my mask over my eyes. I wanted nothing more than to go back to my grandmother's palace. I stood—and heard the bathroom door slam. I didn't know what made me pause, but I did, and peeked out into the powder room that led to the exit.

I covered my mouth and looked away as the red-clad woman laughed. I sat back down, pulled my feet up onto the toilet seat, and hoped I didn't slip into the toilet water. A low rumble of a man's voice came from the powder room and the woman laughed again.

Now I was stuck in the bathroom while those two did...*what*? I pressed my face against the stall door, leaning forward. Just as I'd suspected.

Couldn't they have found a bedroom? I shouldn't have kept looking, but I'd never seen anything like it.

It was the tall man from the shadows. Bronzed and dangerous looking, his head was thrown back to reveal a thick, muscled neck as a short raven-haired woman bobbed her head in his lap, his big hands wrapped in her hair. I had to plug my ears as his soft deep moans were having an undesirable effect on me.

Ugh! Get out!

An eternity passed. Finally, I heard the vibration of the door shut against the wood stall I was leaning against. I opened my eyes and peered through the crack. No one was there. I brought my feet off the toilet and opened the stall, looking around the room. All clear.

I tried to speed my way from the scene of the crime. I was feeling nauseous and dizzy, and I desperately wanted to get back to Tawny.

"Enjoy the show?" rumbled an impossibly deep voice, and I stiffened.

That man was still in the powder room. He was sitting on the counter in front of the vanity and somehow had managed to find the only shadow in the brightly-lit room. I squared my shoulders towards him. His voice was a deep vibrating purr that reminded me of the low sounds he had been making not five minutes past, doing unpleasant things to my insides.

"I have no idea what you're talking about," I said haughtily as I turned on my heel and headed to the door.

"Voyeurism is not illegal. I am not passing judgement," he said, amusement thick in his voice.

I spun back towards him. "Don't flatter yourself. Generally, when people engage in sexual activities, they don't do it in public places." He obviously had no respect for that woman.

He stood up from the counter and I took a step back. The shadows had hid just how big he was. The man was a behemoth. Rippling with muscles, he strode over to me with a fluid-like grace that should have been impossible for someone his size. The man dripped sensual eroticism. His bare arms were corded with thick muscle, not bulky, just jam-packed full of bronze brawn that led down to a trim waist and, from what I could see through his snug leather pants, powerful legs.

Silver, thickly-lashed eyes looked down at me from above the hard planes of his face that were at odds with his full sensual lips. Those lips curled above his strong chiseled jaw, and I froze. It was a predatory smile and every bone in my body told me to run. The carnal look in his eyes, though, told me if I did, he'd chase me down and play with me. I set my jaw and hoped it was convincing; he could probably smell fear.

He walked around me like an animal prowling. His glossy black mane caught the low lights of the powder room and I shivered. His wavy hair was pulled back by random braids with carved fetishes and silver beads threaded through it. It was longer than I'd first thought, falling to his shoulder blades and giving him a primitive, yet polished, look. I couldn't get an emotional read from him and it scared the sugar-foot out of me.

I turned towards the door and wrapped my hand around the knob. I didn't see him move, but he was there, his hand over mine, freezing me in place again. His touch was electric; it took my breath away.

His hard body pressed along the back of mine as he rumbled low and deep in his chest.

"*Sex contains all,*

Bodies,   souls,   meanings,   proofs,   purities,   delicacies,   results,   promulgations,

Songs, commands, health, pride, the maternal mystery, the seminal milk;

All hopes, benefactions, bestowals,

All the passions, loves, beauties, delights of the earth,

All the governments, judges, gods, follow'd persons of the earth,

These are contain'd in sex, as parts of itself, and justifications of itself."

I wanted to turn and gape at him. Did that barbarian just quote Walt Whitman?

Something about the man triggered in me a primal need to flee, one that overrode my curiosity. He ate girls like me for breakfast. The man's breath tickled my cheek as he twisted me around and pointed above my head. I eyed him warily and lifted my eyes to where he pointed.

Who puts a mistletoe over a bathroom door?

I scoffed and realized his body was pressed tightly against mine, his head bent down towards me, the mane of hair falling over his shoulder, and my mouth went dry.

Too much man, too much arrogance. A primordial voice in me shouted to hike up my skirts and let him do what he did best; his palpable virility spoke to my basest urges.

"If you think I'd honor some ridiculous tradition with the likes of you, you are even more of a Neanderthal than you look."

I tried to huff, or to even look serious, but all I accomplished was being doe-eyed and gaping. I barely remembered to shut my mouth after my rant.

"The goddess Frigga's tears changed the colors of the mistletoe from red to white, thereby saving her son's life after he was poisoned. She kissed everyone who walked beneath it out of gratitude for getting her son's life back. Henceforth comes the tradition. You dare disregard the love of a mother for her son?"

His scent was intoxicating: spicy, cloves, earthy, and all man. His body was warm and hard against mine.

My head was craned back, one hand on the doorknob, the other flat against the wood door as if I was trying to become intangible so I could pass through the solid wood without having to turn the knob. My eyes were wide as I scanned his face. Was he serious? He had to be messing with me.

No, he wasn't.

He slowly lowered his head until we were a scant inch apart. I was frozen as his big hand slid to the nape of my neck. Protests died on my lips. One kiss wouldn't kill me. Pearl had said it was tradition, and his speech was very convincing. His other hand pushed up my mask and I saw his eyebrow twitch before he did the same to his own. I nearly groaned. His nose was perfectly symmetrical, and straight midnight masculine eyebrows cut above his silver eyes. No one should be so tantalizing.

When his full lips pressed against mine, heat rose to my face instantly as a soft moan escaped. His lips were sinfully delicious. His hand at the nape of my neck held fast as he deepened the kiss so his velvet tongue found mine and a charge thrummed through me. My palms were sliding up his hard chest to his long hair.

I'd never kissed a man with hair nearly as long as my own, but it was revolutionary. The image of his face framed by those long midnight waves while he moved above me caused me to gasp—bringing myself back to reality.

My fists pushed against his chest and he backed away with a

surprised expression. Did he feel the jolt, too? His silver eyes saw me, really saw me. Had he somehow caused static electricity to shock me when his tongue met mine? I didn't think leather could do that.

I gave myself a mental shake, pulled my mask down, and yanked the door open. My body was locked up and I fell over the threshold and right into another person.

I could feel the shadow man behind me.

"I'm sorry," I started to say as the new person's strong, sure hands righted me.

"I was looking for you," Ash said, his light green eyes locked on me.

I blushed. *He* was looking for *me*.

"I was just using the bathroom," I stammered.

Ash's eyes slid past me and to the man behind me. Those gorgeous eyes hardened.

"I was not aware this lavatory was co-ed." His voice was cold and accusatory.

My cheeks heated; I hoped he didn't think I was in there with that heathen. I mean, I was, but not *with* him. Not really.

"It is not." I could hear the smile in his voice.

I turned as he adjusted himself visibly and I gasped. He did that on purpose! He tossed his glossy black mane over his shoulder like a lion and let his eyes settle on mine before turning away.

My head swiveled back to Ash. "I have no idea who that man was," I told him, feeling the overwhelming need to defend myself and hoping no trace of that kiss still lingered in my flushed expression.

Ash's eyes followed the back of the man and then locked back down to mine. I was acutely aware that he still had his hands on my hips from when I stumbled into him. I bit my lip and scanned what little I could see of his face. He gave me a cocky smile and shifted, lacing his fingers through mine.

My cheeks heated again as I let him lead me back into the main ballroom. Normally, I didn't like to be touched, but tonight I was making all sorts of exceptions.

With the party in full swing and adults noticeably drunk, Ash persuaded me to let him take me out onto the shimmering dance floor where bodies were pressed against one another like sardines.

Ash deftly led me around the marble floors; he was a superb dancer. His body led me effortlessly, leaving me awed. He caught more than his fair share of glances as he beamed at me, and I found myself smiling back. He was handsome and charming and obviously a catch. I felt like Cinderella.

I lost track of time and danced in Ash's arms until my feet ached. He spun me one last time, my aquamarine dress fanning out around me, my reflection glittering in the mosaic pieces of mirror of the cavernous ballroom. My eyes caught on three figures standing still against one of the massive columns. Shadow man with two other equally tall, dark-haired men. I could feel their eyes.

I faltered in my spin and Ash caught me easily, but not before my body crashed into his. He didn't seem to mind in the least—in fact, he held me there and lifted my chin with a long finger until my eyes rested on his full, sculpted lips. I licked my own subconsciously before I could stop myself.

"I'm very tired. I should head home. Do you think you could show me back to the portal room?" I asked, hoping to prevent the imminent kiss.

I wanted to kiss Ash, but having been kissed by that knuckle-dragger in the bathroom made for one too many kisses for one night already. Ash's smile twitched. I could tell he was disappointed, but he reached for my hand and laced it in his again as he led me off the dance floor and right past the three men.

I kept my eyes averted until the last second, and they snagged on a fourth man.

Jett stood with the three dark-haired men, his Batman mask resting on top of his shaved, dark blonde head.

"See you around, Scarlett," he said as I walked past him, close enough to touch.

His eyes glittered as they flitted past me and rested on Ash, who cocked an eyebrow.

"Yes, I hope to see you again, Jett," I said with all the politeness I could muster, with the other three men glaring at me from behind their masks.

Men just weren't naturally made the way these men were. Their bodies looked like they were built from hard labor or professional fighting; the only place you'd find similar ones in Chicago would be at a powerlifter's gym.

"Do you now?" Jett teased, and I blushed furiously as one of the dark-haired men chuckled.

Ash led me away quickly until we reached the hall, where he slowed down to walk alongside me. He was jealous, I could *feel* it. I didn't know how to reassure him. The idea that he was even jealous was foreign to me. Ash could have any girl at the masquerade—what was he doing with me?

We passed through the yellowed stone halls and all the carved alcoved doors as he told me about Valla. His voice was even charming; it made my ears perk up and want to listen. Even though I wasn't retaining what he was saying, I was enraptured.

Finally, we reached the portal room. I was disappointed not to have found Tawny or the rest of the family on the way back; I didn't know where my room was and I'd probably spend the night wandering the halls like Pan's Labyrinth with a kind of earthy scent to it.

"Thank you," I told Ash as we reached one of the plain wooden doors.

Plain for Tidings, I realized, but not plain at all. Every door was beautifully carved with vines as if each one was done with love and care.

"You are very welcome, Scarlett. Will you be needing an escort to your room?" he queried.

It was such an innocent question, but I *felt* what he intended, and it made butterflies beat in my stomach.

"Thank you, I will be fine. I had a great time tonight," I added to soften the rejection.

He couldn't come back to my room. I'd be helpless to him.

"I would like to see you again. Where are you staying?"

He didn't seem surprised I'd turned him down, and he still wanted to see me. I couldn't help but be flattered.

"In Thrimilci. We're staying at the palace," I answered, hoping there wasn't a slew of palaces in Thrimilci so he'd know which one.

His eyes widened. "The Sumar palace? What is your surname?"

"Yes. Tio."

His lips curled and his celadon eyes glittered. "Scarlett Tio, I am Ash Straumr. It probably does not mean much to you now, but it will. Your mother is Wren Tio?"

"Yes," I answered, surprised he'd know her.

"She is the only Tio woman known to have daughters, and I heard someone say she had returned from the dead. I do not suppose your father came with you?"

"Very alive and very well living in Chicago. You've been misinformed." My cheeks heated. "I have never met my father."

"I am sorry. I did not realize you did not know. From what my cousins tell me, Lark was a good man. I will see you again very soon," he purred, and lifted my hand to his well-formed lips.

I bit the inside of my cheek to keep from swooning and gave him my very best smile. It had the desired effect: he smiled brightly at me. Maybe I was drunker than I thought. Ash must have been mistaken...but there was that name again, Lark.

I walked to the door and glanced over my shoulder to give him a wave before crossing through, thinking of the Sumar palace as I went.

Past Ash stood one of the tall dark haired men watching me leave alone. From what I could see of him, he had shoulder-length dark hair and broad muscled shoulders that led to a trim waist. Powerful legs were clad in black leather and absolutely gorgeous amber eyes glittered at me. I was struck again by how attractive the people here were.

A set of plump lips with a defined Cupid's bow curved and—his arrow might have struck me in the heart if I'd hesitated. I looked away and hurried through the door.

Maybe my family wasn't out of danger yet. Maybe we shouldn't have returned. I was being stalked.

"Little rabbit."

I stirred in the big bed.

That voice.

"Home safe, little rabbit, and all alone," he rumbled, very close to my head.

I rolled onto my back over the satin sheets that stayed cool in spite of the heat, and looked out into my pitch-black room. Silver glinted back at me from a man's eyes and I narrowed mine at him, flattening the pillow under my head.

The dark poet.

"I knew I'd dream of you," I told him huskily as I tried to dampen my throat.

I was the burster of bubbles, but I also knew my poets. Walt Whitman was one of everyone's favorites, wasn't he?

I'd give him a treat.

"Mong the men and women the multitude,

I perceive one picking me out by secret and divine signs,

Acknowledging none else, not parent, wife, husband, brother, child, any

nearer than I am,
    Some are baffled, but that one is not—that one knows me.
    Ah lover and perfect equal,
    I meant that you should discover me so by faint indirections,
    And I when I meet you mean to discover you by the like in you."

My lips curled at the shadowed man that was lying in my bed next to me. His eyes glinted in the moonlight at my words. His ascot and waistcoat were undone as he gazed down at me while propped up on an elbow. His chuckle was deep and rich and made my skin prickle as his lust rolled hot and heavy.

Who knew a chuckle could do that?

"I thought I would have to bind and gag you."

He used a part of his throat that only he had discovered that made his every word a cross between a growl and a purr.

"Now there's an idea," I said saucily.

The shadow man was much less intimidating in my imagination than in person.

His grey eyes widened infinitesimally and a sly smile spread across his chiseled, bronze face. "Tomorrow we will meet officially. I am going to offer to train you, and you are going to accept without reservation. Clear?"

I sat up, the thin black strap of my silky chemise sliding off my shoulder.

"Crystal," I purred.

I'd never had a dream of a man in my bed—well, celebrities yes, but not a real person. I was beyond intrigued. It must have been a side-effect of watching him and the red-clad woman in the powder room. I had felt all sorts of uncomfortable sensations then, but now I would welcome them.

He raised his dark, masculine brows at me and let his gaze trail south over the swell of my chest and the thin material covering it. I breathed deeply for him.

"Are *you* enjoying the show?" I teased, and chuckled.

His eyes flashed silver in the moonlight coming through my windows, and brought them back up to mine. "Perhaps not a rabbit, but a torch."

"A torch?" I asked, and I scooted myself up farther so I was scant inches away from him.

"Yes," he responded. His voiced had dropped so it sounded like he spoke from his stomach.

I gave him a puckish grin and raised my hand to touch his face. His eyes watched me carefully as the pads of my fingers traced his jaw and ran over his full lips.

"You're not so scary," I purred.

His eyes glittered and I ran my fingers back up the nape of his neck and into his hair. *Oh!* It was like black silk. I gave it a tug, my fingers wrapping in the few braids and beads, and he growled, making my breasts bead against the satin.

"Are you frightened of me, Rabbit?"

I nodded and moved myself closer. "Not now, though. Now, you're..." "What am I?" he whispered.

When did his face get so close to mine?

"Tempting," I breathed.

His lips were so close they brushed mine. He smelled like cloves and crisp fallen leaves.

"I draw you close to me, you women
I cannot let you go, I would do you good,
I am for you, and you are for me, not only for our own sake, but for others'
sakes;
Envelop'd in you sleep greater heroes and bards,
They refuse to awake at the touch of any man but me."

I nodded and his sensual lips curled. I closed my eyes. I wanted another kiss, one without consequences.

I felt a sharp pinch and my eyes sprang open. I could taste blood in my mouth. The man ran his tongue against my bleeding lower lip, and I gaped at him.

"Tomorrow. Training. Do not forget," he rumbled, and my mouth fell open.

His hand reached to cup my face and my eyes slid shut on contact.
By far the weirdest dream ever.

CHAPTER 5

Someone had glued my eyes shut. How could a room spin if your eyes were closed?

My brain was pushing against my skull to escape, the pounding in my head causing me to wince. I remembered the shadow man dream and popped my eyes open to find my enormous bed empty.

Bile rose in my throat, and I ran to the bathroom, where evidence of my wild night escaped my body. I rested my forehead against the cool seat of the porcelain, which would normally be completely disgusting, but felt good against my pounding head.

I replayed the night's events in my mind and couldn't help but cringe. I'd watched a couple being intimate in the bathroom, *gah!* What was worse was then I kissed him, then dreamt about him! The anxiety in my stomach forced another deluge into the porcelain toilet.

I leaned against the wall next to the toilet, to weak to pull myself up. Tawny strolled in, dancing in her midnight blue glittering evening dress.

"I think I'm in love," she said, humming and twirling.

Her shoeless feet attempted a pirouette. She tossed a blue dragon mask at me.

"Oh my goodness, stop spinning before I barf all over you and your happiness." I tried hard not to sound petty and jealous.

"What crawled up your butt? Long night? What happened after I left?"

She stopped her twirling and obnoxious humming. Was she humming the love song from Cinderella?

I sighed and fought back some more bile. I sort of smiled thinking about Ash, but then it was replaced by a scowl.

"I had a weird night. I think I saw my father arguing with my mom, and I'm like ninety percent positive some man had his girlfriend go down on him in the bathroom—and wanted me to watch. *But* I did dance the night away with Ash. He's kind of amazing. Then I dreamt about the man. Also, I'm hungover like, *whoa*." I definitely didn't tell her that then the man had kissed me; it sounded even worse out loud than it did in my head.

Tawny rifled through her purse and found some painkillers. She handed me three and a glass of water. I downed them greedily.

"Dreamt about Ash? Your dad? Ugh, that sucks. I'll try to tone down my ridiculousness." She gave me a small smile, and I was glad that there was no bitterness in her tone.

"No, no, I'm sorry. I feel like a pile of garbage. I dreamt about the guy from the bathroom. It was weird."

I reached up and touched my lip, finding that it was puffier than usual. I winced. Did I bite my lip in my sleep?

Tawny knew my boyfriend tally was a big fat zilch. She nodded in understanding and started running a bath in both sides of the double bathtub, adding vanilla scented bubble bath.

"When I went out to get some air I heard mom talking to some guy. I eavesdropped, but I don't remember exactly what they said. I heard enough to know they weren't getting along. But Tawny, he loves her *still,* and he was…warning her. Like she was in danger or something. I don't know. I was so drunk last night, it's embarrassing." I pulled myself to my feet. "Then I told Ash my last name and he implied my presumed dad was dead. Some guy named Lark."

"Scarlett, it's alright. We're good here. Nothing will happen to your mom.

Have you met her brother?" Tawny smirked. "My dad wouldn't let anything happen."

"True." I dried my eyes on the edge of my nightdress; I felt dirty and wanted to pry it off my skin.

She shook her head and I helped her out of her dress, and slipped out of my nightdress and into the bubble bath. The sloshing water spilled over the edges when she climbed in the opposite side, and we were faced each other in our side-by-side baths.

"Tell me about Prince Charming."

She started to hum "So This is Love" again and I rolled my eyes.

"Scar, you know I've never been one for falling in love. But he's different. I'm going to marry him. I wonder what the weddings are like here."

And she was humming again. This guy had really gotten to her. She'd never talked about a guy like this before—in fact, she'd never been anything but dismissive about a guy she'd met.

"Who is this stud?" I quirked an eyebrow at her.

"I didn't ask his name!" She giggled wickedly.

I sat up, raising my head. "Tawny! What the fiddlestick?"

She sank down in her bubble bath and popped back up, water spilling down her hair, makeup from last night smearing under her eyes. She nodded.

"Tawny!"

I couldn't believe it. This was what happened when I let her run around with beautiful strangers on a magical island.

"It was *amazing*. We danced all night, and when people started to leave, he showed me the greenhouse at the back of the university. We had grabbed a couple drapes from that water pipe room and a few cushions. I don't think that he had a plan or anything. We walked through the maze of flowers and stopped at a small pond filled with pink lotus flowers. We placed the drapes down and rested the cushions against a cherry blossom tree. It was so beautiful, Scar." She sank into the bubbles so only her face floated above the water.

"He could *call* the air so the flower petals would float down from the tree like pink snow. He could *call* heat into his hands when he touched me, a trail a warmth... We made love beneath the tree and swam in the pond with the pink lotus flowers, then made love again. We fell asleep under the tree, me in his arms. When we woke up, he kissed me and we made our way back here. I'm supposed to meet him after breakfast back in Valla. Scar, I'm in so much trouble. I can't keep my head with this guy." She sat back up and started to wash her hair.

"Maybe you could catch his name this time."

I splashed water at her as I wrapped up my bath and climbed out of the tub, wrapping myself in a towel. I felt a lot better after the soak, but I was worried for Tawny.

"It didn't seem important at the time." She blushed.

I could see the red spread all the way to the top of her chest. I started drying off my body and my hair. My stomach, completely empty, started to grumble. I was trying not to be jealous..

"I might be in love with this guy, too. Does he have a brother?" I started using my blow dryer. I was surprised it worked; someone must have activated our power plate while I was sleeping.

Tawny laughed and yelled over the roar of the dryer, "He might."

She rinsed her hair and climbed out of the tub, wrapping a towel around herself and pulling out her own hairdryer. "Are you going to see Ash again?" she asked with mischief in her wide hazel eyes.

I bit my lip to hide a smile. "I hope so. He was really charming."

"Good. He couldn't tear his eyes off you. Wouldn't hurt to explore it some. Ask Pearl if she knows him.," she suggested.

It wasn't a bad idea; he seemed particularly delighted about my last name. I wondered why that was.

Tawny was positively glowing, and I smiled at her. "Love becomes you, Tawny. I'm a little jealous," I added begrudgingly. She bumped me with her hip, and I made my way to my closet to get ready.

My limbs felt like putty. My technicolor upchuck had sapped my energy. I didn't want to look like I felt on my second day here, so I braided my long, light brown hair and pulled it over a shoulder. I pulled a heather grey maxi dress over me; its light jersey fabric was just the ticket. A pair of sweats would have been better, but it would do. I walked back into the bathroom and dabbed on some lip gloss and a couple swipes of mascara, hoping it would brighten my eyes some.

Tawny glided into the room, still on cloud nine, and started applying a full face of makeup. She had on a short, red, belted shirt dress and cork wedges. She didn't look like she'd been out all night. Whatever she was on was contagious because my mood perked at her happiness. I watched her get ready and slipped into a pair of black gladiator sandals. I planned on crawling under a rock once breakfast was over anyway—no point in getting all dolled up.

I'd been sighing all morning. Even I was annoyed with myself.

"Ready!" Tawny bounced into the room.

I briefly toyed with the idea of tripping her.

We meandered through the halls. It was late morning already, and I wondered if anyone would be eating still. We heard talking before we entered the dining room.

It looked like everyone was having a late breakfast. Pearl sat at the head of the table with Gypsum, and Sparrow. My mom and Hawk sat on the other side, waiting for us to start breakfast.

Pearl stood. "Come in, girls!" She said it so joyously that a smile blossomed on my face as I sat down next to my mother.

Tawny sat next to Sparrow across from me.

"Did you girls enjoy last night?" Pearl asked cheerily.

"Yes," Tawny said, her eyes dreamy, and Pearl gave her a speculative look but didn't ask any questions. I nodded and piled scrambled eggs and toast onto my plate.

"How are you feeling?" Pearl asked me, and I gave her a reluctant smile.

"Not very well, actually," I admitted, ignoring the look my mother was giving me.

"We heal upset stomach with *calling* if you're interested," Hawk offered graciously. He, too, ignored my mother's death stare.

I stood up to go to him, fighting a laugh, but froze as three men entered the room. Bile rose into my throat again. I knew even without their masks who the three men were. Shadow man, Jett, and blue dragon mask. They swaggered in like they owned the place.

Jett and the shadow man were the same height, but the shadowed man had slightly broader shoulders. Blue dragon mask was tall, but shorter than the two giants. Jett and Shadow's eyes rested on me, but blue dragon mask was on Tawny, who looked confused but elated at the same time. The three men were dressed the same, head-to-toe black. It almost looked like a uniform of sleeveless V-necks and snug black pants with matching boots.

"I can soothe that for you," Jett said and he strode right up to and rested his hand on my stomach without being asked.

I stared back at him with a blank face.

The emotions in the room were smothering me. I swallowed hard. Suddenly, my stomach went warm and the acid stopped roiling. He'd just used *calling* on me. My breath caught, and I realized he was searching my eyes, then he smiled and confirmed what I had already suspected. He was possibly the best-looking man to ever grace Mother Nature's green Earth.

"Thank you, Jett," I murmured, blushing and taking a step back.

My mom nearly choked as she crossed over to us where I stood awkwardly trying to reverse back to my seat. Shadow's eyes burned holes into me.

"You've met?" she asked, hesitancy in her voice.

It snapped me out of my stupor. "Mom?" I asked.

My mother's eyes were just for the men though. Jett looked back at her, and I suddenly felt like I was intruding.

"Scarlett," my mother started, then wrapped her arms around Jett and Shadow's waists.

Jett looked down at my mother fondly and I shook my head.

I pictured the blonde man my mother had argued with in the hallway, the big blonde mountain of a man, and swallowed convulsively as I raised my finger to point at Jett.

"You're my brother. That was my father last night, wasn't it? Ash was wrong, it's not Lark."

I was going to puke on everything.

"Where did you hear that name?" Hawk asked, but my mind was trying to fit pieces together and I barely heard him.

My mother's mouth snapped open as if she'd forgotten I'd seen them together, but I was on a roll. An angry roll.

"And who are these men?" I turned towards blue dragon mask.

He was lean, but powerfully built like Hawk, with that same swimmer's body, but taller. My eyes fluttered.

"You're my other brother?" I asked.

"Steel." My mother uttered.

"Steel?" I repeated.

At that, everyone's faces seemed to lose color except for Jett's—who laughed. "Uncle, but might as well be brother."

Then I turned to Shadow. Pearl rose gracefully to her feet.

I was vaguely aware of Tawny's yelp, like she'd been pinched, as she ran from the table.

She knocked over her heavy chair as she escaped from the room. I wanted to chase after her, but the room was spinning again and black spots were forming in my vision.

"This is a lot." She fidgeted. "Jett *is* your brother, Steel is your uncle. This is Slate...my adopted son. He's offered to train you before your course starts." I could tell my mom was trying to make me feel better, possibly even try to calm me down, but my head was underwater.

I slow blinked at Slate. "My brother?" I shook my head.

"Adopted. You look sick, Rabbit," he rumbled.

Rabbit? My mouth opened to say something scathing, but suddenly, I was looking up at the ceiling and Slate's arms were lifting me.

CHAPTER 6

JETT

Nothing would be the same.

"Sit down, Jett. You're making me nervous." Steel was looking nervous himself.

The plan was to spend the day in Valla, but Jett couldn't wait to see his mom and his sister. The prodigal son was returning with his family and heir. He couldn't just wait around while they were at home.

Slate had strolled in late—even after Jett sent the message to his favorite spot, Shadow Breaker headquarters. Jett fixed him with a glare and sat back on his couch to cross his ankles on the coffee table.

"I saw your sister," Slate rumbled.

Jett immediately despised the tone in his voice. "She's your sister, too. Don't forget that."

Slate's lips curled mockingly. "I will leave her to Quick. I do not like them so young and inexperienced. She is little more than a girl."

Jett took a deep breath. He was purposely irritating him.

"You read Mom's letters. She *is* a girl." Jett gave them his back as he smiled.

"A maiden, no doubt," Slate continued.

The door to his room had opened and he held his breath as a petite brunette entered; she was even shorter and kinder than he thought she would be. Her big brown eyes welled with tears as she closed the door behind her. Steel and Slate both rose to their feet. Slate looked to be regretting his disheveled appearance. "You look so much alike. I don't know who is who," she said, knitting her brows as she looked between Steel and Jett.

"It is good to see you, Wren," Steel said, and Wren slapped her hands to her mouth with a whimper.

She launched herself at them, hooking her arms around both their necks as she peppered their cheeks with kisses, forcing them to hunch even though she was on her tiptoes.

Jasmine and roses. He had not imagined her scent.

She leaned back and Jett hoped she didn't think he was a pansy for tearing up at the sight of her. Her eyes scanned both their faces.

"I cannot believe how handsome you both are—and so much alike. Steel, you look just like Pearl's mother, but Jett, you are built just like your father. I love you both. I am so sorry I left you."

"It's okay, Wren," Steel said thickly.

Jett nodded but had lost his ability to speak.

My mom pulled back and laughed through her tears as she swiped them from Jett's cheeks and then Steel's. She turned to take in Slate; he was a few feet away, and had never looked more nervous. Wren watched him, her hands partially covering her face, her tears coming down harder.

Finally, she rushed him and Slate's brows drew down when she forced him to suffer her embrace. She didn't linger as she had with Steel and Jett, but let him sit down, and sat so close she was leaning against him as she cupped his jaw.

"By the Mother, you look so much like him," she said in disbelief, and sat back to take him in. "Tall and handsome." She smiled and cupped his face again, knitting her brows. "My little stoic," she whispered.

After two hours of her probing for details about their lives and a lot of her staring blatantly at the three of them, she gave them all chest-crushing hugs and left the room.

"You should've told her you already had bodyguards watching Scarlett. Pearl must have told her to come to you," Jett said wryly to Slate, who looked dryly at him.

"She's going to marry us all off," Steel said, settling back.

"Not Slate. She's going to wrap him in swaddling and put him in a bassinet next to her bed," Jett teased.

Slate gave him a flat look as Steel chuckled. "She only feels bad for me because I am an orphan."

Jett had gotten up and patted Slate's shoulder. "Not so. You're my brother; you have a mother."

Jett shook himself out of his memories of the day before. Scarlett had not taken the shock of all the extra siblings well.

"I could carry her."

After a great deal of fussing and delving from his mother, Jett had walked next to Slate as he cradled Scarlett's unconscious form up to her room. His brother from another mother was surreptitiously stealing glances of her still form as he held her close to his chest. Jett's usual smug smile was accompanied by an arched brow as he watched Slate. Having known Slate all his life, Jett was amused at his immediate fondness for Scarlett.

Fondness...or possessiveness, Jett mused. "Not my fault you were too slow to catch her," Slate replied with a curl of his lips.

His tone was meant to taunt Jett, but he failed since he had stolen a long look down as he spoke. Jett's eyes narrowed as he tried to decipher the look. On another man, Jett would have said Slate looked longingly at his little sister, but that was impossible. Slate longed to do one thing with women and that was to push their thighs apart and plunge into them.

"Our mother had her arm around my waist, and you jumped across the room. If I had moved a moment sooner, I'd have your bootprints on my back," Jett said, and opened Scarlett's bedroom door so Slate could bring her in.

Slate led the way through the royal blue and gold room, not bothering to hit the energy plate. Jett followed behind Slate since the two big men wouldn't fit through the archway into the bedroom abreast. Slate laid her down with the utmost care, taking the time to add a second pillow behind her head before resting her lolling head back.

Jett knit his brows with a smirk on his lips as Slate lingered before straightening. Jett ducked his head to hide his smile as the two men switched positions and Jett plopped down on the bed beside their sister.

Had Slate breathed her in before he rose? No way.

Slate sat down at her feet and Jett fought that smirk again. It wasn't like him to linger with women. When he was done with them, he would leave. He never made any promises, never led them to believe it would be anything other than physical.

Jett had been the same way until he'd met up with Cerise and Amethyst. The girls had grilled him after Scarlett had walked away. They hadn't taken kindly to Jett's unusual attention to her. Jett smiled inwardly; it *had* been strange when he'd leapt over the table to lift her mask, but he couldn't help himself. He saw Scarlett's mane of caramel brown curls...and those eyes. There was no mistaking those turquoise orbs for anyone but his sister. Only he and Steel had eyes that color, and he'd seen the pictures his mother had sent of them and knew beyond a doubt that the blushing young woman who had come in on Ash Straumr's arm had been his sister.

Ash Straumr. Jett shook his head. Scarlett had walked right into that one. Ash must have had a sixth sense for power. There was no way Scarlett would know how to play the subtle games all the greater families played. He'd known just by watching her how gullible and naive she was.

When he'd lifted her mask, her almond eyes had gone wide; she clearly wasn't used to being touched. She wasn't comfortable with it. He knew she had felt confused when he had embraced her, but when he told her she was breathtaking she'd nearly spluttered.

He'd felt an odd sense of pride when he'd lifted her mask to reveal the beauty underneath. Not that you couldn't tell even with the mask on, but Jett wanted to see the whole picture. He didn't like that so many others had noticed her beauty as well. Quick had made more than his fair share of comments last night, and then there was Ash.

The corner of his mouth curved. Jett was usually the corrupter.

Looking at her though, he knew he'd have his work cut out for him. He felt an instinctual protectiveness, like he could sense her vulnerability in a world she wasn't familiar with. He knew she'd be like a breath of fresh, virtuous air to all those jaded men looking for a young, pliable wife.

Jett decided it would have made his job easier if she *had* been hideous. Instead, she had high cheekbones that rounded demurely when she smiled, and full lips—her upper lip was slightly fuller than her lower, giving her a unique look. Her brows had a soft arch and were a shade darker than her hair, the same color of the thick fan of eyelashes that framed her almond eyes.

Jett started when he realized Slate was still sitting with him. Jett knew why *he* was looking at his sister. He couldn't believe she was finally there, after all these years, countless letters, her never even knowing he existed. He had wanted to scoop her up and swing her around last night and demand she tell him everything about herself... but why was Slate still there?

"Why don't you go grab a washcloth?" Jett said, dropping his eyes back down to Scarlett lying serenely on the pillows like a princess waiting to be awoken by a kiss. Slate had better not be getting any ideas.

Slate grunted his assent and stood. Jett quirked an eyebrow; he had expected Slate to ignore him. What was going on with his brother? He suspected it had something to do with the girl lying next to him that was starting to stir.

"I had pictured this morning going better," Jett stated when he noticed her eyes moving beneath her delicate eyelids.

She rubbed her sun-kissed face with pink polished fingers, trying to clear her head. Jett smiled. Of course she'd like pink, pink and natural tones that would suit her coloring. She opened her eyes, trying to get her bearings, as she wasn't used to her new room yet. She angled her narrow chin up to him and gave a sheepish smile with her pouty lips.

"I didn't know I had a brother. My mom only mentioned a half-brother and I'd heard the name Steel before. I know why she didn't, I never would have let up trying to meet you, but this is seriously sugarfoot."

She sounded exasperated as she pushed herself up against the headboard so they sat shoulder to shoulder—well, shoulder to elbow. She was about five and a half feet tall, and Jett was a foot taller.

"Sugarfoot?" he asked with a smug smile. "Is that the dreaded 'S' word?"

She pulled a lower lip into her mouth to stave off a smile. "Yes."

She was enchanting. Jett could understand why Ash had spotted her. "How are you feeling? Bit of a doozy?"

She played with her manicured fingers in her lap. "Doozy is accurate."

Jett wanted to give her cute little nose a pinch, but he figured it would only make her think he was more nonsensical than she'd already suspected. Scarlett would have to get used to his affection. Jett was entirely secure with his masculinity and had no problem giving hugs and kisses out freely. He was a touchy-feely kind of guy.

"How's Tawny?" she, asked looking uncomfortable with his proximity, but she was looking at him just like he had watched her while she slept.

She was memorizing his face, trying to find the resemblance between them; there were many.

Ah, Tawny and Steel. What a mess he'd made of that. Saying it was a bad idea was a bit late...but the thing was, Steel had looked *happy*. He'd said it with awe, and if Jett wasn't completely off-base, with something that looked a little like infatuation. In a single night, the little brunette had ensnared Steel, who'd never had a serious girlfriend in his life.

"Hmm...after she punched Steel in the face outside of the dining room, she ran into her rooms and has locked herself in. Don't worry, only Slate and I saw it. He was carrying you up here when we saw their lover's quarrel," Jett told her, and she squeezed her eyes shut making a grimace.

Poor Steel.

"Tell me he didn't know who we were," she said.

"He certainly wouldn't knowingly sleep with his family, if that's what you're implying." Jett was hinting at what would need a deeper explanation at a later time. "Lark isn't our father. Everyone in Tidings assumed he was because he and our mother were close. They grew up together and when his wife died, our mom married him. I go by the surname Sumar, but they think I am a Haust bastard. Lark and Mom adopted Slate here. After the Red King Massacre, Pearl kept us boys together and mom took you."

"My mother was married!" she gasped.

Jett tried to not visibly wince. In the letters his mother wrote them, he knew she'd kept her very sheltered, from herself, her abilities, her past. Their mother had a lot of secrets.

"Out of convenience. Our mother and Lark were in love with other people, but because they were fertile greater family, they were highly sought after." Slate exited the bathroom and Scarlett went rigid.

This kept getting more and more interesting.

"I thought my mom—*our* mom—and I didn't keep secrets from one another," she mumbled, sounding hurt.

Jett watched as Slate sauntered over to Scarlett's bed, her eyes trapped on their brother. Jett suspected Slate was used to women looking at him with lust and desire, *not* like he was a rabid beast who'd barreled its way into her bedroom.

Slate unfurled himself over the bed, just missing Jett's boots. His own boots were off the side of the bed, but his upper body curved around her legs. Jett watched as Slate reached a long arm up and dabbed at Scarlett's face. He hadn't thought it was possible for her to go more rigid, but she managed. She started trying to lean away from his attentive hand—but he leaned with her so she was nearly pushing Jett off the bed. Jett wanted to laugh out loud, but he settled for taking a deep breath to stave off the laughter. What was Slate doing?

"He won't bite," Jett said, smiling his usual smug smile.

Slate snapped his teeth with an audible click. Jett chuckled; *that* was the Slate he knew.

Her fingers flew up to her bottom lip and Slate's lips curled. Jett knit his brows, wondering what that had been about, and watched as she snatched away the washcloth. Slate let it go easily and let his hand fall into her lap. Jett narrowed his eyes at Slate's hand resting against the thin jersey material of his sister's dress as if by will alone he could get him to move it. Scarlett had stiffened again, all too aware of the hand in her lap.

"I can do it myself," she huffed as she wiped her forehead.

"Of course you can," Jett said, and he snaked his arm around Scarlett's shoulders, wanting to be close to her.

Wanted them to talk about their mother and find things they had in common. He'd waited years for this. Slate acted like he wasn't as interested, but he remembered a boy who missed his mother when they were little. Once they'd received word Scarlett and Wren were coming, Slate's usual nonchalant attitude faded whenever they were spoken of. Jett acknowledged that Slate had a legitimate interest in them too.

"If our mother kept secrets, it was not to hurt you. It was not under ideal circumstances that she fled. Pearl does not discuss those times either." Jett nodded along with Slate's assessment.

She didn't look comfortable. Jett had been right to assume she didn't like being touched. She was eyeing Slate again as if any moment he'd tear out her throat. As far as Jett knew, downstairs in the dining hall had been their first interaction, but now he was doubting it. It had been Slate's idea to have Brass watch as Ash escorted her to the portal room in Valla to make sure he wouldn't follow her home.

"Do you two normally spend a great deal of time in women's beds?" she asked peevishly and her eyes went wide.

Jett laughed at her embarrassed expression. She was adorable.

"Only my lovers'. We have read about you in letters and seen you in pictures; I wanted to take care of you. Besides, we're family, surely that calls for an exception to having men in your bed?"

Jett nudged her with a shoulder, trying to be playful. Under no uncertain terms would he keep his distance from his lovely sister. Jett wanted to pick her brain until there were no more secrets between them.

She started to smile at Jett, but her almond eyes flickered to Slate and it fell from her face. Jett sucked on his teeth as he assessed Slate. Something had happened between them that he'd have to press Slate for later.

"I guess, but I don't have men in my bed *ever,*" she said, and lifted her eyes to meet Slate's. "*Brother.*"

Slate's full lips curled and she was pressing against Jett again. Jett squeezed her shoulder; he liked that she sought him out even subconsciously as her protector. He didn't like that it was *from* Slate. Was the man trying to make her run screaming for the hills with that smile? Jett gave the same smile when he was facing a particularly difficult challenge, whether it be a sparring opponent or a woman who had been resistant to his charms. There had been a precious few of those—most women couldn't wait to be bedded by Jett.

"Don't worry about Slate, he always looks at women like they might make a delicious snack," Jett joked.

Slate had better not be looking at his sister like the latter.

"Yes. I saw his version of a snack last night," she snapped, her turquoise eyes turning intense.

Slate's grey eyes glittered. "Not all women."

Slate pushed himself up and Jett watched as he let his hand trail down her leg, such an innocuous move but deliberate. Everything Slate did was calculated. Jett didn't like the subtle move, and wondered if Scarlett had any idea that Slate was interested in her. Jett doubted it, or if she did, she had told him unequivocally that she didn't want him.

Yes, that must have been it, Jett decided. It would explain why Slate was off-kilter today. Slate was like Jett: women did not tell him no. It was a simple truth.

Still, Jett gave Slate a look that told him he wanted time alone with her and to get lost. After a moment, Slate conceded and left, while Scarlett narrowed her eyes at his retreating back as if he'd suddenly change his mind and lunge at her.

"Mom wanted us to take you shopping. Get some new clothes, pick up your university things," Jett said, trying to draw her attention away from Slate.

"Yeah, that sounds good." She sounded dreamy; still getting used to having a brother, Jett guessed.

"I'll take you. Some brother/sister bonding time. We'll drag Tawny out when she feels better. My girls would love to go shopping." He gave his smug grin.

He watched her intently for her reaction to his mentioning his two lovers. People sometimes had a hard time with the three of them together. They didn't understand that as much as he was Amethyst and Cherry's lover, the girls were also lovers. Admittedly, he had been lucky to find a relationship that he could fully invest himself in. Two years ago, he'd met the girls at the first induction ceremony after Valla U reopened and his world had never been the same.

"I'd really like that. I bet Tawny would like to get some fresh air too," she told him, giving him a small smile that rounded her high cheekbones prettily—too prettily. He would have his hands full with her suitors.

"My room is on the floor below yours, same wing. Just knock on random doors until you find me."

Jett winked and almost laughed at her flushed cheeks. Jett knew he was a good-looking bastard, and he couldn't help but flirt with just about every woman he encountered. He'd have to try to tone it down with her; she wasn't used to his sense of humor, men in general, and certainly not a brother.

"This might be a stupid question, but how do you pay for things here? Assuming they don't take credit cards."

Jett's chest shook with silent laughter. "No dollars here. We have marks—coins for you. We have careers here as they do everywhere else, where we earn marks. The Sumars have wealth, but it comes with responsibility. We manage the land, and work with the native tribes. We have a seat on the council also, which helps Tidings keep its balance. Pearl will have a purse brought to you. She will arrange a weekly allowance for you, Tawny, and Gypsum."

"Big brother? Your name is a color name. We're not twins, are we?"

She chewed on the inside of her cheek and Jett got a glimpse of how she must have looked as a little girl, with that golden mane of waves and big turquoise eyes and lips too big for her then-tiny face. She'd grown into herself extremely well.

"My birthday is January first," he said with a subdued version of his smug smile. "Yours is before Samhain." The corner of her mouth quirked at his knowledge of her.

"When is Steel's?" she asked, and Jett's brow twitched.

"Early spring. He's four years older than us. Year of the alloy. It goes: precious stones, color, stones or rocks, which is very vague in my opinion, fish, amphibians, alloys, insects, reptiles, trees, Canis, *er* dogs... Anyway, that's the gist of it.." Jett's dropped the hand he'd been ticking off names on.

"My head hurts from all this information. I can't believe she didn't tell me she was married. This whole time...were they married long?"

"No. Married on what you would call Labor Day and he died at the Red King's Massacre that Yuletide," Jett told her.

It was when Wren had left them and he'd lost his mother. Steel was old enough to remember it, and even he didn't talk about it. It had been terrifying.

"Lark and my—*our*—mom were married when I was born? She never...I feel like I don't even know her. She had this whole other life and the woman I know..." She gave a tight smile. "I'll stop by Pearl's room and get the purse from her. My wardrobe doesn't quite fit in," she said nervously as she ran her hands down where Slate's had been.

Had she done that self-consciously, or to erase the feel of his hands? She didn't seem to realize she'd done it. Jett looked down at her as she gazed up at him through her lashes and felt an overwhelming love for her.

"I think you'd look gorgeous in whatever you wore," Jett said, trying not to jut his jaw arrogantly as he normally held it.

She dropped her eyes and fidgeted. "Thanks. You're only saying that because you're my brother."

"Say it again." Jett couldn't help but smile smugly. He'd been waiting a very long time for this.

"Brother." She bit her lip to stop the ridiculous smile blooming.

"Baby sis," he said with a lift of his brows.

Oh yes, this was very nice indeed.

CHAPTER 7

 My reflection wasn't half bad as I walked through the bathroom to Tawny's door on the other side. I loosened my braid and let my golden hair fall in crimped waves around my face. That would do.

Her door wasn't locked so I let myself in. She stopped me with a hand before I could speak.

"Nothing happened last night. I never want to talk about it again. Don't feel sorry for me, I knew exactly what I was doing," she said curtly.

"But not *who* it was with," I said softly.

Despite her tough look and hard voice, I could see the puffiness of her eyes under all that makeup. I could tell when she was hurting inside so bad it took everything she had not to curl up in her bed and cry.

"Not another word!" she yelled at me.

I knew she didn't mean it. Her eyes were starting to water, so I walked over to her and squeezed her as hard as I could. It didn't bother me that she didn't hug me back. This was what I knew she needed.

I whispered, "Okay," and that was that. "Do you want to come with me to get purses from Pearl? Jett wants to take us shopping. Also...I have a brother," I added.

She smiled and it didn't look as forced. "Yes. Definitely. You have a brother, *and* an adopted one. Possibly a half one."

I nodded. "And I think he bit me."

She gave me a look and I dismissed my random comment with a wave. Slate had definitely bit me.

We walked in silence, not an uncomfortable one, but a quiet one just the same.

We found Pearl's room at the highest level at the very back of the gold and blue mosaic-lined palace. Her double door was exquisitely carved, a blazing sun the centerpiece, half of which was on each door. When we knocked, Pearl swung the doors out and revealed her room.

Our bedrooms were big, but Pearl's room was sprawling. Her massive white bed sat under a backlit, recessed arch. Ivory silk fabric draped on either side of the massive bed. She had an alcove that held a flight of stairs which I imagined led to the top of one of the many domed turrets. She gestured to an oversized cream chair that we could comfortably fit side-by-side in. It felt like cashmere when we sank into it.

"Have I told you how happy I am to have you here?"

She must have told us a hundred times.

"The boys are happy to have you girls and your mother back."

She sat across from us, her curvy figure draped across the cream chaise lounge. She kicked off her shoes and pulled her feet up. She looked like a Golden Age movie star. Her coppery hair was in her usual big, shoulder-length, wavy curls, and her long maroon dress was ruched at the middle, drawing attention to all the right places. I doubted she owned a single pair of pants.

"Your mother said you saw her last night with Alder." She said it as a fact. She wasn't asking.

Alder. Another name to add to the slew.

"There is a long history between your mother and father. None of the way it happened was her fault. If it had been up to your father, he would have stayed with her. Stayed with you and Jett..."

I *felt* hesitation.

"She wants you to all know each other, but Alder is married with a family of his own. They know nothing of you or Jett. Imagine being one of *those* children. It is a sensitive situation. I am not saying not to be upset—I certainly would be, having my father so close but unable to get to know him. However, it may be possible with time. It has always been hard to keep Alder and Wren apart even when it was in their best interest. Lark Haust is assumed to be your father. We plan to keep it that way. Jett has taken the Sumar name, but you are considered legitimate, Scarlett. Not that that matters with too much with Guardians, darling. You understand?"

I was leaning forward, I wanted to learn everything that had never been discussed for over nineteen years. I was starved for information. I must have looked crazed, my eyes wide, not wanting to blink in case I missed something. Tawny was just as enthralled as I was. As it turned out, we truly knew nothing about our parents' past.

She got up and went to the wall that had a mini kitchen—all white marble, of course—and brought back a pitcher of ice water and three goblets.

"You and Jett were born while Alder was already engaged and then married."

I was appalled. The shock must have shown on my face.

"Scarlett, your mother had only been with Alder until she and Lark married." She ducked her head, and I had a feeling it was about the Lark I knew so little about. "She loves your father still, and I believe it is too hard for her to talk about him. That is why you have been left in the dark about the subject, that and more.

She patted my hand after she filled our goblets. I took a big swig and held it between both hands in my lap.

"Pearl...er, uh, *Grandma*, why didn't my dad just marry my mom if he loved her so much?"

All I'd heard about them was how much they loved each other, but he was still married to this other woman.

"Grandma, if you wish, but Pearl is fine. Alder's marriage was arranged when he became tried and true, which is our equivalent to graduating from the university. Jett was born while your mother was still at the university, and she never had a chance to finish. She was with child again a month or so after that. That is what I meant by not keeping them apart. I think they had a meeting place in Ostara, out from under my nose. You do not break betrothals here. Even if Alder had not been promised to someone else, he and your mother could never have been. Alder's uncle is a spiteful man; he and I have never gotten along. He despised Flint, your grandfather. Alder's father is under his brother's thumb, he would never go against him. There was a lot of politics in their marriage also. Your mother and father thought love would prevail. Alder left to tell his father and uncle he was choosing his own bride. They denied him. He returned here and they did run away for three days with Hawk, but when they returned, he left. I do not know for certain, but I fear they threatened him. Alder and your mother did not see each other again until Jett was born. He was there, both him and Lark, when Jett was born."

She sipped her water, shaking slightly. Not from sadness—well, maybe a little sadness, but her eyes were angry. If I were a betting woman, I would have said it was adrenaline, her fight or flight instinct ready to fight.

I *felt* loathing.

"I tell you all this because you should know. It is your history as much as it is Wren's. But it is also because being here for her is undoubtedly bringing all those emotions long buried back up. Try, if you can, to be kind."

I wanted to cry for my mother. How she must have lived with this sadness for all these years. In love with one man who she couldn't be with, married to her childhood friend. I was starting to draw a picture of this *Lark* and it painted him the hero. He saved my mother from the disgrace she would have undoubtedly fallen into if he hadn't stepped up to marry my mother. I understood why everyone seemed to feel his loss so strongly.

"Is that why she left with me? Because of the threat from his uncle?"

"Partly. After the massacre on Yuletide, it was not clear who was involved. All the doubt, the questions...many people believed one of the greater families was involved, but there was no proof."

"Why did Jett stay if we were in danger?" Tawny asked.

Pearl smiled sadly. "Alder would not make the same mistake twice. No one besides him and our family ever knew you were not Lark's. Some knew Jett was Alder's son, and we feared they would try to find them. Scarlett, all these years we have acted as all that left Tidings had died the day of the massacre."

My head swam. Tawny's mouth had dropped open. That one or some of the wealthy aristocrats from last night be so deadly frightened me.

"Jett knew the threat to him while he grew up, but since our Prime closed the university, he was not under any risk from the Red Kings or whomever gave them access. But now that Wren and Hawk are back, attention will be drawn to them and to you. Others knew about Jett so he wasn't as easy to hide. We decided keeping the boys together was smartest."

Pearl frowned into her goblet then. She seemed to be mentally debating if us coming back had even been worth it.

"I am so happy to have you all here," she said again.

"I love it here. I love having a family. My mom never seemed complete in Chicago." I shrugged and leaned back in the oversized chair. "I think she still wants to be with my father. She never gave up the hope that he'd come after her. I think she is willing to risk it, and so am I. I...I want to be a Guardian." I didn't realize how much I meant it until it popped out of my mouth. Tawny nodded in agreement.

Pearl was tearing up. She pulled out a kerchief and dabbed her eyes. "Come here, my girls."

She held us like that for a while. We held her back, inhaling her floral musky scent.

When we let go, she changed the subject entirely. We sat on the chaise lounge and talked about life in Chicago, and how it was to grow up there. A perfectly normal conversation about nothing.

We found the hall Jett said his room was in, each of us with a heavy in our hands. I didn't recognize a single coin inside.

"So...he said just knock on some doors."

I shrugged at Tawny.

There were six doors in the hall, two in the same spots as our doors were in our own hall. Tawny tried the one that was directly below where her door would be.

Slate opened the door, surprise flitting through his grey eyes for an instant before he crossed his arms and leaned against the frame. "Fall down the rabbit hole?"

The shock was all ours. He was shirtless, fetishes woven through braids hung over a bronze shoulder. What my imagination had conjured up under his shirts didn't do him justice. I wanted to run my fingers down his rippling torso, stopping at his belt buckle where the "V" of his muscles led into his black pants. I wondered if his flawless skin felt as silken as it looked, or tasted as spicy as his scent suggested. My mind had run amok.

I *felt* embarrassment.

It was coming from me.

My face burned, I felt for my eyebrows to make sure that when my face lit on fire, I hadn't singed off my eyebrows. "...Jett?" My mouth had gone dry.

Tawny laughed. *I* thought it sounded fake. She was a big fat liar if she wasn't at least half as impressed as I was.

"Down there." He pointed to the next set of doors with a muscled arm. "First door on the right."

"Thanks," Tawny said, and then she winked.

Winked! Slate was unfazed as he watched us walk down to Jett's door and knock.

"Come in!" I heard Jett say from inside the room.

I met Slate's eyes for the first time; you couldn't really blame me for not tearing them away from that chest and those abs. Tawny went into Jett's room, so I was in the hall alone with Slate. I urged my legs to take a step, but he was firing off that intense look that made me hold my breath and stand perfectly still.

"Enjoying the show, rabbit?"

My eyes widened instantly as I watched his countless muscles flex while he laughed deep and rich, my skin prickling in response. His teeth pulled along his lower lip and suddenly, I blinked.

Broken of his spell, I stumbled into Jett's room.

It had the same layout as mine, and the only difference was the furniture. It was all dark blue and black, masculine, and was surprisingly clean.

We couldn't see him when we walked in, but he yelled from the bathroom, "In here!"

We turned the corner into the bathroom and ran smack into Steel, wearing only a towel around his waist.

"It's going to be a minute, training ran long. Gyps won't thank us for it in the morning unless he gets some healing." Jett, also wearing a towel, gave us a devilish grin and pushed past us into his room.

His eyes twinkled, beads of water still resting on his tanned skin. Jett was ripped—six-pack abs, chiseled pecs...well, he was ripped.

I wanted to turn and gauge Tawny, but she was nearly standing on my heels. I *felt* pain, longing, love, betrayal...there was an emotional storm brewing when she spotted Steel.

"We share a bathroom. I did not know you were coming here," Steel said in a rush.

Steel was lean. He had the type of body I'd seen while watching the summer Olympics swimmers. I idly wondered what type of training they had done, and what my body would look like when we started.

I *felt* a wall building in Tawny. I didn't know if it was a good thing or not.

"Hey, *Uncle* Steel," she said coolly and headed back into Jett's room.

I winced at her tone. I wouldn't want to be on the receiving end of Tawny's vehemence. From Steel, I felt anger, love, and hope.

What kind of sick soap opera had I stumbled into?

Steel's anger wasn't directed at Tawny, but the love and hope was. I wanted to be grossed out by his incestuous love, but...it was weird. Admittedly, he was one of the beautiful people the place had strolling about as if oblivious that regular people weren't supposed to look that good all the time. I didn't find him attractive like Tawny obviously did; there was something in his features—and Jett's for that matter, since they looked nearly identical—that were like mine. The same tanned skin tone, the same greenish blue eyes. It was a natural expunger of all things romantic. I knew we had some sort of connection from the moment I saw them. I wished then that Steel had been my uncle from my dad's side so he and Tawny could be together, and it wouldn't be so creepy.

Steel walked over to me. "Sorry about all this, it's not what it looks like."

He tried not to smile inappropriately; it seemed like something he did when he was nervous. He looked like he wanted to hug me, but I knew he wouldn't in only his towel after things had gone so poorly with Tawny.

"I missed Wen. She raised me with Lark like her own son. I was only four when you left." That same sadness that came over everyone was etched his handsome features.

"Wen?"

He blushed, creating splotches of red on his tan cheeks. "Wren. I couldn't say her name when I was little so I always called her Wen."

I loved hearing about my mom and her old life. So much was missing from the image she'd always shown me, and Steel was a big part of that. I shook myself. He was related to us somehow. He'd taken advantage of Tawny.

"You knew. My mom told me she sent pictures."

I wanted it to come out angry, to yell it in his face. I couldn't; the look on his face was like someone had just run over his puppy.

He dropped his eyes and rubbed his jaw where she must have socked him earlier. "It's a big mess."

Um, okay. Dropping an open box of cereal on the kitchen floor is a "big mess"; this was a *catastrophe*. Tawny would never be the same.

His tone and his choice of words caused a bubble of anger to burst on the surface. This guy might have been my uncle/brother, but Tawny was my sister from another mister. No one should hurt her this way.

Then again... I felt pain and love coming from him. It confused me.

I tried to keep my tone level. "Look. Just stay away from her. We all have to live here." Something much more frightening occurred to me. "What if Hawk finds out you took her to the greenhouse?"

Hawk was the most level-headed, even-keeled man I'd ever met. But when it came to his little girl...I just hoped it never got out.

"You don't understand." He turned back to the mirror and was using electricity to remove hair on his poster boy perfect jaw in some kind of electrolysis procedure.

I had to ask. "I don't want to pry. It's not really my business, but it sort of is. Pearl said things are sometimes done differently here, an older set of rules. So, *um*, do family members sometimes...keep it in the family?"

He looked at me quizzically, clearly not picking up what I was putting down, so I just blurted it out.

"Do immediate family members sometimes marry? Like if I married Slate? I dunno, to keep the bloodlines strong or *something?*"

I threw in the bit about Slate and me because, A) it was utterly preposterous to me and, B) I wanted to throw him off the scent of me asking about him and Tawny.

I mentally punched myself in the face. I was just throwing a net hoping to catch something that would logically explain what happened. The look he gave me was of utter disgust.

"It was just a question," I muttered, barely audible.

He bent down to look me in the eyes. He was clearly having a hard time controlling his face. I felt disgust and amusement. Amusement?

"Scarlett, frowned upon would be the lightest way I could describe the uprising that would be caused by immediate family attempting to get married. It happened to one of the greater families within the last century and it was an outrage. *But*, you and Slate aren't blood related."

He flashed me a smile that belonged on a shirtless model I occasionally saw at the mall. "You aren't his type, and he isn't the marrying kind, but I saw how he looked at you."

It didn't help me dissect what happened between him and Tawny. I made a disgusted face at him.

"A lot of second cousins marry, but usually for the benefits it offers, such as land, keeping names, power. Power is always a reason."

It was my turn to be confused. Was he telling me he'd slept with his niece for power? No, that didn't make sense. He said it so I'd know it, but I had no idea what to apply it to.

"I'll be back in a minute." He strode over to his room, so I went into Jett's room.

That horribly awkward conversation didn't clear up a single thing, except now he may or may not think I had a crush on Slate. I sighed as I plopped down into the black sofa chair across from Tawny. She had a look in her eyes that I had never seen before.

Is she jealous?

I wanted to laugh, but I had a strong suspicion that would upset her. Even as ridiculous as it was to me, she had very real, very *hurt* feelings.

"Enlightening conversation?" she asked slowly, quirking an eyebrow.

"Not really," I huffed. "I'm pretty sure he thinks I want to marry Slate now, and that I believe this place runs like medieval times." I gave a mock grimace.

And she smiled.

"What did he say about your proposal of marriage to Slate?" "He said I wasn't his type." I wrinkled my nose.

Jett walked out of his fitting room/closet, that smug grin of his on his too-handsome face. "Ready to roll, ladies?"

His love of movies had affected his way of speaking. It was more like a typical American teen than anyone else's around here; it had even influenced Steel's speaking, I'd noticed. I liked it, it was homey. He was wearing a sleeveless lightweight tunic. It had a "V" collar and closed at the side of his chest with a couple toggle buttons. The cream, lightweight shirt was tucked into brown fitted pants, and soft-looking, cuffed brown boots. It had a casual feel, like it was something he wore every day.

"Ready," Tawny and I said, lifting ourselves out of our comfortable chairs.

"Ready," said Steel, coming out of the bathroom.

He was coming too? I shouldn't have been surprised; he and Jett seemed to do everything together.

Steel was wearing a near identical outfit, but his shirt was olive. I felt like a bum in my grey maxi dress, code name young woman's moo-moo.

"*Fantastic.* The girls are meeting us at the portal door in town. Let's go." Jett's girls: Cerise call-me-Cherry, and Amethyst.

"*Great*, can't wait," Tawny said, sarcasm oozing.

She pulled the belt of her red shirt dress, ready for battle.

I'd never seen Tawny around a guy she cared about. Throw in a couple aloof hot chicks and it was a recipe for disaster.

We took the portal door in the palace to the one at the market.

When Jett had said "market," I envisioned mules with packs and dirty stands of people selling fruit. Maybe a scampering street rat running from a patrol.

I'd watched way too many movies.

There were horses, but they seemed more like pets than beasts of burden. Everyone floated their items along in the air like the hair-dressers Cricket, Katydid, and busty Bronze had. Occasionally, the wares bumped into each other before the conveyor belt of floating items simply gathered back up around the obstacle.

The portal door behind me was less of a door and more of a fifteen-foot gate. It had a high mosaic arch, done in whites and blues. Spiraling ironwork below the mosaic radiated from a blazing sun and below that, an iron patchwork door. There was a door for people in the middle of the gate, but during the day it looked like the gate stayed open.

"Are the gates always guarded?" I asked, noticing a man in the blue and gold house colors, blazing sun sigil on his chest.

"It's not so much guarded as it is monitored. It never used to be, but after the attack from the Red Kings, things changed. People lived in fear of another massacre. Twenty years later, things are finally back to normal, sort of," Steel said, leaning against the white plastered wall of a building.

I guessed we were waiting for the girls.

Tawny was simultaneously trying to look uninterested while leaning forward to hear Steel. It was comical. It would've been so normal if he hadn't been her uncle...I shook off the thought.

"My birthday is in two weeks, what are you getting me?" Jett said with a lopsided grin, breaking me out of my jumble of confused thoughts.

He was trying to change the subject, I figured. The yuletide massacre was something no one wanted to discuss. I couldn't blame them. For Jett, it was the day his mother decided to leave him and take her infant daughter to safety instead. I was surprised he and Slate didn't hate me.

"What do you want?" I wanted a relationship with my brother so badly, I hoped he couldn't see how desperate I was for it. I tried to be casual.

"What do you have?" His smile broadened.

He had this way of making you feel constantly hit on—a lech, I decided. I doubted he took anything too seriously.

I opened my money purse within the purse I normally carried and moved some coins around with a finger. "I have no idea. None of these coins have the monetary value on them."

"That's easy. It's gold, silver, nickel, and copper." He dug through my purse.

Didn't he know you were never supposed to go through a girl's purse? He didn't seem to notice my shock.

"This is a Daymark, the gold one." It was divided with lines like eight slices of pizza, little etches stemming from the center.

He held up another. "This silver one is a Crescent."

It had a circle on it, half a blazing sun, half a crescent moon.

He dug through my purse some more. "This one is what most people carry around; it's called a Hunt, and it's nickel." Three dog-shaped figures chasing one another were imprinted on the coin in a circle.

"Last *and* least is the copper coin, a Skoll. The wolf that swallows the sun." He flicked it back into my open purse.

"You won't normally carry that much around; it's quite the little fortune you have there. My guess is Pearl gave you so much so you could buy some clothes more in trend with local customs."

Steel side glanced at Tawny's legs, looking lean in her short dress and high corked wedges, then at the women shopping around us. The locals wore dresses like the ones we'd seen the palace staff wearing. Long flowing fabric that reminded me of the bedsheets Tawny and I wrapped around ourselves in as a children pretending to be Grecian goddesses. I remember thinking that my mom looked surprised when we'd danced around for her in those. Back then I attributed it to our super stylish skills. Now I thought it was because it reminded her of home.

"You want us to try on clothes for you?"

Was Tawny talking to Steel? My stomach knotted for her.

"You don't have to try it on, but we could help so you know what is in style," he said, kicking an invisible rock.

"I'd like to see you try it on," Jett said, pushing off the wall, circling around Tawny with what I deemed an inappropriately lecherous look for a cousin.

"Flirt!" Before I could see where the voice came from, a tall, thin girl launched herself into Jett's arms and proceeded to make out with him.

I looked away, uncomfortable with their very public affection. She plopped down and leaned past Tawny to give Steel a kiss. Cerise aka Cherry planted a wet one on Steel's mouth and turned around to wink at Tawny. Jett was currently holding babe number two, Amethyst.

Both girls donned long dresses with sheer panels in their stomachs worn off the shoulder with sheer sleeves and gold torques at their throats to a type of halter. They looked like supermodels in something out of ComicCon.

"Steel," Amethyst said in a voice like a purr.

Tawny was not going to have an easy day.

"Girls! Let me introduce you again to my sister, Scarlett, and my cousin, Tawny."

The attitude of the girls changed in unison from competitors to cohorts. Just like that, my brother had let them know to make us feel welcomed.

Amethyst reached out for me and drew me into a hug she didn't seem all that comfortable with, but did it for Jett's sake. "Nice to see you again."

She had big, dark bedroom eyes, a wide mouth with full lips on a diamond-shaped mocha face. Amethyst moved on to Tawny, embracing her too.

"Scarlett, we're going to be like sisters!" Cherry squealed, kissing me on both cheeks.

She had bright blue eyes, fair skin, and a red pouty mouth: Snow White. It popped into my head every time I saw her. I had the feeling she was harmless, and I couldn't figure out how she fit into the complicated relationship my brother was having with these two women.

Amethyst was under my brother's arm speaking in hushed tones when Cherry swung her attention over to Tawny. "I've seen Steel with plenty of women who go gaga over him. I've never seen *him* go gaga, period." She tapped her finger to her chin. "Nope. Never. Anyway, no harm, no foul?" she asked, her slim arms opened, waiting for the okay to give her a squeeze.

Tawny nodded; she didn't explain that Steel was her uncle/cousin and just how complicated the whole scenario was, she just hugged her back.

Steel stood stiffly, his lips pressed in a solid line. I guessed Cherry wasn't as quiet as he wanted her to be. He looked like he wanted to say something. We'd been gone five minutes and this was already a miserable trip; something needed to change, and fast.

"I thought you were here for me?" Jett gave Cherry a pinch in some unseen place and she jumped.

"Naughty!" She giggled.

"Let's shop," Jett said, Cherry falling in alongside him.

We walked the shiny roads made up of white stones compressed into a flat surface that shimmered. The market street was lined with shops. White stucco buildings with gold embossed signs and blue mosaic patterns that stretched as far as I could see.

I looked around, trying to find the palace. As it turned out, we were standing at the very bottom of the mountain the palace sat upon. The white palace covered the entire precipice. Several pointed domes and turrets in metallic blues and golds glittered in the sunlight. Its hundreds of arched windowless windows were sculpted into the face of the palace. I could see two rivers that flowed to the waterfall behind it. I realized then that it wasn't so much a mountain—it only looked that way from the way the homes were built around it. It was really a cliff. The cliff ran at the same level as the rivers and then fell off the side where the waterfall was. That had to be strategic—it would be fatal for an enemy to attack from land this way.

Jett caught me looking. "The rivers Mani and Sol loop around from the ocean and back into it behind the palace. It's mostly Merfolk territory inside those patches of land. Steel here is the Merfolk aficionado."

Steel's Olympic-swimmer-like body made more sense now.

Steel puffed up, proud of his association with the Merfolk. "I am ambassador to the Merfolk. Mermaids are real." He flashed us a bright, poster boy smile.

"They're called *folk* for a reason—some are half octopus, half shark, you get the idea. But the mermaids...they love the man who puts the *ass* in ambassador." Jett and the girls laughed as they led the way into a shop.

I could only see the back of Steel's neck but it was bright red. I wondered if humans could have a physical relationship with a half-fish as Tawny seethed next to me.

We entered a shop lined with dresses of all different colors, but seemed to all have the same flowing style. The guys found a sofa by the fitting rooms as Amethyst and Cherry fretted over us and our dress choices. They were in their element, and since I had no idea what I was doing, I didn't mind. Tawny didn't seem to care either. She was trying not to be obvious about stealing glances of Steel, hurt in her eyes. I couldn't fathom how she felt.

Sitting side by side, the similarities as well as the differences between Jett and Steel were more apparent. As well as my own similarities, I thought ruefully. They said they were uncle and brother, but I never once heard my mom or Pearl say it.

After nixing several extremely revealing dresses the girls had picked for us, we arranged to have some slightly more modest ones sent back to the palace, and we paid with our Guardian currency. It was nice not to swipe a plastic card.

We then stopped somewhere for the guys, seeing as they were such good sports at the dress shop. Not that Steel seemed to mind. Amethyst and Cherry had insisted on us trying on the dresses in case they needed to be altered, and he drank in Tawny every time she emerged in a new dress. He looked disappointed when she refused a particularly revealing black one.

It was a weapon shop. I was surprised the shops felt air conditioned, but Jett told me it was one of those things the *calling* allowed them to do. It kept constant cool air flow with the activation of a metal plate.

Fluorescent glass cases lined the whole shop, and the guys walked through, checking them out. I had a hard time imagining the need to use any of the weapons. The men working there were dressed similarly to the guys—light sleeveless tunics with fitted pants tucked into soft, folded-over boots. I was surprised there weren't any scars on them after all their use with blades and bows. They did have tattoos, but I thought they were paint at first because they were such a bright blue. I watched as they brought out knives to admire. Both men had on torque bracelets, one gold, one silver. The same ones Steel had on with the pendant that settled in the hollow of his throat.

Without thinking, I reached out twisted one of the bracelets on the big man's wrist. It didn't twirl; it was fitted to the shape of his thick wrist. The man's Oxford blue eyes—so dark they were nearly black—were watching me. People probably didn't often reach out and try to play with his jewelry.

He took me in, weighing me. I felt a bitterly cold breeze caress my chest and my skin prickled in response. He was leering at me! I realized why and crossed my arms in a huff as he chuckled darkly.

"They are from the university. He has passed both the Wild Hunt and Ragnarock, and has been proven tried and true," growled a voice from behind me.

I knew who it was without looking. He was so close I could feel the charge of his body.

The man behind the counter smirked. He must have known Slate. The girls had dragged Tawny over to the other side of the shop, convincing her she needed something, and I was on my own. They had warmed up a great deal to both of us, apparently determined to make us their new best friends.

Slate stood too close behind me; I could feel his breaths shift the hair on the top of my head. I spun around to give him a tongue lashing about personal space, but was hit by the storm in his eyes. I wondered if they were always waiting for the storm to break or if it was some horrible gift I had, that I could make him so arrogant and angry.

I stood frozen by him, trying to remember to breathe.

"Liked that, did you, Rabbit? Your naivety draws them in like sharks when there is blood in the water."

I wanted to slap him.

He walked away from me and I followed, trying to think of something brilliant to say that would shut him up. He stopped suddenly and I ran into him; his body was like a brick wall.

He grabbed me by the waist to stop me from bouncing onto the floor. My stomach did a flip, my heart ran a marathon, and my brain went blank.

Smooth, that was me.

He steadied me, but my knees were rubbery. He held me out at arm's length, and a million things ran past those eyes that were locked on mine again.

"You bit me," I muttered mulishly.

He turned around, ignoring my comment. Jett had healed me so I couldn't confirm that my lip had been split, but I was seriously starting to doubt that it had been a dream.

I looked at his back and groaned. Silky midnight hair fell in waves halfway down his powerful back, with little etched fragments or fetishes of stone and silver beads through it, the front pulled back by a black leather strap. The other night, I'd wrapped my fingers in it and pulled. The responding growl had done embarrassing things to me.

"This would suit you."

I jumped to attention at the sound of his voice, then mentally scolded myself. I would not dance to the tune that man played. It was the first time he'd said something to me that sounded remotely congenial without a hint of lechery.

I did my best saunter to where he pointed and leaned over the case. He shifted his body so I could press closer. It was a black handled, single-bladed knife like the one Hawk had given Gyps. I didn't have any interest in knives, but it was beautiful.

Its black handle was carved into the shape of a woman and etched in gold. Its black, hand-stitched scabbard had gold-embossed wings and gold buckles. It was barely as long as my forearm, but it looked wickedly sharp.

"It's beautiful. Who is she?" I asked breathlessly.

I was in complete awe. Did the cavemen working there carve this thing of beauty?

"Freya, queen of the Valkyries, among other things," Slate whispered too near my ear.

I stiffened when I realized he had placed himself behind me, his hands on either side of me, and was glancing over my shoulder. He signaled over to the pervy-cool-breeze-guy who gave me a shrug that said, *Sorry, not sorry*. Slate slapped down a couple gold Daymarks and pressed his front against my back as he took the blade off the swath of black velvet.

I held my breath. His front was as hard as his back, and my cheeks flamed thinking about my own innuendo.

He moved and his missing body heat left me oddly cooled. Strong hands on my hips shifted my body and Slate knelt in front of me, starting to raise the skirt of my dress. I pushed it back down with a tomato face, wrestling with Slate's big hands, and he held up the seax I'd been admiring with an arched brow. I still wasn't sure what he was implying, but instead of trying to hopelessly wrestle his hands away I just watched. He handed me the hem of my dress roughly and reached between my legs, then buckled the knife to my thigh.

Slate's fingers trailed on the inside of my thigh for a second longer after he'd buckled the seax. Something inside me pulsed in response and I firmly stamped it out. I wondered if he saw the prickle of my skin since he'd been so close to it. He sat back on his heels and took my hem from my hand, letting it drop back to the floor. He nodded and gave me an appreciative smile. I gaped at him as he rose.

He spoke with the guy behind the counter for another minute and bought himself a series of little knives that looked like they'd fit perfectly between his knuckles. He stuck them into an invisible belt he was wearing under his charcoal grey shirt like the ones Jett and Steel wore. He saw me trying to catch a glimpse of where he was shoving them, and he arched a dark masculine brow. Slate lifted his shirt so I could see two belts that crossed his chest that held a dozen of those little knives...and a perfect dark pink nipple.

He looked profoundly amused. I wondered what he could've done recently that he'd needed to replace those knives.

Jett and Steel walked up together.

"I'm glad you made it. Did you get something?" Jett was asking me.

How would I tell him my boundary-inept adopted brother had bought me something?

"She picked out a seax," Slate said, neatly avoiding the fact he'd bought it for me.

I lifted my dress enough to see the tip off the scabbard. He smiled at me, perfectly aware of how uncomfortable I was with having three men and the leering salesman staring at my fully exposed leg.

"Good choice. Fits you perfectly. We've got to help Tawny pick one too. The girls are trying to cajole her into buying some little kitchen knife."

He shook his head and laughed. He slapped a hand to Slate's shoulder, he knew he'd bought it or that he'd helped me. I couldn't be certain.

I admired my knife under my dress and how you could barely see it under the jersey fabric. In those flowing gowns I'd bought, it'd be near invisible. I smiled and started to join the group, huddled around Tawny.

I caught Slate watching me, and wanted to say my thanks, but those intense eyes stopped me.

I kept my eyes averted.

In the end Tawny bought a seax like mine, with a blood-red, studded handle, the matching scabbard embossed with a tree that had a woman's shape. Mother Earth, Steel had told her as he strapped it onto her thigh. Jett and Slate conveniently stood at the other side of the store when she asked for help to put it on. Tawny stared straight ahead the entire time, even as Steel lingered at the last buckle, willing her to look at him. To feel anything but anger towards him. He sighed as he stood and walked to the storefront.

I knew Tawny wasn't adopted; she was Sparrow's daughter through and through. I sighed in resignation. Maybe she and Steel would run away together and live in sin where no one would know. Oddly, that idea made me happy.

We strolled along the bustling shop streets as Amethyst and Cherry gossiped about the people at Valla U. Amethyst was a second year; I noticed the silver torque at her wrist after the fact. The silver was for surviving the Wild Hunt challenge. It turned out her brothers all worked at the school and were high up like her father. I was slightly in awe. Jett was obviously a good-looking, witty guy, but she could probably have anyone she wanted. I'd bet she would get a very powerful marriage.

I balked at my own thinking, but then I realized it was true. What was she doing sharing my brother?

Cherry was a more understandable match for him: she was fun and loving, she cared about Jett in a way Amethyst could probably never allow herself. The dynamic was fascinating the more I observed it.

Slate and Steel walked behind us, Jett and the girls in front. We passed at an equipment shop and went in. The mannequins were armed to the teeth in garb I'd never imagined myself wearing in a million years.

"What's all this for?" I asked.

I hated being the one doing all the talking—besides Amethyst and Cherry, of course. Tawny was usually the one to speak up first, but she was lost in her own thoughts. I left her to them.

"Battle. It's the only time you get to pick your own clothes, being a tyro. Otherwise it's the same old same old black dress for the girls and black jerkin and pants for the boys. Dull if you ask me, but it's easier to identify the students at the university that way. We do get red belts as first years, yellow as second. Since most of the guys wear all black anyway, it works out just fine for them. The blood doesn't show on black," Cherry said matter-of-factly.

It was the longest I'd heard her speak without giggling.

"I have no idea where to begin," I said, gawking at all the crazy gear, trying to ignore her blood comment.

I would need help to figure out how to put all these things on. It'd take forever.

An exceedingly beautiful man caught my eye through the racks and flashed a provocative smile our way. Even though I was blushing, I started to return it.

Slate stepped into my line of sight and I lost track of the hottie.

"It's easier than it looks. We wanted to bring you by so you can start getting ideas on what you want to get in the future," Amethyst noted.

"We can always come back whenever and help you try things on. It's hard to do it alone your first time."

Cherry's innuendo was not lost on me. My face blushed accordingly, as did Steel's and Tawny's. Perhaps Cherry only played vapid to disarm people.

"We should get back. We must head over to Valla for Butterfly's son's *Ausa Vatni,*" Steel said, attempting to guide Tawny back out the way we came.

She pulled her shoulder away from him in a sharp tug.

We headed back to the portal. Amethyst went first, as she lived in Valla. After making out with my brother for an uncomfortable amount of time, Cherry skipped through the portal next; she lived in Mabon. The rest of us could all walk in together since the gate was open, but Jett held me back, his hand on my shoulder as we watched the other three walk through. Tawny, head held high, not wanting to acknowledge Steel to her left, and Slate glancing back as he walked through, the bright light making him look like an avenging angel.

I snorted internally; a *fallen* angel more like.

"What's up?" I asked Jett.

"Let's grab a cup of tea. We can't take long, we'll have to head to the *Ausa Vatni* soon. I just wanted some brother/sister time."

He smiled and hooked my arm in his. My arm was slightly lifted into the air, and he tried to hang his arm lower so I'd be comfortable. It was funny; if I didn't know any better, I'd say *he* was uncomfortable. I could see now why he'd always slung his arms around Amethyst's and Cherry's shoulders.

He knew a cafe around the corner; we went to it and sat outside on black, wrought iron seats with our tea, watching the crowd hustle around us.

Jett looked at me meaningfully. "I want to tell you something important. It's not mine to tell, but I feel it is imperative you know. The deal is, you can't tell anyone. *Ever.* I need you to vow you'll never tell another living soul. Not unless it has already been revealed."

I nodded. I didn't see the big deal. "Okay?"

"Vows are different here. It's binding. You will literally never be able to speak, write, or pantomime what you've sworn not to tell."

I thought he threw in that last bit to try to keep it light, but what he was saying was heavy. It was something big.

"What does it entail? The vow."

"Hold out your hand."

I gave him my hand. He slid a knife out of who knows where and sliced my palm open. He did the same to his own. "Now repeat after me: *By the name gifted to me by my ancestors, I give my word. May I never stain it. From my blood, I vow with the voice of my forbearers. On my honor, and the honor of my descendants, I hereby swear to keep it.*"

I said it word for word; it felt surreal. The words seemed to sink into my skin. Jett held his wound to mine and at the end of my oath my skin felt tighter, and then it was done. I felt my oath settle over me, and I took a deep breath.

What did I just promise?

Jett's eyes locked with mine under his thick masculine brows. "I'm sorry I made you do that, but if it slipped out unintentionally, Pearl would have my hide."

"Okay, so now that I swore your blood oath, what's this big secret?" I was still feeling uncomfortable from the oath.

"Scar, do you think Steel is a good guy? I know you just met him, but what's the vibe you get from him?"

I shifted uncomfortably in my seat. He had to know Steel and Tawny spent the night together, that had to be what this was about.

"He really does seem like a good guy," I said aloud, and it felt true.

A small smile played on Jett's lips. "Do you think a genuinely good guy would purposely spend the night with his brother's daughter?"

I hadn't thought of it like that. I'd thought of him as her uncle/cousin and her as his niece, but not Hawk's brother purposely taking his daughter's virginity. That hadn't crossed my mind at all.

"Sparrow and my mom sent you guys pictures." "Our mom," he corrected gently.

"Sorry, I'm not used to having a brother." I gave him a nervous smile. "Are you sure Steel isn't our brother? And shouldn't Slate be here for brother/sister time?"

"You mean after four hours you haven't bought into the whole sibling thing? Regardless, uncle or brother, Steel is *family*." He smiled jokingly then got serious again. "I don't know how to say it, except how it happened. Bear with me." I nodded.

"Sparrow wasn't there with Tawny at the massacre. They left beforehand, after

Ridge Vetr was killed, and supposedly his infant daughter and wife."

He gazed out at me, but my brain was mashed potatoes. I couldn't put the pieces together except that I was finally hearing about this Ridge person, so he continued.

"Things were really sketchy the days leading up to the massacre; people were uneasy. When Ridge was attacked while out with his family, everyone assumed the whole family had been killed. They weren't. Sparrow fled and escaped with their daughter. She and Ridge's daughter, Tawny."

I couldn't move. Couldn't think. Tawny, my would-be sister, not even my cousin. Hawk wasn't her father. Steel wasn't her uncle/brother. Steel knew he wasn't her uncle.

"Who all knows?"

I sounded like an old smoker trying to talk past the lump in my throat. I didn't know why I'd be upset. I wouldn't lose Tawny; she was still a part of our family. I was upset because the one thing that would alleviate her pain from not being able to be with Steel would cause a different kind of pain—i.e. finding out the man whom she thought was her father all these years wasn't.

"Everyone but Gyps and Tawny. Hawk and Sparrow had a thing before Ridge came along, and he never got over her, I guess. He helped set her up in Chicago, and came back in time for the massacre. When that happened, they decided it wasn't safe for you or Mom, so Hawk moved you out to Chicago and I stayed here with Pearl."

My mom knew Tawny wasn't really Hawk's daughter and never told me. I couldn't blame her.

I would have said it in a heartbeat this morning when she thought Steel was her uncle.

I played with my teacup, letting the facts sink in, taking fortifying breaths. When *would* the right time be to tell Tawny? Probably now. But now that I was under oath, I couldn't tell my mom, or Hawk or Sparrow to tell Tawny. I couldn't even mime it.

I took Jett's hand. "If you knew how sad mom was without you, you'd know how badly she wanted to be back here. I've never seen her more herself than she has been since we arrived. I didn't even know she *was* sad before, so incomplete. I'm sorry you had to grow up without her. She's a wonderful mother."

He shook his head as if what I was saying wasn't necessary. I looked at him quizzically. "You really didn't know anything about me, did you?" he asked.

I shook my head.

"Mom wrote me, Slate, and Steel every week since she left here. Before I could even read, I had letters from her...pictures of you. I cared about you all before I'd ever met you." I took a deep breath to keep from weeping in such a public place. "Don't ever be sorry. I've always felt loved." He took my hands off my teacup and held them.

Things were way too serious for me, and Tawny wasn't here to lighten the mood.

"You sure *do* get enough loving, don't you?" I joked.

He laughed sat back and wiped a hand down his face. "I was wondering when you'd get to that."

I quirked an eyebrow at him and gave him my best disapproving sister look.

He laughed again. "It's simple. Amethyst grew up thinking she'd be married off to the highest bidder. Her dad has serious influence, so people would be fighting for her marriage. Her mom passed during the massacre, so she's grown up with her three brothers and her dad. She's been spoiled rotten, it's kind of messed her up a little. Not for me, of course. She's perfect for me. But for someone who would want her to settle down, be a wife, have kids, the works—it's not for her, she's not wired that way. And Cherry...*well,* she's got enough love for all three of us. The two of them don't get jealous over one another because they love each other, too. I don't know what will happen, but I know if I got married, it'd have to be both or neither. Amethyst would be good at running a household, she's tough as nails, and Cherry would love to be a mother. I suppose I love them. The three of us. It's all or nothing." He shrugged.

That had to be the most he'd ever explained it, to himself or out loud. I thought Amethyst could be maternal, but maybe I was misreading her ability to control a situation.

I wasn't sure what to say, so I just nodded.

"Do you think Steel really cares about Tawny? She's never acted like this about a guy, obviously. I think she's heartbroken. How do we get Hawk and them to confess?"

He held his hands up and twisted his lips.

"I don't know. I guess they'll do it when they're ready. Hopefully, that'll be soon. As far as Steel is concerned, that guy has fallen *hard*. He's hopeless. Of course the only girl he has a thing for would happen to be his adopted niece!" He laughed as if there was some joke there. "I mean, the Merfolk...if they found out how hard he's fallen, they'd probably try to drown her." He laughed again.

My eyes were bugging out of my face.

"Sorry, I guess that requires some backstory. Mermaids are jealous creatures—you'd never catch me messing around with one, that's for sure.

I gave him a *I still have no idea what you're talking about* look, and he sighed.

"Yes, people—" he pointed to himself, then me—"can have a *type* of relation with other tribes. You wouldn't want to bring them home to Mama or anything..." He caught the look of disgust on my face. "Sorry. It's common and those mermaids aren't like the cartoon kind. I'll take you to see them one of these days. Hook you up with a Merman." He poked my middle from across the table. "They have this drink, rousen. It's what they give to...*ah*, well. You'll find out in time. Long story short, it's used to awaken...certain parts of a person's body."

I was smiling but trying to look disgusted, while secretly intrigued. "Thanks, I have my hands full at the moment," I muttered.

"A little chip off the old brother block." He gave me the biggest, most smug grin ever.

"It's not like that." I blushed.

Had he seen me with Ash? Oh yes, he had.

"Scar, Slate lives a hard life. He changes women more often than he does underwear. I love him, he's my brother, but you're my sister and I've seen how he looks at you. He's not the settling down type; there's a lot there you don't see. Those of us close to him know he sees things, has a bit of a death wish."

"Slate *sees* things? You make him sound like a psychopath."

Jett gave me a wry grin. "I don't have memories without him. He has a talent that's hard to describe and I'm not comfortable telling you about it without him knowing. He plays his cards close to his chest." He shrugged. "Anyway, I just wanted to tell you so you wouldn't get hurt. You're my sister." As if that explained everything. "Maybe I'm wrong. He did buy you that seax, and you live at our home. He's never brought a girl home, but don't worry about it. I heard you've got guys beating down the doors. *Tsk, tsk.* Shouldn't go playing around with boys' hearts, you might break one."

I scoffed. "No one has *ever* accused me of breaking hearts. I did meet someone last night, Ash Straumr. He was very charming, and I plan on seeing him again. Slate, not a chance. I saw some older woman and him in the bathroom doing unscrupulous things." I didn't hide my disgust.

Jett laughed at my face. "Ash is trouble, Scar. He hangs out with all those greater families and he has a reputation for breaking hearts. He's Amethyst's cousin. He's one of those guys who'll be looking for a powerful marriage. *You* come from a powerful family." He lifted his hands as if he was putting two and two together.

He thumbed the direction of the portal door and we got up to leave.

"I'm nineteen. I'm not looking to get married!" I almost yelled it.

"You should, because they'll be looking at you that way. A Sumar/Tio girl whose father is suspected to be a Haust? Oh yeah, sold to the highest bidder."

"Mom would never do that."

"Even if it meant you'd be well taken care of for the rest of your life by some stud? Come on, you've seen the gene pool. Whoever created the first Guardian knew what they were doing. Think of it this way: if you want kids, you have less than ten years to get that done from now. Might want to start looking at things differently. You'd better believe most of our fellow students will be betrothed, or very possibly married, before we're proven tried and true and become true Guardians."

We walked arm in arm to the portal and went through together. I was still digesting Jett's information.

The drapes were thrown open so the stained glass showed its colors through my room and I could hear the waterfall below. The boxes of dresses were already waiting on my sitting area table.

"Scar, that you?" Tawny yelled from her room.

"Yup, just got in. Have you talked to your mom yet?" I asked as I walked into our shared bathroom.

"Uh-uh, been waiting for the dress delivery to get ready. What do you think?" She spun in her lemon-yellow dress, a gold torque securing the fabric in a halter neckline.

"Gorgeous, as always. I had a nice chat with my big bro."

"You're never going to get sick of saying that, are you?" "Never," I said, beaming.

I filled her in on our talk, everything except what my oath prevented me from saying.

"That Slate is sure making himself at home with you. Hands all up your leg," Tawny commented out of nowhere.

I blushed to my toes. I'd hoped no one had seen that.

"He's just one of those guys who wants all the women to want him indiscriminately. I'm fresh meat. No worries here, I can handle him," I blustered, and she guffawed.

"Sure you can. That robot thing you do whenever you're in his line of sight is *very* convincing. Don't lose your head over some cache hole." *Cache hole*, our slang. "Get up, we have to get ready."

I GROANED in mock protest and she led me back into my room. She let me sit on the couch, and went through the boxes until she found a blush pink strapless dress that, despite all the folds of fabric, was very light.

"This with your nude strappy wedges. I'll help with your makeup. Your hair still looks good.

I pretended to stomp my feet into the closet. "What would I do without you?"

"Thankfully for you, that'll never happen."

Even though I'd found out less than an hour ago that she wasn't really my cousin, she would always be my sister.

CHAPTER 8

 When we met the family at the portal door, my mother stood near Jett and Steel under the blue starry lights. It was strange watching her talk to Jett, who towered over her. Pearl glowed watching them, her smile from ear to ear as we walked through the portal door. I knew she was happy to have us all with her, doing regular family things...

As we walked through the magic door.

We arrived at the Tio palace, Pearl's brother's home, her childhood home. I looked behind me at the portal door; it was becoming a habit of mine. The walls were all cool grey stone, the top of the doorway was a large, stained-glass clock. Very appropriate for the Tio palace. The door was blocky stained glass with a blazing sun peeking over wavy hills, sunflowers reaching up on either side of the door. I thought it must have been designed by a woman because it had a very feminine feel to it.

A woman with curves that rivaled my grandmother's and fiery red hair met us in the portal room. She had a warm smile and hugged Pearl the second we were all through the door.

"Pearl, *oh* my, how happy I am to have you all here. Reed will be delighted to see all of you."

She looked to be around my grandmother's age so I took her to be my great uncle's wife. She started hugging and removing nonexistent pieces of lint from us with her long-nailed fingers.

"Fern, you remember Wren. This is Scarlett. Hawk is here with Sparrow and their children Tawny and Gypsum. You know all the rest," Pearl said proudly.

It was her first time introducing all of us. It was a big moment.

"I remember, I remember. Now, try not to get overwhelmed. We wound up inviting all of the Straumrs; they don't have any children to welcome to the world this year so I thought, why not just come over here? We shall make a grand feast of my grandson's blessing!"

Fern had a rushed, excited way of speaking. I couldn't imagine her ever being angry a day in her life, she was so perky.

"And then Moon's daughter invited her friend and his eldest son invited his friend. So we shall have a big mix here today. Butterfly is just *so* excited!" I doubted she could be more excited than her mother.

Fern was like a classic southern woman, incredibly friendly and hospitable. I liked her already. My heart skipped at the mention of the Straumrs. I'd get to see Ash sooner than I'd thought.

"Butterfly married Robin's eldest son?" my mom asked with a smile.

"She did—Coyote. Such a wonderful young man. All the Regn are here." Fern turned to us and gave Tawny and me a mischievous look. "You know what they say about those Regn boys." We didn't.

Tawny leaned into my ear. "*This* is going to be interesting."

Fern fluttered around us like a redheaded hummingbird, ushering us into their formal ballroom. It was lovely; one wall was all windows, letting in bright sunlight. The walls were paneled with mirrors making the room look huge, and two tiered crystal chandeliers hung from the ceiling.

Even though she said it would be quite the party, I was still surprised to see all the people. I had never been to a baptismal, but I'd always imagined one to be an intimate affair. What was most notable were all the redheads; I'd never seen so many gathered in one place.

Fern brought over an older gentleman, and by older I thought *maybe* fifties. He had a small mustache and a thick head of coppery brown hair perfectly quaffed into a pompadour. With them, they brought a dark eyed man with shoulder-length dark hair, the front pulled back, and a petite redhead carrying a baby.

"Scarlett, Gypsum, Tawny, this is your great Uncle Reed." Fern pointed to the mustached man. "Butterfly, our daughter, your future provost of tribal affairs and her son, name soon to be announced." Fern was teeming with maternal pride. "And her husband, Coyote Regn." She gestured to the man with the dark hair and eyes.

Coyote's eyes were intense and soft at the same time; something about them made me want to stare at him for hours. We said our *hellos* and *your baby is so cutes* and began to wander around. Jett made a beeline for his ladies, who were already together. Amethyst was Moon's daughter and Cherry, the friend.

Steel stood fidgeting next to Tawny, clearly hoping for a reconciliation, until he gave up and went in Jett's direction. Tawny and I stood together sipping to kill the time.

"I want to go find out what they say about Regn boys. If they are half as scrumptious as Coyote, this party may be looking up."

I had to agree with that sentiment. Coyote was positively dreamy.

Slate had disappeared and I tried not to crane my neck to find him. Hawk and Gyps were talking next to a table filled with appetizers while my mom, Sparrow, and Pearl hovered near Fern and the baby.

"I didn't expect to see you again so soon."

It was Ash. No mask, nothing between those gorgeous light green eyes and caramel skin. He'd snuck up behind me and put his arm loosely around my waist.

"This is my great uncle's home. Fern told us your families are close?"

He seemed disappointed I didn't say anything about him. He let his arm drop from my waist and I tried to hold in a sigh of relief—the last thing I needed was my mom to ask questions. But, *fiddlesticks,* Guardians had a toothsome gene pool.

"Very. They run the university together. We all live on Valla, the only greater families who do." He said it like I should be impressed, but honestly it meant nothing to me.

"Very cool." Tawny picked up where my brain had malfunctioned.

I felt Slate's eyes on me, I tried to look casually over my shoulder. He didn't bother hiding the fact he was staring, eyes like gunmetal. He stood with two other dark-haired men, probably the two from the masquerade. His *spies*.

Why on earth would he have a reason to keep an eye on me? The man with shorter hair flashed me a dazzling smile and I blushed a deep crimson. That one was trouble. Before I could get a good look at the amber-eyed man, he turned to refill his drink. I wanted to see his face without his mask. I must have imagined how inviting those eyes were.

Ash noticed he didn't have my complete attention and put his arm back around my waist. I didn't try to pull away. I liked Ash's attention. No boy or man had paid me attention that way before. It was beyond flattering...and, he *was* gorgeous.

"Let me introduce you to a few people. Tawny, I would be honored if you came along."

There he was again, Ash with Tawny on one arm and me on the other. I wondered if he was trying to work a *Jett* on us.

He brought us over to four redheads. They held their conversation when we joined them.

A man that looked around his late twenties spoke up. "Good afternoon, Ash, who have we here?"

The redheaded man smiled, probably to make us more comfortable, but he was intimidating. He had a dark red beard and hair that brushed his shoulders with piercing blue eyes.

"Provost Sky, this is Scarlett and Tawny. They will be first years at the university."

That got Sky interested in us.

"Then we will be seeing much of one another. I teach Counter Calls. These are my sisters Magnolia and Wisteria. Mags teaches arithmetic and Wisteria teaches about Energies and Spirits."

I was thankful for the naming ceremonies in that moment; I knew just from their names that the women were twins.

He went on, "This handsome gentleman is Ford. He will teaching you about magical beings; which happens to be the name of his class. This is essentially a university party. Nearly everyone here has something to do with Valla U. Do not worry, I will not expect you to remember all our names this time."

He asked about where we came from, what Chicago was like, and listened with a great deal of interest. Provost Magnolia was the only one to learn most of her subject outside of Tidings, so she nodded knowingly at the things I said.

Magnolia had the curves of her mother, tall with blue eyes, while Wisteria was very slim. Both had fiery red hair and skin so fair it was nearly translucent. Wisteria had a coolness in her demeanor that Magnolia didn't have. I had a feeling she'd be a tough teacher.

Tawny was bored, so she went to play with the baby and see where Gyps had run off to, leaving me alone with Ash. He was a great escort. He introduced me to his cousins, the battle instructors, and their father, the Prime and Overseer of Valla U.

A young man with the same caramel skin as Ash, but with sky blue eyes, put his arm around Ash's shoulders. Tried to, at least—Ash was just over six feet while the caramel-skinned man was average height like the man who looked to be his father.

"Ash, who is this beautiful woman you have ensnared?" he asked, blue eyes sparkling, and smiled.

"Scarlett, this is my cousin Fox, and may I introduce you to my uncle Prime of the Guardians and Overseer of Valla University, Moon Straumr."

It seemed appropriate to introduce me to the most important man in Tidings before his sons, but it was strange to greet one man before all the others.

"It's a pleasure to meet you, sir." I smiled at Fox in acknowledgement.

Moon Straumr was an ebony-skinned man with dark eyes. He was the first person I'd met in Tidings that looked his age. I knew it had to do with the death of his wife and the Yuletide massacre. He had the air of someone used to making big decisions and bore the weight of those decisions' consequences. He was the same height as Fox, and looked to have once been heavily muscled, but not as physically fit as he had been.

His tone was measured and thoughtful, as if each word meant something to him, and cost him to say.

"The pleasure is all mine, Scarlett. A Tio?" I nodded.

"The last Tio girl." He smiled sadly.

The last Tio?

Another ebony-skinned man cleared his throat, so I turned my attention to him. He had sharp, dark eyes and a full mouth that appeared to be always pursed in contemplation. His cheekbones looked like they'd been chipped away from a cliff, they were so sharp.

"I am Crag Straumr, this is my brother River. I believe you are familiar with our sister, Amethyst?"

I smiled and nearly sighed at having some common ground with the intimidating men. River was mocha like Amethyst, taller than his brother Crag, about six feet, with dark, depthless brown eyes. Each of the three brothers was uniquely handsome.

Amethyst and Cherry budged their way into the circle of men.

"You've met Scarlett, I see. She's Jett's younger sister." Cherry smiled wickedly.

I got the impression it was a juicy tidbit from the way the men's eyes widened for just an instant. "Ash has been escorting her all over Valla." Amethyst added.

"She comes from a very old family. You make a smart pair," Moon said matter-of-factly, and Ash preened.

What the hell just happened?

Ash led me away, his hand on the small of my back. He deftly introduced me to the barrage of redheads, sons and daughters of the provosts. I noticed that the girls' last names were Rot and the boys' were Tio, and there were the Regns, Litrs, Blomis, and Sandrs, Amethyst and Cherry in the mix too. Finally, I asked Ash about it. Faces became a blur until names became white noise.

He led me over to a balcony outside. It was winter in Valla. I hadn't realized the seasons were in step with Chicago's—I didn't think Thrimilci had a season other than summer. Through their magic, they were able to keep the balcony warm despite the snow.

"You're the first person to introduce me to people using their last names. I hadn't even noticed it. Why do the women all have different last names?"

He kept constant physical contact with me, his light green eyes piercing. His fingers were sliding up and down my arm as we leaned against the balcony. It was sweet, like he thought I needed constant soothing.

"Women always maintain their maiden names, and their daughters after them. Your grandmother is Pearl Tio, her husband was Flint Sumar. All their sons are Sumars, and their daughter Wren Tio. It keeps the old names longer, so they do not die out. My last name is Straumr, my sister is a Natt. In rare cases, when a greater family name is going to die out and it can be prevented, a daughter will take her father's name. Right now, there are no Vetrs. Old man Vetr is the last one; his son died before he could pass on the name. He is desperate to name an heir, but the only sons born of those lines are Heir Haust and Heir Var and the eldest daughter is Heir Natt. It only leaves one alternative."

"Names are a pretty big deal around here." I gestured towards the ballroom where at least a hundred people were gathered for the naming ceremony of an infant.

Ash nodded. *"By the name gifted to me by my ancestors, may I never stain it."* His quote from the blood oath sent shivers down my spine. "It is part of an oath, the most severe you can make. You are cold, let us go back inside. The ceremony will begin soon."

Things with Ash were escalating just by being seen with him. My mom came over and introduced herself, giving me looks she had *never ever* given me before in my life. Looks that said, *good job* and *he's cute*. I shifted uncomfortably, his hand on the small of my back the entire time. Even Hawk and Sparrow got in on the action, making me wish I could walk away and they could swoon over him for me.

He was making quite the impression. He was very good at dealing with people, knew just what to say and how to act with each person. I noticed his subtle changes with each group; he was who the person wanted him to be in that moment. I found it intriguing and wondered if he did that with me, knew just how to get me to do the things he wanted.

I quickly dismissed it. I was being paranoid. What did he possibly have to gain from that? The only person who didn't seem as taken with Ash, besides Tawny, was Pearl. She wasn't particularly rude, but just friendly enough not to be so.

The ceremony was about to begin. We were being ushered into an arboretum. It was an indoor orchard, floral and citrus scents mixing in the sweet air. It had a calming effect. There was a small pond and a white plush blanket laid out in front of Butterfly and Coyote.

We gathered around the pond. I managed to squeeze next to Tawny who had been hanging out with Jett and the girls.

"Are you married yet?" she asked, quirking an eyebrow at me with a sassy smile.

"I'd call you a fanny pack, but that hardly seems appropriate right now." I gave a fake huff.

Cherry was giggling.

Butterfly removed the baby boy's swaddling and placed him bare on the white blanket. Coyote stood over his kicking baby boy and nodded. Butterfly picked up the bare-bottomed baby and dipped him in the still waters, cupping her hand in the pond and letting the water fall through her fingers onto his head. The baby smiled and played with strands of his mother's hair that hung by his face. Butterfly laughed and took her son out of the pond and wrapped the soft white blanket around him before handing him to his father. Coyote made a gesture with his fist across his chest in the shape of an inverted "T."

Coyote then announced, "We own this baby for our son. He shall be called Copper."

I tried not to giggle. I guessed Copper *would* be a popular name. Tawny was trying to hide a smile too.

Coyote and Butterfly stood with their son, beaming with pride as a little dark-haired girl that looked like her father ran up and held onto her mother's skirts. Fern and Reed walked up and laid a gift at the feet of the little family. Everyone left an offering for little Copper. Even I was swept up by the ceremony, and I left the bouncing baby boy a few silver Crescents. Butterfly and Coyote smiled appreciatively. Not that I thought they needed the money, but it felt right to give something to thank them for sharing with us.

The group wandered back into the dining room. The air felt alive with the buzz of the new life we helped welcome into the world. Everyone was a little happier—the joy was contagious. That was when the real party began. Punch bowls of wassail were brought out, a band came in and set up. Dinner was served.

I sat with my family near the rest of the Tios and Sumars. Ash's family sat at the other end of the ridiculously long table, with the Straumrs. I was glad for the reprieve from being Ash's trophy. I liked him, but things were moving too quickly. I sighed. Maybe I shouldn't have been sabotaging something that hadn't even started yet.

I pulled my lips between my teeth and looked across the table. Slate sat there, and I watched the tightening of his bronze jaw as he ate. The muscles moving under his flesh, flesh I knew was softer than it looked because I had touched it when my fists had pushed him away. My lips were parted, heart thumping...I might as well admire his eyes while I was at it. His grey eyes reflected silver while burning a hole right through me.

I closed my gaping mouth and averted my eyes, like *oh I was casually looking everywhere.* I lifted my eyes to see if I'd fooled him. *He* had stopped chewing and was still looking at me. He took a deep breath and shook his head, then returned to eating. I felt like I had disappointed him somehow, and the look he'd given me made my stomach sink.

I saw Coyote's family sitting in a dark-haired group; it was easy to pick them out with all the redheads running around. They looked like a dangerous lot: something about Coyote and his brothers reminded me of Slate, but I couldn't put my finger on it. I turned away when a short-haired one turned my way and gave me a dazzling smile I felt to my toes. Trouble again. So the two dark and dangerous companions of Slate's were Coyote's brothers. Good to know.

I thought I was beginning to understand what they said about those Regn boys.

Jett was sitting between his two leading ladies, ignoring the glares from two of the three brothers of Amethyst. Surprisingly, the oldest brother seemed fine with their relationship. Crag was sitting next to a tall, thin blond man with blue eyes. He looked strong in a wiry way, and I realized neither of them had brought a wife to the occasion. Magnolia was alone too, so maybe it was commonplace to come without dates.

Amethyst was sitting next to a younger girl with light green eyes and chestnut hair, her skin the caramel cream I'd come to expect from the Straumr family. She wasn't as willowy as Amethyst, but just as elegant. I kept catching her sneaking peeks at me when she thought I wasn't aware. Finally, I smiled at her, and she blushed and made her way over to the seat my mom had just vacated. I was ninety percent positive they were either arranging my marriage or trying to find one for Tawny. Plotters.

How did my life change so quickly? I should've been planning for my Masters, working to save up for mine and Tawny's apartment. Definitely not learning that my family is much bigger than I'd known and we could use some kind of magic. I kept waiting for the reality of it all to hit me. So far, I'd been bombarded by a constant flow of new information; now I was holding my breath for the undertow.

The girl sat next to me and gave me a shy smile. "Hi, I am sorry. I did not mean to stare. I am Diamond, Ash's sister."

She didn't need to say younger, I could tell. "It's a pleasure to meet you." She giggled in a cute girlish way.

Then she looked embarrassed. "I am sorry, Ash told me you had a

Chicago accent. We do not really have accents here unless they have left Tidings before. I like it."

Diamond looked about twenty, but for what I knew about the way people aged here, she was probably about sixteen, and she acted like it. It was refreshing.

"Do you like my brother?" she blurted.

"I guess so. I just met him." She looked disappointed, so I added, "He is very handsome."

"I knew it!" She was positively gleeful. "You should marry him. You are so much nicer and prettier than wretched Jonquil."

"I'm a bit young to be thinking about marriage."

She looked at me like I sprouted a third eye. Then I wondered if they had a Cyclops here.

"*I* am betrothed. He is really handsome. Have you met Sterling Haust? He has dreamy indigo eyes and brown hair you can run your fingers through."

I lost her in her fantasy world. I hoped someone was keeping an eye on her. *Run your fingers through...*I never thought that way at her age!

"I have met him. He is very handsome."

Green scaled mask at Ash's table. I didn't have a chance to speak with him. He didn't seem to want to be around Nova and Quartz.

She must have known what I was thinking, because she was smiling and shaking her head. "If you met him with his sisters, forget it. They are evil, he is completely different alone."

She tittered and I blushed.

The twins did give off a wicked witch vibe. Maybe their younger brother wasn't so bad. I was glad Diamond had made the effort to come talk to me. I felt a little bad about Jonquil. She didn't leave me with a good impression, but if I thought a girl was making the moves on the man I loved, I'd be vicious too. At least I thought so. I'd never been in love before.

I looked over at Tawny, who didn't bother pretending like she hadn't been eavesdropping.

"I'm Tawny, I was listening. You seem like quite the matchmaker; you should find me husband too. No one I'm related to, thanks."

Tawny shot her with her finger gun. It was a joke for my benefit, but

Steel was *definitely* eavesdropping on the eavesdropper. I saw him wince. I was going to have to have a talk with my poor uncle/brother.

Diamond loved the idea of finding a match for Tawny. "Oh! I would love to! Hardly anyone is not related though. Sterling is my second cousin, his grandmother and my mother are sisters." She shrugged, like *no biggie.*

Tawny's face was smooth. I would have expected some exaggerated reaction from her.

I decided to break the silence. "I'm not related to you and Ash, am I?"

She thought for a moment, furrowing her caramel cream forehead. "Not within the last three generations. After that I would have to look it up."

"That is not enough for me," I murmured.

A big hand with a platinum pinky ring grasped my shoulder lightly. A crescent moon shown on the obsidian ring face. I turned towards the ring's owner.

Ash's celadon green eyes sparkled at me. "Would you ladies mind if I escorted Scarlett to the arboretum?" he asked kindly of Tawny and Diamond.

Tawny cocked an eyebrow at me, and I blushed. As much as I hated everyone acting like we were already a couple, I could do a whole lot worse than Ash.

I raised my hand to his at my shoulder and he laced his long fingers through mine before he led me away. I could feel my family's eyes on us. As well as someone who was adopted into our family. Slate and his dark haired dynamic duo split apart as I glanced over my shoulder.

Ash walked me into an archway tunnel made of grape vines. I wanted to ask questions about the orchard/vineyard, but I was sure the answer would be magic. It was going to be hard to wrap my head around *that* being the answer to some things.

It was an impossibly romantic setting; all it needed was a few butterflies, and I didn't mean the ones in my stomach. Ash turned me around with his hands loosely wrapped around my waist so he could look down at me through lowered lashes. I was glad he was holding me. Men didn't look like *that* at me, and I could feel my legs getting rubbery.

"Scarlett." He said my name like a benediction.

I breathed deep, afraid my brain wasn't getting enough oxygen. The floral citrus scent flooded my nostrils. If he was going to kiss me, this was the time. I couldn't imagine a better moment. He ran his hand up my spine, and my chin lifted of its own volition.

"Yes?" I breathed, and the smile he gifted me was supremely cocky.

He knew he had me.

"In our short time together, I find myself smitten by you," he said in a low voice.

Butterflies beat furiously in my stomach as his hand ran up to the nape of my neck and found its way into my hair. His other hand brought my waist closer to his hips so my neck was craned to look up at him. My blood thundered in my ears.

I was at a loss. What should I say in response? I wasn't *smitten*; he was super hot, and the attention he showered on me made me feel like the most precious thing on the planet, but I just *liked* him. I licked my lips to answer and he took that as my signal.

Ash's mouth closed over mine and my eyes fluttered closed. *Oh!* His well-formed lips were skilled as they parted mine easily allowing him to deepen the kiss. My arms lifted languidly from his shoulder to wind around his neck. His hands alone held me upright.

It was *some* kiss.

His hands tightened around me and pressed me against his hard body. I wondered if was all that training that made his body feel like it was chiseled underneath his stylish clothing. I wondered what that body would look like without all those clothes. I blushed as a soft moan purred from my throat and felt Ash's smile on lips.

I blushed even deeper when I heard a girl giggling.

I wanted to pull away and see what the girl was laughing at, but Ash was holding me firmly. He moved his to investigate the sound himself and buried his face at the crook of my neck. I felt a wave of pleasure crash over me as his breath fanned my bare skin and he pressed a light kiss on my neck. Thank goodness he was holding me. My eyes were still closed.

"We should go. The room has gotten crowded," he whispered, blowing my hair along my skin.

I was afraid to try speaking. I knew my already gravelly voice would come out husky and reveal my innermost emotions if I tested it so I nodded and slowly opened my eyes, hoping he wouldn't try to make me walk that instant. He didn't.

My eyes took a second to focus and when they did I bit down on my lower lip. Ash was looking decidedly pleased with himself. He didn't exactly leave me breathless, but he did make my pulse quicken and I definitely went weak in the knees...who was I kidding, that kiss was the best one of my life. All other kisses paled in comparison, and Ash knew it.

There had been a brief moment of insanity in a bathroom the night before, but that didn't count. I was sure I had only been left breathless then because I had drank so much.

Ash took the opportunity to nuzzle me while I gathered my scattered wits, and he kissed my neck again, not once, not twice, but thrice, and my wits were slipping through my fingers.

The girl's giggles were shadowed by a low chuckle, and I heard the unmistakable sound of a feminine moan. My eyes shot open again. I turned towards the sound rapidly, Ash's hands still around me, but just enough to keep me upright.

I saw through the grapevines a tall dark figure with a strawberry blonde woman I could only see from behind, but the man was unmistakable. I flushed and felt angry for some inexplicable reason. The girls' moans grew louder and I couldn't stand it.

Ash was waiting to see what I would do: would we rival the other couple, or would we leave? I opted to leave.

"We should get back to the celebration," I said, not bothering to hide my irritation.

Ash looked over my head at the couple, and his eyes were doing that glittering thing. But I was *not* going to do *that*. I couldn't believe I'd seen Slate *twice* doing things better left to the privacy of bedrooms in public areas.

Ash tilted my chin up to him again and kissed my lips chastely before lacing his fingers through mine and leading me back to the main ballroom. I was grateful, although it didn't prevent us from hearing the final calls of the girl's pleasure that chased me from the room.

The wall of windows revealed the late hour when we returned. Music reverberated off the walls and despite my foul mood, I agreed to dance with Ash. It was hard to say no to him. He was his best on the dance floor, leading me around effortlessly despite my poor skills. I'd need dance lessons soon to keep up with all the events in Tidings. You just knew dance lessons were one of those things they were forced to take at a young age, especially the children that came from what they called *greater families*.

My mood improved substantially once I had a chance to dance with Hawk, Jett, and even Steel. Tawny had grudgingly allowed Steel to glide her around the dance floor after he had interrupted her dance with Hawk. It was smooth on Steel's part. I had to give it to him, he wasn't giving up. Although I did see Tawny stomp on his foot more than a few times.

I found myself in Coyote's arms. The intensely handsome man had a sort of Latin flair, but then I guessed there were a ton of different ethnicities that had bred into the Guardians.

The song finished and I smiled warmly at Coyote who inclined his head and lifted my hand to my next dance partner who'd come up behind me. His big hand took mine and I froze.

I was starting to think he enjoyed making me uncomfortable. "I hope you washed your hands," I bit off as the music started again.

I was as trapped as Tawny had been with Steel; if I ran off now, my dislike for my adopted brother would be obvious. Slate chuckled as he pressed his hand flat against mine, it was surprisingly soft where my fingers touched, but his palms were rough and hard.

"I saw you scamper off, Rabbit. Can you not handle a little competition?" His voice was a barely-audible rumble in my ear.

I made a face and quickly shed it in case someone else viewed my disgust. "Competition for what? To grunt like an animal in public?" I snapped, and inwardly grimaced at my rudeness.

His cool grey eyes finally caught mine and I fought the urge to freeze again.

"Now, that is not very nice. She was not grunting, it is called *moaning*." He spoke to me like I was an imbecile and it incensed me.

Slate's fingers dug into my waist as he pressed me against his body. I was going to snap at him again, but his eyes warned me to shut it.

"You know, precious little Rabbit. Do not think for a second that your *boyfriend* would not have had you on your hands and knees, grunting like an animal, as you call it, if you would have let him."

Why was he so angry? My mouth had gone dry at the venom in his tone. This guy was crazy, and yet, his body had drawn me in, caught me in his web. I bet all the girls felt that way with him. He had a definite draw to him; his skin sizzled mine where it touched the back of my hands, and I was horribly aware of where his hands squeezed around my waist. He was too much; when he was close I was drowning in his savage sensuality so heavy around me I felt myself want to breathe deep to fill my lungs, but that would be worse. His spicy scent would intoxicate me.

He was the bane of my young existence.

"I'll keep my *moaning* reserved for my bedroom with my *boyfriend*," I gritted out, finally getting my head on straight.

His big hand squeezed harder on my fingers and I thought I could hear the delicate bones in my fingers protest. His eyes flared and I almost groaned as my eyes went wide. What *was* he?

"You are a silly little rabbit, playing big games. When you are neck-deep in trouble, do not expect me to save you," he ground out.

I half expected him to gnash his teeth at me or lock his jaw around my throat.
"I'd rather drown than ask you to save me." Now where did *that* come from?

His eye twitched and I thought he was going to throw me down and maul me. Instead, his lips curled and loosened his fingers so the blood could flow again. He shifted my hand so his chin rested next to my head.

We were dancing much closer than what was respectable. The smell of his skin permeated my clothes and I got the impression he was rubbing his scent on me intentionally, which was ridiculous. Spicy and masculine, and all Slate. Some terrible noise emitted from my throat and my eyes snapped open. 1) When did I close my eyes, and 2) Did he just hear that noise?

Please God, no.

After a few moments, the tension in my body eased. He must not have heard it, because he would've made me feel like a complete fanny pack for it. The song ended and I realized we hadn't said one mean word to one another in a full minute. Slate held me back and I blinked at him; his face held an unreadable expression. I had melted against him. He probably thought I'd lost my wits—maybe they were still scattered on the arboretum's floor.

We were still holding hands and the music began to pick up again as the next song started. He could hold me another few minutes. All the anger had washed from me, and I could be pleasant.

I offered him an apologetic smile, hoping he wouldn't make me say the words.

"Slate." The sound of a mature woman's beckon made me take a deep collecting breath.

It was the raven-haired beauty, not the same girl in the arboretum. So many women; he was playing a dangerous game. I yanked my hand free and left the dance floor. His eyes followed me until I reached Ash's side who wrapped an arm around my hips in a possessive gesture. At the moment, it was just what I needed to bring me back to reality.

My lack of sleep the night before combined with the retching I'd done that morning had left me drained; throw in a whirlwind of confusing emotions and I was ready for bed. It was already late, and the celebration would last long after little Copper went to sleep, but I was done for the night.

When the last group of people tapered away, I pulled Ash aside. "I'm going to head home. It's been a long day," I said, mustering a smile that I hoped would let him know it had nothing to do with him.

"I shall escort you home." His tone brooked no nonsense; it seemed pointless to say that it was literately a door away.

We walked over to my mother who gave me an approving look as she went all gooey at looking at the two of us together. Honestly, my mother had never seen me with a boy and she was all atwitter. Some insane part of me found it irritating.

"Thank you, Ash." My mother beamed one of her warm smiles at him.

"Of course, Mrs. Tio," Ash said formally and linked his arm through mine as he led me from the hall to the portal room.

Unseen eyes burned into my back, and I spared a glance over my shoulder as we passed through the blocky stained glass of the door. One of Coyote's brothers let himself be seen for the briefest instant.

Molten amber eyes, then he was gone.

A shiver ran through me.

On the other side of the portal, Ash paused. I thought he was going to question me about the Regn brother.

Instead he said, "I have never been to the Sumar palace."

I was so relieved not to be pummeled with questions that I managed a smile. "I'm not really in a hostess mood, not that I would know where anything is...I've only gone from my room to the dining room, my room to this one, and from my room to Jett's and Slate's. But I could show you the halls." I tried to keep the conversation light; I was so drained that I knew I would fail miserably at a serious one.

I sighed. "This way."

I led him through the blue and gold mosaic halls slowly, letting him get a good look around, not that I was in a rush to get back to my room. I had no idea how I was going to go to bed with Ash hanging around.

We got to my door, and I opened it straight away. I could tell from his body language he wanted to be invited in.

I tried not to fidget. "Would you like to come in?"

He'd follow me in even if I didn't invite him. He *felt* determined. Not in a way where my red flag was flying, more like he had business to handle. I hoped he didn't think of me as business.

The lights were off. I couldn't even see my hand in front of my face. Ash could've *called* energy into the panel, but instead he ignited a flame in his hand.

I was in awe. Soon, I would be able to make a ball of fire appear in my hand. He held it between us, and it cast wicked shadows across his face. He snuffed it out and used his other hand to hit the panel so the lights came on.

"Thanks," I said.

I didn't want to be cliche and "slip into something more comfortable," so I put my shoes and purse in the closet and came back. He was walking around the room checking things out, looking through the windows, and running his hand along the bedspread.

"You can change if you would be more comfortable," Ash said absently.

"*Um*, okay."

It was easier to agree. I had no idea what to put on that wouldn't be too suggestive or too casual. The idea of wearing sweatpants with him in his dark blue brocade waistcoat just didn't work. Did he mean pajamas? Maybe he meant my day wear, like jeans and a t-shirt?

I was definitely overthinking. I had a few satin nightgowns I'd bought with a gift card from my birthday. In the closet, I picked one that was black, ankle-length, with lace trim and a slit. I held it up: it felt somewhat appropriate. I rolled my eyes at myself and slipped out of my blush pink dress and threw on my nightdress. I wouldn't normally wear a bra with it, but I had to draw a line with comfort wear in the presence of a teenage boy *somewhere*.

I walked out of the closet and I didn't see Ash anywhere. I thought he must have gotten frustrated and headed home, but there was no way I'd taken longer than five minutes. I saw his black boots resting on my bed. I walked over to the bed and quirked my eyebrow at him.

He moaned appreciatively at my choice in comfortable clothing, and I blushed right on cue. Things were not going as planned.

I stood to the side of my sapphire bedspread, he had his hands behind his head, legs crossed on top of the comforter. "It is very comfortable. Your room might be even bigger than mine. I will have to show it to you some time."

His waistcoat was undone. He patted the bed next to him and I shook my head. I had to get control of the situation. Ash narrowed his eyes and shrugged his shoulders. His legs swung over the side of the bed and he scooted himself to the edge of the bed while pulling me closer. I stood between his legs while he sat on the bed, his arms around my waist. He was looking up at me, eyelids lowered. He buried his face in my stomach, holding tightly.

It was sort of sweet. I stroked his head as he held me. I still didn't want to get into my bed with him so I angled myself away. He clasped my hands and stood up.

I gasped as he pinned my wrists at the small of my back and lifted me off the floor. He held his forehead against mine until we reached my chaise lounge, where he laid me down gently. I was taken aback by his strength: he was obviously much stronger than I was, but he wasn't even out of breath from that!

The power of his body had left me speechless. His knee fit between my legs, the other foot planted on the floor, his arms to either side of my shoulders.

"You are a rare beauty, Scarlett." He was running his fingers through my hair. "I want to show you what *calling* can feel like," he said, his voice low.

A wave of excitement coursed through me, and I tried to scold myself to no avail. He placed his hands on my shoulders and gently eased his other foot off the floor. He still held most of his weight. I was thinking it was the strangest make out session of my life—not that I had more than two to reference—when I felt it.

Cool invisible fingers slid from the nape of my neck, down my breasts, over my hips and down my legs to my knees. Even after the invisible fingers were gone, my skin was prickled with attention. My body rose of its own volition, pressing against Ash's contrasting warmth. My eyes popped open—I didn't remember closing them. My red flag was up; I had to stop no matter how *amazing* that felt.

"Ash..." I blushed. My voice was low and came out much steamier than I planned.

"Yes?" he breathed.

I swallowed hard. Mentally, I knew we had to stop for proprieties sake, but fiddlesticks, my body wanted more. I managed to move my arms and wrapped them around his neck. I titled my chin to his and he obliged. He tasted like delicious ripe peaches. No more invisible fingers, but now it was a much different type of danger.

His hips had pushed my legs apart and while one hand was wrapped in my hair, his other ran down the slit at my thigh.

Did that moan just come from my mouth?

Red flag! Red flag!

My body was a terrible traitor, and my hands were everywhere on him. I couldn't get them under control, and the way he moved on top of me...*oh*, I needed help.

Somewhere there was still some semblance of common sense. I pulled my mouth away from Ash's.

"Ash. Not yet," I breathed.

Yet?

Irritation flashed in his eyes, but he squashed it and peppered my swollen lips with a few more kisses before standing.

"I forget you are not from here. Forgive me if I overstepped," he said, the perfect picture of decorum despite the *huge* bulge in his snug pants.

My eyes snagged on it, widening, and I *felt* his pleasure. I stood as well, straightening my satin nightdress.

"No, it's my fault. I shouldn't have invited you into my room. I didn't mean to, *um*, tease you." I balked at my own frankness.

Ash chuckled darkly. "Scarlett, I can restrain myself." He kissed my cheek and I followed him to the door. "I hope this will not deter you from inviting me back. I enjoy your company immensely."

I licked my lower lip. "I enjoy yours as well."

I kicked myself mentally—that was *way* throatier than I'd intended. One taste of a real man and I was reeling. Something was wrong with me.

His celadon eyes glittered. He was clearly pleased with my admission and bent down to give me one last kiss before leaving.

"Until next time," he whispered before I closed the door.

I pressed my back to the door after he left and chastised my wanton ways. Shuffling to my feet, I went into the bathroom. I didn't look any different. You'd think after a serious make out session that there should be something that changed in your appearance that said, *Yes, I am becoming a woman,* or maybe just, *I have a sexual appetite.*

Looking at myself one last time in the wall-to-wall mirror, I realized I did look different. My hair was tousled; every strand had been thoroughly felt up by Ash's big hands, my lips were swollen with what had escalated into very hard kisses, and my tan skin had a flush to it. I gave myself a wicked smile and got ready for bed.

The night had gone very well, and I'd managed to hold my own with Ash, although when he had used *calling* I'd been nearly helpless. I didn't like that very much at all.

I fell asleep feeling like a girl on the verge of womanhood.

CHAPTER 9

 "Little rabbit." A deep voice rumbled and I squeezed my eyes tighter.

It had to be a dream.

"Come now, Rabbit. I know you are awake," Slate's deep voice teased.

"This had better be a dream because if you are creepily crawling into my bed every night, then we are going to have a problem," I tried to snap, but my voice was raspy when I woke so it sounded more like a sensual promise.

His low laugh answered my concern. He didn't take me seriously for a second.

"I am surprised to find you alone, Rabbit."

I turned around rapidly and immediately regretted it. We were nearly nose to nose. His grey eyes glinted silver in the thin stream of moonlight from the stained-glass window coming from the other side of my bed. Words died on my lips as I froze. Those eyes. They were dark with promise, if only I chose to ask for what he offered.

I gave myself a mental shake. "Where are your little girlfriends? Shouldn't you be in one of *their* beds? You aren't needed nor wanted in this one."

"My women aren't my girlfriends, nor do I spend the night with them. Are you sure I am not wanted?" he growled, his lips so close they were nearly brushing mine.

"That was a *girl* you were with in the arboretum. Make no mistake, you will *never* be wanted in this bed while it is *my* bed. You might be only my adopted brother, but that is as far as this relationship will ever be taken." I turned back around, feeling as if I'd won that round.

I *felt* a flare of frustration from Slate which nearly made me gasp because he kept a very tight rein on his emotions. It was like a shout from any other man, and I held my breath. I shouldn't have turned my back to him; it seemed like a dangerous idea now that I couldn't see what he was plotting.

It happened in a blink. One moment I was turned away, thinking he must have stealthily left the room without me noticing and the next I was on my back, my arms pinned high above my head with the weight of Slate's body crushing mine. He held my wrists in one hand, his face hovered, a midnight sheet of wavy hair falling over his shoulder, silver flashing in his eyes. I took in a shuddering breath. I wasn't going to bother struggling. It would be laughable.

I relaxed my muscles under his tense ones and waited for what he planned to do next. He hadn't thought it through. What could have possibly instigated a full assault in my own bed? If I was calm, and he was being irrational, I would come out of this looking like the bigger person.

I gave him a look that said, *Now what, big boy?*

I saw his strong jaw flex at my goading. No, he definitely hadn't thought this through.

"Where is Ash?" he ground out.

Scoffing in his face would only enrage him, so I did it. "You mean he left already? I hadn't noticed since I passed out *after*," I said in my most aloof tone.

Slate let loose a growl that wiped the smug look off my face as his teeth met the skin of my throat. I froze. His velvety tongue flitted out to run along my jugular. I knew my blood must have been pumping hard —I was paralyzed with fear. *And* yet...I didn't think Slate wanted to hurt me.

"He left ten minutes after he brought me back," I said with calm I didn't feel.

His teeth still rested on my skin, but he'd brought his tongue back into his mouth. Slowly, he sheathed his teeth and his hand loosened on my wrists so my fingers tingled as the blood began to flow again. His other hand had slid alongside of me so most of his weight was on it and his legs as he bent them over mine so I couldn't move.

His lips puckered over my vein and pressed a searing kiss to my skin before he rested his cheek against my chest. I felt his kiss shoot straight through me to settle steamily low in my belly. He moved his hand from my wrists completely. Whatever flare of rage he'd felt had subsided. I didn't know if I was out of the woods yet, but I felt him start to calm.

I dragged my arms back down, but instead of rubbing my wrists like I desperately wanted to, I placed my hand at the back of his head and stroked those silky midnight waves. It defied logic—I had no idea what made me do it. He seemed to need comfort, and despite that he obviously wanted to tear my throat out, I wanted to comfort him.

His body sighed on top of mine. My fingers twined in his dozens of scattered braids that clicked as the beads hit one another, and I felt my own body truly relax. I ran my nails along his scalp, like scratching behind the ears of an oversized puppy. If that puppy was actually a five hundred pound, weak, starved tiger. As long as he didn't turn those predatory eyes on me, he was just a confusing man. Or a confused man.

"You do not understand the game you play," he said, his voice muffled by my chest.

"I'm not playing any games," I whispered back.

He leaned back on his elbows to either side of me so I was cocooned by his body on the plush bed. His face rose above mine. Grey eyes full of that unreadable expression. *Oh*. It wasn't easy to forget how breathtakingly handsome he was, but when his head had been down I'd grown bold and some idiotic nurturing part of me had felt the need to soothe the beast within. With him looking at me, my hands stilled in his hair. His weight on top of my body caused my nerves to dance excitedly at the anticipation of being touched. He let out a breath that smelled of cloves and I felt my eyes shift to his full lips and back again. Mustn't do that.

"*That* is the problem, Rabbit," he rumbled, and it did undesirable things to my body.

"I don't like games," I retorted.

Did his eyes just shift to my lips? Surely not.

"You must at least learn to play them. So you know when you are being played yourself. You are not allowed to show weakness, especially when you are."

His weight shifted and I thought he was going to roll off, but no, just getting more comfortable. I let my hands fall; it was too intimate a gesture with him looking at me.

"Am I being played now?" I breathed.

There I went looking at those full sensual lips again. There was so much to look at. I could stare at the way the muscles of his jaws flexed as he spoke, the chiseled planes of his bronze face, the way his dark lashes were so thick and long they nearly touched his brows. He almost looked like he was wearing eyeliner—it wasn't fair that his lashes were so lush.

"Oh, Rabbit, you have no idea," he growled, and I blinked at him.

Did he mean with Ash or him? Or something unseen? All three?

Slate's eyes flitted down again to my lips, there was no mistaking it this time, and I realized I had parted them as I breathed. It must have been because his weight was crushing me. Panic surged through me and I started wriggling under him. I couldn't shake him off for the life of me and he raised an eyebrow at me in amusement.

"I do not think this is having the effect you desired." He pressed his hips against me and my breath caught. "Unless it was?" He let the question hang and I froze, gaping at him as he rocked his hips.

"Most definitely not! Get off me you...gorilla! I let my guard down for an instant and the only thing you can think of is *that*!" I shouted, even though he was inches away from my face.

Cool amusement was all I got back. He was staring at my lips again—that, or the blood he'd just caused to sprout onto my lower lip.

"Not on your life," I said, pushing as much defiance into my words as I could.

He leaned back and gave me a wry grin. "As if you would stop me, Rabbit."

"Is that the kind of man you are?"

I set my jaw. When in doubt, launch an attack on a man's honor. Men are prickly about their honor, no matter where they're from.

Slate bristled, but then he leaned in close. "You are going to want it. You are going to beg me for it. I am going to say no," he growled, no purr in his voice this time.

I leveled my cool eyes. "As if you could."

Was I daring him? Taunting him? The man who just restrained me with a single hand? I must have lost my mind. I'd need to go back to the arboretum and pick up the wits I'd obviously left there in the soil.

His rich deep laughter surprised me and I nearly kicked myself. Did I just challenge this man? Oh, dear God, help me.

"Torch. I would hear you sing your song one day."

Slate's massive body rolled off of mine, and I sucked in a full gulp of air, not caring that he was eyeing me...until I realized what he was eyeing. I scowled as I blushed and adjusted the top of my nightdress, then pulled the blankets up to cover myself further.

"Training. Tomorrow. I do not want to catch Ash in this room, Torch."

He slammed the door behind him and I thought about getting up and locking it. *Like that would stop him.*

He probably broke down doors to warm up for his training. What was his problem anyway? He obviously didn't like Ash; I wondered if they had fought over a girl at some point and trying to seduce me was Slate's revenge. But no, Slate wasn't seducing me, was he? More like terrifying the fiddlesticks out of me.

I was walking through carnage. I felt her, heard her, but I didn't see her. She told me I could fix this. I tried not to look at the bodies, the battleground alongside the castle. Not everyone was dead. Angry frozen faces stared up at angry faces atop the castle. I couldn't tell if the faces were human; they all looked like monsters to me.

The wind was whipping at me. I looked up at the sky—even the sky was angry. Black clouds, lightening without rain. She was all around me. "You are night."

I stood in the middle of a circle, people around the edges. Slate lay in the center of the circle, blood pooling around his body. Light and gushing wind blasted from my body, my hair, my hands, shooting up into the sky. My mouth opened in a silent scream.

I was stuck to my pillow, every pore releasing perspiration. I tried not to thrash, so I pulled a pillow over my face blindly and screamed into it.

"That good, huh?" Tawny mumbled from the doorway of the bathroom.

I pulled the pillow off my face and took a long look at her and shook my head.

"We need to get you healed after all that alcohol. You look like sugarfoot."

Tawny rolled her eyes and winced. "No need to remind me, I have eyes. Did you and Ash leave together?" she asked as she crossed the room and sat down next to me on the sprawling bed, pushing aside the panels of the sapphire blue satin form the canopy.

"We did."

I told her the rest of the night's exploits with Ash. She even blushed.

"Holy crap, Scar."

"Holy crap, indeed. And then...Slate showed up in my bed." I confessed to the kiss under the mistletoe when we first spoke.

Tawny's eyes bugged out. Slate was the antithesis of my type, if I were to have one. "*Um*...we've only been here two days, and you've seen him with two different women."

I agreed. "Bad news bears. One does not simply *let* Slate into their bed. I woke up and he was in it—and hostile. I let him know under no uncertain terms that it wasn't happening."

He could take those unreadable looks of his and shove them right up his fanny pack.

"What'd you wind up doing last night?" I asked her.

She winced as if thinking about it hurt her physically. "Drank with Amethyst and Cherry 'til my mouth couldn't perform the necessary function to drink more in order to get drunker. Everyone was pretty wastey-faced. I saw Diamond sneak some too; you know she's eighteen? I thought she was younger after I spoke with her, but she looks like she's in her twenties."

I was going to say that it was weird she was marrying her mom's great nephew when I remembered Tawny's predicament.

"We should head downstairs. Jett's promised to kick my butt in training. Gypsum trained with them yesterday. I'm sure they can kick your butt, too."

I decided I would shower post butt-kicking, so I headed into my closet. I had no idea what to wear to a butt kicking. Someone had put away the dresses we'd bought yesterday so I picked a seafoam green one out and slipped into it. I knew why the women loved these dresses, despite all its chiffon pleats, it was like wearing air, and it felt oh-so-glamorous.

Next on the agenda: fix Tawny's stomach.

Pearl was the only one sitting at the table.

We smiled warmly. "Good morning."

"Good morning, darlings. I am so glad Jett took you to House of Gres. You both look stunning." She kissed us both on our cheeks.

"House of Gres? As in Madame Gres?" Tawny beamed.

Pearl nodded sadly. "She left Tidings and fell in love. She always kept in touch, and her grandniece runs the shop now."

I was clueless, but Tawny was the fashion nut. "She was a famous designer in

Paris. Jackie O wore her dresses!" She sighed at me. "You're fashion disabled."

SCARLET SORROW

Pearl laughed in her elegant way. "We will help her as much as we can." She patted Tawny's hand. "I hear you two are going to start training today?"

"We are. They're going to take it easy on us, it being our first day and all right?" I asked jokingly.

"I would not count on it, darling. Slate and the boys had a trainer brought in especially. They take it very seriously. I would not expect much sympathy from them. I would help settle your stomach though, Tawny, so the punishment will not be doubly so," Pearl offered and Tawny nodded as Pearl set a hand on her stomach and *called*.

Tawny visibly relaxed and sighed. "Thank you, Grandmother." It still sounded awkward to me, but there would be plenty time to get used to it.

My mom came gliding into the room, feet almost floating off the floor. What had gotten into her? Was she still drunk from last night? I had never seen my mother drunk, so I wouldn't know either way.

"Have you thought any more about the Faunelle?" Pearl asked my mom.

"I have. Since Scarlett will be in school and there isn't much for me to do around here, being away for extended periods will not be a problem." She said this in a serious tone.

I couldn't believe she hadn't told me about this; how long was *extended?*

She saw my face and added, "You'll be so busy with classes you won't even notice my absence, I promise. It will most likely be a month at a time, with long breaks in between. We have an excellent relationship with the Faunelle, so I won't be in any danger."

"What would be dangerous about being an ambassador?" Tawny asked tentatively. Hawk was going to teach at Valla U, but we didn't know what Sparrow would be doing.

"Not all tribes are friendly. We have to maintain a relationship with even the volatile tribes to ensure just treatment for their people. Not everyone in those tribe is a danger—some are as vulnerable as we are." My mother sounded rehearsed, as if she had argued this point before.

"Do some people not want to send ambassadors?" I asked, hoping to learn a little more. Knowledge was power.

"Some people would rather they destroyed themselves so we would not have to bother with them." Pearl shook her head in irritation. "We have the ability to *call* in order to maintain balance. Those tribes were put on the islands with us so we could help them maintain that balance. If they refuse our help, it is no matter; we then make sure the weak are not their prey."

I was starting to see why we needed all the battle training.

"I wouldn't worry, Tawny. Your mom will not be an ambassador," said a deep voice. Steel. Tawny's back stiffened at the sound of his voice.

He kissed Pearl's cheek before he took the seat next to my mother and across from me. "Good morning, all." Steel smiled broadly at my mother before giving her a kiss too.

Uncle my *fanny pack*. Steel was my brother; I just needed to find out why they were lying and get proof.

"Are the Merfolk dangerous?" Tawny asked.

Steel blinked at her.

It was possibly the most uncomfortable ten second silence *ever*.

Pearl had to clear her throat to wake Steel out of his stupor. Pearl started to merrily eating her breakfast; she was always blissful with her family around.

The range of emotions I *felt* wafting from Tawny and Steel was starting to affect my own. Hope, surprise, pain, anxiety, all wrapped up with overwhelming love.

Tawny was still looking at Steel through her lashes, waiting for a response. Steel's turquoise eyes looked bewildered, then suddenly brightened.

"They can be. They're all emotionally fickle so you have to tread carefully. I've spent years swimming in their waters, trading with them. Having grown up with them, it made sense for me to treat with them."

Tawny gave a small smile in thanks for answering her question and Steel was in heaven. It was a baby step, but the hardest one to take was always the first one.

Jett came in next and gave a round of kisses to the women. My mom clasped his hand and smiling warmly. Tawny was surprised to be included in the kisses, but Jett wouldn't have left her kiss-*less*. He was in one of his smug moods, teasing us mercilessly of how bad we're going to get our fanny packs kicked.

Slate came down for breakfast, his body moving like a large black panther. I almost laughed when my mother made a point of being in his way to steal his kiss. It may have been the only time in his arrogant life he looked uncomfortable.

"We heal after training. Our healing methods work on nearly everything, just do not lose your head. We do not know how to grow those back."

I rolled my eyes. He had a flair for the dramatic. Slate caught my eyeroll and his grey eyes flashed with promised retribution.

Hawk and Sparrow came down with Gyps, they ate and went about their business. Gypsum lingered with us so he could train. He *loved* training. He was even wearing the seax at his hip. Calling him my little warrior would probably undermine the look he was going for, so I held it back.

"*So*," my mother started and I knew that tone.

It was the same one she used when I'd taken a big test in school and she was tired of waiting to hear how I'd done.

I was already blushing.

Internally, I prayed fervently she'd let the subject drop and we could talk later. I hung my head hoping to melt into the chair. Tawny, Hawk, and Sparrow knew what that tone meant and I could see Tawny's shoulders shake in my peripheral.

"Tell me what happened with Ash," my mom prodded, and I turned beet red.

"Nothing. He's very nice," I said trying to send a telepathic message that now was not the time or the place.

"He's very handsome, and he comes from such a good family. Are you going to see him again?" she asked, oblivious to my death stares.

"Yes," I ground out.

"Did he ask you to meet him soon?" she pushed.

She wanted details. Back in Chicago, we would sit around the dinner table with Hawk and the rest and joke about things. I was a late bloomer. My third kiss was with Chris the night we had gone to prom, and I had sworn off boys...until Ash. Slate had snuck one in under the mistletoe, but that didn't count. She didn't know about the last two and I was praying she wouldn't ask about them.

No such luck.

"Yes, Mom." I tried not to sound too annoyed.

We generally didn't have barriers between us, but this was different. I was sitting with four other members of our family who didn't know that I'd been an ugly duckling until college. I never minded when we spoke about it when it was just us, or maybe it was that my dates were usually atrocious and therefore hilarious, not like last night's at all.

She gave me a conspiratorial look and I knew what was coming so I tried to be preemptive.

"Yes!" I shouted without meaning to, and Tawny and Gypsum started laughing outright.

Glad someone was entertained.

My mom clapped her hands gleefully. I understood all her fretting about my lack of love life; they wanted us all married by the time we were twenty.

"He kissed you!" my mom nearly squealed.

Even Sparrow looked delighted. My mortification meant nothing. Sparrow never had to worry about Tawny finding boyfriends. She'd never had one, but they had lined around the block in wait.

"Your first boyfriend," Sparrow noted wistfully.

I groaned aloud when I heard Jett laugh.

"Yes!" Tawny chirped with mock excitement, adding to my embarrassment.

I shot Tawny a withering glare and she shrugged as she smiled. This was what my family did: we embarrassed each other mercilessly and then supported one another ruthlessly. Not an entirely bad deal, and I should have been used to it, but for some reason it was much *much* worse today. They'd always teased me about my lack of boyfriends, and I usually instigated the joking; so what was my problem?

"Okay. Enough. Yes, Ash and I shared a few kisses. It was a lovely night, and I hope to see him much more. It's...different." I regretted my words as soon as they left my mouth.

"Different?"

My mom's warm eyes shimmered. This was what she'd been waiting for since I'd hit puberty.

I let out a long breath. "Different, but he's not my boyfriend."

"*Future* different?" she asked, fighting a smile.

I nodded and my mom clapped her hands.

Obviously, she was not hearing me.

"Let me enjoy this, Scarlett. I've waited too long for this." Mom glowed. A new door opened filled with more bonding moments for us.

There were many choking sounds across the table. I wanted so desperately to drag Tawny under the bus with me. I shot her a look that said she better shut up or I'd reveal she had still never had one, and I saw her eyes plead. Of course, I didn't, and I took the brunt of my mom's excitement.

"Now we need to find Tawny a good match." Sparrow turned to Pearl. "She hasn't had a boyfriend either. These girls of ours are nothing like the teens you hear about. We had to *encourage* them to go out and meet boys. They don't."

Tawny's face was now as red as mine was and I gave her a commiserating look. I chanced a glance at Steel and he was red-faced. He obviously hadn't gotten that detail from Tawny during their night together.

"Tawny and I can find our own dates. Besides, good things come to those who wait. We're waiting for the best ones." I said it much too defensively.

"All the world loves a lover. Are you an innocent, or do you have casual lovers?" Jett asked, pointing a fork at me.

"Jett!" my mother exclaimed, but she watched me for my response.

I couldn't help but blush. "I do not have *lovers*. My first kiss was when I was fifteen. I sort of dated a boy when I was sixteen, and then there was my prom date. Now Ash. I'm picky," I sniffed ticking them off on my fingers.

"Okay..." Gypsum said, and I flushed again.

I may or may not have gotten carried away.

"You forgot about me. I will try not to be insulted," Slate rumbled as his silver eyes glittered at me while he chewed.

My eyes widened.

"That was because of the mistletoe. It doesn't count," I spluttered.

I felt like the record had stopped. Jett and Steel were craning their necks to look at Slate while the rest were looking at me in disbelief. I wanted to shout at them that I would *never* have let that brute kiss me under normal circumstances!

Slate raised his brows at me, furrowing his bronze forehead. I wanted to punch him. Training would be good. I could work off some of this frustration and copious amounts of embarrassment. My eyes lifted to see if anyone was still paying attention to me, praying that they weren't. My mom was looking at me like I'd lost it completely; maybe I had. Jett had some horrid mischievous look to him that made me think he was devising ways to find me a man to seduce me.

Steel was staring at his food as if it held the answers to all life's riddles, or more specifically, Tawny's.

My mom excused herself and I got up with her. "Be right back, don't start without me," I said as I hurried after her.

"Wouldn't dream of it!" Jett yelled after me. I could hear everyone chuckling at the table.

"Mom," I said, and she paused in the hall and smiled at me.

"It's hardly been two days, but you're adapting here better than I could've hoped. You want to walk with me?"

We started strolling together, and I realized she was giving me her own personal tour of the palace. "So, I have some brothers." It was an accusation; I was hurt, and I thought she wasn't worried about me.

"I spoke to Jett, Steel, and Slate that first day and after you were told. I know you, Scar. I knew you'd be thrilled to have long-lost brothers. I knew I'd just have to give you time. I never finished at Valla U and I need to be proven tried and true before anything else since we've come back. I'm sorry if I've been preoccupied. Our entire purpose, starting with being gifted the ability to call, is to become a tried and true Guardian. From there we can really help the tribes and our people."

I wasn't upset that she was preoccupied; I'd barely had a moment to myself since we'd arrived. I only wanted a little mom time before I headed to Valla U until summer.

"I'd really like to spend some time with all of you before you leave. The boys have big plans to get you up to date as much as possible before you head to the university, so I doubt you'll have much free time," my mom said.

"That would mean a lot to me. I kinda love having brothers," I said as she put her arm around my shoulder. "You didn't tell me you were married," I whispered as we walked, and she swept my golden hair from my face.

"I never realized how much you remind me of my mother. You're so strong

Scarlett, you don't realize it yet, but you will." She smiled fondly at me. "Lark."

She said it wistfully. "I loved him very much. It started out very innocently. I'd made many mistakes and he helped me regain my honor so I could face the other greater families. He was a wonderful man and I miss him every day." My mom swallowed hard and I wished I'd never brought it up.

I thought of the mountain of a man I'd seen with my mom the night of the masquerade. "Mom, was that my dad? I have to know."

My mom's face paled; it wasn't a conversation she was prepared to have yet, but I craved information like a sponge craved water. Anything about my dad would be welcomed. One look at my face and she could tell I wasn't going to accept anything but the truth.

"It was." I expected more, but I was afraid to push. "He's married, Scar, he has kids of his own. It is a lot more complicated than it seems."

"It seems pretty complicated."

"It's *worse*. Lark saved me from the disaster I'd created by...being with Alder. If anyone asks, you pretend Lark is your father. Alder knows the truth. He's not a bad man, Scar. If we could've been together, we would have."

I just nodded. The tidbits I'd overheard and the obvious fact that they still loved one another was pretty darn complicated. I let it go. There would be plenty of time to meet him. We had just gotten to Tidings and I'd already had more interaction with him than I had in my previous nineteen years. "Ash Straumr seems taken with you." It was my turn to pale.

"He likes to show me around, and he's nice enough."

She was watching my expressions. "Do you like him?" she asked.

"He's cool. Gorgeous. He's just so...I don't know, aware of himself. He *knows* he's gorgeous."

She was nodding. "The men from the greater families are like that. I only ask because I noticed he escorted you yesterday and yet didn't introduce you to his family. Diamond introduced herself, and when Dahlia would come close, he'd lead you away. It struck me as odd. I am sorry if I embarrassed you at breakfast."

I'd met so many people yesterday. It was a little odd; he seemed so eager to treat me as a trophy, so why not to his parents too? I smiled at my mom anyway. I had been embarrassed, but it was probably long forgotten by now.

"Mom, we're not dating or anything, I just met him. I'm not offended. A little surprised though, because he does seem genuinely interested in me."

I didn't know what my interest in Ash was just yet. My mom knew me too well...

"Is there someone else who you're *more* interested in?" she nudged.

I stammered. "What?"

"He's very handsome," my mom pressed. "You two would make a lovely couple."

"I have no idea who you are talking about. I'm only interested in Ash," I spluttered. "But even if I was interested in someone else—not saying I am—the men here seem to have slews of women after them. I'm not the kind of girl who fights over a guy."

My mom stopped and grabbed me by my shoulders to face her. "Listen to me, Scarlett Tio. You are amazingly beautiful, you are strong, and you come from a loving *powerful* family. I'm sorry I've sheltered you so completely that you don't know those things already. But you will, so help me." Her speech was so impassioned, it surprised me.

"Okay, Mom." I looked into her eyes. She was somewhere else in time.

"You'd better head to training, Jett isn't the most patient person." She smiled fondly as she spoke of her son. "Scar, one more thing. I know it'll be hard, but please don't hunt down your father. It's in your best interest to let us work things out first."

I nodded. "I love you, Mom."

They weren't kidding when they said they kick our fanny packs—sometimes literally.

The training room was huge. It was a conservatory the size of my high school football stadium. All types of plants and trees lined the gravel track. It was divided into several sections, an obstacle course, a weightlifting section, an area that held all different kinds of weapons with mats, and a section for archery. It was daunting.

The guys showed up in full regalia. Their theory was, what you practice in is what you were most comfortable fighting in. Slate gave us lightweight sleeveless tops and black fitted pants. He also found us each a set of soft black leather boots to wear.

Slate's grey eyes followed us as he made us run laps. Jett was running backwards, yelling things I could only assume he meant to be encouraging. Gypsum was forced to run with us, but he wasn't having a problem. He had that natural endurance gifted to athletic teen boys. Tawny was struggling, but she gritted her teeth and refused to give up.

Slate's muscled body rippled as he ran the obstacle course, making it look like a child's playground. He made us do it over and over. We couldn't get through it without him making us restart. We sucked at it. He told us we wouldn't spend much time using weights because we needed to focus on our endurance first, and I wasn't going to argue. I *couldn't* anyway; I had to save my energy.

He showed us a few hand-to-hand combat moves and that was where all the fanny pack kicking came in. He was insanely quick. He'd block every hit I'd try to throw, knocking me back without even breaking a sweat.

We didn't use any weapons that first day, except for the archery. It turned out Tawny had a gift for it. Jett thought that with *a lot* of practice, she might actually be good one day. Tawny beamed at that.

Gypsum ditched us after that to go lift weights with Steel. It was surprisingly modern. We didn't lift weights in their training boots; they had soft-soled boots they slipped on when they were in the weight area. We would've joined them, but I swore, I could already feel the soreness setting in. At the end of our training session, he wanted us to cool down by doing laps in the pool. I didn't even know we had a pool.

Despite my wanting to strangle Slate several times throughout the three hours of grueling torture, I thanked him for his time. It was like last night had never happened.

"Do not thank me yet, Rabbit. I took it easy on you today. Every day I will push a little more, and it will be a little harder. Soon you will be devoid of weaknesses." *Weaknesses?* I was suddenly very grateful to be starting academic classes in ten days.

"Dagr." Tawny turned to face Slate.

Dagr was Sparrow's last name. I felt like an idiot for never questioning that fact. I assumed they didn't feel the need to change it to Hawk's last name after they were married. I did know that Hawk and Sparrow hadn't been married until after she was born. I mentally miffed myself. You'd be surprised what you could explain away. At least now I knew it was the tradition in Tidings.

"You are going to want to get a bow for yourself. A borrowed one will only get you so far," Slate rumbled.

Tawny nodded eagerly, and a small twinge of jealousy sparked inside me. I wanted to be good at something.

"Tomorrow. Same time." Slate returned to his weights with the other guys.

"I am so glad not to be lifting any weights today," I said as we walked into the locker room. Well, I called it a locker room, but they called it a "preparation room."

"I wouldn't mind working out some."

She sent a last lovestruck look over at the men. Steel was rowing his way to a sculpted body. Steel had been making moon eyes at Tawny all morning, but clearly not wanting to interfere in case she snapped at him.

We'd brought our bathing suits with us in case by some stroke of luck we got a chance to use them.

Tawny slipped into her leopard print bandeau topped bikini and me in my seafoam fringe topped halter bikini, then we walk out of the preparation room and into the pool.

It was. How was the pool not the first thing we were told about?

I loved swimming. The usual smell of chemicals didn't greet us; I assumed it had something to do with being magical. The pool was huge. The walls were the royal blue that matched the rest of the Sumar palace, with gold trim. The ceiling was done is gold landscapes, and exposed gold rafters spanned it. Plaster sculptures of people lined the pool, as well as globed lampposts, already lit, thank goodness. The pool itself was tiled in royal blue with gold blazing suns.

We walked in and I swore I heard angels sing. I immediately dropped my towel and cannonballed into the pool. I could hear Tawny laughing at my retreating back.

By the time my head bobbed at the surface Tawny was already sinking to the bottom in her own cannonball. She came up laughing.

"Let's get these laps done." I said. "I wonder if they have any floats around here." She laughed hysterically at that, but I thought it was a legitimate question.

We decided to race each other to the minimum thirty-two laps Slate charged us with. Somewhere around lap twenty, four big *plops* submerged in the water. It was Jett, Steel, Slate, and Gypsum.

Tawny and I stood on the shallower end of the pool.

Jett smiled a big, infectious smile. "Couldn't let you have all the fun!"

His short dark blonde hair spiked straight up with the water, and we couldn't help, but smile back.

Surely twenty laps was the better than nothing. I secretly hoped Slate didn't ask us.

Jett was smiling mischievously. He dove into the water quick as a rocket, which had to be assisted by his magic, until he sprung up in front of me. I tried to dodge out of his way and escape his grasp.

Tawny let loose a squeal and swam for the edge. Jett tossed me into the air and dunked me into the water. Tawny plopped next to me a second later. I saw another set of men's legs next to Jett's from under the water. Steel's super-swimmer form was grinning from ear to ear. He looked too wholesome to be Tawny's type. His green eyes were inviting, and he had a big uplifting smile of perfect teeth. Tawny and I tried to team up to dunk Jett and Steel, but we were failing miserably. We weren't very graceful coughing up bouts of pool water, but we were all laughing so hard we didn't care.

Gypsum and Slate were doing laps from the center of the pool, the spoilsports. We leaned on the edge of the pool catching our breath. I may or may not have been admiring the view.

"Do you guys have games here? Like volleyball, or maybe some inflatable rafts or a beach ball?" Gypsum asked.

Steel held out his hand and he floated on top of a raft made of bubbles using a bit of his calling. "It's air. We're going to have to teach you three some basics." His big perfect grin leveled at Tawny.

"You came to the right man." Jett launched himself out of the pool and opened a door, and came back out with a net and a ball. "Picked up some myopic items on my last visit." He gave his smug grin, chin held high, showing just a sliver of teeth.

It made me sullen to think he had been around and not seen us.

"What's myopic?" I asked finally. "Ash said something about it too."

Jett, Gypsum, and Slate started setting up the volleyball net. Gypsum's full lips pulled down in the corners. "It refers to someone from outside of Tidings, an average Joe with the inability to *call*. They can only see what is up close, they fail to see the bigger picture. I got into a fight that first night when some jerk called me a myopic. Ash didn't say you were a myopic, did he?"

When did Gypsum start to look so disapproving? The seventeen-year-old was scowling at me like an older brother, and I didn't miss the approving looks Jett and Slate were giving him.

"Of course not," I snapped. "Come over here Gyps, I think bad manners are rubbing off on you."

I gestured for my cousin to come over to the bright and shiny side and away from those two bad influences. The three of them only laughed at me.

I heard a door shut and we all turned to see who came in. Ash strode in, taking in the scene. Slate was the only one who looked back at me, his eyes glinting silver like a knife's edge.

"I was told I could find you here. Mind if we join you?" Ash's eyes skated over to me and his mouth broke into a heart-stopping smile.

Tawny had floated over to me, eyes bugging out at me. *What are you going to do?* I clambered as gracefully as possible out of the pool to Ash to greet him.

I opened my mouth, but as soon as I got close, he laid claim to it. P.D.A. and me was like eagles and those creepy fish that live in the deepest darkest parts of the ocean. We were never seen together, and we didn't even know the other existed.

His big hands on my bare skin sent a shocking thrill through me and he held onto me for an extra second after he laid that kiss on me. I tried to duck my head to hide my blush but he held my chin and reveled in it.

"We are about to play a game; we need to keep the numbers even."

Even *I* was shocked that Slate spoke. Slate and Ash clearly didn't get along, but I hadn't yet asked if there was a history there or not.

Ash pursed his lips, and then smiled big and steamy...right at me. I wanted to sink up to my nose in the water.

"I guess it is a good a thing I brought some people with me."

Right on cue, Cherry, Amethyst, and Diamond burst from the preparation room.

"Jett!" squealed Cherry.

She was wearing my bathing suit; in fact, they were *all* wearing my bikinis.

"I hope you don't mind...when your mom told Ash you were training, he came back to get us so we could train with you, but instead you were in here. He knew where your room was, so we raided your closet."

Amethyst looked better in my bathing than I did. I only had a small amount of satisfaction over the fact she didn't fill out the top as well.

"This is *much* better than training." Cherry beamed, already hanging off Jett who wasn't complaining.

Gypsum wasn't complaining either. Diamond floated over to him to introduce herself. She looked dazzling, brown hair piled on top of her head, and wearing my light pink bikini. Gypsum was a goner.

Ash, looking particularly pleased with himself, walked me down to where Tawny and Steel were bobbing in the pool. Those two were trying and failing not to keep bumping into one another.

Ash started stripping right then and there, his light green eyes locked on mine.

"I hope you don't mind; there was not anything for me to wear in your closet."

He was down to his navy blue skivvies. He stood there watching me, knowing it was impossible not to take in him in. He had chiseled abs, and the "V" that drove me crazy. He looked like an underwear model; I would've signed him.

"You can touch if you want," Ash said too loud for my taste, with a quirk of his brow.

My eyes popped back up to his face and he had a cocky grin that spoke volumes.

Oh yes, he knew I thought he was gorgeous—it was probably written all over my face. He scooped me up under my legs so he cradled me, and I squealed after he gave me another kiss and tossed me into the pool. When I popped up, wiping water from my face with a big smile, Ash was in front of me, and he grabbed my head by my nape and pressed our lips together. I didn't fight him this time as I twined my arms around his neck. I felt his kiss in my toes. It was what I imagined my first boyfriend would be like; it was perfection.

I *felt* competitive.

"Are we going to play or what?" Ash turned to the guys who'd just finished putting up the net after he broke away from our kiss.

"Okay, hit the ball over with your hands; if you miss the ball, it's a point. No holding, and no *calling*. Outside the pool is out of bounds," Jett said loud enough for all of us to here.

"We will take Tawny, Steel, and Gypsum against you, Diamond, Cherry, Amethyst, and him," Ash said to Jett.

We was apparently him and I, and *him* was Slate. A fact that Slate looked like he wanted to punch something over.

Gypsum looked disappointed not to be on the same side as Diamond. I gave him a half smile that said *buck up*. He realized he didn't have anything to be upset about once we all got to jumping around.

They were all so athletic. Giggly Cherry even had abs. Not that I was in bad shape—I was toned from years of sports and had a pair of stems that would give a supermodel a run for her money.

Steel and Ash were dominating the game, mostly because Jett was distracted. Slate and Diamond were doing well, Amethyst could set the ball with the best of them, and Slate had no problem spiking. Years of volleyball gave me an advantage. I stood between the guys setting the ball for the guys' spikes. Tawny was giving it her all, trying to keep up with everyone taller than her. Gypsum was laughing, having a great time.

Even I was having fun—when I was ignoring how aggressive Slate and Ash were being, their teeth gritted, muscles tense.

Cherry even floated up to the net and whispered, "Thanks for the show." She nodded towards the increasing competitive dup.

They were slapping the ball so hard they were going to take someone's head off. Thankfully, we were only playing until one of us reached twenty. It looked like my team was going to win, until Jett quit playing grab fanny packs with the girls to score a few more times. Then we were tied at nineteen; it fueled the fire building between Ash and Slate. It got so intense that we all started to float away and we weren't missed.

"Just let me know who wins!" Cherry called, clearly amused.

There was now only Slate on one side, Ash on the other. Tawny slid up next to me. "Holy crap, dude."

"Holy crap, indeed." Not that I wasn't enjoying the show, but someone was definitely going to get hurt.

They were ignoring the no *calling* rule Jett had laid down. The ball was soaring so quickly over the net I could hear it whistle through the air. Back and forth and back and forth. I didn't know all the capabilities of *calling* yet, but I thought they were using something to assist how quickly they were moving themselves; they were swimming so fast that my eyes couldn't keep up.

Ash slipped and that was that. Slate whipped the ball right into his nose. It broke with an audible *crunch,* and I swam to Ash to comfort him.

Slate tossed his head, letting the beads in his hair click. At least he wasn't *too* smug.

Steel was healing Ash's nose, and Slate was taking down the net. Ash didn't seem like the type who liked to lose so I was surprised he wasn't pitching a fit. He was quiet, and that to me seemed more frightening.

"Well, *that* was interesting, but I think we were all disqualified since *calling* was involved," Jett said, stepping out of the pool, a beautiful wet woman under each arm.

Slate and Gypsum finished taking down the net and started to carry it out of the pool, Tawny and Steel following close behind. Diamond was checking on her brother who was looking daggers at Slate. I felt a little guilty.

"How's your nose feeling? It looks perfectly perfect." I said with an easy smile, reaching up to touch the newly-fixed nose.

He encircled his hand around my wrist and pulled it down. Diamond took that moment to vacate the premises.

"We heal quickly. I wanted to see you again. I know I saw you last night, but not like this."

He clasped my other wrist and pulled me to him. My bikini clad body against him and his wet underwear. I swallowed hard.

That wasn't the only thing that was hard.

Something inside me had been awakened last night, and not with Slate, I was sure. He nuzzled my neck, taking my head in his hand. I felt like the odds were stacked against me.

He tilted my chin up to meet his and I parted my lips to receive him. Ash teased my lips with his tongue before giving me his kiss. Waves crashed over me attempting to make me lose control. Ash's hands pressed against my back and down to my hips while he pressed his own hips against me. I felt like I was underwater. "Ash, let's join the others," I breathed, breaking free.

There, I said it. I had barely uttered the words, but I got them out.

He loosened his grip on me and bent down to my mouth and pulled my lip into his mouth, sucking on it softly. I might have let him continue, but he pulled away and set another chaste kiss on my lips before leading me out of the pool by my hand.

I helped carry his clothes into the preparation room. He didn't seem too disappointed, and I was beyond grateful. One thing I was learning quickly about Guardians: the men were as dangerously erotic as they were beautiful.

Jett's girls were barely clad in bras and panties in one of the aisles we passed. Slate, farther down in that aisle, lifted his head to see Ash leading me by the hand. We passed Gypsum and Diamond talking,— fully clothed, *thank goodness*—down the next aisle. Steel and Tawny were in the following one, where we had both put our clothes.

He was leaning into her, her back against the cubbies we kept our clothes in. Her hair was fully dry.

"Oh!" she cried out when we she saw us.

Steel only looked slightly embarrassed. Tawny touched her dry hair. "Look what they can do," Tawny said, red-faced.

"See you girls at lunch. Ash." Steel nodded and left, still not dressed.

I gave Tawny a *What are you waiting for?* look, but she dropped her head. I'd have to corner my mom and tell her they needed to come clean to Tawny, and soon.

She walked away anyway. "Later."

"I can dry your hair for you," Ash said to me.

"If it's not too much trouble." I straddled the bench and he sat behind me and moved suspiciously close.

He placed his hands on my head gently and I could feel heat and wind. He had made his hands into blowdryers. He ran his hands through my hair while they emitted the gentle blowing heat, massaging my scalp, running the back of his hands down my spine. I didn't know that hair drying could be so sensual. I was going to have to start keeping track of all the things I didn't know.

I will not moan, I will not moan.

I was already closing my eyes as I leaned into his palms.

I could *feel* his satisfaction.

My hair soon dried into its usual waves. I'd seen Gypsum and Diamond pass by, making exaggerated suggestive faces at me together, and Jett and his lady loves strolled to their cubbies, all of them completely dry. I was abundantly aware that Slate was still somewhere in the prep room.

Ash grabbed the back of my hair at the scalp and pulled my head back to kiss my mouth. It sounds like it might've been painful but, it was horribly, wonderfully hot. I thought I was developing a thing for being manhandled.

He smiled down at me, his hand still firmly in my hair. "All done."

He released my hair and I took a second to catch my bearings. He stood up and peeled off his underwear.

I heard them hit the floor, and I averted my eyes. Ash chuckled wickedly. I tried not to be completely immature and cover my eyes with my hands, so instead I buried myself in the cubby that held my dress. I was trying to be somewhat cavalier about changing in front of him, but I was just too awkward.

Slate chose that moment to walk past me and shoot me that smooth look of his, his face completely emotionless. Ash pulled on his linen shirt and gave me a quick kiss on the cheek before following Slate out. I didn't even want to know the outcome of that confrontation.

I turned my back to the door and peeled off my semi-dry fringe bikini top, then tried to wiggle my dress on over my head. The weight-less material was sticking to my skin and bunching up almost as awkwardly as I constantly felt.

Strong hands slid under my dress at my hips, surprising me—I thought he'd gone! His hands slid languidly my up to the sides of my breasts to pull down the fabric that was preventing me from pulling it over my head. He came very close to cupping my breasts and I held my breath as a crash of pleasure rolled over me, my skin tingling at his touch.

I still managed to be embarrassed. Ash had caught me half-dressed, hands flailing above my head like an idiot. I didn't say anything; I *was* appreciative and feeling something deep inside me I'd never felt before. He zipped up the back of the dress. Then he did something I was *not* expecting. He slid his hands back under the dress, fingers sliding leisurely up my legs, my back still towards him. His hands skimmed none too gently over my wet bikini bottom and he hooked his thumbs into them, kneeled down, and pulled them down slowly over my trembling legs. Tsunami sized waves of heat washed over me, and I fought not to moan aloud as tension coiled deep inside me. I had to stop him before he did anything else with those fingers.

I stepped out of my bottoms and turned to face him; he was still kneeling, my bottoms in his hand.

My breath caught.

It was Slate. My body was on fire. His eyes were glinting that reflective silver.

So many things passed through my mind. What'd it be like to press myself against his body was number one. What it'd be like to wrap my legs around his waist was number two. Number three was pure, raw indignation. It was obviously some way to get even with Ash for some prior slight, it had to be.

I took a step forward and slapped him hard across the face and tried to yank my bikini bottoms out of his hands, but the man had a death grip.

I blinked at him. I didn't slap people, that wasn't me. I started to apologize, but he leapt to his feet in an instant and crushed my back against a closed door of a cubby. His hands held me at my throat and sternum, while his lower half pinned me to the wall. My feet dangled inches off the floor, my hands wrapped around the wrist that held my throat.

Slate's jaw flexed as he pushed his face close to mine. The smash of the cubby at my back had hurt, but the way he had me pinned left most of my weight held by his hips. The added pressure of his hands kept me still.

"You've lost it," I gasped as he shoved his leg between mine. "You can't keep manhandling me like this, Slate," I gritted.

Slate's eyes burned into me. "You did not have to slap me."

I jutted my jaw out in defiance. "You copped a feel and slid your hands over my fanny pack. You had no right. I appreciated the help with the dress, but you took off my *bottoms*," I emphasized. He had raked his hands over my skin, causing me to feel...

He burst out laughing and I stared at him indignantly. "Fanny pack?"

He let me down on my feet, but he didn't take a step back, so my head was still against the cubby door as I looked up at him.

"You treat me like some ignorant plaything because I'm not one of your eager worshippers, and I don't cuss. You're the one who keeps coming back even though I could not have made it clearer that I will never *ever* sleep with you. So who's the ignorant one?" I snapped.

Slate dangled my wet bottoms in front of my face and raised them out of my reach when I tried to pull them away. "Tell me you did not enjoy my hands on you." He caught my hand that swung out to slap him and bent my hand back to kiss my wrist, his full lips lingered.

"Irrelevant. It was inappropriate and I don't want to be felt up by you!" I admonished.

"So you say."

He pressed his hard muscled body against mine again, but gently, so I could have pushed my way free. He was warm and his scent filled my nostrils, so I held my breath.

He was daring me. We both knew it, but I wasn't that girl. I looked up at him with cool eyes.

Eyes said much more than he could control. The ones that told me just how badly he wanted to either tear my clothes off, or tear my throat out. For a second, I thought he would take that kiss, and much more. He lowered his face, his glossy black locks falling around his face, beads clicking, our noses nearly touching. He was daring me again to come the rest of the way.

I wouldn't. Never would. I didn't care how his eyes ached for me then. *Nope.* Didn't care at all.

I pushed him back with a hand and he moved easily as if deflated. "You don't put your hands on me again unless we're training," I said with my back to him.

He grunted acknowledgement. "You forgot your bottoms."

I started to briskly walk away, not wearing anything underneath, and we both knew it. "Keep them as a reminder."

Slate was chuckling as I left the prep room.

He must have chased after me. Slate tapped my shoulder as I turned the corner of the hall near the dining hall everyone would be eating lunch in.

Slate was still chuckling. "What?" I snapped.

Why did he find me so amusing? It made me irate. He held up my shoes and something else.

"I think you will want these."

He dropped my shoes to the floor, and I slid into them, blushing. I was so discombobulated I'd forgotten about shoes!

Then he held up the lace in his hand with a sly smile. My underwear. A white lace thong. I turned plum purple and tried to snatch it out of his hand. He kneeled in front of me and I stifled a scoff—I didn't want someone in the hall to hear me and come investigate.

"You will need to balance yourself to put them on. Use my shoulder," he offered, his grey eyes twinkling, closer to my eye level now than he was when he stood.

Two choices: 1) Use his body to block my wiggle into my underwear since something told me he wasn't going to go to the dining room without me, or 2) Not give him the satisfaction of seeing me put on my panties. No one could see my fanny pack through the dress, and I only had to make it through lunch until I could go to my room and get a new pair.

"No, thank you," I said haughtily, and felt somewhat satisfied when his grey eyes widened.

He was still kneeling in front of me, though, too close for comfort. He looked at where my panties should be, and I wrapped my hands in the hair at the top of his head and jerked his head up. His silky hair slid between my knuckles and I imagined myself with that hair over my thighs. I gave myself a mental shake.

"What are you going to do with them? You do not have any pockets on that dress," he rumbled, lower than usual.

Sugarfoot. I hadn't thought of that. "Don't *you* have pockets?" I asked, irritated that I'd have to ask him for a favor, but it was his fault anyway.

He gave me that unreadable look and I watched as he pushed my white lace thong into his pocket. I realized I still held his hair in my hand. I bit my lip.

"Sorry." I let his hair trail through my fingers as I attempted to smooth it back down.

He took my hand away and held it as he stood. He lifted my wrist to his lips and pressed his full lips to the inside. Slate never gave up. He pressed his lips even higher, and then higher again to my inner elbow. I yanked my arm back and his grey eyes glittered as if he'd just discovered something precious.

"You are incorrigible," I rasped.

His full lips curled. "Only while chasing rabbits."

Ash and the girls stayed for lunch. It was the first time Pearl or my mother had seen Jett with his girlfriends. The mix was very entertaining. Jett was a hard one to embarrass, so I thought he enjoyed himself just as much as I did.

Ash sat next to me, ever the adoring escort, but I was done for the day. He asked to see me again tomorrow and I agreed to come visit him if I could bring Gypsum. Gypsum really liked Diamond, and she liked the idea of him coming by. Besides, I knew I would need an out, and Gypsum would be perfect for that.

My mother kept beaming at Ash, and Ash was ever the charmer, even with Hawk who held his own talking about Hawk's favorite subject, U.S. history. Ash's hand rested in my lap as we sat at my grandmother's table. I was acutely aware of my lack of panties. It had been a terrible idea.

It became a worse idea when Slate decided to use a familiar looking pair of white lace to dab at his mouth. *At his mouth.* I stiffened as he held my gaze; he had some serious balls on him. Ash noticed my change in posture and I was sure I'd been found out, but Ash just squeezed my thigh and gave me a cocky smile.

After I walked Ash back to the portal room, he gave me a swoon-worthy kiss and I trudged back to my room. I couldn't ignore that every movement I made hurt, that was a very bad sign.

I opened the door to my room; it was only midday, but I needed a cat nap. I went to my closet and slipped out of my dress and shook my head at my bottomless state.. I had been rash this morning, totally unlike me.

I rummaged through one of my boxes and pulled over an oversized Chicago Bears t-shirt, and put on a pair of white boyshorts with a fuzzy pair a blue striped socks. Now *that* was comfort.

I walked past the alcove and to my bed while I pulled my hair into a pile on my head. My feet stopped in their tracks. *No fiddlesticking way!* I crossed over to my bathroom door, and sure enough, there was moaning coming from Tawny's room. I covered the stupid smile that blossomed on my face and hurried out of the room and closed the door behind me so the sounds were muffled.

My smile was still plastered on my face when I reached my bed. I scanned the clothes on my floor. My white underwear lay on top of the pile of black clothes.

I shook my head. "No."

I toed the pile of clothes and weapons.

His hair was undone, and he was shirtless. His black mane was spilled over my pillow.

"No," I said again, and he pulled down the blankets to reveal that he did in fact have his underwear on.

They were tight black boxer briefs. What I noticed most though was the "V" shaped muscles that disappeared below his waistband, and the strong muscled legs that extended from the black briefs. They were thick and sculpted, even though he was just lying there. I took a deep breath.

"Come to bed, Rabbit," he said huskily, and something inside me tugged me to him.

"I won't sleep with you." I wished my tone had been more stern, that my back had been held straighter.

Slate's lips curled. "Only *real* sleep, Rabbit. Do not be indecent," he rumbled in a teasing tone.

I put my knee on the plush pillow top and watched as it bowed. It was just a bed, and he was just a man. My adopted brother, whom my mother adored, to my neverending frustration. I was not promising to do anything. Slate's eyes watched my bare legs as I climbed into the bed and suddenly it didn't feel so innocent anymore.

"I can't be in a bed with you if you're going to keep looking at me like that."

There was no safe place to look so I kept my eyes on his. What I found there made my mouth go dry.

"I shall have to close them then." Slate closed those grey eyes and I crawled under the blankets next to him, unable to tear my eyes off his face.

A permanent mocking smile etched his bronze face. My head fell upon the pillow and his eyes opened simultaneously—and my breath caught. His black-lashed eyes peered at me and I opened my mouth to protest, but he placed a long finger to my lips and I searched his eyes.

"Do not scamper away, Rabbit, I will only chase you," he growled.

I liked Ash, I honestly did, but sometimes, if you squinted real tight, it kind of looked like I wanted Slate to tear my clothes off with those teeth he kept biting me with. *But* I wasn't squinting; my eyes were wide open and I remembered the other two women I'd seen him with, one of them just yesterday.

I turned around and broke myself from his trance and folded my hands under my cheek. My willpower grew like the Grinch's heart and I sighed deeper than I'd intended.

I felt Slate's hand on my back and warmth flooded my muscles as they relaxed and the pain disappeared. His hand moved up to my head and he *called*.

"Sleep tight, Rabbit."

CHAPTER 10

A big hand squeezed my bare breast and my eyes shot open. I struggled to clear the fog from my mind. Where was I, whose hand, what had I done...all questions that I tried to clutch on to answers for.

Ever so carefully, I turned my shoulders to face the man in my bed.

His hand slid over my nipple and over the other under my shirt as I turned. I was so close to him that my shoulder pressed against his chest as I moved. This was not how we fell asleep. Did he unwittingly curl up around me or was it intentional? That was what mattered.

Slate. Despite his hard body, he was very comfortable to sleep with.

His face was so peaceful when he was asleep. No mocking smiles, no salacious looks, just the stress-free, flawless skin of a young man. Our bare legs were touching under the blankets and I shifted towards him. I shouldn't have, I knew it. I lifted my hands to his sleeping face and trailed my fingers from his wavy locks down his strong jaw. I ran the pads of my fingers along his full lips and gasped when I felt his fingers move under my shirt.

He'd touched more of me than I'd let any man before, and my skin prickled in response.

How did I forget about his hand? His fingers brushed the swell of my breast until it reached my nipple and he tugged gently on it. He was definitely awake. I pushed at his hand slapping his arm wildly.

"What do you think you're doing?" I shouted at him.

His lips curled as his eyes opened. "You touched me without permission. I returned the favor."

"Ah!" I cried as I sat up and tried to pummel him.

He started laughing, the cache hole!

He spun me around so my back sunk into the bed and he pinned my arms above my head with one hand as he kneeled above me, his eyes like gunmetal. I struggled and he parted my legs with his knees. My shirt had been wrestled up so my stomach was showing and he knelt between my legs.

Slate wasn't even breathing heavy as he looked down at me. "No more slapping me, Rabbit."

"Let go of my wrists. Pinning me down isn't going to earn you any brownie points. All it tells me is that you can't control your temper," I ground out.

Slate's eyes bored into me and I licked my lips. H growled as he lowered his sculpted body onto mine.

Somewhere in my head was a brain that worked, but not with Slate between my legs. Not with his hair falling around his face like a dark halo, and his ridiculously muscled upper body flexed above me. Certainly not with his powerful thighs tensed between mine. I couldn't find my voice; did I still have a head that used a mouth to speak?

Slate's big hand kneaded my thigh as he pulled my leg up and his hips sunk against mine. My lips parted and a gust of air expelled from my mouth. He was hard against me, fitted to me. He shifted his hips and my skin flushed with the clench I felt that sent pleasure spiraling through me, muddling my already muddy mind.

I shook my head and he arched a dark eyebrow at me. "What was that, Rabbit? Scampering away?"

He lowered his head so his waves brushed my face and he watched me as he pressed his lips down against my jaw. Then trailed down my throat as his hand slid from my thigh and under my backside. He pushed his hips into mine, a moan slipped from me, and I found my voice.

"Stop." It was hoarse, but firm.

My body wasn't listening to what my mind knew had to happen...or not happen.

Slate blew out a breath and rested his head against mine. His heavy body pushed me deeper into the mattress, but his hand released my wrist and I straightened my leg.

"I want you, Scarlett," he breathed, and my own breath caught as my heart skipped.

His tone made me believe it, but his actions told me just what part of him wanted me.

"Get dressed; we have to show up to dinner," I said, sounding much more sure of myself than I felt.

I nearly patted myself on the back. He thought using my name would make me weak in the knees, well, he was wrong...for the most part.

Slate lifted his head. He almost looked hurt.

"Scarlett, I..." he started.

I couldn't stand the look he was giving me, cutting me to the quick, playing on my compassion. "If this is where you tell me that you care about me, or that those other girls don't mean anything...spare me. I've seen you with two different women in two days. I was waiting to see if there was a third girl for a third day, but maybe you planned on that girl being me."

His grey eyes searched mine. "You give me far too much credit."

He growled as he rolled off of me. I sat up quickly and pulled down my shirt. I slid off the bed and stormed past where Slate was dressing to the bathroom.

"I was with a woman today."

It shouldn't have hurt, but it did. When did he find the time? Was it the strawberry blonde or the raven-haired woman? Did he spend the night there after he left my room?

"Rabbit?" Slate rumbled, and I nearly crushed his fingers in the bathroom door as he tried to reach me.

I locked the door and sank down to the floor. He'd had his hands on me had kissed down my neck and pressed his body against mine...and I was the *second* set of legs he'd knelt between.

I shoved my wrist into my mouth to stifle the cry that wanted to come out. No. I wouldn't give him the satisfaction. I just needed some air.

"Open the door, Scarlett." Did he sound anxious?

"You've made your position perfectly clear. Between any woman's legs at any time. Please go away. You have been playing a game with me. You win, Slate. I don't know how to play. I don't know the rules."

"Open the door. Scarlett, it is not like that." I could hear the restraint in his voice, but I didn't care.

"Please, just go. We can pretend it never happened," I pleaded.

"I cannot do that. But I will walk away right now, this once." I could sense his hesitation as he did as I asked.

The next morning, I almost wanted to be sore, the sweet soreness of a hard day's work. I rolled out of bed hating the world, and stumbled into our bathroom. I was peeing with the door open when I saw a bare backside run past Tawny's open door.

It surprised me, so I yelped.

The owner of the bare backside did not check to see if I was okay. I heard her door slam, and the muffled sounds of someone moving around a bed.

I couldn't resist. I walked into Tawny's room. She was searching frantically in her bedsheets when she saw me.

It was her turn to yelp.

She hung her head. "It's exactly what it looks like."

She looked like she was on the verge on tears. How could she do something that made her dislike herself so much afterwards?

I had to fix it.

"Is it safe to sit here?" I asked in mock disgust. She made a face. I held up my hand. "That's alright, I'll take my chances."

I plopped down on my stomach and I realized she was naked as the day she was born under those sheets. "Oh, dear God!" I shouted, pretending to shield my eyes.

"You are a fanny pack."

"I have a *fantastic* fanny pack, thank you." I threw her a familiar looking tunic that wasn't hers at her head.

"Scar, seriously. I think I'm in love with him. And there are serious things wrong with this picture here!"

"At least the family will save money on the guest list for your wedding." She definitely tried to punch me then, but settled for kicking me from under the blankets.

I could make light of it, because I knew under no uncertain terms that they were *not* related. I couldn't imagine what she must be going through—no one could because she was the only one who still believed he was her uncle.

I sighed. "Tawny, I am your moral compass, am I not?"

"You used to be before you became a hussy," she chided. And she didn't even know about Slate yesterday.

"I resent that. But let's pretend I still am. Would I *ever* condone something as reprehensible as incest?"

"No."

"I think you and Steel make a lovely couple and I hope you have adorable little babies together."

She looked at me, her head cocked as if maybe at this angle it came out differently. Then she threw up her hands.

"You're no help! I am going to rot for this."

"Look, maybe keep it under wraps for now. I won't judge you, I promise. And we'll see if things sort themselves out."

"You're an idiot, you know that, don't you?"

"I will try not to take extreme offense to that." I hopped off the bed. "It smells like sex in here," I said as I walked into the bathroom.

"How would you know?" she yelled.

Training was going to suck. I didn't know if Slate had tried to come visit me last night because I'd locked the door—not that I would've heard him anyway over the two at the end of the table who couldn't stop blushing this morning. Jett kept side glancing at Steel like he'd lost his mind. Pearl even asked if he needed healing because he looked *fevered*. That sent them into a tomato face tailspin.

I was running laps before Slate came into the training room.

I enjoyed being in the training room; the blooming trees and plants gave the masculinity of the workout area a much-needed feminine air.

Slate ran alongside me awhile before speaking. "I will not take it easy on you if you are having a bad day, Rabbit."

Tawny was heading to the market in town for a bow with Steel and Jett, which meant the girls were meeting them. A double date, sort of.

I ate lunch with my mom, Pearl, Hawk, Tawny, Gypsum, and Slate. They wanted an update on our training from Slate, and I wanted to crawl under a very large rock.

"Despite the fact that they were not raised here, they show promise. Tawny shows the potential skill for archery and I am certain that Scarlett is an empath." Everyone's eyes slid me in interest. At least no one looked frightened.

My mom spoke up since Slate didn't elaborate for me. "You can feel people's emotions. You know how they feel by being in their presence.

You probably always attributed it to being really good at reading faces. I had my suspicions, to be honest."

I was shaking my head no, but what she said was dead-on. I *felt* people. I could even turn it off, or if I was highly emotional it would mute everyone else. There had even been times when someone was so upset that I became upset. It was very inconvenient, come to think of it.

"It is hereditary, darling. I myself am an empath. It is a good thing too, since Hawk and Wren were so used to hiding their emotions from me that I am sure they did it from you also," Pearl said sympathetically.

I could only read my mom when her emotions were boiling over, and Hawk, sometimes when he was really happy.

"Can you feel my emotions then?" I asked softly.

I felt like I'd just confirmed everything they were saying about me.

Pearl nodded. "You are quite capricious, my darling. It has been an interesting few days. I can teach you to control what you put out though, if you like."

I smiled shyly. "I would."

How embarrassing. My grandmother knowing how sullen I've been since yesterday. Then a thought: she knew about Steel and Tawny. If anyone was taking people on an emotional rollercoaster, it was those two.

I finished eating and excused myself. I sulked back to my room and got ready for my date with Ash. Gypsum met me in my room, so no funny business went on.

He was bummed everyone went to town without him because he hadn't gotten to go yet. He wasn't so bummed out after finding out Diamond would be present.

Ash met us at the portal room. The faux starry lights cast their blue glow on everything they touched. I wore my hair in a single thick braid, and had on a cornflower blue dress. Gypsum was really taking to the Tidings lifestyle. He had on a brown jerkin, gold embroidery wound up the front buttons, and dark brown pants tucked into matching leather boots. His long dark hair fell past his shoulders, and his olive skin freshly scrubbed. He looked nervous. He was dressed up by Tidings standards.

"Thanks for coming with me, Chief."

I felt like Gypsum had somehow grown into a man since we'd arrived.

Ash hooked an arm through mine and led me through the portal door, Gypsum on our heels. We arrived in the Straumr Palace a moment after stepping through the door.

A woman in her fifties with strawberry blonde hair and light green eyes stood in the wood paneled room. A large antique chandelier hung from the ceiling, casting a warm glow.

I put my knowledge of my ability to read emotions to work: Ash was *irritated*, the woman, *eager*. I stored that for later.

"Scarlett, this is my mother, Dahlia Natt." He held me out from him, my hand in his as if I was on display.

She briskly walked over and daintily shook my hand. "Pleased to meet you, Scarlett." She smiled hesitantly.

She wore a green and white silk caftan inspired dress, a full white moon on the center of the wide belt that cinched it. She was pretty, but I was surprised that she appeared to be around the age of my grandmother.

"And you." I smiled; she brightened at that.

"Very nice to meet you. I am Gypsum Sumar." I felt bad we had forgotten about Gyps.

"My cousin," I added. Dahlia smiled and bid her greetings.

She led us to a round parlor with green, embossed velvet chairs. She gestured to them and sat down across from us. Diamond walked through the door and squealed at the sight of us.

"Gypsum, Scarlett, I am so happy you came!" She kissed Gypsum on the cheek, gave me a hug, and sat in the chair next to her mother.

"Oh, Diamond. Please be appropriate," she quietly chastised her.

Diamond blushed and poured us tea.

"So, Scarlett you will be starting at the university with us this year? I am headmistress of first years and the provost of history—Tidings history, that is."

She scrunched her face, as if any other history left a bad taste in her mouth. Diamond rolled her eyes behind her mother's back.

"My father will be provost of American History this year," Gypsum inserted.

He must have missed the face she'd made.

"Oh. I hadn't realized Moon had been looking to fill positions." She sipped her tea.

I started to see why Ash hadn't introduced me before.

A man with skin the color of creamy coffee swept into the room. He stood behind the blonde woman and rested a hand on her chair. He appeared to be in her fifties, like she was.

"Basil, dear. These are Ash's friends Scarlett Tio and Gypsum Sumar. Did you know Moon hired another history provost? *American* History." She said it in a pinched tone.

"Did he now? Well, that will be an interesting class." He smiled warmly.

I liked him much better.

I wasn't sure I was going to like having Dahlia looking over my shoulder my entire first year. She had made up her mind about Hawk and Gypsum after hardly a sentence.

"Do you work at the university also?" I asked Basil. I wasn't sure what to call him.

He had a wide, open smile. "I work in the offices there, but I am not a provost. I am claviger, or the record keeper. I preserve and record all of Tidings' history with the help of my beautiful wife." He patted her shoulder and she held it with a spare hand.

"Dahlia, I think we have bored the kids enough. They will not be able to escape us in a few days, with us being at the university full-time." He smiled again.

Dahlia pursed her lips and stood up from her chair. She stood for a moment, eyes shifting between Gypsum and Diamond.

"Come along, dear," Basil said, and he gently led her away.

Diamond grimaced. "Sorry, my mom is very traditional. She disapproves of Tidings folk leaving, or worse, bringing back myopics to live here!" She said it wide-eyed and excitedly. She seemed completely disconnected from the idea that she could be hurting anyone's feelings, with naiveté of someone sheltered.

Gypsum was chewing the inside of his cheek; he had caught the gist of it. Ash's family thought they were better than us and people who came from outside of Tidings. Gypsum was *born* in Chicago. His feelings were hurt.

Diamond sensed his onset of gloominess. "Oh! Sorry Gyps, I did not mean *you*!" Her apprehension at him possibly being upset with her washed over me.

"Stay out of trouble." Ash stood up, clearly tired of the spectacle his family was making of themselves and pulled me up after him.

"You cool, chief?"

He gave me a halfhearted smile.

"Chief. I like that. Can I call you chief?" Diamond asked in a timid tone.

Diamond was practically sitting on Gypsum's lap. I was unsure if I should leave these two alone together so I mouthed, *Be good,* feeling like I'd done my cousinly duty.

Ash took me to his room; I should've predicted that. His room was surprisingly modern. The rest of the house was the height of gothic architecture, but his room was white-walled with gold patterns. The bed was just as massive as mine, but it had a black upholstered head-board and footboard. The bedspread was even black. He has recessed lighting along his ceiling with a small black chandelier. One wall was a panel of windows; it looked as though on sunny days he could push the panels in and it would lead to a balcony. Heavy gold drapes hung to the sides of the paneled windows.

"So this is where the magic happens?" I said stupidly.

It could have been taken any way really; he *was* magical for crying out loud!

He smiled, cocky. There was a difference between Jett's smug smiles and Ash's cocky ones. Jett had a sense of humor, sometimes self-depre-cating, but I hadn't heard Ash joke once.

He *did* have reason to be cocky, I couldn't deny that. We've estab-lished that he was gorgeous with a great body, but he was also smart and came from a *greater* family. Although after meeting his mother, I thought "greater" may have been a term thrown around too loosely.

"Thank you for coming. My family can be quite trying," Ash said as he led me through his room.

"That's okay, I love your sister. Your dad seems nice too. I don't know if this is an indelicate question, but if it is feel free not to answer. Why are your parents so much older than everyone else's?"

The question didn't seem to bother him at all, even though I was *feeling* irritation from him. "They tried for a long time. Then when they stopped trying, and instead dedicated their lives to our history, they were lucky twice. We were quite unexpected."

I thought it was sort of sweet that they were so interested in history together; it was the only thing I thought was sweet about his mother.

"Your sister told me she's betrothed; why aren't you?"

I was thinking about marriages and what introducing me to his parents meant, and *BAM,* it just popped out of my pie hole.

He gave his best, most cocky smile. "I do not *need* anyone to arrange my marriage."

I didn't have anything left of the room to inspect, so I was standing idly not wanting to sit on the bed first. He sat down and motioned me over.

"You are at a disadvantage; that is why I invited you here. I want to help you *call.*"

I perked up. "You can do that? No one's offered.To be fair, there's been a lot to absorb."

"I can, and I will. We shall start with something easy. To turn on the lights, you *call* electricity, or if it helps, lightning. We harness that bit of electricity from lightning and use it to power Tidings. Close your eyes and clear your mind." I sat on his bed and he took my hands before turning my palms up.

"Now envision lightning, only a small amount, in your hand."

I breathed deeply trying to relax my mind. *Rainclouds, storms, flashes, thunder, lightning...*nothing.

I opened my eyes. "It's not working," I said glumly.

He took a deep breath himself. "You are trying too hard. Try to relax. If I may?"

I nodded and he opened his hands; my muscles relaxed immediately. I didn't even know they'd been tense.

"Thanks, what'd you do?"

"With our ability to heal, we can also manipulate the body. However, it is not always the body that needs healing; sometimes it is the mind. It requires a willing participant, that or unconscious."

I thought he was joking, so I laughed, but he was serious.

I cleared my mind again and held my palms up. *Flashes, thunder, lightning, lightning, lightning.* And...*poof!*

I was not aiming my lighting very well, and I *called* a wee bit too much of it as it soundlessly shot through one of Ash's pillows behind him. A spray of singed feathers was the only indication that the call went awry.

"I'm sorry! Are you hurt? That was awesome!" He enjoyed my attention, if his smile was any indication.

"Get up, try to turn the lights on."

I walked over to the panel...*lightning, a little bit.* The lights came on.

I was positively giddy. I jumped like a schoolgirl and clapped my hands like a seal. Ash was laughing too, more at me than with me, but I didn't care.

"It was a lot easier the second time. Why is that?" My heart was racing—I was exhilarated!

"Once you find the place inside yourself where you *call* from, you can always find it. You did extremely well; you are impressively powerful."

I cocked my head. "What do you mean?"

"People have been known to go through quite a few sessions before being able to *call* and they are usually very weak. Some people remain very weak. My mother can barely make a plant grow. I myself happen to be very strong." He was bragging, but he also said it as a fact.

"You could probably channel any element you wished to now. Not with very much control, and you would have to watch your strength, but I am sure you could do it." His eyes got a devilish gleam to them. "I could show you how I did that trick from the night of the Ausa Vatni..."

He let it hang in the air watching for my response. I didn't want to fool around; I wanted to learn more magic! Although he probably would have been repulsed if he knew I called it "magic."

He smirked, and then, as if having an *ah ha* moment, said, "For teaching purposes, you can do it to me. I will coach you. You will have to use heat and air, and when you are ready, divide your paths." He started to remove his waistcoat.

I wasn't sure if I was ready to use my *calling* on a person. Especially something that I knew from personal experience was so intimate, but I was practically bouncing with anticipation to use it, so I agreed.

He lay down next to me on the bed, bare from the waist up, chiseled abs at the ready.

"Okay, very carefully, imagine heat."

I relaxed my body, crossing my legs at Ash's side and thought, *fire, flame, heat*...and there it was. I'd managed to create a ball of hot air in my hand, no sparks or anything. My face hurt from my idiotic smile.

He smiled, reassuring me. "Now *call* air."

It was trickier; I could only think of wind, and that kept blowing out my hot air ball. So once I had my warm air back together I thought, *gentle, air, pressure.*

I knew I had it before Ash said anything. It felt right to me.

"You are doing incredibly well," he praised.

"Try not to sound so surprised." I was captivated by my own magic.

He smiled. "Now the difficult part. Divide your call into paths. However many you want. Start small. When you are ready, I am here."

Oh, I bet he was. I was looking forward to using my magic on him.

I closed my eyes and thought about the warm air pressure I had ready for me to use right at the tips of my fingers.

I thought *divide,* and it did.

I started with ten paths, connected each to one of my fingers, and I reached out to Ash's chest with my invisible digits.

"Why did you take off your shirt?" I asked suddenly.

He'd used invisible fingers on me over my nightgown, and I might as well have been naked.

"Just in case." He closed his eyes and relaxed, then prepared to be pleasured.

"In case what?"

"I want you to be able to see how much pressure you are applying in case it is too much, and if it is too hot, you will notice."

I didn't like the sound of that at all. I hesitated.

"Scarlett, it will be fine. Diamond will heal me if something goes wrong."

I nodded; I was way too eager to use my magic fingers for a little thing like burning gouges into him to stop me.

I realized then that I didn't need to keep my palms up; I looked like I was meditating. So I spread my fingers out and placed them on the bed. I had complete control over my *calling.* I mentally raised my paths and ran them slowly, seductively, from the nape of Ash's neck to his knees. I knew by the way his skin moved that it was the appropriate amount of pressure, just enough to see his skin prickle as they glided.

"Scarlett, that was excellent." His voice was low.

I blushed. "I could do it again," I offered. "Maybe change it up a bit?" His eyes sprang open. He liked that idea a lot.

I thought, *breath, ice, blow, cool.*

I mentally divided my magic paths again and ran my invisible fingers from his neck down his chest and to his knees again. It was getting easy.

I went back to my warm pressure; I wanted to get the paths to go to different directions, not all down. I thought it would feel like a few different hands then.

Genius!

I started five paths at his lips, five at the nape of his neck, and five from his knees. I had them all move toward a center point: his belt buckle.

He gasped and clenched his fists as the paths reached their point. I could see how much he was enjoying it. Admittedly, I was getting a bit squirmy watching him.

One more time, I told myself. Something good.

I thought, *pull, air, wet, warm, moist.*

I kept the paths going in the same direction since I was calling so much already.

I started at his ears; he moaned. I trailed the paths along his jawline, over his mouth, down his neck. I crossed my warm, moist air over his hard pecs and down his rippling abs. And the pièce de résistance, down below his belt. Then stopped. Ash shuddered with a moan.

The blood had rushed to my face so rapidly, I thought it was on fire. He was so helpless, letting me do whatever I wanted to him. I'd felt disconnected from the intimacy of it, I didn't think of the repercussions. I suddenly felt incredibly guilty. I wasn't even sure why I hadn't actually touched him.

Ash's breathing evened out. "You are something special. I have to make you mine." I blushed again.

My heart was beating in my chest, partly because I was turned on myself, and partly because I was beyond mortified, and to top it off, he'd either just proposed or asked me to be his girlfriend. In Tidings, I had no idea which.

"Give me a moment." He slid out of bed somewhat stiffly and went into his closet.

I lay back on the bed. I shouldn't feel guilty about doing things normal people did. Well, maybe not with magic, but whatever!

Ash came back out, eyelids heavy. What I did had either made him want more, or want to take a nap. He smiled down at me over the bed and pulled me up to my feet.

"What do you say?" he asked me.

His light green eyes twinkled as he held me against his bare chest.

"To what?" I asked blankly.

I knew he'd just asked me to be his, but I needed him to go into detail.

His eyes hardened so quickly I thought I imagined it, but then they softened again and he said, "To be mine. Be with no one else. Promise yourself to me. We can take it slow, and if we are happy, promise yourself to me forever."

"Like a girlfriend?" I asked.

I'd never had a boyfriend, never been asked to be someone's girlfriend. Was that how it's done? That was awfully ambitious for a couple of nineteen-year-olds.

"Maybe we can start by dating for a while first? I've never had a boyfriend before," I confessed, feeling like an idiot.

He appraised me for a moment and gave me his most charming smile. "I will be your suitor. When you are ready to take our courtship to the next level, say the word."

"Ash, thanks for showing me how to *call*." My voice was small.

"Someone would have done it sooner or later, so I wanted to be the one to do it." He *felt* triumphant.

After a time, I told him I should go find Gypsum and head home for supper. He invited me to stay, but I politely refused.

I knew there would be trouble when I left Gyps with Diamond, but I thought *maybe* since she was betrothed, she was under contract not to do anything with anyone else. Hence my surprise at catching them *on her bed*. I tried not to mom it up, but I wanted to spank Gypsum.

I opened the door, and caught my chief...well, I caught him with a girl with a fiancé so I said, "Stop that!" while I shut my eyes and slammed the door, waiting for him to leave the room.

She called after, "Please don't tell my brother!"

I had left Ash waiting at the portal door, thankfully. I gave Gypsum a minute to get his wits about him and shoved him through the door. Ash, ever the gentleman, kissed my hand and opened the portal door. I shoved Gyps through in front of me.

"Are you insane?" I held my hands up. "Okay, okay. Sorry. I have...I don't...Dude, Gyps, I don't think you can go around fiddlesticking girls who have been engaged probably as long as you've been alive!"

He shrugged. "They won't get married before he graduates. A lot can happen in two years."

"Gyps, I don't think they take those things lightly. She shouldn't have led you on." I was trying to be sympathetic, but something I'd said ignited lit the anger in his eyes.

"I'm not a child, Scar. She didn't lead me on, I knew what I was doing."

It was hard not to see him as my little chief, but if ever I was going to see him as an adult, it was that day.

"Let me ask some questions before you see Diamond again." I shook my head when he started to object. "No, let me do it. I don't want anyone who doesn't need to know knowing. I'll be clever." I waggled my eyebrows at him.

When had his jaw become so square?

He nodded grudgingly.

He looked at me with those dark, puppy-dog eyes of his. "Scar, you didn't...agree to anything...with Ash? Hanging out with the guys, I've heard things. Just don't go giving away yourself away to the first guy who comes around."

He gave me a kiss on the cheek and scuttled off. When I say scuttled,

I mean he was developing a manly swagger, but I felt better calling it a scuttle.

I found myself excited about the idea of having a suitor, if not a boyfriend. Still felt a weird guilt about having taken *calling* so far with him, but I could convince myself that it was only slightly worse than thinking about it. I didn't actually come in contact with him, my *calling* did. Although, if some guy said, "Hey baby, I didn't actually touch her, my magic fingers did," I'd be none too happy. I shook off the guilt that was trying to make a comeback and made my way into the dining room.

My mom and Pearl sat chatting happily, waiting for everyone to arrive.

"Good evening," I said. I wasn't going to show off, but the itch to *call* again was too great.

Pull air. I spread my fingers and pulled out my chair.

They stopped their conversation and watched me sit into my chair smoothly, twin amused smiles on their lips.

"Good evening, darling. You have been busy." Pearl rested her polished, long nailed hands on my arm.

"I have!" I said excitedly. "Ash showed me how to *call*. It was surprisingly easy. He said I was powerful! I don't know what that means, or in comparison to what, but it's awesome."

They were both laughing.

"Your mother was ten the first time she *called* intentionally. If memory serves, she did not do a single thing with her own two hands for a month." They started laughing again.

Jett and Slate strode into the dining room, kissed us all, and sat down next to Mom. Slate even made a point of giving me a kiss on the cheek and I stiffened, much to his never-ending amusement.

"You all look in good spirits," Jett said, raising an eyebrow and smiling.

"They're telling stories about when mom started *calling*," I told him.

"Oh, I'm intrigued. Do go on."

My mom laughed. "It's nothing, really. Just me being silly. Ash taught Scarlett how to *call*."

"Really now?"

Somehow Jett made that sound like *I bet that's not all he taught you.* Slate had a similar expression on his face.

I tried to control the emotions I projected in front of Pearl, but she clearly picked up on something.

She must not have thought it was embarrassing because then she asked, "Did something happen while you were there?"

The night's events ran through my mind, his mother, *calling*, *calling* inappropriately, him asking me to be his, and catching Gypsum making out with a girl on her bed. I had to give her something.

"Ash sort of asked me out." I gave a shrug.

My mom and Jett raised their eyebrows, expecting more. Pearl placed her elegant fingers over her lips, as if to hide a smile. Slate's face had gone completely unreadable.

"And?" my mom asked. We'd never had this conversation before.

"I said I wanted to take it slow, so he said he'd *court* me." I suppressed a moronic smile. "He made it sound like he was open to something more permanent."

"Permanent?" Jett asked, no longer looking amused.

"Damn it, Rabbit. I hope you did not do anything rash," Slate growled, and Jett blinked at him like he'd grown a second head. Pearl noticed Slate's outburst as well and was gazing at him speculatively.

My mom looked excited. I didn't think she cared much for Ash in one way or the other, but I knew she wanted to see me happy. If Ash made me happy, then she was happy. I appreciated her enthusiasm. Pearl put on a smile, but it didn't reach her eyes. I didn't think she had anything against Ash; she was only looking out for my well-being. It felt wonderful to be cared about so much by my family.

"He said—and I quote," I said, making a face at Jett that got him to give a half smile, "'We can take it slow, and if we are happy, promise yourself to me forever.' I didn't make any promises, I just agreed to date him."

"Darling, he knows he would have to consult the head of your family before making a serious proposal, or his father would. Until he speaks with Hawk about it, it would not be binding." Pearl said it to reassure me, but I didn't like how it sounded.

"That's so archaic. What if Hawk didn't approve and I still wanted to?"

My mom was beaming at that, like I'd just admitted I'd wanted to marry Ash. Jett looked perturbed.

"That almost *never* happens. Do you think Hawk would turn down someone he thought you would be happy with?" Mom said it with an air of personal knowledge, her and my father were one of the *never* cases.

"No, he wouldn't. Why Hawk? I mean, he's basically my dad, but that makes him the head of *my* family?"

"Hawk is the patriarch of Sumar palace now. It is his whenever he wishes to claim it. I act in his stead, for now. He is being a bit stubborn about it, really." Pearl smiled indulgently thinking about her son. "When Hawk is ready to step down, Gypsum will be head of the Sumar family." My little chief, the head of a family?

"If your father was around, he would be handling any marriages." My mom averted her eyes after glancing at Jett and me.

Pearl searched my mother's face, but she was blocking her emotions.

"What about you, Jett?" Pearl asked, happy to have finally cornered him on the subject.

"What *about* me?" he asked tentatively.

"Any marriage proposals in your future?" Pearl asked.

"No one's asked me yet," Jett said with a sly smile.

Pearl made a slap gesture, but was smiling.

My mom was smiling again. "I wouldn't be disappointed about a few grandkids."

Jett choked on his water. I couldn't help but laugh. I didn't think the comment was directed at me.

"Cerise and Amethyst have talked about it; I'm not against it."

Polygamy was not against the law, but that didn't mean it was entirely accepted either. I liked Amethyst and Cherry—sure, I thought they could give Jett a little breathing room every now and again, but they loved him. That was the best thing you could wish for someone, for them to be loved unconditionally.

"Whenever you're ready, we'll arrange a meeting with Moon Straumr, and..." My mom didn't know Cherry's father's name.

"Viper Enox," Jett said as he ran his hand down his face.

"And Viper. To make sure things are done properly. You never know."

A conversation starting with, "My son would really like to marry your daughter and her friend," was not going to go well.

"What about you, Slate?" I jerked at the sound of my own voice.

Pearl and my mother were skipping right over him, but I figured he deserved to feel just as awkward as the rest of us. I must have missed something because Jett and Pearl had similar looks of discomfort on their faces.

Slate's eyes narrowed at me as if I was dense and then let his lips curl. "I have not caught a woman whom I love more than myself."

I narrowed my eyes at him. "That sounds about right," I murmured.

"Do not listen to Slate. There is someone for everyone." My mother looked at

Jett with a cheery smile. "Sometimes several someones."

Sparrow and Hawk came down next and my mom burst out the news of my suitor. I felt like they were making it a bigger deal than it was, but it was becoming clear whatever I wanted to call it, I was one step closer to a marriage. Gypsum came down and they brought out the platters of food. It was horribly obvious that Steel and Tawny weren't at dinner, at least to me. Jett said something about them wanting to go to bed early; I mentally inserted *together*.

Slate was monitoring what I ate. Gypsum and Tawny were going to be on this special diet too. I wanted to punch something.

After everyone heard my recount of the important parts of my date with Ash, juicy bits omitted, Gypsum demanded someone start showing him how to call also.

I couldn't agree more. I was glad Slate volunteered to include it in his training. Hawk was extremely busy setting up his office in Valla and making up his lesson plan for the year.

"Sparrow and I have been speaking, and we have something to discuss." My mom's tone was serious. "I *do* want to become an ambassador, but not to the Faunelle. I was told that our relations with the Aves have all but been cut off completely. I plan to reestablish *that* connection. Sparrow would take over the daily dealings of the palace, since she despises it." She grinned. "And we'll find someone else for the Faunelle. Perhaps one of the kids would want to do it in a couple years."

The table was silent. Sparrow was nodding in agreement, but seemed somewhat reserved about it, as if even she had been convinced to agree.

There was a swirl of emotions, but what I picked up most on was *danger.*

"Are the Aves dangerous?" I asked.

"The Aves are not dangerous. They have always been the easiest to treat with on Ostara," my mom said, bolstering herself.

"Why are they not communicating then?"

"No one is sure; it's been about fifteen years since they've broken contact. I think I can fix that."

"Ostara lands are especially dangerous for you," Hawk finally said. He was trying to broach the subject delicately.

"It's dangerous everywhere, Hawk. They're short ambassadors on every island. Relations with the tribes are in jeopardy. We have found a way to keep the Faunelle covered and hopefully the Aves too. I would volunteer for the Risar myself if Gypsum was going to Valla U this year, but he isn't, so I want to stay close to home."

Sparrow was my mom's woman until the end, she'd support her anywhere. Same as their own daughters.

"You could be ambassador to the Risar, Wren," Hawk offered.

"I don't understand. Why can't Mom be ambassador to the Aves?"

It was obvious Hawk and Pearl did not like the idea. Jett looked just as confused as I did, which gave me a little solace. At least I wasn't the only one out of the loop.

"The Aves' home is one of the few places the old *calling* still exists. They live in a tree that is rooted in a floating mass that is never in the same place, and continuously revolves around Ostara. The Aves themselves are not dangerous, as far as we know, but the tribes around the land are. I'm not saying she can't, I just think it's dangerous and we've been away so long..." Hawk said in earnest.

I had never seen my mom and Hawk disagree on something besides what to order for dinner on a Friday night. I was feeling conflicted. I wanted my mom to do something she was passionate about, but I didn't want her to be in any kind of danger. Hawk was right, it'd been almost twenty years since she trained.

"So, what are they?" I asked, I was afraid of the answer.

"They're human-bird hybrids," Jett told me.

He seemed to be the only one still listening to me as a battle of wills began across the table. They sounded beautiful. I imagined a half-peacock, half-human, and thought, *yes, I must see this.*

Something dawned on me: when they had told me about the native tribes, I envisioned humans. I now knew that they meant...something else.

"Wait a minute. Ash told me there are fairies, and Steel treats with mermaids. Now Mom wants to go work with bird people? And what are the Wemic?" I asked in astonishment.

Slate gave me a feral grin that showed far too many teeth. "They're big cat hybrids."

"And the Faunelle?" Gypsum demanded excitedly.

Hawk was trying to suppress a smile. "The simplest way to describe them would be deer hybrids, but they're more than that. They have elk, moose, antelope and gazelle hybrids as well."

"You *have* to take me to see the native tribes here. I'm serious," I said to no one in particular.

"I can take you during your summer break," Slate answered, and I realized he *would* be the one to show me.

I tried to loosen the knot in my chest. He was acting like a normal adult; I could do the same.

"No, *promise* me," I beseeched.

Slate laughed richly and I felt it somewhere low in my stomach. "I promise."

The mood in the room had changed. Everyone was entertained by our interaction.

"Will we learn more about the tribes at Valla U?" I asked, dragging my eyes from Slate's glittering gaze.

My mom nodded. She wasn't finished making her case.

"I have the inside track to becoming ambassador to the Aves; I know someone who is helping me get in. I start right away. I'm telling you as a courtesy."

I knew that tone. That was my mom's no-nonsense tone. She wasn't going to budge.

Even if I wasn't sensitive to people's emotions, I would've felt the tension in the room. The swirls of pattern on the table top suddenly became very interesting.

The lanterns were dim, setting a peaceful mood, for all the good they were doing. The morning glory vine was still thriving in its little pot. It reminded me of our first day here. I liked that reminder. I was rapidly getting overcome with emotion.

My big family was sitting here together arguing about work. I relished it. I was so happy I was crying, I tried to nonchalantly wipe my tears.

"Scar?" Jett said gently.

I tried to scoff, but it came out in a sob. I shook my head.

"I'm fine. It's just...I never knew we had this family here, and there's just so much love." I'd finally succumbed to my new reality.

After a lot of tears, and not just from me, I headed to Tawny's room to fill her in on my long, exhausting day.

I changed out of my cornflower dress and threw on a pair of grey jersey shorts and a matching racerback. I did my nightly routine...and then quietly listened at Tawny's door.

I felt a little perverse, but I'd rather hear it than see it. All was quiet on the western front, so I quietly opened the door and peeked in. It was dark, but the drapes weren't drawn, so under the moonlight I crept over to Tawny's bed.

Steel was lying on his chest bare-backed, sleeping. Tawny had her eyes closed, propped up on some pillows, gold bedspread so much like my own pulled under her arms. I could tell she wasn't sleeping, or rather, I felt her euphoric emotions.

"It's creepy when you stand over me and breathe like that."

I stifled a laugh. "This is weird, isn't it? I'll come back later."

"It's a little weird, but Steel sleeps like a rock. It's about to get a whole lot weirder." She lifted back the blankets and motioned me in.

I shrugged and climbed in next to her. I'd always thought that men looked so much younger when they were sleeping; Steel was no exception.

"What's up?" she asked once I had settled in.

"You first. Is this now a thing?"

I pointed around her to Steel's sleeping form. Her dark hair was piled on top of her head in a sloppy bun, and she wore a black tank and boy shorts. She was lying on her side, hands tucked under the pillow her head rested on, not a stitch of makeup on. She was glowing.

"Scar, if we weren't...who we are, I think...we would probably just elope." She sighed deeply.

"Well, good thing you're only nineteen and your dad would kick your fanny pack if you eloped. I would too." We didn't bother pointing out the pink elephant in the room.

"Ash is my suitor now," I blurted.

Her eyes widened.

I told her about him teaching me to *call,* his inference of a proposal, and I told her what Slate said about me being an empath. Her eyes just kept getting wider.

"Scar, do you even like him?"

"I do. He's handsome and sweet to me. I don't know if he's *the one,* but I can give him a chance, right? He's not like, my fiancée. I told him I wanted to take it slow."

She shrugged. "I don't think I'm the one to ask for dating advice."

"I just need a few boring days to get my head together. I never would've thought I could get a guy like Ash back home. It's weird...it's like he's the good-looking quarterback everyone wants to be around who asked me out, so I said yes, because, you know. Who wouldn't? But..."

"He is literally the first guy you met?" Tawny asked, and I nodded. "I think you *like* Ash, you're attracted to him. There's no harm in hanging out with a guy cause he's smoking. *But...*" She smiled naughtily and gestured to Steel.

"That's a big but."

Tawny leveled her eyes at me. "*But*, you've been all moony and brooding over—"

"Don't waste your breath," I said in disgust. I filled her in on what had happened yesterday, to her growing dismay. "I'm a stupid girl."

Steel raised his head. "I know you cannot possibly know this because you just met you-know-who, not that I was eavesdropping, but if it makes you feel better, he doesn't normally act like this. He-we-do-not-name is used to women throwing themselves in his path, but he seems taken with you. I still wouldn't waste my energy. Ash is a good match, even though he has a similar reputation to...whom-we-allude-to." He paused for a moment. "Then again, for the right woman, anyone could change."

That sent us into a fit of giggles and Tawny threw the blanket up over our faces. I was caught up in Tawny's joy and shoved his comments into a locked box and threw away the key. I would not analyze anything about Slate; that would be like admitting there was something to analyze, and other than a heaping helping of animalistic lust, there was nothing. He couldn't even muster a kind word to me.

Steel pulled the blanket back off, and we squealed.

"So, you obviously know about us." He was struggling with the situation.

That much was clear. He knew Tawny still thought he was her uncle, and she went through bouts of self-loathing because they couldn't stay away from one another.

I lifted a finger to my lips, leveled my gaze at him, willing him to catch my whole meaning. "I know everything," I told him with stilted words.

He searched my eyes, and finally he nodded. He *felt* relief. I couldn't imagine keeping their kind of love a secret. Not that if she didn't think he was her uncle her parents would be okay with him spending the night in her room.

"So Ash is courting you now?" he asked, voice still thick with sleep.

"How long were you up for, eavesdropper?!" Tawny sat up against her pillow.

"You guys really don't know how to whisper. Somewhere around eloping."

His smile was slow and smooth. His eyelids were heavy as he leaned into a blushing Tawny for a soft kiss.

"Well, this officially got weird." I slid out of the bed.

"It was weird long before you got here," Steel said, in a tone that told me I should leave much faster.

I made sure to shut the door behind me—both of our doors. It helped a little.

CHAPTER 11

 I spent the next two days training hard. I trained all morning and *called* all night with Tawny and Steel. He'd taken up permanent residence in her room. I got to know Steel, and found that he was very much like my Uncle Hawk.

Tawny was a littler slower at *calling* than I was, but she still got it within her first session. She couldn't divide her paths yet, but she could hold two different *calls* at once. She put those to good use; two doors was not enough between our rooms.

Gypsum was even *calling*. His physical training was also beginning to show. It had barely been a week and his arms were more toned, his abs were even more defined—a feat only men could accomplish with such ease.

I couldn't tell with myself: mostly I was aware that I should be aching, but wasn't. One night at dinner I asked since we could heal ourselves, then why couldn't we just grow muscles for ourselves? My family looked at me like I had two heads. They said it was the same reason you couldn't make your breasts a cup larger—I should note that Jett was the one who said this.

Jett, Mom, Steel, and I made a point of having lunch together in the sitting room after training. Jett told us stories of life here, most of which I thought were terrifying or inappropriate, and Mom told stories of us in Chicago. I sat back and enjoyed. Things, while still brutally hard, were starting to get into a routine.

The one thing I hadn't addressed was my new suitor. I'd avoided him since the day he taught me magic fingers. He'd come by on the second day after training, when I was on my way to my mom's for lunch. I didn't invite him and he seemed offended, but I wasn't sure what I was going to do about him just yet. We had a date after lunch at his house. He wanted to show me around Valla, so I was to dress for the weather.

I let my long waves hang loose down my back and wore softly-lined black leather pants tucked into fur-lined black boots that had just a hint of heel. I tucked a white, long-sleeve shirt into my pants and buttoned a padded jerkin, its cut-out hole exposing my cleavage. My mother had a black cloak with removable fur lining still in her closet from her teens that she gave to me, and I was ready to go. There's something about leather pants that make you feel just a little bad fanny pack.

Ash met me at our portal door. I couldn't for the life of me remember why I was avoiding him. He was wearing the hell out of his leather pants.

He smiled when he saw me, cocky as always.

"You look stunning." He grabbed a fistful of my hair, his eyes locked on mine as he took a deep breath.

"Thanks. Ready when you are."

He pursed his lips. I knew he was disappointed I hadn't said anything about him, my hot quarterback.

His green eyes narrowed slightly, and he pulled me to him, lifted me off the floor. He kissed me deeply and I felt warm invisible fingers slide across my skin down to my toes. My back bowed. He was happy.

There were four different portal door rooms in Valla. One room was in Valla U, the Tio and Straumr palaces each had one, and the market in Valla had a portal gate. He took me out through the portal gate.

It was in the end of December there: snow had fallen recently and the entire town square was covered in its pristine whiteness.

"Welcome to Valla, *again*." He flashed me his perfect smile.

He remembered one of the first things he'd said to me! Flattered, I smiled back genuinely. There may be some hope for him yet.

"This is the town square?"

I looked behind me at the portal gate. It was a free-standing stone gate with sculptured tree branches twisting up it, and a sculpture of a woman crested the top, her hands extended and becoming branches.

"Technically, it is a hexagon." He smirked.

The *hexagon* was completely devoid of merchants. From each point of the hexagon I could see a road and people milling about.

"It was designed in a star formation. There are three gates that exit the city.

The six roads have roads that link them that lead to the gates, Urd, Verdandi, and Skuld—past, present, and future. Urd gate leads to my palace, Verdandi to beyond the city, and Skuld leads to the Tio palace. Urd and Skuld both have paths that lead past the farmlands and up to Valla U."

I loved information. I was absorbed in his description, trying to remember every piece. He relished in my attention, I *felt* it.

He kept going: "They are named for the Norns, our fates. We are taking Verdandi to the beyond."

He pulled his dark hood up and shoved his hands into gloves. Thoughtfully, he'd brought a pair for me too, which I pulled on as well. I followed his lead and walked alongside him. We took the narrow road not made for vehicles in the direction the gate faced.

Stone buildings never higher than three stories lined the streets. Glass storefront windows that reminded me of a little European city were cramped side by side along the cobbled road. It was compacted as tightly as asphalt...*magic.* The design was artistic and functional, and I had a strong inclination it was built as a fortification.

I was wishing I had brought a scarf by the time we reached Verdandi gate.

A guard stood monitoring the gate, three joint triangles in silver on his thick cloak. He nodded at us as we passed through, his breath puffing into the frigid air in little white mist bubbles.

"Does Tidings have a standing army?" I asked as we passed.

"We are all trained. The most desirable positions are for those proven tried and true. When needed, we all answer the call. Each town center has a contingent of Guardians, and most belong to a greater house. We have a few Guardians at the palace specifically for guarding."

"What was the symbol on that guard's cloak?" I asked.

"The three interlocked triangles?" He asked giving me an *Are you really that daft?* look.

Yes, yes I am. I nodded

"I forget how little time you have spent in Tidings. It is a Valknut, the sigil of the Guardians. They guard all of Valla under that sigil, while the family guardians will wear the sigil of their own houses." He *felt* preoccupied.

"I've never noticed a guard at home." I chewed my cheek in contemplation, or maybe to make sure I had feeling in it.

"*She* is there," Ash said matter-of-factly.

I tended to agree with him; I couldn't imagine Pearl leaving the portal unguarded. I wondered who it was as I looked behind us and noticed the ridge of mountains that spanned the entire city. At the very top of the highest mountain was a castle. I knew the castle must be Valla University. I could make out rounded, stained-glass domes of what was most likely a greenhouse.

We walked on flat land as the road disappeared, the city behind us slightly elevated. Ahead, there was a promise of rolling hills to come.

The hills were devoid of other people as the sky grew darker. It was only three in the afternoon. Despite there being no other people, I had the sense of being watched. I kept my eyes open, but I didn't find anything amiss.

We crossed over a stone bridge and I could make out a dark forest straight ahead; I hoped we weren't headed down the ominous looking path. He took me along the river until I could make out cottages nestled against the river. He wanted to spend the night with me, and all I could think was, *I didn't ask my mom.*

I was frozen and grateful to get inside. Apparently, Ash's family had a cottage for summer vacations, which seemed ironic since they lived on the island. I wondered which one was ours, assuming my family had one too, or rather, the Sumars did. I couldn't make out the other cottages in the dark.

Ash *called* heat into the cottage and lit the fireplace, which was kind of romantic. I was still feeling watched, but it could have been Ash. His eyes had been following my every move since we got into the cottage.

"You know, I didn't tell anyone I was staying the night away from home," I told him, letting a hint of irritation show through.

He smiled wickedly. "That is half the fun."

A traitorous shiver went through my body. I was still wearing my cloak and gloves. Ash had taken off his, and was leaning against the mantle, assessing me. The home was surprisingly quaint, what I'd expect from a cottage back home.

"You are cold. Let me help you," he said, crossing the room to where I sat on a grey striped sofa chair.

His eyes flickered in the firelight, little blooms of color in his cheeks.

It made him look boyish and gave him an air of vulnerability he didn't usually have.

He unclasped my cloak carefully and pulled my gloves off, one finger at a time, relishing in my willingness. Ash kneeled, his hand along the side of my head, and grasped a handful of my hair, taking a deep breath into my exposed throat. He released it, running his fingers through my golden strands. His eyes were on the skin revealed by the cutout in my jerkin as he slid it off my shoulders.

He softly ran the tip of his tongue along my lower lip, parting them, gently probing for my tongue. It was an exquisite kiss, soft and sensual.

"Are you still cold?" he asked, voice low and deep.

I meant to make the *nuh-uh* sound, letting him know, *no, thanks, pretty warm right about now.* It came out as a moan and he smiled against my lips.

"Are you hungry?" he asked.

He was a saint. I liked it. Until he mentioned it, I didn't realize how hungry I was. He brought in crackers, meats, and cheeses and I tried not to stuff my face. He poured me a goblet of warmed wassail and it was just what the doctor ordered.

I was feeling warm and fuzzy as we sat on the couch sipping our wassail while he played with my hair. I dozed off to the sound of a crackling fire against the shoulder of my suitor.

Internally, I did a happy dance.

In the morning woke up to something different entirely. I was alone on the couch, the fire reduced to glowing embers. I pulled on my jerkin and went in search for a bathroom. Behind one of the doors, I found Ash asleep in bed. I closed the door behind me and kept searching for a bathroom. Waking up alone without even a blanket tossed over me bothered me.

I wanted to chalk it up to how some women always joked about how aloof their husbands were, but Ash was *not* aloof. I wondered if he was angry that I'd fallen asleep on him. He probably had big plans for our night alone. For me, falling asleep in his arms was even better. We were laying the foundation for something more.

So I thought.

I snacked on leftovers from last night and waited patiently for Ash to wake. I was ready to go as soon as he was up. I didn't have to wait long. He strode in with a fresh change of clothes on and clasped on his cloak.

"Ready?" he asked.

That was the first thing he said to me, not even a *good morning*. I was boiling inside.

"Yeah, my mom is probably pretty worried." He nodded curtly and began the trek back.

I wanted to curse. Just when I was starting to actually like him.

The scenery was even more beautiful during the bright morning sun. I didn't want to stew in my anger, but I didn't want to be the first one to talk. I was thankful when he did.

"It is a good thing you did not venture out last night. A large animal must have been drawn to the cottage by the firelight."

I shivered. What kind of large animal had been stalking outside where we slept unaware?

"How do you know?"

He scoffed. "I can see the tracks."

I didn't know what to say to that; I didn't even see any tracks. Wow, this day was sucking.

"Forget it. We should get back in time for you to go to training. I can train with you while I am there."

He was being short with me, but I didn't want to fight the entire way to the portal.

"Where did you learn tracking skills? Is that something they teach at the university?" He slowed so I could keep pace with his long strides and watched me out of the corner of his eye.

"No. I do not think they will teach you tracking there either, but I can teach you."

Control. He was a serious control freak. He was probably pissed I'd taken it upon myself to fall asleep before he gave permission.

He continued, "The cousins I introduced you to, Crag, River, and Fox? They taught me. They have taught me almost everything I know."

"What about your dad? He's so into history, he must have a ton a cool information."

His face looked pinched, and it reminded me of his mother's. "My father always has his head in his books. He does not have time for the *now.*"

"I never knew my father. Jett either," I confided.

Snow crunched under our boots as the wind tugged on my mother's cloak. It was a magnificent morning despite Ash's sour mood. If it wasn't so bitterly cold, I could have laid out on the snowy blanket that covered the fields and watched the fluffy clouds float past the clear blue sky.

He noticed me shivering and asked me how my feet were. They were freezing. He knelt in the snow and *called* warmth on them, letting me balance a gloved hand on his shoulder.

Ash was a difficult one to read; he scared me just a little. His moods were unpredictable and yet, if he was in control or if it was centered around him, he was happy. I thought there was worse things in the world than being selfish.

The walk back through Valla was bittersweet. I wanted to get home, but I also wanted to explore more.

"Will you take me back here one day?" I asked.

He stopped in his tracks, reading my face. Whatever he saw made him happy, and he smiled his cocky smile for the first time that morning.

"I would love to."

I *felt* content. We were back where we usually were in our relationship.

He was right; we got in a few minutes past when I usually start training. I brought Ash to Jett's room and grabbed some things for him to train in, and we changed side by side in the prep room. He'd already seen me in my bathing suit so I didn't feel too bashful, plus I changed in about thirty seconds. Good luck getting an eyeful at warp speed.

He was right behind me when I burst out of the prep room. We jogged over to the weights where the guys were lifting. Jett's eyes darkened when he saw us together.

"You're late," he said coldly.

What crawled up his fanny pack?

"Sorry," I said, feeling childish.

Ash's face was cool, but that made me nervous.

"Ash is going to train with us today," I whispered. "Play nice, please?" Jett rolled his eyes.

Slate was yelling at me before I even reached him.

Training was punishing. With all the walking I'd done with Ash, my legs were already in pain. I wasn't healed and Slate gave me extra laps around the conservatory. Tawny waited for me in the prep room before heading into the pool, which I totally would've ditched, but Slate must have read my mind because he decided to join us. I filled Tawny in on our short night together and miserable morning. She didn't know what to make of it either.

"I did not realize *he* was training you." Ash had said in a cool tone when he met us in the pool.

I inwardly rolled my eyes. Slate was hardly friendly while he barked orders at me during training. In fact, he seemed like it was something he did often and well, and didn't have a problem separating his personal feelings from his professional ones. He trained me the same way he did Tawny with the exception of the morning I came back from my night with Ash.

Ash was competitive—everything he did was a competition. I could tell the other guys weren't particularly fond of him, but he was friendly enough so they were amiable.

Good thing too, because while I may have been considered an adult in Tidings, my mom grounded me for being out all night without telling her where I was. Ash came over twice that week to train with and join us for lunch. Ash was making an effort to soothe my mom, and luckily, he did everything right. By the night before the induction ceremony, he'd be back in her good graces and I'd no longer be grounded.

"Wake up, Rabbit."

My eyes sprung open. I'd locked my bedroom door every night since our altercation; how in the world did he get into my room?

I rolled over, grateful I'd worn my big girl pajamas, a dusky pink satin and lace camisole set that proudly displayed my curves. I looked to him dreamily and stretched my arms out languidly over my head while pointing my toes. I had a good idea of how I looked.

Slate's grey eyes were greedy and caught on the pearls formed from the rub of satin over my sensitive breasts. His gaze made my skin prickle, and I realized I was tempting fate.

"Enjoying the show?" I purred before my common sense kicked in.

Slate's responding gaze was all the answer I needed. Not that it was a big accomplishment to be desired by man driven by the little head between his legs, but it felt good to be reminded of my feminine wiles.

"Careful, Rabbit. I would not want you scampering off." He growled low in his throat.

If I hadn't been wearing thin material, perhaps he wouldn't have noticed my body's response to his growl, like a call to my wild side. He made a noise in his throat that sounded a lot like appreciation. I sat up and kicked off my blankets. Things were spiraling out of my control.

"What are you doing in my room? I locked the door," I snapped, swinging my legs over the side of the bed to sit next to him.

Was he *sniffing* me?

"I did not notice. Get changed, time to put your training to some practical use.

Tawny and Gypsum declined so it is just us."

He gave me a devilish grin, but it didn't touch his eyes. Those eyes kept flitting down to my satin camisole.

Great. A day alone with Slate. Ash was just going to *love* this. I got up and started towards my closet when I *felt* something from Slate for one of the first times ever. His wall had opened a window into his emotions and I'd stopped in my tracks. He knew I *felt* it—he'd done it on purpose. He let me slightly inside his carefully crafted walls he hid everything behind.

I stood frozen, deciding whether or not to glance back at him and acknowledge it. If I looked back at him after feeling *that,* I might let him do what his emotions implied. They were so intense they must have confused themselves with my own. I shivered and started walking again. Better to ignore it. If I didn't, I'd be back in my bed and my camisole would be a puddle of pink lace at Slate's booted feet.

"Should I wear something warm? Or are we staying in Thrimilci?" I shouted as I clasped on my light pink bra with lavender leopard print that matched my boyshorts.

"No need to shout. We are staying here. Something light and breathable will do. No dress." Slate leaned in the doorframe with his arms crossed, midnight waves flowing over his powerful shoulders, and I wondered how long he had been standing there.

I covered my chest with my hands. It was a push-up bra—don't ask me why I'd bought it. Even though it was pink, it wasn't like me. I was grateful for my long hair at that moment; it helped hide my body as I was trapped in my closet with Slate fully dressed and looking at me...like *that.*

"Stop looking. How long have you been standing there? Go sit somewhere." My words stumbled out of my mouth.

Slate enjoyed making me uncomfortable, that much was clear. "Long enough. Do not worry, Rabbit. You do not have anything I have not seen before." He didn't move a muscle and I sighed.

"You sure know how to make a girl feel special, Slate. Thanks for reminding me that I'm like one of probably a hundred women you've seen in their underwear." I sounded defeated even to my own ears and I turned away to rifle through my clothes.

When I turned back around he was gone. I pulled over a beige tank top and slipped into a snug pair of chocolate-colored pants, tucking them into brown, mid-calf leather boots with just a hint of a wedge heel. It seemed in-tune with what people wore here...*that,* or I was some kind of tomb raider.

I sighed. I'd never fit in.

Slate assessed me when I exited the closet, his expression unreadable. I may have humbled him somehow. I didn't know how, but it was a revelation.

"That should do. Where is your seax? You will need a weapon if your *calling* falters. Can I assume you have been practicing?"

His tone was the one he used in training. I found myself answering him his demands in a snap when he used it. I found this especially disconcerting in my bedroom.

"I have."

Slate lifted that strong bronze jaw and leveled his eyes at me, letting me know that if I lied, he'd know. "With someone *other* than Ash?"

My cheeks flushed, but I answered. "Steel has been training Tawny and I after dinner." I buckled my seax to my thigh, glad to not to be captured by his hard gaze for a brief respite.

Slate inhaled slowly; he looked like he was counting to ten. "Good. We will eat in town. Come."

I was used to dealing with this version of him in the conservatory, but not outside of it. I was wrestling with my urge to do the exact opposite of what he said...but another part of me wanted to learn everything he had to offer. My pride would have to take a backseat.

It was another beautiful day in Thrimilci. The townsfolk seemed to always have a faint hint of a smile as they walked over the shimmering white roads. Slate escorted me to a cafe and we had breakfast together, and I tried not to read too much into it. He wouldn't have devised this whole plan just to get me alone for the day. That would have been ridiculous. How would he explain it when we got back and my family asked where I'd been all day?

No, it was what it was. Another training exercise.

He ordered for me—my favorite breakfast of two scrambled eggs, two slices of thick-cut bacon, and wheat toast. It was a safe bet, I decided; it's not like he would remember such inane details like what I ate in the mornings.

"I had a dream the other night—a nightmare, really. I've had it a lot, except this time you were in it," I said.

I scowled at my plate. Telling him about how he died in my dreams wasn't breakfast conversation.

"Really?" He didn't make it sound as perverse as he could've.

"It wasn't a pleasant dream," I admitted and he sat silent for a moment. "I'd rather forget it."

"I have had many dreams about you," he rumbled, and I rolled my eyes. He gave me a small smile, "Unfortunately, they never end well." *Oh.* Why did I feel disappointed?

"There have been reports of a bauk in the old buildings just outside of town. It is a large, dangerous creature. Fortunately, it has not attacked any people yet, which leads me to believe this one is small, but livestock has gone missing. We will find where it is hiding and dispatch it," Slate said as we started our trek.

He had packed us a lunch, which I assumed meant we'd be gone for a while. My new muscles were ready.

Slate made small talk by saying *nothing*. Maybe he worried about saying something that would aggravate me, but I was a nervous chatterer. I yammered on and on about Chicago and when I tapered off, he'd ask a question to let me know he was listening, if disinterested.

We were having a normal conversation like two adults and I felt myself relaxing a bit. It wasn't bad at all. I didn't know what I'd been dreading. Telling Ash about today, yes, but hanging out with Slate, not so much.

I'd just finished telling him about my exceedingly awkward first attempt at a kiss after a movie theater debacle when I was in ninth grade. I shook my head. "I just don't have that *thing* that Tawny seems to have been born with. The harder I try, the more hopeless it is." I shrugged. "I've given up."

"Is that why you have never had a lover?" he asked, glancing at me from the corner of his eye.

I pinched my lips together. "I didn't say that. Just because I've kissed only a few guys doesn't mean I haven't taken it further."

Why was I offended? Was it because he assumed I was inexperienced? I bet I looked as clumsy as I felt. My heart plummeted; I thought I had been hiding it well.

I decided to direct the subject towards him. "I bet you've had a plethora of late night dates.."

Slate stopped and knit his brows. "What makes you say that?"

I blinked. I thought he'd be flattered, but he seemed offended.

"I'm sorry. I didn't mean anything by it. You're a handsome man and you have something about you that draws women in."

I felt it whenever he was in the room, as if my feet tried to start towards him whether I wanted to or not.

"Something that draws them in?" he asked, arching one of his dark brows.

I nodded. "Like a tug. Like you have your own gravitational pull and they can't help but find themselves near you…" My words trailed off.

He wanted me to admit I felt something—anything—for him.

I started walking again. "I heard one of the staff girls talking about it. Probably one of the many notches on your belt," I lied.

Slate caught up easily. "I do not sleep with the staff. Neither would I bring women home."

I made a disgusted face at the sand below my feet. I regretted where my conversation had led us.

The sun beat down on us, but Slate assured me that if I burned, he'd heal me.. It didn't stop me from being uncomfortably hot. Slate had pulled a light tan scarf from his pack, and I wrapped it around my head. It did help a great deal.

Slate hardly sweated at all. Most likely because his perspiration was afraid to do so without his permission. I wondered if he ever lost control of himself, aside from when he was crushing me against things. We walked the desert for another hour outside of the main part of town. The road ended and it turned into tightly-packed sand, and then loose sand, and my every step sunk as my muscles worked twice as hard to walk.

"We will stop for lunch once we reach the buildings."

He apparently used the term "buildings" loosely; they were more like multilevel shacks. We reached them around late afternoon. When he took off his pack and we leaned against the side of one of the dilapidated buildings, I decided to attempt making a palatable sandwich. With my magic, I now even knew how to reheat the meat. I was pretty proud of it.

"Ash has you make sandwiches after? Something the two of us have in common," Slate said, taking a massive bite out of the sandwich I'd made him.

I'd stiffened...but maybe this was playful banter? Tawny and I teased each other constantly and I never felt the resentment that I felt towards Slate for saying things she would have. It was time to change that. Slate was family, after all.

"Actually, we try to incorporate the eating *during,*" I said in my most suggestive voice.

It was a just a joke, but Slate stopped his hand midway to his mouth and shut it. "I have lost my appetite," he said coolly as he started to put down his sandwich.

I was at a loss. "Slate, don't. I thought we were joking, like friends. Teasing one another?"

I hated sounding like I was backpedaling or that I cared so much about his feelings. What feelings? He just wanted to sleep with me, so why would he take this jest to heart? Men were so confusing.

The front of Slate's hair was pulled away from his face with a leather strap, and his skin seemed even darker that usual from our hours in the sunshine. "I do not want you to joke about fucking Ash. Get indignant and huff, scurry away like the little rabbit you are." The hard planes of his face seemed harsher to me as his grey eyes flashed silver at me.

He'd used the "F" word. I didn't like that word. I blinked at him trying to think of something to save the rest of the day.

"I won't always be a rabbit," I whispered, and he nodded.

"You have made that clear," he said gruffly.

I forced my sandwich into my impossibly dry throat. After a few minutes, Slate taught me how to *call* water and I drank it from my index finger like a fountain—after getting it up my nose several times, much to Slate's delight. Fed and full, we leaned against the building, letting our food digest.

I hated the silence, but I was afraid to say something that might upset him again. Joking like I would with my friends didn't work, and I didn't want to hear about his *sex*capades. I had told as much as I could come up with about my childhood. That left me blank.

His eyes were closed when I looked at his profile. His long muscular legs were stretched out in front of him and crossed at the ankles. It looked like he was completely relaxed but there was something just under the surface that was constantly moving.

Slate had a glorious profile. His nose was straight and masculine, his lips curved deliciously from his mouth, leading to that strong jaw and corded muscular neck. The terrible urge to lick his Adam's apple as he swallowed made me squeeze my eyes shut.

Slate looked at home in the desert. There was no doubt about that. I chanced another peek at him and he was peering at me from the corner of his eyes.

"I can feel you looking at me. Have something you want to say?" His words rolled from his full lips.

"Just thinking how upset Ash will be when he finds out I was out training with you all day. He doesn't much like you for some reason, but I guess the feeling is mutual."

Slate grunted scornfully. "I may have had many lovers, but I do not break hearts and I am always honest about my intentions."

I furrowed my brow at his cryptic words. "Ash breaks hearts?"

Slate appeared to have some internal struggle. "Ask him yourself."

"Is this some sort of guy code? You don't say bad things about him, he won't say bad things about you, but you two can't stand to be in the same room together?" I'd never understand men.

Slate got to his feet, ignoring my question, and packed up what was left of our lunch. I couldn't help myself; I chewed my cheek.

"You have had a lot of lovers?"

I inwardly chastised myself. Not an appropriate question, nearly as bad as asking me if I made Ash sandwiches after we made love.

Slate lifted the pack over his head and turned towards me, his expression unreadable. "Does it matter?"

I thought on that for a moment. It didn't matter to me, not really. I just didn't like *seeing* it. "It might matter to someone who falls in love with you."

Slate's gaze turned cool, and it froze me to my core. "Any woman who falls in love with me is a fool. There is no future with me." He turned his back to me and started to head into the building expecting me to follow.

"Love makes fools of all of us," I murmured as I trudged behind him.

He had stopped so suddenly I bounced off his back and fell onto my backside.

"Would you believe that I have been a fool?" he said with his back to me.

"Don't worry, I'll help myself up," I said sarcastically as I dusted off the back of my pants.

He hadn't moved. Was he expecting an answer?

I huffed. "I guess anything's possible."

He spun on a dime. "Is it?"

My mouth fell open as I tried to find my words. I knew those once, not always around this man, but I *had* a vocabulary.

"I suppose," I answered in a small voice.

The ends of his lips quirked as he turned back around. I shook my head; this man was more confusing than most. I followed him into the abandoned building. Slate had said there were a lot fewer Guardians nowadays, so people moved closer to the town's center and these buildings stood empty. No one had the heart to destroy them because it would mean the end to an era.

It was once a town, but the entire place had been abandoned. I couldn't believe that there were thousands of people who had never come to refill the places that their ancestors had left. It felt like a graveyard and it gave me the creeps. The walls may have been strong and sturdy once upon a time, but I was sure if I pushed with enough air, I could probably blow one down, or at least drive a hole through it. The buildings had a unique design. They reminded me of townhouses back in Chicago the way they ran in succession to one another; each one had their own little yard with their own tiny yards.

We'd been searching through house after house for the bauk to no avail. I'd never seen nor heard of one, but Slate assured me I wouldn't mistake it and to shout for him the moment I did.

We'd looked down the entire block of a street with many more to go. Slate said we'd probably catch it closer to night since it was when it hunted. I almost wished it'd attack me so we could kill it already.

I sneezed what felt like a hundred times in another dusty building. Slate shot me a look that said, *Really?* We were both getting irritated. I dragged my feet after him.

"Pick up your feet, Rabbit. You do not want to chase it away before we can dispatch it," he said sternly and I mocked him behind his back.

I did just as he said and stomped it to the floor; I didn't expect for the ground to creak underneath me. Slate spun around fast enough to see my *oh, sugarfoot* expression and my feet broke through the floor. I fought for a way to hold on. I didn't have to, though, because Slate had thrown his body across the floor and was pulling me back up from the hole in a blink.

I laughed nervously as I looked at the scrapes that had shredded the bottoms of my pants. I could see the blood start to well against the fabric. Slate looked daggers at me when he tossed his hair over his shoulder, but then his face contorted into anger as he covered me with his body, slamming my head against the wood planks of the floor.

I could hear the thunder of others' steps as I saw stars and tasted something metallic in my mouth. Then Slate was off me and I heard grunting and *felt* a fury of violent emotions. I wasn't ready for this.

"Time to scamper, Rabbit," Slate growled at me as he fended off three men simultaneously with his blades and *calling*.

My hesitation lasted for only an instant. Slate would sacrifice himself so I could run away. Not a chance, I wouldn't be able to live with myself. My mom and Sparrow had taught me that.

I dug deep and *called*. Wind buffeted the men away from Slate and he turned into a blur of movements, one with the shadows around him. I felt like a doofus standing there blowing air at our attackers. Three more men ascended from the stairs and one came right for me; his *calling* cut through my wind.

"Run, Rabbit!" Slate bellowed as the man knocked me off my feet.

He was bigger than me, but small compared to the other Tidings men I'd seen. It was a small gift, the only way I would stand a chance. I tried to remember my training and it was all starting to go out the window when his dark scruffy face hovered before mine, and I realized why I wasn't dead yet. The attacker pulled a knife and my focus was immediately drawn to it. It was what he'd planned.

A fist hit the side of my face like a truck, and I felt my whole body being knocked aside. Before I could get up, he threw himself on top of me. The thick fingers of the man held the knife to my throat as his other hand tugged on my pants. I had to pull it together. While he still was holding my face, I slid my seax from its sheath. I didn't give myself time to process what would happen if he caught me because I knew what would happen if I didn't try.

I once read that everyone was capable of murder. I didn't consider the thrust of my seax anything, but self-defense, but I'd taken a life. I wouldn't have delivered such a devastating aim if it weren't for the muscle memory from all of Slate's training.

The knife's edge stuck out from the back of the man's throat and his eyes rolled to mine with astonishment on his features. His blood pooled over me and I rolled him off me with air and pulled my knife from his throat. I got shakily to my feet and looked for Slate who was fighting two of the men, keeping them at bay while trying to back up to where I had been lying a moment ago.

Two more men had joined the three attacking Slate and were circling around him with one dead or dying on the floor.

I stumbled forward clumsily—I had to stop them. I couldn't let them hurt Slate. Other than a few cuts that left his shirt hanging open to reveal thin wounds underneath, Slate had stayed intact as he kept the other men away from me. But who knew how long that would last? I *called*. Slate thrust forward, driving his knife into one man's heart, and slit the throat of the other on the back slash when the attacker had thought he was vulnerable. Didn't he know that Slate was never vulnerable?

Two heads rolled from bodies that took a second to crumple at my feet and his head snapped up to where I stood. It was just a bit of air and it'd done so much damage.My legs trembled as I walked towards him. The closest I'd come to killing something that lived and breathed was when I got crazy with the fly swatter in the kitchen.

Slate was at my side in an instant. His eyes scanned the bodies and that of my lone assailant. He seemed unsatisfied, as if he wanted to kill them again. Slate had killed three times as many men as I had and he hadn't even blinked an eye. Was this the kind of life teenagers were used to here?

"Rabbit, you did not listen. Why did you stay?" Slate's voice shifted between irritation, frustration, and admiration as he led me down the stairs of the building.

My mind was in a tailspin. I'd *killed* people.

"I couldn't leave you," I rasped and Slate held me closer.

I could tell he wanted to carry me, but I was making a point of walking on my own two feet. That was how I wanted to walk away from it. On my own two feet. I had held my own, and I'd walked away.

Slate hurried me into one of the buildings we'd checked earlier. It had a mattress and a basin so we could clean off the blood and heal each other. Slate shredded some curtains and *called,* filling the basin with water. He dipped the curtains into it and started to dab at my face. It hurt to the touch.

I pushed his hand away and he growled at me. "I can do it," I said and he gave over.

I was trying to be pragmatic. I'd taken the lives of three men, but they had been attacking us. It was us or them. Still, they had all been someone's sons. I opened up my little box of emotions and shoved the deaths of the men deep down, hoping those feelings would never resurface, or maybe they could once I grew accustomed to my new life. I had killed someone. *Three* someones.

I gingerly wiped the blood off myself and peeled off my blood-soaked tank top, drained the basin full of red water and refilled it before dunking my tank top back in and scrubbing the blood away. Slate sat next to me on the bed doing the same until we could see all the cuts and bruises caused by our attack.

Slate wasn't half bad. Most of the blood on him was the men's, and other than my legs, which had been sliced from the wood shards, I was only bruised. Any other day I would have been modest about sitting in my underwear next to Slate on a bed, but not today. Today I was feeling very mortal and small, completely insignificant to the powers that be and my state of undress was inconsequential.

"Why do you think they attacked us?" I asked finally as I washed the blood off my legs.

"They wanted to capture us. For ransom, most likely. They came in force—they must have expected us. I will double check on who gave the tip about the bauk," Slate said in a tone that made me sorry for whoever the messenger was.

"So there might not even be a bauk," I murmured.

That was good. I couldn't do any more fighting. The dirty mattress I sat on was looking much too inviting.

"Rabbit."

Slate's tone made me stop drying my pants. Was he sad?

I turned to him and his lips quirked. "You have it in your hair. Here."

I put my fingers to my hair and there were dried clumps of what I hoped was only blood. He rinsed out the basin and refilled it, helping me hang my head over the side and rinse out the blood. His fingers deftly moved through my strands and ran across my scalp with ease.

"I hope I am not making a mess of this. I would not want to knot your hair."

I hummed an agreement and something inside me did a happy dance. So *not* used to washing women's hair. Good to know.

Slate wrung it out and started to dry it while my head was still upside down. I didn't argue for once. I didn't want to sit with damp clothes and wet hair. I closed my eyes and let him work focusing on breathing. When he stopped I could've fallen asleep on the spot.

"All done, Rabbit," he said in a low rumble.

I slowly brought my head back up and opened my eyes. It was going to be a terrible walk back to the palace. I looked back at the bed and hoped it looked less inviting.

Nope, even more so. I groaned.

"Do you know how to heal?" Slate asked and my dreamy eyes shifted to his.

I nodded, lifting my hand to his chest where his wavy hair spilled over his shoulder and *called*.

Watching the wounds seal themselves up was fascinating. His skin worked like a time-lapse video right in front of my face; it was nothing short of amazing. He pressed his hand to where I'd been socked and I felt the warmth flood through me as he cupped my face.

"Do not ever be brave for me again. I am not worth dying for," he said softly.

"I couldn't live with myself if you died fighting so I could run away," I scolded, knitting my brows thinking of how my mother and Sparrow bore their deep sorrow for decades.

"If you died today in that fight, I could not look our family in the face and tell them what happened. You are precious, Scarlett Tio."

It was a side of Slate I had never seen. Tender and soft. The pad of his thumb had slid over my lips.

I smiled ruefully. "If you died in the fight, I'd probably roam the desert forever and died anyway, so call it self-preservation," I chided.

The corners of his mouth lifted into a small smile. "You are tougher than that. You would find your way back," he said softly and his thumb pulled down my lower lip.

My breath hitched.

Heat blossomed in my stomach and our eyes searched one another's. That man intended to do a number of hideous acts to me I couldn't even fathom, and the only thing that I had thought besides *survive this* was...I wished I had made love to Slate.

Anticipation pumped blood hotly through my veins like liquid fire as I parted my lips for my tongue. Slate watched with rapt attention as I ran the tip along the pad of his thumb, his lips parting to inhale a sharp breath.

Who knew the body could contain so much heat?

He was waiting for me, I could see it in his eyes. What did he see in mine?

Realization struck me. I had frozen *him*. He was afraid to move or I might change my mind. I shifted on the bed, his hand falling from my face until I sat on my heels in front of him. I slid my hands along his bronze jaw, into his silken hair, my fingers running into his braids, and brought my lips close to his.

Slate loved Walt Whitman, so I whispered one of my own favorite poets, Robert Browning, knowing he'd understand.

"Out of your whole life give but a moment!
All of your life that has gone before,
All to come after it,—so you ignore
So you make perfect the present,—condense,
In a rapture of rage, for perfection's endowment,
Thought and feeling and soul and sense—
Merged in a moment which gives me at last

You around me for once, you beneath me, above me— Me—sure that
despite of time future, time past,—
This tick of our life-time's one moment you love me!
How long such suspension may linger? Ah, Sweet—
The moment eternal—just that and no more—
When ecstasy's utmost we clutch at the core
While cheeks burn, arms open, eyes shut and lips meet!"

Those big muscular arms wrapped around me so tight I couldn't breathe. When our lips met, heat burst through me in a way I hadn't known possible. I wanted to taste every inch of him. Our kisses were frenzied. The near-death experience was making me feel more alive than I had ever been, and I wanted to be alive with Slate. I wanted to devour him, to feel with my body in ways I never had before, for Slate to make me feel what I had in our brief interludes and then some.

His hand fisted in my hair as he pulled me into his lap, and kisses rained down my jaw and down my throat until I was nearly hanging off the bed with his mouth tasting and kissing over the swell of my breasts.

I moaned aloud, throaty and full of need. Need for Slate, need to be filled by him. He swung me back up and slanted his lips to mine as his hands cupped my breasts, kneading at my soft skin.

"Scarlett, I *need* you," he growled, low and slow so my toes curled.

My hands found his shoulders, hard and broad. I wanted to lick every bronze inch. I pulled his hair back to expose his throat, and he let me. It was such a vulnerable position that I found myself smiling against this skin as I ran my tongue along his collar, gently nipping with my teeth.

Suddenly, air punched through my body. Pain replaced fear as it exploded through my nerves stemming from my stomach. My wide eyes met his, full of alarm, as a warm wetness poured over my stomach and onto him. I had enough time to look down and see blood before I was ripped off Slate's lap and into the air. And then whatever it was had me in its mouth and was running.

Slate was chasing after me in his black boxer briefs and nothing else. Something had me so tight I couldn't move. I broke through wall after wall and I could hear its animal grunting as it fled Slate.

I looked down numbly and realized I was in shock. I could make out the tips of the jagged black claws that were hooked inside my stomach just below my ribcage. I'd barely felt them slide in. I looked up at Slate; he wasn't catching up, but he wasn't slowing down. The creature slowed every time it had to break through the walls, but it didn't want to lose its meal: me.

"Fucking faint already!" Slate bellowed at me.

Slate's skin looked dark, he seemed to be swelling as he ran. Did he have fangs?

Slate bellowed again, but this time it sounded more like a roar. I gave into the darkness.

I came to.

"Hold on, Scarlett. You are not allowed to die."

Slate's red-streaked face hovered into view. His brows turned down in concentration and an edge of something—panic. I reached up and *called*. He slapped my hand away, dark blood coating his arms to his elbows, and cursed me.

"Do not waste your strength healing me!" he growled, and I went back under.

Where was that mumbling coming from? I lay on the dirty mattress with Slate running his hand through my hair, sitting on the floor beside the bed.

"*Passing stranger! you do not know how longingly I look upon you,*

You must be he I was seeking, or she I was seeking, (it comes to me as of a dream,)
I have somewhere surely lived a life of joy with you,
All is recall'd as we flit by each other, fluid, affectionate, chaste, matured,
You grew up with me, were a boy with me or a girl with me,
I ate with you and slept with you, your body has become not yours only nor left my body mine
*   only,*
You give me the pleasure of your eyes, face, flesh, as we pass, you take of my beard, breast, hands, in return,
I am not to speak to you, I am to think of you when I sit alone or wake at night alone,
I am to wait, I do not doubt I am to meet you again,
I am to see to it that I do not lose you."

There he went quoting Walt Whitman again. My dark poet. What were those words?

My eyes felt soldered shut. I literally had to use my fingers to separate my eyelids to open my eyes. I mentally probed my body: aside from extreme exhaustion, I felt whole. My fingers did a physical inspection, I wiggled toes and felt for my stomach and chest, and last but not least I ran my fingers over my face. I let out the breath I'd been holding. I *was* whole.

My wandering fingers swept around me until I found a nest of matted hair: Slate. Only his head rested on the bed. Adrenaline pumped through me. I hopped off the bed and used air to pull Slate on the bed, he went on limply and I panicked. I delved into his body. He was fine, completely wiped out, but healthy. I let loose a choked sob and it tapered into a relieved, slightly hysterical, giggle. Ash had been the one to teach me how to delve among other things.

If this wasn't instant karma, I didn't know what was.

I looked around and prayed it was early in the evening. It was pitch black out, maybe ten or eleven I hoped. I chewed my lip and decided on what to do next. I wanted to curl up next to Slate and sleep, but I couldn't leave him covered in blood. If he slept through me washing him, we'd stay; if he woke, we'd go.

I was nearly naked anyway, so I showered myself creating my own hot water with my *calling* and briskly scrubbed myself down until the water ran clear right there beside the bed. Then I slowly and carefully washed Slate's body; he didn't even groan.

I unbraided his hair carefully, removing the silver Celtic beads and etched white fetishes, which I supposed were bones or ivory. Then, I washed his hair, running my fingers languorously through it and drying it once my water ran clear. I braided his hair with deft fingers and reattached his fetishes and beads.

I didn't know what made me do it. He had a single jade fetish that was carved into something canine with fangs barred the size of a copper Skoll mark, and I braided it into my hair at the left side of my head behind my ear so it was visible just above my shoulder.

I got to touch his unconscious body in ways I'd only dreamed of, making me feel like a total pervert. There wasn't a line I didn't cross, as I used *calling* to pull off, clean, then put back on his, *um*, underwear, then I found his pants, shirt, and weapons. I got his pants on and his shirt over his head—none of which would have been possible without *calling*.

I hunted for my own clothes, thankfully all dry and bloodless except for my underwear which I took off and washed in a hurry. A scuffle of noise made me stop drying and I pulled on my clothes at breakneck speed. If it was another beastie, it was going to feel a world of hurt when I found it.

I pulled Slate's belts of knives over my chest like he wore them and adjusted the belts the best I could so they wouldn't slide right off me, and buckled my seax to my thigh.

Tiptoeing, now scrubbed and fully dressed (if a bit rumpled and torn), I searched out the source of the sound.

"They should have been back by now. They said the man would be hard to take."

It was a gruff man's voice. I halted in my steps and tried not to hold my breath; they could only be referring to one person.

"We are not getting paid enough to be led to the slaughter. The girl is an unknown, but they said she was his weakness. Get the girl and he would follow. Simple," a second man said irritated.

"We should not have allowed Gator to go with. He likely tried to take the girl during the commotion against orders. Let us hope they are both too injured or wiped out from their healing. If they are not..." A third man's voice let the comment hang.

"We will bring back his carcass. They said alive, but there must be a price for the bodies and if he killed the others," the gruff voice of the first man ground out.

My mind was running away with me, I was imagining all types of frightening looking men, but they were probably regular old murderers, not wearing signs that said, *We kill people for money!* It didn't offer me any solace.

I peeked through the curtains. Six men stood in the moonlight. They hadn't even bothered hiding. If Slate had been awake, they'd all be dead by now.

Maybe that's what they were counting on, that he would have been so worn out after fighting that he'd be defenseless. Slate was helpless in the bed upstairs. I had one chance going for me against these men.

Surprise.

I silently thanked Ash for his lessons as I popped up from the window and threw both knives in succession and used *calling* so they'd find home in two men's throats.

I didn't think, I acted.

I kept moving, flinging blades of air slicing through the night to where the men had just been. From the sound of the high-pitched screeches, I figured I had taken someone down. I couldn't stop moving. I didn't know how to counter-cast and the world around me was exploding with fire and earth as they tried to get ahold of me.

There was this moment of clarity for me when the last two men decided they were going to kill me painfully and slowly, and they stopped aiming for the ground in front of me and started aiming for my middle. *Been there, done that.* I'd found out the hard way that water thrown at a ball of fire hurling towards you only makes boiling water hurling towards you.

I faltered as my skin bubbled with blisters, it had caught my left arm and my nerves screamed. It was worse than the impaling, I immediately decided.

Every breath the breeze shifted, every grain of sand was pure agony against the arm. I let loose a scream that would've made a banshee proud as I exploded the earth beneath their feet, shooting spears of sand through their bodies until none of them stood. I gagged at the gurgling noises their bodies made on the sand that soaked their black blood. I fell on my face, exhausted and retching bile.

Just breathe, now move your hands, I told myself.

What if whoever hired these men kept sending men all night? Their friends wouldn't try to capture us next time—they'd be out for blood. I held my left arm delicately. The searing pain never ceased, it only increased as I searched around the men I'd just murdered. They must have had a way they planned on getting us back.

Sure enough, they had metal cuffs attached to a makeshift stretcher.

I shambled back to the building Slate was in and nearly collapsed on the stairs. I lay there breathing until I gathered enough strength to get to Slate.

I was really worried. He was still out and hadn't so much as moved a finger. I *called* again and did something I'd never admit to in a million years. I tore what fabric I could find on other windows and fastened it around Slate's body and slowly guided Slate's limp body out the window with my feet braced against the wall, down two stories to the stretcher below. I knew I wouldn't be able to *call* him through the halls and down the stairs, but down the window with the help of fabric in lieu of ropes? Sure could.

I stumbled down the stairs afterwards, tossing the last of the fabric out the window. I wrapped the curtains around Slate's body, securing him to the stretcher as best I could and rifled through the men's packs and took whatever looked interesting, just in case. I rinsed the blood off my hands and stood with my back to the stretcher. I knelt down and picked up the handles and with great effort, started forward and prayed a strong wind would cover the trailing marks from the back of the stretcher.

We *were* lucky.

I had no idea where I was going, especially in the dark. To say I was navigationally challenged would be like saying that Ray Charles was visually challenged...or maybe that *would* be accurate. In any case, I finally hit the hard-packed sand signifying what would be one step closer to the city.

Then I saw the low lights of Thrimilci's town heart. I wasn't completely off, but I did have to sharply change the angle I had been coming in at.

If those men found us on the road, they'd kill us. I couldn't let that happen while I had an ounce of strength left. As it was, by the time we reached the first houses I was bawling with frustration. I wished I was stronger; if I'd been Slate instead of myself, I wouldn't have been on my knees on the road sobbing uncontrollably, but I was.

I couldn't *call* even a drop of water; my last feat of strength was used to push the stretcher against the side of a house deep in the shadows, and make a place for us to rest overnight. I hoped the owners of the house wouldn't freak out in the morning. Hopefully, they *would* call the Guardians.

I was afraid of what might happen if the people who lived there took advantage of an unconscious man and a girl in over her head. The chances were slim, but stranger things had been happening.

I pulled myself on top Slate's sleeping form, cradling my searing arm and burrowed against his chest after I pulled two more knives out of Slate's belt and grasped them in my hands. I'd probably end up stabbing myself in my sleep before anyone else, but I wouldn't go down without a fight. I rested my head under Slate's chin and let myself be carried away by the sound of his breathing.

CHAPTER 12

JETT

Slate and Scarlett had gone out on a routine mission. Slate would let Scarlett hang back as he showed her how to fight one of the rare creatures that found its way out of the wild and into civilization.

It was a little strange that they'd gone alone. Slate should have had Shadow Breakers trailing them in case they got into trouble, but when he'd asked the Regn, they said he'd dismissed them. Jett wanted to strangle Slate. He would as soon as he found them. Slate had just wanted Scarlett alone. Plain and simple.

Jett and Gypsum had paired off to search the roads while Steel and Hawk went straight to the building ruins where the baulk had been reported. Slate and Scarlett should have been back hours ago.

Jett looked over at his grim-faced cousin. The kid was proving a quick study. He would do well using the long seax; the handle of the black blade handed down from their grandfather peeked out from over his shoulder as he walked. He was already starting to adopt the deadly grace the men from Tidings developed from their hours of relentless training.

They'd been up and down all the roads that led from this side of the desert to the buildings. If they didn't find them in the city, they'd have to start to search the desert; that didn't bode well for their survival.

Gypsum stopped and squinted at the side of one of the outlying houses. Jett broke into a trot and then a full run as he saw his sister's caramel hair fanned over the side of a stretcher.

"By the Mother! Scarlett?" Jett shouted as he grew closer.

She popped up wildly and threw a knife she'd had fisted in her hand right for Jett's chest.

"Duck!" Gypsum shouted and Jett pulled his long seax in a blink, deflecting the blade with a spark.

Scarlett blinked groggily at them, seeming to recognize their voices, but she looked dead on her feet. Jett didn't even know how she'd managed to throw so well having just woken.

"Scarlett, what on earth happened?"

Jett walked into the moonlight aside the house and she made this nervous laughing, crying noise. She curled back against Slate's chest clutching over him protectively—and fell asleep in an instant.

Gypsum gaped at the pair on the stretcher. Slate looked well enough if unconscious, but whole. Jett put his hand to his sister and winced. The arm she'd wrapped around Slate was badly burned, and blisters covered it wrist to shoulder. He healed her immediately so it wouldn't scar.

"What happened?" Gypsum said numbly as he looked over the cousin he knew and the trainer he revered.

Scarlett was wearing Slate's knives across her torso, and several were missing. She was covered in sand and her pant legs were torn to shreds. It was obvious that Scarlett had fought and carried Slate's body from somewhere. There was no way Slate would have lain down and gone to sleep letting Scarlett fight for him. All signs were pointing to something very bad.

Had Scarlett carried Slate all the way out of the desert? If she could have *called*, she would have instead of throwing the knife. That meant she had pulled Slate's lifeless form for hours.

It boggled Jett's mind.

"I don't know. Get the other end, Chief. We can guide it as we go and take turns *calling* it back to the palace," Jett said, stroking his sister's hair away from her face. Her fingers were clawed around Slate's shirt as if she was still trying to protect him even in her defenseless state.

Gypsum took a deep breath and took the other end and Jett *called* the stretcher into the air so Gypsum could focus on steering it. Jett noted that Scarlett had tied Slate to the stretcher confirming that she had not only pulled him this far, but had gotten his body onto it. Jett shook his head. Scarlett was unbelievably powerful at *calling*; it rivaled even his own and he was one of the most powerful tyros ever.

Jett put his hand behind Scarlett's back as he *called* to make sure she didn't fall off. They were only an hour away from the palace, but they'd want to put Wren's mind at ease as soon as possible. She had been wringing her hands with worry until the men had decided they'd waited long enough. Wren had hugged Jett so fiercely then it'd almost brought tears to his eyes. While he was the affectionate type, he wasn't the crying kind, but his mother's arms around him with worry before he went to go save his sister had nearly done him in.

"Scarlett?" Slate's voice sounded hoarse and panicked.

"You're safe. We're taking you back to the palace," Gypsum said reassuringly from behind Jett.

Jett turned to Slate and saw his eyes flash silver. He immediately stopped *calling* and Gypsum took a step back. Slate popped up, tearing the fabric that held him like spider's web, with Scarlett limp in his arms.

"She's fine. Put her back down, we've got to get you both back to the palace," Jett said, watching Slate carefully.

Lately, Jett had noticed Slate's temper flaring like it used to when he hit puberty. Not only that, but every time Jett saw Slate and Scarlett in the same room, there was something going on there. The day they'd played volleyball with Ash, Slate was jealous. Scarlett looked at Ash like he had hopped out of a magazine and swept her off her feet. Jett had let it go; he didn't like Ash, but things weren't serious and it kept Scarlett away from Slate.

She deserved better. She deserved more. Knowing when to walk away from a woman who would expect more from him was Slate's most redeeming quality. He slept around, sure, but he kept it to older women who wanted to use him as much as he wanted to use them. No one who wanted a future. There was that little strawberry blonde, but he knew why Slate had picked her up. That, if anything, had let Jett know Slate was playing a dangerous game with Scarlett.

Slate jumped off the stretcher with a feral look in his glinting eyes. "We have to get there now!" he roared, his voice booming in the empty street.

"Put her down!" yelled Jett. "What the fuck happened? She dragged your ass while you took a Gods-be-damned nap. You're supposed to be protecting her! Why weren't Brass and Quick guarding your back? You selfish bastard!"

Slate would die for Scarlett. He'd die for any of his adopted family members, but Jett was pissed.

Slate growled deep in his throat as he cradled Scarlett close to his body possessively and Jett narrowed his eyes at him. "I am taking her. I can run faster than you can carry her," Slate ground out.

"If she wakes up while you're running? Then what?" Jett said lifting his chin at Slate.

"She will be more comfortable if she gets to lie down. If you run with her, she'll be jostled around. It makes more sense to keep her on the stretcher. She's healed, now she needs rest. Let her rest," Gypsum said boldly, stepping between the two men that towered over him.

Gypsum wasn't short, Jett and Slate were just very tall, powerfully built men. The fights they'd had growing up had been brutal and always ended in blood, but that hadn't happened in many years. If they got into a fight now, it would last until one of them were unconscious.

Slate let out a shuddering breath and turned around. He unbuckled the knife belts from Scarlett and laid her back down, then smoothed her hair over her head. Jett nearly tackled Slate when he leaned over her and planted a kiss on her lips.

Gypsum turned around to look right at Jett and gave one shake of his head.

Not the right time. Slate turned around, getting to his feet, strapped on his belts over his torn shirt, and dared Jett to say something. Jett's strong jaw flexed as he narrowed his eyes.

"We can *call,* but I want to guide it myself and I am going to run. Try to keep up," Slate said stiffly as he took up Gypsum's previous position.

Gypsum moved to one side, and Jett to the side as the three men started running with Scarlett's unconscious body. Jett bit his tongue to keep from asking questions while they ran. Slate was a man on a mission and would have ignored him, further enraging Jett.

It was time Jett was honest with himself.

Slate cared about Scarlett and it was a fool's errand. Nothing good would come from it. In fact, Jett was positive it would only end in heart-break. He didn't want Scarlett getting hurt, but Slate getting emotionally involved with Scarlett would be catastrophic. How do you tell someone the first time they care about someone that it will only break their heart? Why couldn't Slate like that young woman or his usual khoraz? Not Scarlett, she would fight Slate every step because of her own fear of the unknown.

Jett sighed and resigned himself to taking it easier on Slate. Scarlett wasn't the girl for him, and Slate was going to need his brothers soon. It was obvious now that Scarlett was more than capable of taking care of herself.

CHAPTER 13

"She is still sleeping, darling. Why not go get yourself ready for tonight, hmm?" Pearl said soothingly.

"I am not leaving." That stubborn growl was definitely Slate.

"You should get some sleep, son. After what Steel and I found at the ruins, you are both lucky to be alive. You need time to rest as well."

Hawk was trying to gain control of the ever-persistent Slate. Fat chance of that.

"Fine." He stormed off.

Hawk let out a breath. "Any idea why he is so protective of our Scarlett all of a sudden?"

Sparrow snorted. "I remember a time when you would have brought the world down about its ears for me. The boy's dealing with emotions he did not expect to have."

"Someone bring me a cot!" Slate bellowed from the hall.

Pearl sighed. "I try, but try as I might, these boys have minds of their own."

Hawk chuckled. "They are three strong, sure men. You did a wonderful job."

"Does she look pale? Maybe I should delve again?" My mother. She sounded beside herself.

"Wren, our Scarlett may look like a delicate flower, but she fought nine men on her own, and dragged Slate's body for hours in the dark and then had the sense to hide themselves until Jett and Gypsum found them. Really, give the girl some credit. I shouldn't even say 'girl.' She's a woman, Wren," Sparrow admonished and my mother sighed.

"I've sheltered her, haven't I? She's so different from the other girls her age, and so is Tawny." My mother sounded sad, like she'd failed me.

There was a grunt and some shuffling and I felt a *whoosh* of air. "There," Slate said, and in my semi-conscious mind I smiled.

"Stoic, this isn't really appropriate," my mother told him gently and I had to agree.

If Ash came to check on me and found him in my on my sheets, death bed or not, he'd pitch a fit.

Slate hesitated. "I mean no disrespect. Your daughter...she saved my life. I cannot..."

Slate at a loss, now there was something. No response from my mom only meant that Slate calling her mother had turned her into one of his doe-eyed admirers and was putty in his hands. She had a serious blind spot when it came to Slate.

"We can understand that," Pearl said with a hint of amusement in her tone.

"What time is it?" my mother asked, jerking herself out of her adoration for her adopted son.

"It's only seven. They have plenty of time to sleep. We can come back later and bring lunch; there will still be plenty of time for dress shopping if Scarlett is up for it. Tawny is throwing a fit in her room because we won't let her in until she wakes up. Steel is trying to calm her, but Gypsum is nearly as bad just in the hall," Sparrow said ruefully, but I detected a hint of pride.

They were their mother's children.

"They can't understand why Slate is allowed in, but they aren't. I tried to tell them we didn't say Slate *could* be in here," Hawk said, and I was sure Slate just loved them talking about him like he wasn't there.

"Please take off your blades and boots," Pearl said and I heard Slate grunt in assent.

With another rustle of clothing and the mingling of the scents of what I recognized as my family, they left my bedroom and I heard the door click. More rustling and the bed bowed beside me as I felt arms circle around my body and Slate curled around me murmuring unintelligible words.

"Did anyone see you?" rumbled Slate's deep voice.

"No, Brass let me know the nature of what you needed," replied a breathy gruff voice I didn't recognize.

"Slate, you poor bastard," said an amused seductive whisper of a man's deep voice.

"I know what this looks like, but it is for her own good."

Why did Slate sound so nervous and defensive? A familiar hand brushed the hair at my head and I fell into a deep sleep.

When I finally woke up, I was alone and starved. First things first: a long hot shower. After a quick check of every inch of my body, making sure everything was in place, I hit the energy plate and took a luxuriously long shower.

I quickly dried my hair and fingered the jade fetish on the counter before braiding it back into my hair. I slipped into a sunny yellow chiffon dress with flowing fabrics and sleeves that fell off my shoulders from the sweetheart neckline. I even put on a little makeup. I looked like sunshine personified even though I felt like mud. Cruddy mud.

I checked the clock before I went to lunch, I'd only be a few minutes late. I hurried down the halls forcing a smile as I went. It was the fake it 'til you make it philosophy. I didn't feel happy, but I would eventually.

SCARLET SORROW

"Good afternoon," I said as I breezed into the dining room.

Everyone was gathered around the table already eating, the smell of roasted chicken mingled with the blooming morning glories and sunshine filled the room. The gold trim of the rafters that lined the dome ceiling glinted in the lantern light.

I started to come around the table to give my usual round of cheek kisses when Slate sprang from his feet so fast his heavy carved chair clattered against the far wall.

He rounded the table towards me.

"Slate?" Pearl asked, and she got to her feet as well.

The rest of us were frozen in place, and everything seemed to go into slow motion. I saw every muscle in his body flex as he managed to be in front of me in a heartbeat without running or jumping over the table. I watched as his arms wrapped around me and crush me to his body. My feet dangled as he didn't say a word, but closed his eyes so his thick long lashes fanned across his bronze cheeks and his full lips met mine. My head swam.

Was I still asleep?

Nope, that was definitely my mother's gasp. Slate was breathing me in, trying to meld our bodies together. I pushed gently at his shoulders. I had to fix this.

My toes hit something solid and I was back on my feet. I laughed nervously as I blushed and licked my lips self-consciously.

"Good to see you survived," I joked and thanked the Gods for Jett and Gypsum who started laughing.

I broke Slate's intense grey gaze as I took him by the elbow and gave my round of cheek kisses to everyone, and led Slate to his seat before sitting next to Tawny across from Jett who had his eyebrows raised expectantly. It was a testament to how off-kilter Slate was that I had led him without objection back to his seat.

"I take it everyone has been filled in on what happened?"

I started to pick through the food on the table. I lifted my gaze and smiled a big fake phony baloney smile at my confused family.

Tawny sat next to me and stared openly like she'd never met me before. I shot her a look that said, *please help me.* That shook her out of it.

257

"Yeah, what happened? Slate said he was passed out for whatever happened after he killed the bauk."

"Actually, I have no idea what happened during the bauk attack. So maybe someone could clue me in as well," I said.

Slate's eyes bore into me and he set his jaw. "I killed it after it impaled you, but not before it shredded your midsection. I was elbow deep in your insides before I could heal you."

My single bite of chicken caught in my throat and I sipped my goblet of water to wash it down.

"You don't say," I said nonchalantly. "I vaguely recall healing you while you were covered in blood. My blood, as it would turn out. Thanks."

"*Thanks*," Slate repeated in a low dangerous tone.

I ignored him and turned to face the long end of the intricately carved table where they were all watching me; clearly they thought I'd lost my mind. I smiled my insane smile again and began to tell them the story. Their faces morphed from concern, to denial, to outrage—it would've been funny, except it was all true and I wasn't sure I was okay, in truth.

Gypsum thought it was the coolest thing ever. To him, I was pretty much a superhero. Jett and Steel looked at me in disbelief, while my mom, Sparrow, and Hawk looked stuck somewhere between relief and rage. Pearl was looking at Slate, and Tawny must have thought I'd been replaced by a body snatching alien. I ate merrily after my story was told though, enjoying those intestines Slate had put together so nicely for me after the bauk gutted me.

"Your family did not know what happened to the men outside the buildings. I did not think you could do it on your own after so much healing. Then you managed to get me onto a stretcher and carried me for what must have been three hours?" Slate's tone was still low and dangerous.

Did he think I was lying?

"It was either that or die. I thought testing myself to my limit was preferable to dying. I have a lot of life to live yet," I chirped without looking up. "I told you I wouldn't leave without you." I was acutely aware of everyone's eyes on us.

I looked up to Slate; I'd been ignoring his gaze.

I sucked in a lungful of air. I was prepared for a lot of emotions, anger being the most obvious, but not disenchantment. I could deal with one of his rages, but not the disappointment in those cool grey eyes.

I cleared my throat and forced out the words that would drive that wedge permanently between us. "Did Ash send a messenger for me?"

It was the last nail in my coffin. Slate had to know we couldn't continue what started in that abandoned bedroom *here*. That was a one-time only offer and karma made her presence known. We shouldn't have done it; it couldn't happen again.

Slate got to his feet and an array of emotions passed over his hard face as his chest heaved.

"Scamper away, Rabbit," he growled before he left the room.

I let out a breath. It was done. Hard part over. I wouldn't be his all-too-convenient bed buddy at his home.

"Slate?" my mom called.

Jett shot me a look and I shrugged as he balled up his napkin. "May I be excused?"

Pearl gave him a nod and Jett followed after Slate. Slate might have a whole troop after him soon from the way Hawk and Steel were looking at Jett's back.

"Care to explain what just happened, young lady?" My mom was using her no-nonsense tone and I felt like ducking my head.

I shook my head. "I don't really know. He doesn't like Ash for some reason."

Hawk leveled his dark eyes at me above his narrow nose.

I made out with Slate and I was impaled and I think he wants to sleep with me, didn't fit into pleasant lunch conversation. I sighed.

"I don't think he wanted me risking myself to save him..." I swallowed knowing that wouldn't satisfy them. "There was a moment that things were confusing between us," I spat out under my breath.

"We're going to look into who gave the tip about the bauk and see if anything suspicious comes up. It will be difficult because it's possible that whoever hired those men only heard that Slate and you were going to be there and sent them after the fact," Hawk said, changing the subject.

"Why would anyone want to kidnap Slate or me? He thought maybe they would ransom us," I added thoughtfully. It wasn't adding up.

"Who knows why criminals do what they do, darling? We are glad you and Slate are back in one piece. You did a truly miraculous thing. I could not say I would have been able to save Slate as well as myself if I had been in your position. It takes a great deal of love to find more strength beyond yourself," Pearl said with a warm smile.

"Of course I love Slate. He's family. I could have done it for any of you." Too much, sounding defensive now.

My mom's brows quirked and I had to untangle this mess in a hurry.

"Is there still time to shop for dresses?"

It was a sneaky trick, but I had to get them off my trail. Tawny picked up what I was putting down and she clapped her hands accordingly. Gods, I loved that girl.

My mom had changed since arriving to Thrimilci; she was happier, but more secretive. My mom had asked me half a hundred times if I was okay. She wasn't entirely convinced, but she let it go. I knew I'd gotten off way too easily and they had something up their sleeves. I would have to wait to find out what it was. I had almost died and they were okay with it? Fat chance. I expected it.

We didn't go to House of Gres, the shop we'd gone to our first time in town.

They took us to a shop called Myriads of Murad; Tawny was shaking with excitement the whole way there. After we each decided on a dress, we went to the cafe Jett had taken me. The Tea-rrfic Cafe, a name so bad it was good.

"We'll find you a suitor, Tawny. The the university is a great place for that. Wren met Alder there," Sparrow said nodding with her teacup.

We'd heard how Hawk fell in love with Sparrow at first sight a million times at the at the age of like five. I didn't know how it had happened with my dad.

"What happened when you first met my dad?"

I expected her to dismiss my question as usual. It had always been too hard for her to speak about him even when she tried, but she actually answered this time.

She sighed. "It wasn't actually *at* the university. He is two years older than me so he was already tried and true. We met *again* at the masquerade, but I'd met him in Ostara at Beltane years before."

It certainly explained why she loved spring and why she'd cultivated the most envious garden in a ten-mile radius at our old house. She'd planted huge obnoxious trees our neighbors hated that had grown at a suspicious rate. She never raked the leaves though. Some of my best memories growing up were piling those leaves up with Gypsum and Tawny and their parents then rolling around in them after a game of tag.

We gossiped all the way back to the palace, and I was feeling much better—not great, but good. Pearl had arranged for our three favorite hairdressers to come back and fix us up, so I was looking forward to their skills.

Steel was in Tawny's room when we got back; luckily our moms weren't still with us. Although it was hilarious to watch him crawl out from under the massive canopy bed when he saw it was just us.

"Getting sloppy," I teased.

He gave me his lopsided, playful smile. He scooped Tawny up and spun her in a circle, begging her to show him her dress.

"No way, it's a surprise."

"You'll be surprised when I tear it off with my teeth." He pretended to bite her neck as she giggled.

These two.

Steel turned to me, and his green eyes gaze turned serious. "I don't know what happened with you and Slate, that's your business, but I've never seen him like this. Not in years, so out of control. Well, he lost it. Your brother and Slate are two hotheads."

I gulped and looked at Tawny. Tawny gave me a sympathetic look. "Slate's just...he only wants me because I say no," I said.

Steel's lean muscled body strode over to me and slung an arm over my shoulder. "No judgement. You're very naive. I don't mean it as an insult, it's a fact. You don't know what you could have with someone unless you try." Of course *he'd* say that. "I only thought I'd bring it up so maybe you'd cut him some slack if you were feeling generous. You'd be doing me a favor, I hate having to play mediator between those two if they get into it. At least now I have Gyps on my side to help."

My chest rose and fell with a big sigh. "I'm with Ash. Slate will forget me in no time. I'm sure he already has."

Steel kissed my forehead in a very fatherly way and he gave me a big brother smile. "Actions speak louder than words. What do you think his actions tell you?"

"That he's a little psycho," I joked, and Tawny laughed until Steel shot her a look. "Things have gotten blurry. I need clear lines."

Steel left before Cricket, Katydid, and Bronze came in. I was thinking about where else I could sleep tonight instead of next door to the love-birds when they started knocking. The frosty blonde Cricket came in with her head full of perfectly quaffed blonde curls, her twin sister Katydid on her heels, her straight blonde hair falling to her waist, her eyes soft under her blunt-cut bangs. Then came busty Bronze, directing their floating arsenal of beauty products. Bronze grinned with her classic sassiness.

Cricket wanted to see our dresses to best achieve a desired look. Bronze and Katydid gushed over them, making me proud of our choices.

"I am thinking, old Hollywood—Veronica Lake?" Bronze told me.

I was thrilled. "You know old Hollywood?"

She gave me a *Girl, please* look as she shot out a hip and put a fist on it. "You have got to know the classics, no matter what the culture." She smiled.

She was much more friendly and at ease this time.

Cricket nodded at her assessment and it was go time. We were cleansed, extracted, trimmed, painted, sprayed, teased, and curled. I admired their stamina.

Bronze's favorite part was the reveal. Once she started our makeup we weren't allowed to look into the mirror. She pointed our chairs away and set to work. They helped us into our dresses and shoes and bid us *adieu*. Bronze and Katydid must have thought they did a good job because they snuck a high-five behind Cricket's back. That sure bolstered a girl's confidence, a much-needed boost after the afternoon.

Tawny and I gave each other big cheesy grins and ran, inelegantly, to the mirror. Tawny's hair was in a bouffant bun, a delicate black jeweled chain dangled across her forehead and disappearing into her hair. Those women were really good at their job. I needed a red carpet to sashay across. My lips were stained red and I had cat-eye makeup. I looked *good*.

The portal room at Valla University was brimming with people.

Entire families mingled around the room, and the party spilled into the surrounding rooms as well. There were a few thousand people at the university, and they were everywhere I looked. People touring wandered through the halls in groups. They stood in the dining hall—the water pipe room from the masquerade was still there, but was now packed with toddler toting families as opposed to young adults puffing away. The pillow-filled room was a big hit with the little ones.

The actual ceremony and feast were held outdoors in huge tents. I didn't feel much like pushing past people to tour the university since in another day we would be living there for the next two years. Instead, we went out into the tents; they were all but empty. There wasn't much of a seating chart, but tables were assigned by family. Since we were a "greater" family, we were in the front.

When we found our seats, I couldn't help but think about the massacre. I saw how easily it would be for someone to attack from behind the stage and how deadly it would've been for people sitting in front. We had two tables next to the stage. Pearl, Wren, Hawk, and Sparrow sat at a table for eight. Gypsum, Jett, Steel, Tawny, Slate, and I sat at the other.

The tents were decorated with garlands of branches with tiny lights twinkling within. They reminded me of Christmas. Shimmering silver covers over the tables matched the chairs, and tree branches with strings of crystals that caught the light sat in the middle of the silver tables.

I wanted to sit next to Slate; I needed to be close to him. Something that needed closure had welled up inside of me. I needed to explain, or at least talk about it, but Tawny caught my eye and gestured to Gypsum. I sat between Tawny and Gypsum so she could sit next to Steel. Slate sat alongside Gyps.

I may have been a sugarfoot adopted sister, but I was the ultimate wing woman.

People slowly began to file into the tents. The ceremony was set to start soon, and I recognized some of the faces. The Straumrs were directly in front, the Tios, my uncle and his family, in the next place of honor. Amethyst waved when she walked in. The Sumar tables were next to the Tios, while the Vetrs and Vars were next to the Straumrs. I recognized the massive blond man at the Var table; it was my father.

Several tables were between us, but there weren't many tall blond men whose shoulders were as broad as a house. He was with a stunning blonde woman, statuesque in a form-fitting stark white shimmering dress. He pulled her chair out for her as she glided into it elegantly. I knew it was his wife. When her back was turned, he scanned the tables rapidly, and they came to rest at the table next to ours, on my mother's back. His eyes met mine for the briefest moment before he took his own seat.

I felt woozy.

"Scar, you cool? You look like you're going to barf," Gypsum said, leaning away from me the little punk.

"I need some air," I squeaked out.

"The ceremony is going to start soon," Tawny said, as a woman I recognized as Dahlia Natt started moving around the podium.

I shot her my best death stare. *Want me to barf here?*

To Slate's credit, he started to scoot his chair out.

"Come with me," said the familiar voice.

If I'd been deaf I would've known it was Ash by the look on Slate's chiseled face.

He took my hand and helped me out of through the nearest tent flap. I gulped air.

He smirked. "You look stunning, even with your pallor."

It was sweet, sort of. I smiled anyway. My dress was a long-sleeved fitted number with golden sequins that tapered away at my knees and gave the illusion of nudity.

"You're just being nice."

"Nervous about crossing the stage?" Ash asked.

Fiddlesticks! I hadn't even thought of that. Another wave of wooziness splashed over me. He rubbed my back through the keyhole cutout at my shoulder blades, slow and tender. My nausea was gone; I knew he'd taken my nausea away. Even my anxiety had lifted some.

"How'd you do that?"

He smirked again, eyes twinkling, "Sometimes it is mental. I am an accomplished mental healer. I soothed your stomach as well."

"Thanks." I smiled.

I used a quick blast a cool air from my hand to dry the drops of perspiration that had sprouted on my face. I was getting *pretty* good at this whole magic thing.

He really enjoyed my use of *calling*. He pulled me to him and kissed me, not his usual soft kisses. It was demanding; he pulled my hair at the nape of my neck sliding his fingers through and nuzzled into my neck. As always, he tasted like peaches.

"We had better get back in." He clasped my hand and smoothed his face.

He could've been walking down the runway at fashion week when we entered. The tables had filled quickly, and heads turned as he led me back to my table. He was walking tall, his broad chest out like a king's. People were staring at me; I was terribly self-conscious. He slowed at my table and pulled out my chair. The entire tent of people faced our way, thousands of eyes looking at us.

He tucked a single finger under my chin, lifting my mouth to his full smiling lips, and gave me a deep kiss. He flashed the crowd his very best smile. Someone whistled. I sat down very carefully, my skin burning up. For a moment, I felt Slate's eyes on me. I leaned forward to see him past Gypsum, but he was already looking away.

"That was a nice *show*," Jett said coolly.

I wanted to throw a shoe at him. It wasn't inappropriate, it was just *showy*. But truthfully, I didn't love it either. I felt like he'd claimed me. Everyone now knew I was his when he was only supposed to be a suitor. Didn't girls have multiple suitors?

Why hadn't this fiddlesticking show started yet?

"Men in Tidings are very possessive," I muttered.

"Yes, we are," Slate said to no one in particular, but his voice did surprising things to me.

Moon, Dahlia, Reed, and his wife Fern sat onstage with the provosts.

Moon stood, his posture that of one used to commanding. His ebony skin and dusting of grey hair matched his dark sleeveless robe with silver and gold thick trim. The crowd quieted.

"Welcome back to Valla, Guardians!"

His deep voice projected to the farthest reaches of the tent. People cheered.

"For those who do not know me, I am Moon Straumr, Prime of the Guardians and Overseer of Valla. Tonight is the third anniversary of the reopening of Valla University for Guardian Mastery. I would like to take this opportunity to have a moment of silence for the ones lost those many years ago."

You could hear a pin drop. It had affected every single person in the room. Even if someone was lucky enough not to have a loved one who'd died in the massacre, the university that trained their Guardians had been closed for sixteen years. I wondered what happened to all the people who were of age during that time. I had seen Steel with his torque bracelets, one gold, one steel, and the necklace. Everyone I'd met over the age of twenty-two wore them, with the exception of my mother which I'd gleaned meant they'd passed the two tribulations at the university and had become tried and true Guardians.

Moon Straumr continued, "During this time of gathering, I would remind you to stay strong. We are aware of the shortage due to the closing. The provosts are expediting the tests as fast as possible for those of you who are eligible. Soon all will be as it should."

"He 's referring to the ambassador shortages, and how bad the tribal relations are getting" Jett informed me just loud enough so Gyps and Tawny heard, too.

I wondered if my mom was already eligible and if the expedited testing was harder without having been taught by the provosts. When I met the provosts at my uncle's, I realized they were mostly on the younger side. Only a few seemed to have been provosts *before* the massacre, like Dahlia.

"I would now introduce this year's inductees to Valla University for Guardian Mastery, and the future of Tidings!" The people cheered again.

"Please come onstage when you hear your name."

There were dozens of students in our year. Reed was standing next to Moon, handing each person a leather-bound folder and Fern was beside him with a pedestal next to her.

"Tawny Dagr."

She nervously stood. She was still holding Steel's hand that they were hiding a second before under the table. She dropped it like it was on fire and headed onstage. Gypsum had a strange look on his face. I hoped he didn't read too much into it.

"Cerise Kaldr."

Cherry trotted across the stage and blew a couple kisses to Amethyst and Jett. When she sat back down, it was next to a man with long greying hair and a close-cut beard. He looked like a hard man.

"Jonquil Kaldr."

Jonquil crossed the stage and sat at Cherry's table. I didn't know they were related.

"Sterling Haust."

Diamond's betrothed. He was good-looking, with big, bright, violet eyes and brown hair. He was athletically built and moved agilely. He sat back down at the table next to us. Haust was a greater family, as in Lark Haust. Gypsum stirred beside me.

"They're our class schedules," Tawny said happily as she set the folder down.

She began looking at the necklace Fern had clasped around her neck. It was a silver tree pendant. I'd seen other people wearing the same necklace before.

"Yggdrasil, the tree of life. It is the sigil of Valla University," Steel told her.

There were less students than in my senior class of high school, but it still took an eternity because some of the students had to walk from farther back in the tent. My anxiety built when they got to the S's.

"Jett Sumar."

Jett strutted to the stage, wearing his big smug smile, chin high. I watched my father for any change in his expression as Jett crossed the stage. It wasn't easy to see from far away, but I thought he smiled. Not a polite smile, but a proud one. I wished I was closer so I could put my empath powers to work.

"Slate Sumar."

He stood fluidly. It was one of the few times I could openly stare at him.

"Ash Straumr."

He sauntered across the stage, his tall muscular frame confident. My hot quarterback. A few people yelled as he crossed the stage and got his leather folder. He knew how to please the crowd, smiling with every ounce of charm his hard body possessed.

Then it was my turn. "Scarlett Tio."

I couldn't hear anything besides the blood rushing in my ears. I crossed the stage, its bright lights reflecting off my gold sequins. I reached Reed and he handed me my leather folder and shook my hand with the other.

"You look beautiful," he said as he handed me my folder, a smile playing on his mustached lips.

Moon turned to me and said, "Find strength in your weaknesses. Have the courage to be brave. While victorious, keep your humility and always strive for balance." He shook my hand.

I searched the crowd so I could wave at my mom. As Fern clasped my necklace, my eyes met Slate's, and I could see his eyes were filled with yearning.

I mentally staggered. Then remembered to smile and wave, not at anyone in particular, *just do it*. I sat back down at the table and Tawny opened her hand to see my leather folder with the class schedule, she had everyone's open in front of her.

I had the same schedule as Tawny, thankfully. Jett and Slate had the same schedule too, the exact opposite of ours. Tawny and I had American History every first day and I wondered if we could get out of it and take another battle class instead. Battle was the only class we all had together because there were three provosts; enough to accommodate the entire year.

I leaned forward to steal a look at Slate, and once again, his face was smooth. Maybe I'd imagined his look when I was onstage; after all, the lights had been in my eyes.

"Indigo Var."

The girl from the party stood from my father's table and headed towards the stage. Indigo was my adopted sister. I was so glad I liked her. I did feel oddly jealous as she came back down and my father kissed the top of her head. That should've been my head too.

"Sage Var."

My half-brother looked familiar, but I couldn't place him. He resembled his mother. He was fair-skinned with blonde hair and round blue eyes, his face somewhat soft for a man.

"Thank you everyone for coming. Let the merriment begin!" Moon said with his hands thrown wide, but his eyes weren't in it.

He struck me as a very sad person.

Plates of food were brought out and the crowd dug in. Tyros chattered excitedly, parents congratulated their children, younger siblings ran about, squealing. I'd never been to a wedding, but I imagined that if I had a ridiculously large family that this would be what the reception would look like. The emotions I was picking up on were all *so* happy— along with a little bit of lust, but no one was judging.

Past the Haust's table were the Enox. Cherry's dad had his cool green eyes on Jett. I checked to see if Jett had noticed him yet, and he had. Jett was trying to eat and would glance up on occasion to find Viper's eyes burning a hole straight through him. Jett's jaw was clenching. I made a face at him that said, *Yikes. That guy has issues.* His smile in response was not his usual smug one.

The one thing that wasn't different in Tidings from home was the food, except the fact that they didn't serve anything fried. They served grilled Cornish chicken with mashed potatoes and carrots, for dessert we had our choice between red velvet cake or angel food cake, each with a side of vanilla ice cream.

While we ate, a team of people magically removed the stage, *calling* to dismantle it into neat piles and as a group, float it away. They replaced it with a dance floor and brought in a band that set up between huge ice sculptures that looked like angels, but later found out that they were Valkyries. I recognized about half the instruments in the band setting up, while bars popped up along the dance floor serving wassail —no soda pop there.

The plates were cleared and people started mingling again. Slate was gone the instant the plates were up, it was like watching him transform as his body went from rigid to lax and loose as he prowled from the table. No good could come from a walk like that.

Ash took away from the table shortly after dinner to introduce me to more people. He introduced me as his *companion*; he was taking his suitor gig seriously.

The most interesting person I met that night was a tall, thin, fair-skinned man who had been sitting with my father. His name was Jackal Var, my father's brother.

"Your lady looks quite fetching tonight. I do not believe we were introduced at Copper's *Ausa Vatni*, but I recall seeing you." He was as tall as my father with the same blonde hair.

"I'm sorry, it was a long day after a long night," I apologized.

I thought I remembered seeing him—the wiry man with Crag.

He had a big inviting smile. "No problem. I do not think your mother likes me very much. I tackled her once when she was trying to look very mature in a nice white gown," he said candidly.

"You know my mother?" It came out in a rush; I'd never get enough of hearing about my mother's past.

"I did indeed. I thought I had seen a ghost when she came to the masquerade; we all thought she had passed away at the massacre. I am glad though. Even when I was being a rapscallion, she was kind to me. Such a shame about Lark." Jackal sounded sincere. "Then again...I always thought my brother was sweet on her."

He was drunk. I didn't mind though, he wasn't being rude. I liked hearing about my mother when she was my age. It didn't hurt that he knew my father. I *did* wonder if Jackal knew I was his daughter.

"You know, funny thing. I knew Lark. He had raven waves and deeply tanned skin. I find it odd he would have blonde children with a dark-haired woman. Do not worry." He leaned in conspiratorially. "Your secret is safe with me." Then he winked so dramatically his mouth also opened and closed with it.

My stomach dropped, but the food in it went the opposite direction to sit in my throat.

Crag Straumr stepped in next to him. "I believe it is time to take Jackal home." The ebony-skinned man nodded to me.

"He frets over me," Jackal said with a sly smile. Crag rolled his eyes.

"Goodnight provost...Jackal," I said.

"I am your language provost too!" Jackal said belatedly as Crag steered him away.

My conversation with my drunken uncle left me shaken. If he made that connection within moments of speaking to me, how long would it take others? Would my mother be shunned for having children with a man married to someone else?

Ash was in his element, and as always, people were drawn to him. He put on that smile and wielded his charm, and the women flocked to him. He was standing around a gaggle of those women, doing just the right amount of touching to make them feel special, but not have it be inappropriate, and they were all tittering. His eyes met mine and he smiled broadly and excused himself from the circle. He didn't seem so happy when he reached me.

"Your stomach still upset? You flushed on stage. I waved to you," he said somewhat coolly.

I interlaced my fingers with his; I didn't want to get into one of our weird silences. I wanted to dance and be treated like the goddess I looked like.

He looked down at my hand in his, and smirked. *That's better.* I reached up and gave him a peck on his lips for good measure.

"You really do look stunning tonight, Scarlett," he said, appeased.

"You *always* look stunning," I told him.

I knew what he liked, but sometimes, I was just too stubborn to give it. It felt like a game and I hated games.

He kissed me sweetly then and brought me outside the tent for some air.

Ash would kiss me, and I'd forget all about yesterday and about Slate's kiss that afternoon. I cringed; it would take a phenomenal kiss to replace that one. I knew it would be the bar to which I held all others.

Curse you, Slate.

There were a few other people getting fresh air outside the white tents so we walked a little ways down to have some privacy. Once we found a darker shadow from the moonlight, Ash jerked me around and pulled me against him. His body was warm against mine. He must have been *calling*; it seeped into me as he cupped my face and stared into my eyes.

Ash's eyes were such a unique color; other than his sister's, I'd never seen the like. They were stunning, not like Slate's light grey that reminded me of a cloudy winter day when you felt the impending snowstorm coming, and then that reflective silver that shone at other times. A completely different pale green.

He pressed his beautifully shaped lips to mine and I *felt* his desire curl up around me. It infiltrated my skin, broke down my defenses as I let myself get carried away. This had to be better than yesterday. I liked Ash, I could replace Slate's kisses with Ash's, his hands for Ash's.

Ash's hands slid under the fabric of the cutout in my dress as he ran his hands down to cup my backside, and I gasped, sucking his air into my lungs. Ash smiled against my lips. Suddenly, his head turned and he slipped his hands from my dress.

Ash's eyes narrowed. "Disgusting. Has Pearl not given him a room?" he sneered, and my head swiveled.

On this side of the yellow-stoned university (which was really an enormous castle) bushes lined the wall, and in those bushes were the unmistakeable movements of a man behind a woman. The woman's moans reached us, and although the man's hair was more carefully braided than before, I'd recognize him even in the blackest of nights.

My stomach twisted and I turned back around to Ash. "We should go."

Ash looked down at me and I tried for a similarly disgusted look instead of the hurt I felt. I had no room to judge: the only reason I'd seen them was because I was having a make out session with my suitor.

"You would think he would at least take her indoors," Ash said, and my chest felt like it would explode.

Ash looked back towards the bushes and wrapped his arm around me. "Scarlett, you are shaking. You should have told me you were cold." Ash's body instantly heated and I leaned into him.

I couldn't summon the power of speech so Ash filled the air.

"If I were your lover, it would be nothing but romance. I would teach you what it is like to make love to a man," Ash promised as he pulled me close, and something stirred inside me.

I pulled my lips between my teeth, I was definitely thinking about it. No, I wasn't like Slate. I couldn't, not tonight at least.

"I believe you." I stood on my tiptoes and led him back into the tent.

He took me onto the dance floor once we entered the silver sparkling tent. The band was playing something classical. The dancers dresses twirled as they spun. There were clearly choreographed steps to the dance and I was hesitant to join.

"Do not worry." He gave me his cocky smile.

I didn't have to. Ash was a god on the dance floor.

We blended right into the fray. Spinning, twirling, stepping, Ash was an accomplished dancer. He led me with ease, and I was finally feeling very good about us.

The other dancers had retreated to the sides while Ash turned and dipped me, our feet intertwined.

When the song stopped I was smiling, and just a little bit giddy. People were clapping for us. Ash took a bow, and twirled me from him, displaying me, and I curtsied. They clapped harder.

"You are quite the man," I told him while we waited for drinks at the bar.

"There is a lot you do not know about me, Scarlett Tio. You must get to know me better." He said it low and deep. There were...many ways to get to know someone.

I felt myself blush. He loved it.

Someone snorted behind me. "Very cute. The myopic can keep up." Jonquil's short blonde hair was styled into a pompadour. She sneered at me with red lips that complemented her tight, leopard print dress.

"Jonquil, such a pleasure," Ash said, unperturbed.

"You two are together?" she asked him, and didn't fully disguise the hurt in her voice.

"Do we look together, Jonquil?" He wielded her name like a knife.

I couldn't stand to watch the argument play out.

"You two obviously need to talk. Ash, I'll see you when you're done?"

He nodded at me and took Jonquil by the bicep, pulling her out of the tent. I was thankful they weren't going to make a scene.

I was immediately approached by Reed looking dapper in his university robe.

"You and Ash make a lovely couple."

Butterfly and her husband were waving goodbye. Probably taking the sleeping boy Copper home, while their little daughter hung over Coyote's shoulder.

"Thank you," I said, then confided, "It is still very new."

He blew a raspberry into the air. "Then you will be married within the year if he has any say. That young man is like a dog with a bone: he always gets what he wants. He will be Prime one day if he plays his cards right."

Reed guided me onto the dance floor, as I mulled over what he said. I could be married to the Prime one day. The idea excited me irrationally; I had no desire for power whatsoever, and it undoubtedly meant long hours and boatloads of responsibility. I would do that, though, if it was what Ash wanted. I gave myself a mental shake. Was I already imagining myself as his wife?

We danced to more classical music, nothing I knew, but he kept the steps simple and led me almost as well as Ash had. He smiled and complimented me, twirled me around some more until Hawk cut in.

Dancing with Hawk was like coming home. I could forget where we were and all the strange things that had happened and just be me. He stayed with me for few songs, and we talked as we danced.

"Are you liking it here?"

"I am. I'm excited and nervous to start at Valla U."

"I'll be there too, there's no need to be nervous. If you have a problem just come see me. Reed is the disciplinarian there too, so he'll be around. You'd better not have to be sent to him," he joked. "How about Tawny? She's been so distant. I worry about her."

"She'll be fine. There's a lot about herself she doesn't know and has to come to terms with." I said it nonchalantly but he searched my eyes for a deeper meaning.

It was as much as the blood vow would let me get away with before I felt its weight over me like a warning.

Steel and Tawny were dancing together *a lot*, too much if you asked me. Any time she was taking a break and it looked like someone was going to ask her to dance, he would pull her back out. My girly side thought it was incredibly sweet. Tawny was laughing, completely carefree. Those two were in trouble.

I thanked Hawk for the dance and traded him for Steel, and I found Tawny and sent her to her father. "You guys don't look like uncle and niece dancing out here." I whispered tightly.

"You're right. Maybe it's because we're not," Steel said bluntly.

"Is that because you're really my brother?" I joked and then sobered. "I know, but *they* don't know that." I nodded towards all the faces in the crowd.

I hated being the bad guy, but things *would* get bad if someone caught on. He sighed and nodded. We headed back to the table; my feet were aching, but I was feeling much better about my dancing skills.

Jett sat with the girls at our table. Their usual fawning was at a minimum. It was a good thing because Viper was keeping an eye on them. I looked around for Gypsum and found him with a few kids his own age. Thankfully, there was no Diamond in sight. That was one mess I didn't want to get into. Ash still wasn't back. I was a little disappointed, we'd been having such a great time.

I heard Cherry squeal delightedly, then cover her mouth. Jett's jaw clenched and he popped up from the table and grabbed my hand.

I saw why once he spun me around. A very angry Viper was talking through clenched teeth with Cherry while Amethyst was trying to placate him.

"Now you've done it," I mused.

"He wants to rip my head off. It's such a handsome head," he said in mock sadness.

He was nervous despite his bravado. His turquoise eyes kept trying to watch events unfolding at the table. Pearl had come over with my mom and they were talking with Viper and the girls. If possible, Jett looked more nervous.

"I might leave this party engaged...or in a body bag."

"They have body bags here?" It was a random question in light of the circumstances, but the image didn't fit in my mind.

"We light a pyre here. No bags required."

The trouble had died down at the table and Viper was now sitting with our family.

"I'm going with engaged. What did you do to piss him off?"

"Nothing he could see. Cherry just squeals easily."

"Seriously, T.M.I."

Jett chuckled like the lech he was.

"I'll see you back home. If anyone asks, let them know where I went. Make sure they think I'm alone." He winked and I shoved him.

The scoundrel left me standing in the middle of the dance floor. Strong hands turned my hips and swept around me as we started to dance.

Slate.

His eyes were shining silver, his jaw tight. His hands held me just a little tighter than they should have. I couldn't stop staring at his lack of white fetishes; at least it gave me somewhere else to look other than his eyes. I was self-conscious of the jade fetish I'd had Bronze tuck into my hair and wondered if he could see it.

"Ash parades you around like a trophy," Slate said, staring down at me.

I was keenly aware of everywhere our bare flesh touched—his fingers on the back of my hand, the callouses of his palm on the soft skin of the curve of my back.

"I am a trophy, something special, something to be *desired*. I'm earned, not given away freely," I said in my haughtiest tone.

"You were giving yourself away freely enough yesterday." Slate's lips curled and my cheeks flushed as my heart skipped.

Steel's plea of civility went out the window.

"How could I have possibly passed up the chance to *fuck* the illustrious Slate on a dirty mattress in an abandoned house? Positively *swoon* worthy." My cold scornful tone surprised even me. I never cussed.

Slate stiffened and he pulled me closer to him so you couldn't push a gold Daymark between us.

"I would not have *fucked* you, Rabbit, as you so eloquently put it. Do you think I wanted to bed you there? I had to take the opportunity as it presented itself. I thought I would only have one chance to show you how we could be together. I did not want you to give yourself to me feeling weak. I wanted you to be strong and choose me because I would worship the woman you are becoming and because you wanted *me*." He scoffed. "I was right."

My cheeks were on fire. That was the last thing I'd expected.

"I'm not an opportunity to be taken." It was the one thing he'd said I could cling to. "And you didn't even give me time to work out how it all made me feel before you decided to push into the first ready and willing woman—no, *girl*. Tell me you won't break *her* heart?"

Slate let out a long breath and his fingers stopped digging into me. "I kissed you in front of our family; if that did not convince you of my intentions, I do not know what would. I was out there falling with no net and you asked about Ash. I watched you nearly die..." His thumb ran down my spine. "Come back to my rooms, Scarlett. Let us finish what we started," he purred.

I needed some air again. My cheeks were flushed, not with embarrassment, but with what his words were doing to me. I pulled it together.

"After you had her, you want me? Can you imagine how that makes me feel? I *saw* you, Slate. If you want to be my friend, I'm here. I'll never make the mistake of letting you into my heart again." I tried to pull away, but he held me steadfast.

We weren't even dancing anymore, and I looked around to see if anyone was paying attention.

Slate's grey eyes glittered. "Your heart?"

I rolled my eyes. "I misspoke. Let me go, I have to go find Ash. I'm sure the girl you fiddlesticked in the bushes is currently having her heart torn out by how inappropriately you're holding me."

Slate let me go with so much reluctance I thought he was going to change his mind and grab me again. I walked away without looking back. I decided to get good and drunk. But I needed an accomplice, and Tawny would be a poor one. I knew because I saw her sneaking off with her future husband—if only we could convince everyone he wasn't her uncle.

Jett had taken the girls back to his room, so he was out of the picture. And I didn't care if it was legal, I would not be drinking with my seventeen-year-old cousin. So Gypsum was out. I spotted Indigo with the evil twins, dark-haired Nova and blonde Quartz. I waved to her and she came over.

"Exciting, isn't it? The day after tomorrow we'll be well on our way to becoming tried and true." Her elation was contagious.

"I'm having a bad night. What do you say you and I get sloshing good drunk?"

"I'm there." She clinked my glass with her own.

Indigo was a great drinking buddy; she was happy and laughed constantly. I asked her about her adoption because, well, my dad had adopted her and I really wanted to know.

"I don't remember anything. As far as I can remember Delta and Alder have always been my parents." She shrugged her slim shoulders. "Sage and I are really like twins. We don't always get along, but he's my brother, blood or not." She smiled.

"Silly question, but do they treat the two of you the same because of it?"

She thought for a moment, "Sage is going to inherit the palace so he gets more attention, and it takes a lot of grooming. My dad though, he'd let me get away with murder." She gave me a half smile.

She asked me about Ash; it was the question *du jour*.

"Yes, we're together. It just kinda happened." I shrugged. "He's cool, really sweet when he wants to be. Obviously he's a walking, talking Photoshop." I smirked.

She was nodding enthusiastically and laughed. "Ash could charm just about any person out of their pants. Not everyone knows about his selfish streak. Are you feeling the pressure yet? To sign yourself away to him, permanently? His sister has a serious marriage lined up already.

For *you* two, it would be huge. Tio and Straumr together again." She laughed. "People were literally clapping for you two."

I didn't know how to take that information; I was already feeling pressured. Mostly by Ash, a little by my mom, but only because she was relishing in seeing me in a happy relationship. From what I knew about the greater families, Tio and Straumr were the top dogs. The two joining would be an excellent match. I was starting to understand the way things worked.

"I've felt a weird pressure since day one. What do you mean *sign yourself away*?"

"A marriage contract signed with a blood vow, but it's not as bad as it sounds. Sort of like a legally binding contract, but you *can't* break it. It's old magic. We don't have much of that anymore. Right now, people are scrambling for marriages. We've been divided for so long that *now* options are open again. Too many people over age, past their prime for children, aren't married. If you think you could make it work with Ash, it would be a big deal." She shrugged. "You'd be the most influential couple, your kids would be Tios *and* Straumrs." She smirked. "They *wait for no man*."

"Are you betrothed, then?"

She wrinkled her nose. "I don't really like the idea of signing myself away before I become a Guardian. I might want to travel outside of Tidings. It'd be near impossible to do with a husband in tow, especially if he's from a greater house. All the demands that come from running those estates are time consuming. My mother, adopted mother, does far more day to day than my father and he's not the patriarch yet." She thought for a moment. " I don't think there are any other eligible boys from the greater houses. There's really only your brother and cousins, your uncle, technically Ash is still available, and Sage is my brother. I think that about covers it. You have the most eligible family and managed to snag the most eligible bachelor. Our age, anyway. Your brother seems to have his hands full, and your uncle, Steel, I'm not really attracted to him. I'm adopted into my family. A marriage to me would be prestigious, but they wouldn't get the benefits of the blood-line even though I have strong *calling*. I've made my peace with it. My father would probably include a dowry if I could get a good one, but I told him not to try too hard. All the seasons are out of my league."

We refilled our drinks. We managed to sneak one of the smaller punch bowls under the table and were drinking liberally. Not that we would be cut off, but now we could gossip and drink, and we didn't want to share. It was rotten, but I wasn't in a mood where I cared.

"What do you mean about seasons?" I asked. All of this was fascinating.

She smiled. "It's funny how you take for granted simple knowledge. You fit in so well here, I forget you don't know anything about it. Where you live is perpetual hot weather. Summer. Sumar. Where I live is perpetual spring, Var. Get it? And so on and so forth. The hope is to always have a greater family in those houses. That's why powerful marriages are in such high demand. I heard old man Vetr doesn't have an heir. It's a big deal. His daughters are married to greater families, so their sons have their father's names. One son to each house, unfortunately for him. If there had been a second son to either, they could've been heir to Elivagar. Not that you'd want to be. It's very possibly the scariest of all the islands. The tribes are the worst. They never have enough ambassadors. Mostly because they always disappear." She shivered. "It is beautiful though. All snow-covered mountains, all year round."

"You're talking about your mom…and she has a sister? Your brother will take over for the Vars, right? Who's the other guy?"

She nodded. "Sterling. His mom is my aunt. He'll take over the Haust house. They are the only two grandsons. Old man Vetr had a son, but he died before *he* could have a son," she said sadly. "My dad tells me my uncle was a really great guy. Not vain like most of the Guardians. Old man Vetr has never been the same since he died, I'm told. He's bitter and angry. Scary. He's my adoptive grandfather and even I wouldn't cross him, not that he ever comes around. He's a bit of a recluse."

She pointed to a dour looking older man. His salt and pepper hair was thinning, his face was lined with deep creases. His mouth didn't look made for smiling, only scowling like he was doing then. He wore a long sleeveless scarlet robe trimmed with white. The robe of the patriarch. Hawk had stubbornly refused to wear our family's. Pearl had joked that it didn't match her dress.

He sat next to a woman who had aged into a great beauty. She had shoulder-length blonde hair and frosty blue eyes. She was speaking with my father's wife and a black-haired beauty who had to be her sister. The three of them had the same frosty blue eyes, colder than ice. They reminded me of Novaculite and Quartzite—I could see the family resemblance.

I wanted to change the subject; talking of the Vetrs left me oddly chilled. "How do the dorms work here? Are we assigned or what?" I asked.

"They can be if you don't know anyone. They have two floors, two separate wings. Women in one wing, first years on one floor, seconds on the other and the same for the men in their own wing. It's four girls to a room. Only the basics. Bedroom, a shared bathroom and sitting room on each floor."

I was nodding so rapidly my head was likely to roll off. I think I knew just the four girls I could live with.

"Indigo, do you have any roommates yet?" I asked, beaming and praying the answer was no.

I really liked Indigo; she would've been my friend in Chicago. Even Tawny would love her and Tawny usually only tolerated girls, at best.

"Not yet. I know girls older or younger than me. Hardly anyone the same age. Why? What do you have in mind?" she asked with a curl of her pretty pink lips.

Indigo was beautiful in a classic, obvious way. Long straight blonde hair with light blue eyes, a lean muscled body, and she was slightly taller than as I was. You wanted *not* to like her. She was always going to be beautiful, life just a little easier for her.

"I don't have any roomies either. Tawny could be one, and I think I know a fourth." I forced a smile trying to pull myself back out of the bad mood I was slipping into.

"Like who?" she asked slowly, lifting an eyebrow at me.

"She's sweet, really. A little annoyingly girly, but she means well. My brother's girlfriend, Cherry. I doubt she has any chick friends either."

Indigo laughed lightly. "I know her. I could live two years with her."

I clapped my hands, elated to have a plan. "Fantastic! Who do I see about it? I want to make sure this pans out."

"Dahlia Natt, she's the first years' headmistress."

I sunk into my seat. "Fiddlesticks."

"What? She's Ash's mom, doesn't she like you?"

"I think so. She's just...different. I don't think she likes my uncle teaching American History and that we come from outside Tidings."

"I can handle it. They're all scared of my mom, they'll do anything she asks."

I looked over at my father's statuesque wife. My father was nowhere to be seen. She did look intimidating, like someone who'd scrape you off her shoe if you got in her way. Well, she'd have someone scrape you off for her.

Indigo laughed at my expression. "She's tough, but she knows how to get what she wants."

I just nodded. I believed her. "Enough shop talk, let's go dance."

The band was playing its usual otherworldly music, with just enough bass that I could dance to it without a partner. The music was directed to the younger crowd. The dance floor was teeming with teenagers. Even Gypsum was dancing with Diamond and a group of her friends, and not inappropriately, *thank goodness.* I didn't think Ash would like Diamond and Gypsum's relationship. Gypsum looked like he may have had a goblet or two of the wassail: his olive skin was flushed, his long hair freed from its ponytail. His dimpled smile lit up the room.

Hawk and Sparrow were drunkenly laughing at a table filled with adults. Diamond and a cute blonde girl I met at the Ausa Vatni brought Gypsum over to us.

"I think he wants to go to bed," Diamond said guiltily.

I tried not to get all judgey on him, I was no role model. I'd taken off my shoes at some point and they were currently M.I.A. I'd be going home barefoot. I had stayed true to my word and fallen deep into my cups, and had brought Indigo down with me. She was nodding off at the table.

The three of us stumbled to the portal doors. Diamond and her friend split off and went back to their little group.

Indigo went first. "See you in two days." She smiled prettily, as if she had any other kind of smile. "I'll have my mother talk to Dahlia tomorrow."

I waved goodbye and headed through another door, Gypsum stumbling over my shoulder. He had moved into a room on the same floor with the guys—the room that shared a bathroom with Slate's.

I got Gypsum into bed. And by *bed*, I mean the the floor, and by *got...fell* would be more accurate. He looked up at me and chuckled, a little too masculinely for my taste.

I left Gyps's room and hovered in front of Slate's door before I quickly tossed the idea. He had invited me to his room, but no good could come from it when I was in this condition.

I turned to the stairs at the end of the hall and ran into Slate and an older brunette heading up the stairway. His arm was slung around her back and her arm was around his waist as she leaned into him while they reached the boys' floor.

I was paralyzed for the briefest moments when I saw her hand grab him below his waist. I turned and started up the stairs.

"Scarlett?" Slate's voice chased after me.

I thought about running or ignoring him, but I had to call him out.

"I thought you didn't bring them home," I whispered as I ascended the mosaic stairwell. My hand slid against the smooth cool rail as I walked away.

It was all that held me upright.

Slate cursed and I hurt something crash, but I kept moving upward and onward.

CHAPTER 14

I had the nightmare again.

I jumped out of bed and ran to the toilet. I went number three. Resting my head against the rim, I prayed for the stomach cramping to stop. I crawled over to the shower and slapped the plate so the water would run. I struggled out of my dress and underwear and into the waterfall of the shower.

I lay on the floor curled in a ball, letting the water rush over me. *I love water.* I was feeling a little better, hydrating my body through osmosis. I managed to do a halfway decent job of a shower and pulled on a terry cloth robe.

I crawled into bed and fell back to sleep thinking about the woman in my dream who now had a form, and I wondered what it meant.

"You missed breakfast." Tawny was grabbing clothes out of my closet and tossing them across the room at me.

She walked over to me and calmed my roiling stomach acids. I had a headache, but using *calling* on the mind was dangerous. We'd only been taught after minor injuries during training and when our moms were *way* to excited to show us how to calm period cramps. There was no way I'd trust my *calling* or anyone else's on my mind.

I was exhausted. The end of the night had been horrible. Thinking about it made my stomach spasm; if Tawny hadn't fixed my stomach I would've projectile yawned at the carpet. I pulled on the clothes Tawny had thrown at me.

"You look like crap. Worse than when you had the chicken pox."

I had the chicken pox when I was eight; it was the only time in my life that I could remember being *really* sick. I'd developed the red pox at school and was sent to the nurse, and then immediately home. My mom had been beside herself. I remembered how she'd looked at me throughout the entire week and a half it took to clear up. I knew now she'd been thinking about healing me, but couldn't without the school thinking something was odd. I had been a *wreck*.

That I was worse than chicken pox was really saying something. I shrugged and went into the bathroom.

By the Mother! She was not kidding. My entire face was puffy from bawling; blotchiness with bloodshot eyes was just the icing on the crap cake. I pulled my hair back into a ponytail, did my usual morning rituals, and met Tawny at the door. She had brought me an apple. I could've kissed her.

I filled her in on the sordid details, including what happened in the abandoned building. I was just *numb*. I appreciated my body's rejection of all things pain. Tawny was dumbfounded, even more so than I was. I was glad. I didn't like to be the only one thinking, *Wait a minute...what just happened?*

"At least now you know. Ash is a better match anyway." Was that supposed to make me feel better?

"Et tu, Brute?"

She leveled her eyes at me. "Steel explained why they're all so pushy to pair us off. I get it, I do. And Scar, outside looking in, you looked really happy last night. I know Ash has his foibles, but ask yourself if it isn't something you can live with. Steel does this thing..."

My brain shut off. She and her imaginary problems with her perfect boyfriend. *Garbage.* I would try to see if there wasn't something deeper than attraction with Ash. Last night *had* been nice. It was too bad he didn't take me home last night; I never would have seen Slate with his latest conquest or if I had, I would've had Ash to keep me company so I didn't allow myself to fall into the abyss wondering where Slate had taken that woman or if he had stayed.

I'd closed the door on Slate. My fingers were stuck in the jamb, but at least it was shut.

We got the rest of our gear from the prep room and headed out onto the training area. Tawny had healed my face, but by mood showed through the now smooth tan skin. I just needed to get through the day and the next I'd be at the university.

I pointedly ignored the guys lifting in the weights section. Then I saw Slate; I'd almost forgotten who my trainer was. He stood there in his snug pants and sleeveless V-neck, his bracers thick around his wrists, and I imagined his hands all over that woman's body and wanted to throw up again.

"Get it in gear. We have a long day ahead of us," he said without inflection.

Jett saw my face as I passed him as I ran along the track, and he dropped his weights. "Freya's burly boar, Scar. What'd you do last night?"

I narrowed my eyes and kept right on running. I had to keep a brave face or I'd never make it through.

We did archery next. Tawny was good. It was amazing what hours of endless practice could do when you had natural talent. She was just going to keep getting better. Her new bow had been delivered that morning; it was lightweight and curved like a "C." She sat down, bent it in the opposite direction, and used air to string it.

She was flushed with excitement. "It's very delicate. I can hit nine out of ten targets at three hundred feet in twenty seconds." She beamed.

Gibberish. I smiled and nodded...that was what you do, smile and nod.

Then we headed to the mats for hand-to-hand combat. Slate was poised for the ready, swaggering around. I wanted to rip his head off. Sure, he had like three percent body fat and had kicked my fanny pack numerous times. But he must have a weak spot, *right?*

Tawny had her fanny pack handed to her eight out of the ten times they started, stopped, regrouped, and continued. But at least two wins was better than nothing.

The guys had come around to watch, their training complete, but waiting for us so we could join them in our pool laps.

Slate and I circled around each other for a moment and then he attacked. Thumbs curled into my fists, I blocked his onslaught of hits. His jaw was set, and I had to keep my cool or I'd turn into a wailing mess. The feel of his skin alone—even just while we were sparring—was too much to bear. I didn't just want to beat him; I wanted to *pulverize* him. I struck out with my legs, my strongest asset. He blocked my kick to his thigh, and landed a shoulder-powered jab with his left hand in my kidney.

I winced visibly and I heard Tawny gasp. I wasn't pulling punches, but I knew he was at least a little bit. I swept his feet out from under him by some miracle and I pounced for the tap out. But he grabbed me by my shirt so I landed between his legs; he locked his ankles around my waist and grabbed my right arm. He swung around so I was facedown on the mat, my left arm between his legs, his right leg pushing my face away. He hooked my hostage arm with the leg that was pushing at my face and grabbed my belt. Then he pushed forward. My shoulder and elbow were screaming, bent in an unnatural way.

"Submit," he said without inflection.

"Slate…" I heard Steel warn.

Training was intense.

"She can submit if she wants," he growled.

I refused to submit. It looked hopeless. He hadn't counted on me being in a slightly murderous rage. Only slightly. I felt my shoulder painfully shift, and barrel rolled out from him, using my unguarded legs to push me. I was on my knees when he tried to get at me again. He went for my waist, but I held onto his head and threw my leg over the arm he had tucked around my waist. I fell back onto the mat and slid the leg pinning his arm to me, across his throat between us. He gripped my leg across his throat, and I wrapped my other leg over his back pressing him harder against my shin, harder and harder.

I was trying to block his airflow. Something had snapped inside me, and there was no holding me back. He tore my leg from his throat, but held on as he slammed my body down on the ground, knocking all the air from my lungs. His body was over mine crushing me to the ground. He didn't seem to be straining at all, to my never-ending frustration.

He got in my face and bellowed, "Submit to me!"

I laughed; it wasn't pleasant. "Never."

I was done for the day.

Slate's face went blank and Jett grabbed Slate by the shoulder, lifting him off me, Steel at his side. Jett looked furious.

"For fuck's sake, Slate. What were you thinking? You almost popped her arm out of its socket."

Tawny helped me stand, the back of my head was pulsing with my heartbeat and my arm was screaming. "We're just training. I could have submitted," I told them in a dull tone.

The three men turned to me as Tawny led me away. "That's not just training, Scar." Jett warned. "What is going on with you two? One day he's making out with you in front of mom and the next he's breaking your arm? Don't think I haven't noticed the jade fetish braided into your hair, baby sis. This is massively screwed up, and *I* know screwed up."

"She's fine," Tawny said leveling her eyes at them.

I nodded. "I've handled it." My fingers tried to push the little jade canine under my hair.

Jett snorted. "The only thing getting handled is you."

He dismissed me and turned to Slate who was looking back at me with disbelief and frustration.

I planted my feet. "I'm a big girl. Don't go lecturing him about taking it easy on me. Those men who attacked me didn't take it easy on me."

I didn't know why I was defending him; I just didn't like the idea of coming between Slate and the guys. Jett arched an eyebrow at me and looked back at Slate.

"Just remember she's only been here for two weeks, huh? Maybe compensate for that a little so you're not breaking her at every turn," Jett said in a more amiable tone.

Slate nodded. "I apologize, *Scarlett*." He put so much emphasis on my name and how he said it that I was taken aback.

"Whatever. Steel, something tore in my arm, could you help me?"

"Sure thing." Steel trotted over to me and placed his hands on my shoulder.

I finished my laps in record time and created an air raft like the guys had shown us our first time in the pool. I let myself soak, fingers and toes getting pruney. Everyone left me alone. Even Tawny said she'd meet me at lunch. I didn't want to go to lunch; I wanted to float there forever. But I was getting hungry.

Everyone was already eating lunch by the time I arrived in the dining hall. "Scarlett, Slate told us the good news. You have found your specialty," Hawk said excitedly.

I frowned. What was he talking about?

"Excellent, Scarlett! What is it?" my mom asked, smiling.

It was a bigger deal than I thought. And I still had no idea what they were talking about.

"Blades," Slate said.

My mom looked on in disbelief. They all looked skeptical. I understood; blades had this implication of stabbing, tearing, blood. Lots of blood. Like an assassin. I was willing to bet she thought I'd take up archery like Tawny or a quarterstaff. Nope, her little girl was going to slit throats. She must be so proud.

Jett and Gypsum were the only two who seemed to accept it without explanation.

I *felt* confusion. But then Pearl said, "Slate uses blades as well. He could help you increase your skillset, darling. How lucky for you." Tawny winced for me. Slate grunted in acquiescence.

My mom spoke up. "That's great, Scarlett. Not what I would've suspected, but still great."

"Thanks, Mom." My tone was dry and as bland as I felt on the inside.

"Mom was just telling us she's taking the expedited testing in two weeks," Jett said, gesturing with his fork.

She gave a small modest smile.

"Do we come to cheer you on, or how does it work?" I asked.

"You wait at the finish line. It's an obstacle course of sorts," she said.

"Obstacle course," Steel scoffed. "Wren, you know people have died doing this *obstacle course*. You're almost certain to have something broken or bruised when you come out, but you'll be healed as soon as you finish. It's a long trek, though."

Hawk and Sparrow were nodding. They were worried about her, and it was sweet to see how much they cared for her. I wanted to support my mom.

"I'll be there. Just let me know where. By the way—I think I have my three roommates for our dorm," I told them all.

"Cool, who are we rooming with?" Tawny said with a sly smile, knowing she'd be one of the four.

"You think Cerise would be willing to room with us?" I looked at Jett.

"Consider it done." He gave me his smug smile.

"And Indigo Var. Her mother is arranging things with Dahlia."

I watched as the chips fell. I was feeling delightfully bad and didn't care if I stirred the pot a little.

"Oh," was all my mom said.

Oh yes, I knew who my dad was. The hush over the table exhilarated me in a terrible way. Tawny and Gypsum, possibly Slate, were the only ones who had no idea why this was a big deal. Jett thought it was evil, but he *did* a little evil himself. "Since we're all here...after a long discussion with Viper, courtesy of mom and grandmother, I've decided to approach Moon about proposing to the girls."

I laughed. *The girls,* I wondered if that would be in the vows in lieu of their names. I walked over and gave him a hug. Everyone followed my lead, giving him pats on the back and hugs and kisses all around.

"Viper's the only one who said yes, so let's not celebrate just yet."

"A Sumar and a Geol, both from the Straumr and Tio bloodlines...why wouldn't he agree?" asked Hawk in a jovial tone.

Jett smirked. "Because there's an Kaldr in there. Besides, they'll get their Tio and Straumr marriage from Scarlett and Ash. There goes our bargaining chip." He said it to be a smart fanny pack.

Instead of balking, I smiled pointedly. "Probably."

It surprised everyone but Tawny. She knew where my mind was.

I would have basked in my intentional drama, but disappointment flitted across Jett's eyes. I'd had enough.

"What's on the agenda for tonight?" I asked, trying to change the subject.

Pearl seemed happy for the subject change; I still didn't know why she didn't like Ash.

"Thrimilci is having a small reception for everyone going tomorrow. It is in town, it would be a good break to go since you have all been working so hard that you have missed nearly all the Yuletide celebrations."

We had hours to kill before our evening out, and I didn't want to spend it *calling*. Tawny wanted to get some more arrows, so we decided to go into town. As it turned out, arrows were code for something for Steel. They were both bummed out about not being able to spend every waking second together any longer. She said many the tyros slept at home and they just had to be careful not to oversleep, and apparently that was Steel's plan. Tawny planned on frequently sneaking back through the portal doors.

I couldn't blame her; Tawny and Steel were deeply in love...a little covert action would only spice things up. I worried about what Ash would have planned for our sleeping arrangements. He didn't ever push to do more than I was comfortable with, but he had a very convincing way about him.

Steel, Jett, and Slate were out and about in town too. We'd planned to meet up at the weapons shop later; maybe we'd buy those arrows after all.

Tawny was having a really hard time picking something for Steel, and I was right there with her. I needed to get Jett his very first birthday gift from me and I was having the same problem. We were probably putting too much thought into it. I vaguely wondered if I was supposed to give Ash something for his induction ceremony.

We ended up getting the arrows at a place called Nock Your Average Bow, *hilarious*. She got a quiver that rested at her hip and filled it full of new arrows. I wished I could have gotten something for Ash's weapon specialty, but I had no idea what it was. I found a black damask sheath with matching handle on a pair of long seaxes nearly three feet long. It cost a pretty penny, but I was sure Jett would love them. I gave up on weaponry for Ash, and instead found pewter studded black bracers embossed with the stages of the moon. He'd look good in anything, so it was a safe bet.

Tawny got Jett black damask bracers that matched the swords I'd bought him. We were feeling good about or purchases. I was super stealthy as I bought gold, jeweled head chains for my mom and Tawny without her noticing. Then I remembered Slate. It felt wrong not to include him in our gift exchange.

Tawny went with more push daggers identical to the ones he'd bought before; he'd need replacements after the ones I'd lost. I was embarrassed that she asked me to help her, and I knew which ones they were by sight. I wanted to get him something special; we were on very bad terms right now, but it wouldn't be forever. Right?

I had given up by the time we left to meet the boys. We were back in the first weapon shop I'd ever been in. The guys weren't there yet, so we hurriedly perused the cases. The burly salesman was there and he gave me a wink. He was okay for a pervert.

Tawny found what she'd been looking for. Steel used a spear, so she found a five-pronged head for it. It resembled a gold trident, which she liked because he was the ambassador to the merfolk.

Burly man came over. "What are you looking for, sweetheart?"

His darkest blue eyes scanned me in a way that made me think he had secretly seen me naked at some point. There was something dirty and bad about this salesman. I was having a dirty bad kind of day.

I let my lips curl. "I want to get a gift for the guy I was in here with last time."

His eyebrows lifted almost imperceptibly. "Slate?"

"Yeah, you know him?"

He nodded and started searching the cases.

"Great tracker. Helped train him some."

"Train him how?"

"Tracking; that is how come he is so great." He gave me a bad man smile. It wasn't *that* bad. "Here it is." He pulled out two things that looked like bracers with a knives. "Retractable wrist blades," he grunted. "Will not buy them himself. I offered to accept some services for them, but he does not like to owe anyone anything."

"Done."

They were better than perfect. Black and dark silver bracers, sturdy for balance and reinforced. The blades looked wicked. Burly man cleaned me out for those. I spent the remainder of the purse Pearl had given me, and didn't feel the slightest bit bad about it.

"Good doing business with you," he said gruffly, holding up one of the several marks I'd just paid him with a lecherous grin that would make Jett proud.

"What's your name, by the way?" I asked as I gave him my best, *You're not so bad when you're not sexually harassing women* smile.

"Hopper, sweetheart, as in Grasshopper."

"My name is Scarlett..."

"Sure it is, sweetheart." He smirked and I rolled my eyes playfully.

My mood had lifted. Not that I was in a forgiving mood yet, but at least I wasn't still murderous. Tawny and I headed to the Tea-rrific Cafe while we waited for the boys. It didn't take long for them to join us.

People were everywhere, setting up a dance floor and long tables with benches for a feast. Watching them work was absolutely fascinating. They used *calling* to do everything. I loved living in a world with magic.

"Who are you thinking about?" Jett teased.

"No one. Despite all my issues, I really like it here."

"It likes you too." He smiled a rare genuine smile, no smugness allowed.

"At risk of sounding too girly, what are we supposed to wear to this thing?" Tawny asked.

She was sitting in her cafe chair, and Steel scooted next to her, his arm around the back, his legs crossed under the table. They looked like they'd been doing it for years instead of two weeks.

"It's casual, anything will look great." Steel's smile was bright white and beaming.

He stroked a finger down her back. They really sucked at being covert. I guessed it didn't matter with this crowd. Jett was going to be a polygamist and I would end up the Prime's wife. I might have been the most normal person at the table, and that wasn't saying much.

"Are the girls coming out tonight?" I asked Jett.

"Nah. Ash?"

"I haven't heard from him since halfway through last night. He just left." I shrugged.

"He was really into you when he had an audience," Steel noted.

"Sounds like love," Jett joked.

"You really are a punk," I told him, giving him a look.

He waggled his eyebrows at me. "You have to adopt the language quirks. I'm not a punk. I'm a bastard or a scoundrel. A blackguard or a knave!" My brother was too handsome for his own good.

"Yes. All those things," I said, eliciting a chuckle from everyone.

We were finishing our teas and getting ready to go.

"Anyone get Gyps a gift? I don't want to all be exchanging things and he gets nothing." Tawny chewed on her lip.

"Sugarfoot, I didn't. I blew my wad on the last gift." Slate choked on his tea.

Jett laughed and as patted his back. "Scar is intent on choking you today." I stuck my tongue out at him, but it only encouraged him.

"I'll be right back. I have an idea. Meet me at the portal door." Steel jogged away towards the shops.

I gave up waiting after about fifteen minutes and wanted to go get ready, and he showed up twenty minutes later, apple-cheeked.

"Sorry. So sorry. It was harder than I thought," Steel said, out of breath, and we started crossing into the portal.

Jett whispered to me, "That's what she said." My brother was a first-class pervert.

Tawny and I took turns helping each other put up our long locks so we looked like we stepped out of a salon. We freshened up our makeup and switched to strapless dresses in the Grecian style synonymous with Thrimilci. I was ready for dinner and dancing; I'd even worn flats so I wouldn't take my heels off and leave them again.

We wrapped our gifts as best we could and rushed to the portal room. Everyone held gifts—only Tawny and I had gone overboard. We went through the town center portal and we heard the music right away.

None of that classical stuff here: all light and fun, designed to keep people smiling, laughing, and in some cases, drunk. It was our last night in Thrimilci before school started so I was determined not to drink. I wanted to be on my A-game for the university tomorrow.

We found a long table and sat down. Volunteers brought platters of food and we served ourselves. We chatted while we ate, the first time the family was at a celebration where it was just us and everyone was smiling.

The time came to exchange gifts.

Jett loved his new long seax swords with matching bracers, which made Tawny and I do a mental high five. I gave Tawny and my mom the jeweled head chains and they promptly put them on. Tawny had bought me a pair of black pauldrons with gold wings embossed in them. Jett gave me a black belt with a gold buckle in the shape of a Daymark, surrounded by small throwing daggers.

Tawny and I received necklaces and earrings from Hawk, Sparrow, and my mom, and even Gypsum had bought us bracelets. "To wear with your fancy dresses," he said, embarrassed because he has gone shopping for bracelets.

Steel gave Gypsum his gift then. Gypsum gave a lopsided smile, dimples showing. It was a blazing sun belt buckle.

Hawk gave us new boots. Mine were black, the leather soft and supple. Tawny didn't give Steel his gift, but he gave her a thick archery bracer that matched her seax sheath with its blood-red color and Mother Earth, tree turned woman, form in black leather. It was beautiful. She tried not to get choked up.

Tawny gave Slate his. He wasn't the type of guy to take gifts or compliments easily. He looked stony-faced when she passed him the gift box with the bracers.

But he had also gotten her something. A back quiver in the same blood-red. I was impressed; the boys had planned their shopping well. She laughed when she saw it and he flashed her a steamy smile that made my blood boil. I wanted a friendship with Slate too.

Slate and I were awkward, there was no other word for it. It could have been my imagination—perhaps he was reluctant and only I was awkward, but there it was. We inconspicuously slid our gifts across to one another, pretending nine other people weren't watching us. I opened my gift and burst out laughing, while he let out a low chuckle.

"What is it?" Gypsum asked.

Instead of telling them, we just held up near identical wrist blades. The whole table got caught up in their laughter. My wrist blades were substantially smaller, and the blades shot out from the bottom of my forearm instead of the top like Slate's. Mine also had solid gold lacework over the bracer so it would deflect, and three blades angled away from the outside of the bracer as the blade shot out, giving me three added blades on the sides of them. I activated mine with a gesture of my pinky fingers, elegant and deadly. We both murmured our thanks, and I laughed at how amusing it must have been for Hopper.

Pearl gave me simple boot knives and black leather gloves. Tawny got a glove that covered the fingers she used to nock her arrows, and a deep red cloak with grey removable lining. Gift exchanging was over after the family gave Jett a series of early birthday gifts. Then we danced.

I was need of some release, more than this morning. It was taxing playing nice with Slate, having him around all the time.

The unbearably gorgeous guy from the armor store we'd gone to asked me to dance and I happily obliged. He wasn't much taller than I was, but he was powerfully built and carried himself confidently. None of that mattered because it was hard to look at anything but his plump pouty lips. He knew just how luscious they were too, by the way he could draw your attention there with a lick of his lips or a flash of a blinding smile. He had one of the few scars I'd seen on a Guardian through his left eyebrow, above deep blue eyes.

He commanded my attention and I thought I was going to have to tell him about Ash soon, but Steel interrupted. "Solder, you're monopolizing my niece's dance card," Steel said with a poster boy smile.

Solder laughed and we all walked off the dance floor. "How could such a gorgeous woman possibly be related to you?" Solder gave me a wink that made my face flush.

"Pleasure to have met you, Solder," I said, starting to walk away.

Solder moved as eerily fast as the other men I'd met in Tidings, he gently caught my wrist. "You have me at a disadvantage, gorgeous. I do not know your name."

Did lines like that really work? His eyes glittered when he smiled, with—*my goodness, those lips...*

"Scarlett," I said, cursing the blush that turned even my tanned chest pink.

He liked the effect. "Lovely Scarlett." His eyes didn't leave mine as he pressed his lips to my hand.

"Okay, okay," Steel said with mock annoyance and Solder laughed and turned to him while I floated back to the table.

"Scarlett, he was handsome. A friend of yours?" my mom prodded.

She loved being able to finally talk about boys. I knew she wanted me to settle down already, but she also wanted me to have more than one suitor so I knew what was out there. I would have loved to talk to my mom about it, but it was far too embarrassing.

"I just met him. I remember him from the armor store, he's Steel's age," I commented nonchalantly as my gaze went back out to the dance floor.

"You remember him from the time we spent in the Armored Armoire?"

Now *that* sounded deceptively jealous. I cast a curious glance over my shoulder to Slate who wasn't looking very amused.

Tawny snorted. "Can you blame her? He's scrumptious."

My mom tried not to look scandalized and Sparrow shot her daughter a look that threatened her to be more of a lady.

"Well, if you already have one *suitor*..." Tawny said as she got up from the table and headed over to Steel and Solder. "I'm sure you won't mind if I introduce myself."

Slate grunted and I turned around and checked to make sure my mom wasn't paying attention. "Your bed must be cold, you should go find another body to warm it. Wouldn't want to go a day without crawling between a new woman's legs." I cursed myself when I turned back around. Now where did that come from?

I kept my eyes on Tawny and Steel, but they were doing a better job of staying apart. What you couldn't change was the look of love in their eyes whenever they saw each other.

I saw Steel lead her away during the dancing. I rolled my eyes and followed. If anyone noticed that only the two of them were gone, it would look suspicious.

He snuck them back through the portal. *Sugarfoot.* I didn't know if I should go back and let someone know we were leaving or not so the family wouldn't know Steel and Tawny were off alone. As it turned out, I didn't have to; the crowd parted and Slate was there.

"I'm going to go wring Tawny's neck. Could you let them know we left, please?"

Please, for good measure. He looked down at me; I was even shorter when I didn't have my heels on. He mulled over my words and turned back.

I ran through the portal. They weren't in the portal room, so I searched the halls. I barely caught them turning a corner and I chased after them. So irresponsible leaving the celebration like that and coming home together—what if someone saw them?

I was trying to catch up to them, but when he led her out onto a balcony I had never seen before, I hung back.

A wide, half-circle of thick balcony hung out over the waterfall. The moon hung surreal in the sky. It was like something out of a dream. I moved closer so I could hear over the roar of the waterfall. I hid behind one of the many huge white columns. If they started doing it, I'd jump overboard.

He led her to the edge and held her, a light mist spraying them. I started to regret my intrusion. He was standing behind her, arms wrapped around her. She leaned into his chest.

"My father proposed to my mother in front of this waterfall."

She turned in his arms to face him, she smiled and kissed him. Tawny probably thought it was the end of the story, but he was pale and trembling.

He pushed on. "Tawny, from the moment I saw you walk through into room, I fell in love with you. Every day, I fall a little farther. When I thought I lost you, I never felt that way before. I never want to feel that way again. I love you." Steel got down on one knee. "Tawny Dagr, will you be mine forever and always?"

He pulled a small red box out and held it up to her. He opened it. A gold ruby ring was nestled in the box. He took her hand and slid it on her finger.

Tears had started to streak down her face. She didn't answer, she just stared at her ring finger and the massive ruby he'd given her. I felt someone step in behind me, I didn't need to turn to know that Slate had followed me.

Tawny was taking shuddering breaths, Steel still down on his knee. It was mortifying, I wanted to pretend I'd never seen it.

"How can you think we can get married when we can't even hold hands in public? You're my *uncle*! Don't you think it's disgusting enough with what we do to each other? Now you want the world to know? I can't do this!" she shouted at him.

Steel started to rise, to grab ahold of her. She shoved him off.

"I can't do this," she said again and she ran back into the palace.

Slate, in all black, stood in front of me so my bright dress wouldn't give me away. Steel was just standing there. I felt utterly helpless. If I comforted him, I didn't know if it would make it worse. He'd know I'd seen the whole thing. He stood for awhile longer and finally left, the moonlight reflecting off his wet cheeks.

I was going to go back to the rooms to check on Tawny, but my body wouldn't move. I realized my cheeks were streaked with tears; I'd been crying and didn't even know it. Slate cupped my face and wiped my tears away with a thumb. I was too weak to fight him off. I was breaking inside for Tawny and Steel. Their love was real, and they couldn't find a way to be together. Jett had made me take that stupid blood oath; otherwise, I would've told them a hundred times by now. Knowing Hawk wasn't her real father would definitely be the lesser of the evils at that point. I concocted an idea.

"Slate, you have to get the family to tell Tawny about..." The blood oath wouldn't let me say it.

He shook his glossy black waves. "There are more reasons you do not understand yet. It is for the best."

After what he witnessed, I was shocked. "How can you say that?

They love each other, it's as plain as the nose on my face! Love like that *should* be celebrated."

"Scarlett Tio, there is nothing *plain* about you. Life is sometimes bigger than love."

I was mentally staggering. The Beatles told me all I needed was love, what was *this* crap?

"You'd give up on love for what? Life? What is life without love?"
"Yes," was all he said, and went out the way we'd came.

I was still reeling. The lump in my throat was making it painful to swallow. I walked over to where they had been standing. A little red box sat on the railing, and I opened it.

The ring was gone. Tawny never took the ring off. I felt a spark of hope.

CHAPTER 15

 The dress code was a black, floor-length caftan trimmed in silver and gold with a wide red belt for first years, and yellow for second years. It wasn't half bad; it was a modern take on the dress so it had a scoop neck and an elegant swishing skirt with a narrow sheer panel that flared at the knees.

I hurriedly got ready and knocked on Tawny's door. She didn't answer, so I tried the handle. It opened, but she was still in bed. I sat down softly next to her. She rolled over, she looked like I had the day before, eyes puffy, face splotchy. I didn't ask, I just did, *calling* to balance her skin tone and sooth the puffiness. It was the least I could do.

"I saw everything. We don't have to talk about it if you don't want." She shook her head and I nodded. Saying it out loud made it real. "We start at Valla U today. *Yay!*" I said in mock excitement, and she gave me a small smile. "See you downstairs," I told her as I closed the door.

One last quick stop; I knocked on the door.

"Come in."

"Hey Mom, just heading out," I said nervously.

It was well before breakfast, and she lounged in a silken robe at the sitting area going over paperwork, her long dark waves falling to her waist as her warm brown eyes checked me over.

"What's all this?" I asked. I couldn't help but notice a sealed envelope sitting half peeking out from the papers with the name *ALDER* scribbled across it in my mother's handwriting.

She smiled up at me. "Sorry, hun. Catching up on my predecessors' work on the Aves tribe before they cut off contact. I can't figure out how I'm going to get to them. I might have to camp out until they acknowledge me. I'll have to find it first." She sighed, not for the hard work ahead, but because things had come to such disarray. "Are you nervous?"

"A little."

First day of school, I hadn't heard from Ash in two days, and I was ready to be a dutiful girlfriend.

"Don't be, you've always been great at school. This won't be any different. Well, the classes aren't like anything you've had before, but you'll catch on. Plus, you have Tawny and the rest of your friends. Your brothers seem like the popular types. Study hard, but don't forget to have fun. And, be careful with Ash... I wouldn't want you to have to leave like I did." She gave me a half smile and patted my lap. She started to get ready for the day.

"Mom, we don't...don't worry. I haven't." She raised an eyebrow as if skeptical. "Really, Mom."

"Okay, okay, but if you do, be careful. There's an herbalist there, she'll whip something up for you. Don't be embarrassed either, it's much easier to ask for that than to explain why you have to leave school. You can't take your battle courses in *that* condition. Oh, and here. I picked these up, mostly because I thought your brother should have them, but you should take some too, that'd make my life easier." She smiled apologetically at me.

She handed me a basket. In it was a mound of lambskin condoms. They didn't do latex there.

"Don't give me that look, it's my responsibility to make sure you're looked after." She smiled. "I thought our talk went very well. Why don't you go put them with your things and meet me downstairs for breakfast?"

I would have done anything to escape the awkward conversation.

I rushed out of her room and headed towards my room, the sooner the better. I didn't think I could be any more awkward—until I ran headlong into Slate when I turned the corner for the staircase, effectively knocking down the lambskin condoms my *mother* just gave me to share with my *brother* so she wouldn't have to be awkward.

Mortified.

I said something that may or may not have been words. I didn't know why carrying them made me so flustered. I guessed it was what they implied.

"Busy school year?"

"They're not mine. They're Mom's. Mom got them for Jett. Only some are mine. Maybe she meant you too."

Gibberish. At least he was only kind of looking like he was going to push me down the flight of stairs. He bent down and started to help me collect them up. It was too much for my fragile state of mind.

"Oh, gods, please stop touching them. Please, I got it. Go about your business." His luscious lips curled at my yammering.

"Guardians do not get sexually transmitted infections. I do not use them because most the women I bed have lost their fertility. I doubt you would use even one of these this year, Rabbit."

My blood pressure rocketed and I lashed out with my words.

"You would probably use them all in a single weekend! I possess a modicum of self-worth to know some things should only be given to those who deserve it, not shared with every single thing with a pair of breasts and a pulse!"

I shook with anger. I slapped the condoms out of his hands and put them back in the basket myself.

"As opposed to everything...without breasts and a pulse?" he rumbled and I thought my eyes had begun twitching.

"You might make certain exceptions," I grumbled caustically under my breath.

"Maybe I already have," he retorted and my head shot up.

Was he talking about me? I had great breasts, high and perky perfect globes I was particularly proud of because I was a late bloomer, and I had a steady pulse, thank you very much.

How did we always end up childishly fighting? I got to my feet and *called*. The condoms spun in a swirling vortex above the basket.

"Impressive. I did not think Ash would show you how to use it in other ways than how to give him pleasure."

What was his problem? Was he purposely picking a fight with me? I could rise to the occasion with little effort.

I cocked my hip and gave him a slow sultry smile. "That was the second thing he taught me. The only man I've used my *extensive* talents on."

"Intimacy is called so for a reason. *Calling* is in addition to, not a replacement for. I doubt you have touched him with your hands like you have done to me. You must have seen much more after I passed out since I woke up nearly spotless. Did you enjoy running your hands over me unfettered? I see you kept a memento." Slate had stood up and was closing in on me.

My lips parted; I'd completely forgotten. It was completely justifiable at the time—he was caked in blood, I cleaned it and dressed him. There was nothing sexual about it. He read it in my eyes and his lips curled.

The shadow man was back. It wasn't easy to forget that Slate was an imposing figure, that he could crush my windpipe with a crunch of his fist if he chose, he wouldn't even break a sweat. When he was pushing me up against the wall while I reversed with that look in his eyes, it reminded me why he called me "Rabbit." Bottom of the food chain and Slate was at the top.

"Do you want to touch me again?"

"Stay away from me, Slate Sumar. You're my brother, and you should act like it. I only undressed you because you were covered in blood. You were my patient and I was your nurse. Family takes care of one another. I'm sorry you misread my good intentions." I was flustered and he took advantage.

"Is that what you called what you were doing before we were attacked?" His grey eyes shone silver like a mirror. My back was against the cool wall and he leaned over me. "When I came to, you were clutching me, curled over my body. Your last conscious thought was to protect me. Would you have done all of that for Ash?"

My breath caught. The answer mocked me.

"I told you what happened before the attack. It was blood loss or something. Just forget it. We can at least be friendly to one another. You can treat me like you do Tawny," I said hopefully.

My head was craned back until it touched the wall to look up at him and he glowered above me.

"I will not pretend it did not happen," Slate growled and all of my hopes of returning to normalcy flew out the window.

"Well, you're going to have to because I'm with Ash and he and I make sense, we want the same things." I shook my head and slid sideways from under Slate. "I'm not sorry we were stopped. It was stupid and impulsive," I told him with finality.

Since coming to Tidings I'd really come to appreciate my family and the love we shared for one another and just how complicated it could be. I hadn't spoken to Ash since the induction ceremony. I wondered if he was dumping me—I'd never been in a relationship before, much less been dumped.

It was time to go. We'd had our few items we were bringing—mostly weapons—delivered to our rooms. We were saying our goodbyes to Steel, the women hugging, the men giving their macho back claps and arm clasps.

Poor Steel. He seemed so unlike his usual smiling confident self; he looked tired and downtrodden. I swallowed hard when I hugged him. I didn't see how Tawny could get out of hugging him in front of everyone's watchful eyes, so I hoped it wouldn't be too painful for her. It was that and more.

Tawny stood in front of him arms stiff at her sides as Steel hugged her so tightly he was clenching the back of her dress. She had taken off the ring, and I wondered where she stashed it. Slate put a hand on Steel's shoulder, and the look of crushed hope when he pulled away from her was heartbreaking.

Jett was talking animately about his birthday, drawing the rest of the family's attention while keeping eyes on Steel and Tawny. No one was paying attention to Gypsum who had seen the awkward embrace. His face was clouded, expression unreadable. I didn't think that was a good thing.

In the portal room in Valla, it was pandemonium. Families with their kids were everywhere. Excited tyros laughing and talking, running around to find their friends.

Jett spotted Cherry and waved. Viper and Cherry joined us as we stood waiting for what was to happen next. Pearl and the parents were speaking with Viper, making betrothal plans, no doubt.

I still hadn't seen Ash. I was frustrated by it; I needed his presence to help me with Slate.

His mom was headed our way. "Pearl!" she said. "I did not know you were coming, but oh yes, these are your grandchildren! Hello again, Scarlett, Ash came here last night. That boy! Always training, he didn't want to break from his daily routine."

"Dahlia, these are my other grandchildren, Tawny, Jett, and I believe you have met Gypsum." Dahlia looked at Gyps with mild disdain; I *felt* the heat of anger spring up around Sparrow.

"Yes, I remember." she said, because she was obligated to speak to him. I was beginning to like her less and less.

"And this is my adopted son Slate, my son Hawk, and my daughter Wren, whom I'm sure you remember."

Dahlia's eyes narrowed. "I do remember. How interesting."

She caught sight of Sparrow angled behind Hawk and Gyps. To say that she was shocked would be an understatement. She forgot herself entirely and gaped. "Hi, Dahlia. How very *nice* to see you again," Sparrow said coolly.

"Oh! I did not realize...your children?" She pointed a long-nailed pale finger at Tawny and Gypsum.

Sparrow nodded. "Hawk is my husband." Dahlia's eyes widened again.

Her eyelids fluttered as she tried to compose herself. "Well, there are surprises all around. Well, I am the first years' headmistress; you may address me as Headmistress Natt. Come along." She turned and headed to another group of people.

Dahlia collected nearly a hundred students and their families. A stern-looking man with long black hair combed away from his face and tilted eyes came to collect the men and their families. Pearl and my mom went with Slate and Jett, although it took some reassurance on my part. I'd had my mom my whole life; she could have this with Jett and Slate.

Hawk and Sparrow came with Tawny and me. Tawny was trying hard not to appear dour, but it was an uphill battle. Cherry and her dad were right behind us, talking his ear off.

Valla University was bigger than I originally thought. We bypassed the only rooms I had known previously, so I was completely lost. Then we went down two very long flights of stone stairs, passing a series of stained-glass arched windows, and down to the left. The girls' wing.

Dahlia spoke as she directed us. "This entire wing is dedicated to the young women training here at Valla University for Guardian Mastery. The entire third floor is for the first years. It is four girls to a room. Some of you have already selected your roommates; for the rest of you, we will assign you as we go. There are two lavatories at the ends of the hall, and this is your sitting room."

Dahlia had led us to the center of the hall that opened out into a large room with several sofas and tables spread out across large Persian rugs. Two fireplaces were lit on opposite sides of the yellow stone walled room. The place looked ancient.

"If you would please follow me again so we can assign your young women to their rooms. I should note that while not against the rules, it is strongly discouraged to have gentlemen here, ladies. The only two rules are no parties of any sort, and no fighting. Save it for the battle grounds." Dahlia said it with her annoying air of superiority.

The third room she called was ours.

Tapestries hung on the walls that weren't occupied by sconces or mirrors. There weren't any windows except for the stained-glass ceiling depicting a woman made of sunlight and a man of darkness embracing. Across from the door were two beds nestled in a large arched alcove. Braided pillars divided the room's three alcoves, another bed to the left, and one to the right.

Indigo rushed in late. "Sorry, we went with Sage first. How's it going? Isn't it exciting? I can't wait to get settled in already."

Alder and his wife came in right behind her. We stiffened. By we, I mean Hawk, Sparrow, Alder, and myself. I hadn't expected to see my father. The thought hadn't even crossed my mind. I *did* visualize Jett and I coming over to Indigo's house one day to hang out and him crying out that he wished he could be in our lives and we all lived happily ever after, but not this. Never this. I'd never seen Hawk angry before. It was frightening. I couldn't blame him for being angry with my father. My mom was his twin sister, he had every right to be upset with him for what he did to our family.

My dad spoke. "Hawk. This is unexpected."

His voice was deep, like it echoed out from a bottomless cavern. He consumed the room with presence.

"You remember my wife Delta." It wasn't a question; Alder said it as a warning.

I could see Hawk's teeth grind as he contemplated speaking to him. "Alder, Delta. I hear our girls our friends."

He *also* made it sound like a warning.

The statuesque woman gave a flash of teeth. Her blonde hair pulled away from her face in waves. Her blue eyes could freeze ice. She was fair-skinned, and quite possibly the most beautiful woman I'd ever seen in person or otherwise. My poor mom: *that* was who she'd competed against...and lost. My mom with her dark long hair and dark eyes, a wide mouth always ready with a sweet smile. No, that woman was ice personified. My mother was warmth and home personified.

I hated to admit that they made a stunning couple. They could've even passed for siblings. I was disappointed that I didn't look much like him.

"My, my, it has been some time," the icy blonde purred.

The ice queen's eyes appraised Sparrow. "It has, and now I'm back. Good to see some things haven't changed."

It didn't sound like a compliment. The blonde's smile chilled me to the bone.

"Indigo, dear, who *are* your friends?"

It sounded polite, but I knew when I was being spoken down to. I wasn't going to let the woman who ruined my mother's life belittle me.

"Pleased to meet you. I'm Scarlett."

My father's eyes were on me. He didn't look surprised.

"Scarlett Tio."

He was trying to see himself in me, I *felt* it. He was controlling his emotions very well. It was frustrating. I wanted to know what he thought of me, be given any sign he wanted to know me better.

Delta looked amused; the expression was in conflict with the *loathing* wafting from her. It threatened to suffocate me.

"A day *full* of surprises. I did not think there were any Tio girls. Your mother is...?" I didn't need to say it, it was obvious.

But I did anyway. "Wren Tio," I said clear and crisp. I wanted my mother to be proud of me.

"I thought so. I was sorry about your father. Lark was a rare man. Who are your other friends, Indigo?"

I *felt* her loathing spike and then it turned cool. It *felt* menacing. The emotions never touched her cold beauty. Alder was standing stiffly next to Delta. Indigo was rummaging through her trunk and managed to miss the entire interlude.

"That is Cerise," said Indigo, and Cherry waved as she lay on her bed, elbows propping up her head. "And Tawny—she and Scarlett are cousins," Indigo continued, turning to her closet.

I felt like it was even *worse* introducing Tawny to Delta than it was to introduce myself and I was my father's lovechild from his affair with my mother.

It must have been a great surprise because shock registered on her face, almost as much as Dahlia's. Sparrow moved to stand in front of Tawny and Gypsum, Hawk next to her. I was suddenly frightened.

"I can see the resemblance," Delta said, softly scrutinizing Tawny with pursed lips. "*This* has been most informative."

Alder and Hawk locked eyes. Somehow Delta had made her statement sound like a threat. I hadn't the faintest clue as to what was going on. Alder kept his face smooth but his emotions were radiating alarm. I wanted to get them out of the room before my mom and Pearl came.

"Indigo, we're supposed to meet in the dining hall as soon as you're settled."

"Sure thing. It's all here, I'm ready."

Indigo gave her mother a kiss and hugged *our* dad. Alder watched me as they hugged. I *felt* a mingling of regret sadness and guilt. *Good.* I didn't know how hard it would be to watch him acknowledge Indigo as his daughter, but not me.

Hawk must have noticed; he turned away from them to give me a squeeze. "Everything will be okay," he said as if he understood.

Sparrow was saying goodbye to Tawny, who looked rattled. Gypsum had his eyes narrowed. I could tell he didn't know what was going on either, but he knew it wasn't good.

The Vars left and Sparrow gave me a hug goodbye. "Be good, study hard," she said, visibly shaken.

Gypsum said his goodbyes and they left. The four of us were getting ready to leave the room when I recognized my mother's voice in the hall. I busied myself near the door so I could overhear.

"The Vetrs know. Now we wait to see what happens. There's nothing else we can do," Hawk said.

"They would have known from Dahlia," Pearl replied.

"No sense in worrying yet," my mother said soothingly.

"I hadn't counted on feeling vulnerable when it came out. Maybe this was a mistake. We were safe in Chicago," Sparrow said, thinking out loud.

"We were always vulnerable. Now they just know how much. It

would not have been right to keep the children from their heritage. This is where we belong," Hawk told her.

"Ready?" Indigo asked me and I jumped.

My mom and Pearl came in. "Sorry it took so long, we'll let you get to orientation."

"Indigo, this is my mom, Wren Tio."

"Pleased to have finally met you," Indigo said, her beautiful face smiling.

I couldn't have anticipated my mom's reaction. She paled and hugged Indigo, not speaking. I couldn't see Indigo's face, but I knew she was uncomfortable.

"I am Pearl Tio, Scarlett and Tawny's grandmother."

Pearl held out her elegant hand and my mom was forced to let Indigo go. She gave me a hug, kissed Tawny's cheek and left the room. Pearl said her goodbyes and then it was just us girls.

"Your mom's a hugger," Indigo said jokingly as we walked to the dining hall.

I shrugged. "Empty nest or something."

The dining hall was much longer than it was wide, with extended tables and benches along its marbled floors. Sculpted pillars lined the rooms and sculptures of people lined the edges of the ceiling, looking down at us. Chandeliers were on each side of the hall, two by two all the way down. The most amazing part was the ceiling. Between chiseled rafters were circular, stained-glass mosaics depicting the phases of the moon so realistic it looked like someone had pressed the moon into the ceiling.

At the head of the hall was a fireplace, with long windows on either side. The head tables for the provosts were before them. The dining hall was teeming with movement. Cherry knew a lot of people, and was talking to everyone we passed. Jett spotted us and waved us over. We sat towards the middle of the hall and were told the left side facing the provosts was for first years, right second years. Our headmistress and headmaster sat at a table directly in front of the first tables. The provosts were wearing their robes, black with a thick silver trim, sleeveless with the university sigil on back in silver. Only the headmistresses and masters wore black robes with gold trim. Moon's had both, his sigil designed with both silver and gold.

Moon sat at the centermost table with my Great Uncle Reed, Fern, Dahlia, and Basil. I was surprised Basil was there, but then again, his offices were at Valla U so I supposed it made sense. Poor Diamond must never have them around. I wondered what it would be like to grow up competing with the past for my parents' attention.

Moon's booming voice echoed over the hall when he stood. "Good morning, future Guardians. I trust you have all been settled into your rooms. I would like to introduce you to some of your provosts and other staff here at Valla University for Guardian Mastery. Some of you have already been introduced; your patience is appreciated. First year tyros have already been introduced to Headmistress Natt who teaches History, and Headmaster Boa Sunna who teaches Nurture and Growth."

They inclined their heads.

"Second years' headmistress is Fern Rot, Mistress of Ceremony, and headmaster is Sky Tio, provost of Counter Calling. To my right is Reed Tio, martinet of Valla University, and you do *not* want to be sent to him. Our librarian and keeper of history is Claviger Basil Straumr. The others you are sure to meet in good time. First year students have been divided into two classes. The tyros with schedule *Ask,* please follow Headmaster Boa, tyros with schedules *Embala,* please follow Headmistress Dahlia. Your schedule names will be at the bottom of the page you received at your induction. Have strength, be courageous, stay humble," Moon said before he sat back down.

"You're in the Embala course?" Jett asked us.

"We are." I gestured to Tawny and myself. "Looks like you lucked out. Cherry and Indigo are with you."

I hoped Jett would take Indigo under his wing, and not in his lecherous way he had women who weren't related to him.

Jett nodded. "Slate's with us too. What about lover boy? Where's he at?"

"Beats me."

I knew who he meant. I still hadn't seen Ash. I tried not to be bummed out that I wouldn't see either Jett or Slate for most of the day.

"You should go—Provost Boa is crazy intense," Cherry said, pointing towards the dark-haired man that other trainees students were standing around.

"See you guys later," Tawny said, and we hurried to our course group.

Our first class was History, and it was on the second floor. Only one wide, beautifully sculpted staircase away. Boa was silent during our entire walk; he didn't seem much like the talking type, which was surprising since he was a teacher. He guided us through heavy wood doors and into a classroom. There were tiers of stone steps with mismatched pillows resting side by side. They were seats—we could pull up a wooden surface from behind the back of the tier in front of us to use as a desk

The room was lit by artfully crafted pewter sconces in the yellowed stone walls. I wondered if all the rooms were rounded like this one was, with no corners. I half expected some great orator to come deliver an enlightening speech in front of Dahlia's desk.

Ash was in my course. I was unexpectedly irritated that he didn't spot me right away. Maybe he was waiting for me to make the first move, but he was the one to leave me at the induction ceremony; I deserved an explanation. Maybe I was starting to like him after all, or maybe I had a thing for unattainable men. Or *maybe* I was still going through puberty and had raging psychotic hormones.

I sat in the third row between Tawny and a pretty redheaded girl. Ash was with Sage, climbing the stairs to the top tiers of seating, when he gave me a small smile. It was hardly a smile, more like a slight curl of his lips. I fumed.

He waved off Sage, who rolled his round blue eyes, and sat at the top tier. Ash asked the redhead if they could trade. She blushed so her skin matching her hair, and quickly got up for him. He gave her his best smile and somehow she blushed deeper red.

It was just a pretty face. Okay, a gorgeous face.

My attraction to him was confounding. He greeted Tawny first. That made it more irritating. He threw an arm around my shoulders and whispered into my ear. Breath tickling my neck, giving me a tingling even more unexpected than the rest of my current emotions.

"I missed you," he cooed.

I could feel his teeth near my earlobe.

I couldn't resist. "I'm sorry, what's your name again?"

Even his cocky smile didn't annoy me. "I could help you remember."

His voice was low, but I still blushed. He ran his warm invisible fingers up my thigh and I gave him a nudge. He chuckled. If he was this man all the time, I could really see us together. But...he still hadn't given me an explanation.

The guy sitting behind us cleared his throat loudly and I blushed again before glancing back and getting caught by a smile so salacious, I didn't make it past his teeth before whipping back around.

Dahlia Natt walked in. She spotted Ash's arm around me and pressed her lips into a firm line. He chuckled and removed it.

She *called* our history books out and passed them to us. "The History of the Guardians. Most of you have a basic background of our origins and past occurrences; I am here to elaborate. I will give a general briefing of what we will learn today." Her eyes passed over me. "Some of you do not." She frowned. "Let me know if you cannot keep up."

I hoped there was another person besides me and Tawny from outside of Tidings there. Tawny was trying to give me a dry look in my periphery without Ash noticing.

Dahlia had a computer—a real computer! It was completely out of place in the castle. The way she looked at it, made me think she hadn't resorted to using it until recently. I guessed there were some things technology was still good for.

Her computer was linked to a projector that displayed the images her computer was showing. The first one was a woman made up of a tree, her arms held out to the sky like tree branches.

"Mother Nature, as depicted in this picture, found herself in need of

Guardians. She asked her Leshys to find a worthy man and woman—Tio and Straumr. To them she gave a gift: the gift of elements. Long before you or I, Guardians could turn into elements. Tio and Straumr were the first elemental humans. Mother Nature knew it would not be enough and so she created an island out of the homes of the endangered races, or tribes as you now know them."

She switched slides to one of a landmass that resembled a hand surrounded by water.

"This island was called *Tidings* prior to the Storm/Wind debacle that separated the islands. Unfortunately for those early Guardians, times were not as easy as they are now. Please read the first chapter silently and have the questions at the end completed for the day after tomorrow."

Our first homework assignment. Contrary to what I would've thought, I was enraptured, and I was seriously thinking of reading the entire history book over the weekend.

We read for the remainder of the class. I didn't know what to expect at the end of class, I couldn't imagine a school bell. The chapter was fascinating: apparently Leshys were the caretakers of the Yggdrasil, our tree of life,we had there in Valla. They are rarely ever seen—one hadn't been spotted in half a century.

A sound like church bells rang.

"That is the end of class. I will see you the day after tomorrow," Dahlia noted.

The students waited another few minutes at the door; we were supposed to wait for Boa to escort us.

Ash was being unusually sweet to me. I really liked this version of him. I even let him kiss me in the hall before Boa gave us a look. Ash just chuckled. Perhaps he'd been possessed.

Note to self: ask if poltergeists exist.

The next class was Energies and Wights. The class was taught by the reserved redhead I'd met at my Uncle Reed's, Wisteria Rot. She taught with the same crisp coolness in which she spoke, brooking no nonsense.

Which was good for me, because learning that when I died I could become a wave in the ocean that guarded the local ecosystem was a lot to swallow. I could admit, it would be pretty cool. I wouldn't want to forget my friends and family though. They said there was even a wight at Central Park! Wights were Guardians who had shown great sacrifice and were given the choice to pass on when they died, or continue to balance nature as nature itself, like a rock formation or a tree. It was a big deal to be chosen.

We went through our Tribal Affairs class taught by the sweet redheaded mother of Copper, Butterfly Rot. There were a bunch of different tribes—I couldn't keep track of all the names. What I did find interesting was that the Red Kings who led the massacre of Yuletide were half crab people, the Crathode. She had slides and they looked positively terrifying. I wanted to think like the Guardian motto and want all living things to prosper, but they looked like they were built for destruction.

Their tribe name was Crathode, which sounded harmless enough. But names can be deceiving, they were five to seven feet tall with as many as six legs! They all had claws, big crushing claws. The Red King Massacre took on a different light for me after that. Imagining a group of attacking half crab people was horrifying.

We had arithmetic with Magnolia Rot, the uber-curvy twin sister of Wisteria. The way Magnolia waved to the pretty redhead next to me made me think she was her daughter; it was confirmed when the girl rolled her eyes.

It was time for lunch after the bell rang. Boa led us back to the dining hall. Platters of food were already laid out. Ash had interlocked my fingers with his own.

"I am sitting with Sage, are you coming? Tawny may come along."

Ash invited us to sit with my half brother. I already had enough of family for the day, new family anyway.

"I was going to see how Jett's day was going, if it's cool?" I didn't want it to come out as a question, but...

He looked around the tables to spot Jett. Slate was with him.

"I will walk you."

I sighed; I guessed it was just how it was going to be. Slate and Ash were never going to be best friends.

As we approached, Slate saw us and his eyes darkened. I fought the urge to release Ash's hand; that would *not* make him very happy.

"Hey, guys!" I said cheerfully as we walked up, Tawny in tow. She sat down next to Cherry. "I'll meet you after lunch?" I asked Ash.

He pulled me to him, pressing me firmly to his body and gave me a slow, deep kiss. More than one person was watching. The provosts present were not amused.

He released me, flashing that fabulous smile.

"Reminds me of spiced apples," Slate said, and Ash stiffened.

What was this?

Ash's eyes swung to mine, and his light green eyes burned. "You and him?"

I was dumbfounded.

"I was talking about the meal." Slate growled, curling his lips.

"Scarlett, would you *please* come with me?" Ash eyes flared against his caramel skin.

"Sorry," I muttered, not exactly sure what I was apologizing about as I got up from the bench I was attempting to slide into and Ash grabbed my hand, leading me away.

Boa guided us to our next class, American History with Hawk. All the classes had the same tiered seating—it made finding a seat easy because you always went to the same one.

Tawny gave me a look when we met up with our course group and I gave a quick shake of my head so she wouldn't ask questions in front of Ash.

Tawny and I approached Hawk. "Excuse me, Provost Sumar," Tawny teased.

He gave her an indulgent smile. "I didn't know they had set you guys up with this class. Seems a bit redundant. We won't really be learning any history, more like a general idea of the outside world so kids wishing to go to college have some basic information. I can't tell you how hard it was when we first moved to Chicago."

"That's what we came to talk to you about. We were thinking we could take another battle class or something to help make up for the time we've lost not having grown up here?"

Way to go, Tawny; truth with a sprinkling of guilt.

"That should be fine. I'll write you a note."

Not that sitting through Hawk's class would've been bad in the least; we would have aced it, but I liked battle training.

I walked over to Ash. "Looks like you'll be on your own. I know my American history." I smiled.

He looked annoyed. "I had not thought of that. I should have seen if my father could have put us in something else."

I knit my brows. "What do you mean?"

"I made sure our classes were together. My father does the schedules."

"Oh. That must be nice. Not sick of me yet?" I said playfully.

"Not yet." He was serious.

Hawk told us the battlegrounds were at the back of the school, so we went down to the first floor and began looking for them. Turns out there were a myriad of rooms on the first floor. After finding two bathrooms, a massive kitchen, and the dining hall, through a different door than we usually used, we found a preparation room, *finally*.

Like most things at the university, there were two prep rooms. We gambled with which one was ours and entered. No urinals; good sign. We changed into our black pants, boots, and close-fitting drawstring tops. Our gear was still in our rooms, but it wouldn't take long to grab it if we needed it. I *did* have my black seax Slate had bought me. I wore it almost every day now, trying to get used to it. I strapped it over my pant leg.

The battlegrounds were, well, *insane.* I expected gladiators to come racing out at us. A track spanned the tiered stone seating, but an enormous globe of a dome capped the room. Also like ours, there was a section for weights and archery. The combat ring did not have padded floors. I hoped that would change or I was going to need a ton of healing.

"Ladies, what can I do for you? Ditching on the first day?" It was Fox, the youngest brother of the Straumr men. He was caramel-skinned with big, playful, blue eyes. "Scarlett, and your cousin, right? Tawny?"

Tawny smiled for the first time all day. He was pretty cute and he had to be year of the Canis. Not too old for us to flirt with.

"Hey Fox! We got permission to opt out of American History since we grew up there, outside of Tidings." I may or may not have given him a flirty smile. I didn't really know how to flirt so it didn't count.

Please let him be the Hand-to-Hand Combat provost.

"I see." He said reading Hawk's note. "Well, I guess I do not have much going on this period so your welcomed to train with me. What are your specialties? I do not have the list your trainers sent over on me."

"Blades and archery," I told him, pointing to Tawny.

"Hmm...what do you want to work on?"

"I've been in a fight before, but I'm not entirely comfortable with my blades." I confessed.

"Yeah, you look a little soft for a cutthroat." Fox laughed at his own joke. "How about I teach you some holds and Tawny can do some stationary target practice? Go get your gear and you can store it in the prep room permanently." Tawny and I took off at a trot so we could get our weapons.

When we came back he was ready for us. Tawny strung her bow, sitting on the ground as usual, then headed towards her target. Fox brought me over to the combat circle. I'd switched into the boots Hawk had given me, tucked my boot daggers into them, and buckled my belt of throwing daggers. Fox helped buckle on my wrist blades.

"Quite the arsenal. You said you have only just been introduced to it?"

I nodded.

"The last day of training, my trainer told me I should pursue blades. So here I am."

He led me over to the rows of combat dummies. "Who trained you?"

"Slate," I informed him, and he began to chuckle, making me grimace.

"I bet he decided on blades. Has he offered you any late-night training yet? Let us see how you do, and I will speak to your trainer to make sure his assessment was not influenced by...other matters."

I could only nod, as embarrassed as I was.

"First things first: you need to be comfortable with your specific blades. Are you?" I shook my head reluctantly. "I did not think so. No problem, everyone has to start somewhere. There are two common holds, forward and reverse grips. Let us start with two of each for now. This is the hammer grip." Fox took out his own seax and held his fingers around the handle like you would a hammer, pretty self-explanatory. "This is the saber grip." He wrapped his hand back around the knife but moved the thumb to its spine. "Or this way," he said, his thumb now resting on the flat side of the handle. "Reverse grips,. This is a slash attack." He held the edge away from himself knife pointed down in his fist. "And finally, for now, ice pick grip." He held the knife the way they did slasher flicks; I could almost I heard the *ree ree ree* from *Psycho*.

"Got it. What about these bad boys?" I held my wrist blades up and moved my pinky fingers to let the blades spring.

"Whoa, buddy. Start small first. We need to work on your flexibility and reflexes before you start brandishing those."

"I'm quick as a cat!" I told him, hopping from foot to foot, flashing him my biggest megawatt grin.

"Okay, okay, killer." Fox laughed. "We will improve them then. Just work on getting comfortable with them. Today Crag is teaching both courses. After dinner, you can come back and get some more training in. Either my brothers or I will be around." He smiled. It was a killer smile.

I bet girls who weren't a decade younger than him really fell for it, you know, because it wasn't working on me.

Boa came in, leading our class, so Tawny and I put our weapons back in the prep room. Crag was in the battle room when we returned.

He had sat everyone on the stone tiers. We snuck in down front. Dahlia was leading her class in now, and I waved to Jett. Indigo was with Sterling, and they headed up to where Ash and Sage were, Jonquil on her tail. *Ugh.* Slate joined my brother next to us.

"Most important part of battle training is to know your weaknesses," Crag began without preamble. "If you are big and strong, chances are you are slow, so to compensate, be stronger, be bigger. If you are small, you might be quick, so be faster. Then work on your weaknesses. While you are with me every third day, I will have you divided into weight training and cardio." He gestured to the track. "During the course of the lesson, I will call you up one by one and do hand-to-hand combat. Ask course you are on weights first, no slacking. Embala, better get running. You do not stop until I say. Do not forget to stretch first."

When it came time to fight Crag, I lasted about two seconds—the amount of time it took to cross the combat circle. There were no pads. My back slammed on the bouncy grey turf. I was *definitely* going to need healing after that.

More than a few of the guys held their own. A couple landed more blows than they took, but still lost. I was only a little surprised that Sterling and Sage did so well. Sterling was built like Steel, lean but toned with a broad chest. He was fast. Sage was lightning quick, even faster than Sterling; he was wiry strong and thin. Jett did really well—I felt bad for not expecting him to, but I had never seen him take anything seriously before. He transformed in the combat circle. He became a fighter. He still had that smug smile while he fought, but it was taunting.

Then there was the Regn guy; I had decided to start calling him Trouble with that smile of his. Watching Trouble, Ash, and Slate battle Crag was frightening. I kept thinking that someone was going to get seriously hurt. They were the only ones to beat Crag and earn bragging rights.

Tawny was nowhere to be found so I went to find Indigo. She found me first. She healed my back, thankfully, just a scrape, and we headed to the dining hall. I felt bad about the morning so after I found Ash and planted a very convincing kiss on him, I went to have dinner with my brother and Tawny.

"That man of yours is a fox," Cherry, said giving me a *Am I right?* face as I sat down across from the trio next to Tawny.

"Hey!" Jett said in mock protest.

"Not foxier than you." Cherry leaned into Jett.

Amethyst smirked on Jett's other side. Being the Prime's daughter had perks: she sat wherever she pleased.

Slate scoffed from the other side of Tawny. "How did lover boy take it?" I breathed and counted to five. I was going to ignore him.

"How was everyone's day?"

Slate interrupted. "Better after Ash knew I had been with you."

Jett narrowed his eyes at Slate. Tawny was taking my rabbit approach of freezing perfectly still. Amethyst was right there, and Ash was her cousin. Cherry laughed.

"I was never *with* you," I tried to say as evenly as possible. "And Ash knows that. What was that apples comment?"

Slate chuckled. "You taste like vanilla and spiced apples. Ash knows that." The insides of my ears burned.

"Just what have you done with my sister?" Jett asked out of genuine curiosity.

Slate had implied a lot. Jett gave me a look like, *What's said here is between us, Amethyst included.*

"Nothing!" I said in a shouted whisper. "Slate, have we had sex, ever, in any way? Tell him honestly!"

"No, but there are many other things to do besides sex, Rabbit. You should know that by now," he growled.

Jett narrowed his green eyes, so much like mine at me. I was shaking my head in disbelief. Jett turned back to Slate and pointed at him with his fork.

"You *like* her." Jett laughed again. "Too late, brother. She's made her choice. Ash already has her jumping when he says to."

"What?" I asked, my temper flaring.

"I'm not judging. This afternoon, when he said jump, you didn't even ask how high, you started jumping until you found the height he was satisfied with. I wish these two listened that well." Jett gestured to his future wives to either side of him with his fork.

"Don't listen to this buffoon," Amethyst said, rolling her eyes.

"She will come around," Slate interrupted.

"Ash is possessive and spoiled. Even I can tell you aren't the kind of girl who will be controlled easily, it is probably part of the appeal," Amethyst continued.

"I could control her easily, it worked—" Slate started.

"Enough!" Tawny yelled, slapping the tabletop.

My face was on fire. My appetite had completely vanished. The clinking of silverware on glass plates was going to drive me insane. I wanted silence.

"Scarlett can do whatever she wants with her beau or whomever. Ash is her first suitor, it's trial and error. Cut her some fiddlesticking slack!"

Tawny fair, heart-shaped face was red. I didn't think this was just about me, but I appreciated the fervent support.

Cherry's red lips parted so her jaw hung open. Her bright blue eyes widened as she leaned in, but the concept of whispering was entirely foreign to her.

"You mean you've never..." She made an obscene hand gesture that made Jett laugh and I groaned.

I pushed my plate away and straightened my dress over my hips as I stood.

Tawny seemed to be looking everywhere else but at me.

Tawny was the only person I'd ever told. Even though my high school had started rumors, it was only speculation, and I'd never confirmed it.

"Scar, I've healed you enough times to know..." Tawny said giving me an awkward smile.

"To know what?" I asked peevishly.

"A maiden. I knew for certain when we fought the bauk," Slate said matter-of-factly.

"It is nothing to be ashamed of—though you are the only one at Valla U." Cherry gave Tawny a wink, and I had heard enough.

Everyone was too busy eating to notice my purposeful gait towards the back of the hall where Ash ate with his friends and Indigo. But suddenly my hand was yanked back and my feet almost flew out from under me.

"Come back to the table. We are going to celebrate Jett's birthday. You would not want to miss your brother's birthday the first year you have a chance to celebrate it." Slate's big hand gripped my wrist like a vise.

There was a protracted silence. Neither of us wanted to give. "I may not have slept with the whole island of Thrimilci, and I know it's inconceivable to you that I *had* had sex and still wouldn't want you, but did you have to make me feel like such an idiot?"

Slate's broad chest rose and fell with a deep steadying breath. "Are you finished?" I opened my mouth to say something else biting, but he placed a firm, strong finger over my lips. "Do not say or do something you might regret, Rabbit."

Slate possessed an uncanny ability to perceive my thoughts and predict my actions. I'd have to learn to keep my cool around him, control my facial expressions—I had a feeling my face betrayed me. I let Slate lead me back to the table. Tawny looked like her shoulders relaxed. Jett watched where Slate's hand clasped my wrist.

His chiseled tan face looked at me, his arrogant jaw jutted. "Will I ever get to meet the boyfriend who had the gall to try to deflower you?" Jett asked as if I'd never gotten up.

"He was never my boyfriend. I saw him the night before we moved here and unless we go back to Chicago, I never will again," I muttered.

"*You* had a one-night stand? No, I don't believe it," Jett said, incredulous.

"It's in the past. I don't want to talk about it." My emotions were struggling free and I fought with the want to run and hide. "Does anyone care if I invite Ash tonight?" I asked changing the subject.

"Yes," Slate said immediately.

"Anyone other than Slate," I said, exasperated that I even bothered.

"I think that's a great idea," Amethyst chirped, her dark eyes narrowing at Jett who didn't look so keen on the idea. "His birthday is in two days so it can be a joint birthday celebration."

I had no idea when Ash's birthday was, so I was glad she mentioned it and that I hadn't given him the bracers I'd bought yet.

"I guess he *is* your boyfriend. It would be weird if we didn't invite him," Jett conceded.

CHAPTER 16

 Ash thanked me with a very passionate kiss for his birthday/induction ceremony present and had delighted in the invite. I let him know we would just be hanging out in Jett's bedroom at home and drinking since we couldn't party at the university. He said he wanted to see me in my element.

Very good, Mr. Straumr.

Steel waited for us upstairs in his room. The doors between the bathrooms were open so it was like a hotel suite. Steel was stupefied upon Tawny's entrance. Tawny was *trying* to ignore him, *trying* being the operative word.

Steel had brought up a water pipe and a half dozen pitchers of wassail.

"There's more where that came from," Steel told Jett and they started drinking.

The guys were feeling good as we sat around Jett's sitting room laughing. Ash sat on the rug and leaned against the chair Tawny was in, with his legs splayed so I could sit between them and shifted against his chest. His charm was on full throttle; he could fit in whenever he wanted to, and it helped that Amethyst made a point of including him.

"We should play a game. I would suggest flip, sip, or strip, but my little sister is here."

Jett gave me his best lecherous grin. The girls giggled.

"I would not mind." Ash gave me his cockiest grin and kissed my cheek as it heated.

Slate sat across the low table from us and his grey eyes burned. I wasn't sure if Ash noticed or not, but I couldn't *not* notice.

"Quarters," Tawny blurted.

She wasn't talking, she was barely even moving. It was a good thing too, because every time Steel *thought* she moved his gaze turned to her.

"We don't have quarters here but we do have silver Crescents. That should work," Steel told her, probably hoping she'd look his way.

He pulled out a silver Crescent and held it up to her. She opened her palm and he dropped it in with a sigh. Steel put a half-filled pitcher in the center of Jett's table and round and round we went, aiming to get the Crescent into the pitcher.

We were all feeling slap happy. I wasn't sure if we were going to head back to our rooms tonight or not. I felt a little guilty we didn't invite Indigo, but with luck, she'd forgive us. She would spend her first night away at school alone since Cherry was here with Tawny and me.

Things started to get awkward with Jett and the girls. Their playful petting turning heavy. There may or may not have been some moaning. It was time to leave, and the rest of us did. Jett kicked the door closed and all we heard was giggling and growling.

Steel shut his bathroom doors and that did little to help. It was Steel, Tawny, Slate, Ash and I in Steel's sitting area. I thought Tawny would want to leave, she and Steel not being on the best of terms, but she was still there. We played another round of quarters with the Crescent and Slate gave the pitcher to Tawny. He hadn't given it to me or Ash once.

Steel and Tawny were getting closer and closer on the couch. I could see their fingers straining for one another's hands. I felt like I was blocking on my girl Tawny. I had to get Ash, Slate, and myself out of here.

"Hey guys, we should go get some more pitchers. We're all out."

I tried to give Slate my *You're supposed to be his wingman, we should let them get to it* face. Slate was amused, his full lips curling. He stood up and, lo and behold, had to straighten himself. Slate might have been wasted. It gave me some weird satisfaction, as if until that point I thought he might not be completely human, and I now realized that he did have flaws.

Ash's eyes were hooded as he looked at me and I chewed the inside of my cheek. How did I get myself into this position?

"We'll be back," I said, with no intention of doing so.

Before I closed the door, Steel had scooped Tawny up.

"What is your plan?" Slate asked, dangerously close behind me.

I turned from the door and looked up at him. Ash was in front of me; he hadn't seen Steel and Tawny, thank the Gods.

"I hadn't thought that far ahead. We could go train?" I asked, somewhat skeptical of my ability to run, fight, or move.

Ash laughed. "If I did not know better, I would think you were afraid to have me in your bedroom." He raised his winged eyebrows at me, his sculpted lips curling.

"I could train," Slate interrupted.

The moaning could have been coming from Jett's room, but I was sure it was coming from Steel's, so I started walking. When I stopped at Slate's bedroom door, I could feel him bristle behind me.

"Goodnight, Slate," I said firmly and took Ash's hand to lead him to the stairs.

Slate watched us until I turned the corner.

Ash was still in my bed when I woke up. I wiped condensation from the mirror and felt the love bites along my neck that led lower.

Ash lay naked in my bed. I could see the top half of his back, while his head rested on his arms. Every time I looked at him, I couldn't believe we were together. His back managed to be defined even as he slept, and the curve that led under the blankets...I shook my head. I had first-hand experience with just how tight those buns were.

I sat on the satin comforter next to Ash and kissed along his spine. He stirred and turned to me. Even just waking up, his smile was cocky, and for good reason. He rolled onto his back and saw that I was ready.

"What time is it?" he asked, sleep thick in his voice making it deep and sexy.

"Classes start in an hour. I wasn't sure how much time you needed to get ready," I said with a smile.

He ran a long-fingered hand over his dark, shaved head. "About fifteen minutes. Although I did not get much beauty sleep last night." He raised his brows suggestively and pulled the top of my robe down to kiss me. His lips were oh-so-soft. "Do we have time for an encore?" he purred.

I blushed furiously. "I should really see how Indigo's first night went alone. I feel terrible that I didn't invite her to come with."

Ash sat up and my blue satin blanket pooled in his lap, exposing all those lean muscles in his chest and abs. "You should have; Slate would have liked her."

He left it at that. He was in a good mood, no disparaging remarks about Slate—that was a first.

"Do you mind if I shower here?" he asked, seeing I'd already showered and looking disappointed.

"Of course you can. Make sure you lock the door to Tawny's room so she doesn't get an eyeful," I teased. It would much more than an eyeful, I'd discovered last night.

He slid off the bed and gave me a long kiss as he strode naked to the bathroom. The man had more confidence in one finger than I did in my entire body.

I lay back in the bed going through what had happened last night. I had wanted all of it, every bit of it, and it had surprised me. That didn't stop my stomach from roiling this morning, though. I felt guilty, no regret, just horribly guilty.

By the time I was ready to go, Ash was out of the bathroom, his body glistening with water.

"You are certainly a sight in the morning," I told him with a smirk.

"Of course. I spent the night with the most beautiful girl at Valla U, possibly in all of Tidings. I have reason to be in a good mood." He let his towel drop, and yes, he was in a good mood.

My eyes widened as he grabbed me and pulled me towards him. His hand wrapped in my hair as his lips found my throat.

"Flatterer," I breathed, and he smiled against my skin.

It was like a scene from *Mission: Impossible*. I was peeking around hall corners and making Ash trot with me so we wouldn't run into anyone while we walked to the portal room. Ash laughed when I exhaled as we entered the empty portal room. We'd made it completely unseen.

"Whoa! What do we have here? Are those the same clothes from last night, Ash?" Jett was nearly shouting and I whipped around to find Jett, the girls, Tawny, and Slate walking into the portal room.

"They are. Though your sister was kind enough to let me shower," Ash said flashing a cocky smile.

Under the blue lights of the portal room, Slate looked demonic. I kept my gaze from him out of sheer fear. Amethyst was giving me a knowing smile and Cherry was waggling thin, black eyebrows at me.

"She let you spend the night?" Slate asked as if it was any of his business.

"We did not exactly sleep, but yes, I was in her bed if that is what you are asking." Ash kissed my neck and it shifted my hair that I had strategically placed over my shoulder to cover a portion of my cleavage.

Jett's eyes fell right to my neckline and he took a step forward. "I'll heal that for you. Wouldn't want people talking," he said, keeping his voice light, but his eyes were hard.

"I am sorry, Scarlett. Forgive me." Ash slung his arm around my waist, and we walked through the portal door, but not before I saw Slate's snarl as Jett held up an arm against his chest.

At lunch, I sat with Ash, Indigo, and their friends for the next two weeks. The university took up all of my time. I didn't even go back to see my family on the weekend, so I told Tawny to tell them I was swamped with homework. Which technically wasn't a lie.

Tawny didn't ask what happened that night, and I didn't tell her; she knew I would if I needed to talk. Word had spread fast that Ash had spent the night. It was like high school all over again. I couldn't believe the rumors of the things that had been said that we'd done—some of which I didn't even know what they were.

The hardest part about dedicating myself to Ash was seeing Tawny and Jett together at lunch and not being able sit with them. I could've, but I was avoiding Slate (who ate with them) like the plague. Thankfully, he was so tall I could usually spot him coming and run the other way.

I *did* ask Tawny what had happened between her and Steel that night, as if I didn't know. They were secretly engaged. She wore the stunning ruby ring he gave her on the chain from which her Valla U pendant also hung. Steel had done a great job with choosing the ring. It was a large oval stone with diamond laurel leaves in a gold setting, totally Tawny. I was happy for her. Her self-loathing was minimal once she'd gotten over the initial shock of their engagement. I wondered if she would hate all of us when she found out that we all knew he wasn't her uncle. I hoped not.

Ash was enjoying my undivided attention. He'd gone back to parading me around like his trophy. I didn't mind; I was eager to please.

The provosts were stern but fair. I liked Fox the best, and then, Jackal, my uncle. He taught languages, focusing on the tribes. It was painfully hard for me, never having heard them in person. He assured me that hardly anyone had. Jackal was fun and sly. It made what could have been a painful experience in his class into one filled with laughter if nothing else.

My mom's testing came up fast. I knew I wouldn't have been able to get out of going home for it even if I'd wanted to, but I wouldn't have missed it for the world. Those of us at university met Friday night after battle training to head home together. It would be the first time I'd seen Slate up close in eleven days; I was keeping track of every aching second, I realized. My heart was thumping rapidly at the prospect.

Jett and Tawny were already waiting in the portal room for us when I got there. I'd been healed after training, but I was still exhausted. The idea of interacting Slate was draining me.

He'd be all dark and brooding, from glossy black head to shiny black-booted toes.

"By the Mother! Is that my sister? I barely recognized you without your lover attached to your hip," Jett teased as he slung his arm around my neck and gave my head a kiss as I stumbled into him. I loved having a brother even if his sole purpose in life was to make me feel more awkward than I did all on my lonesome.

"Very funny. We had to undergo an emergency surgery to pry us apart, but I made it."

Jett laughed and Tawny even smiled. "I feel like I haven't seen you in ages."

"You guys are so dramatic. It's been like two weeks. We're in our honeymoon period, it'll burn out soon and we'll be boring like the rest of you soon enough."

"Speak for yourself. Slate has taken it as his personal mission to service every tyro of the female persuasion singlehandedly. I'd be envious, but two are enough for me." Jett winked.

"Why doesn't that surprise me?" I said, ignoring Slate.

"When you meet the right person, you don't need to bed-hop. You just met the right person first. It's a good thing," Tawny chirped, and I gave her a curious glance. I had a feeling she wasn't really talking about me.

"Enough sap, we're ready." Jett stepped through the portal, then Tawny.

Slate grabbed my arm when I started through and yanked me back.

"You are avoiding me." It wasn't a question.

I pursed my lips and gave him a patronizing look. "You're very hard to avoid, Slate Sumar. I see you every morning leaving the girls' wing, a different room nearly every night. I'm not avoiding you, I'm just not between any of their legs so you don't see me."

"Do you know that Ash is the one who told everyone about that night?" Slate asked, his grey eyes managing to be soft and hard at the same time.

Not all the rumors were untrue. There'd been only two people who knew what happened in my bedroom, and since I hadn't told a soul, that only left one person.

"I know that." I shrugged.

"He should not have said anything about you," Slate admonished.

I gave him a look. "Slate, don't feel obliged to defend my honor. Some of what they say *is* true. I'm not denying it, you shouldn't care." I dismissed. "He's asked me to marry him a half dozen times already. My eyes are on the endgame. Marriage, kids, a future. What do you find in your revolving door of women? Lust? Pleasure? I have that too, and more." I ticked my priorities off on my fingers.

"You will really marry him?" Slate's voice was dangerously soft.

"I know this is unthinkable to you, but some people only have sex with one person, for their whole life. Usually their spouse, that's how it works," I said in an acerbic tone.

His light grey eyes were predatory, almost feral. I tried not to do my rabbit thing.

"You do not have to be so damn condescending. I was asking because you do not love him." Slate's mouth tightened when he found confirmation in my own eyes. "You think you are better than me because you have only let one man push between those supple thighs? You are not. You are no better than I am; I at least do not lie to myself, or them for that matter. We give one another pleasure for the moment and promise nothing. You make promises you do not want and give pleasure out of obligation." He shook his head. "You should have been in love."

He had backed me up against the cool wall next to the door. His body made the great room seem small—there was just so much man compacted into one body. Slate was a man who knew he could intimidate with that body and had no qualms about it.

He had done it to me at every available chance.

I scoffed. "I don't do it out of obligation. I enjoy making him come hard and often. *And* look who's talking. You wanted my first time to be with you? Did you think I was in love with *you*?"

I blinked and my fire was quelled. I'd never been so rude to anyone in my life.

I slid sideways and hurried through the portal.

Dinner was awkward. My mom kept prodding about Ash and I kept deflecting. I didn't want to tell her about the marriage proposal, any of them, or what we'd been up to, so I kept it to school talk. How great it was, how busy I was, and how much I was learning.

My mom pulled me aside after dinner and told me that she and my father were making plans to arrange a meeting for all of us. I was flabbergasted; I didn't even know they were in contact. I should have known. I'd been away too long.

I went to bed that night dreaming of picnics with my dad and mom, Jett and Indigo laughing at something clever our father had said. My mom and dad finally married, like they should have been all those years ago.

It was the morning of my mom's test. The Ragnarock test. We ate silently at breakfast, already ready to head to the course.

"It's a death maze," Jett told me when I asked. "It's different every year and you're not supposed to talk about it with those of us who aren't tried and true." He pointed at all of us around the table still in classes.

"A death maze?" I asked softly.

"That is a bit dramatic, Jett really. It is a series of tests designed to make sure you have conquered your knowledge at school. If it gets out of hand, you shoot a red flame into the sky and they save you. Simple as that," Pearl reassured me.

It wasn't reassuring that they needed a rescue plan. I felt panicked. I wanted my mom to do this and excel, become the ambassador to the Aves and show all her naysayers what's what. But she was my *mom*. I was struggling with the idea of her running willingly into danger and me sitting in the stands twiddling my thumbs waiting for her.

"Don't worry. I've had an extra nineteen years to prepare." She smiled at me. I loved my mom's smile. Her dark eyes twinkled.

We took the portal door to Elivagar where they did the test every year. Since the university reopened, they had been staging this particular test every six months and they would keep doing it until all those who fell within the years it was closed were proven tried and true.

The town center in Elivagar was a snowy mountain town nestled in a valley below the castle Vetr. The town's buildings were made up of a variety of different shades of red brick and split granite cottages. Chimney smoke blended in the air above the town. I imagined if Santa Claus came from a village, it would look like Elivagar.

Elivagar's portal gate was a freestanding iron gate with square pillars on either side. The gate was fascinating. I could see through the iron bars, but every time a person went through it, it would light up. The bright white light made me think we were traveling through it at the speed of light.

As soon as we arrived through the portal, we could tell there was an important event happening. People had a little more hustle in their step than I was used to seeing, and were rushing about. A few signs directed us around the stony town to a mountain path that quite a few people were going up and down. It was fairly cold with all the snow, the ground was frozen. We wore fur-lined cloaks and thickly-lined boots— thankfully it wasn't windy.

We reached the stadium at the top of the mountain in little time. It was really a half stadium, one half being completely open to the forest before it. The stadium was heated, the seating warm. It was nearly empty, but I could imagine it filled with nervous parents waiting for their children to come out the other end.

What I had gleaned about the Ragnarock challenge was that they threw everything you had learned at you in real-life form. It had been deadly in some rare cases. More often than not, people got hurt. They claimed it still wasn't as bad as being unprepared for what *could* happen out in the world. I was not convinced.

There were several other competitors walking around nervously. The start was also the end. You traversed the mountain and back again using the skills learned in at Valla U. There were twenty obstacles you had to collect flags from in order to complete the course. The good part was if you took the challenge with your class, then you were allowed teams up to four. If it was easy for you, excellent. If not, then you hadn't absorbed enough at Valla U and could retake the final. No one chose to give up. To be untried and untrue simply did not happen. You would leave Tidings because the shame would be unbearable.

My mom was at a serious disadvantage going at it alone. She joked about her nineteen years to prepare, but it was really nearly two decades half trained, getting soft and not using skills she'd barely learned. My stomach was in knots, but I couldn't show it. Everyone disliked the idea of her doing this, but me most of all.

We sat in our seats waiting for the event to start. "Steel, did you have to do this course?" I asked, hoping he might provide more insight.

He shook his head. "Sorry, wish I could say yes. I did do the Wild Hunt expedited, but Valla U was opened for my second year. It was probably the hardest year for the Guardians because they were still working out the kinks, but the Wild Hunt isn't as bad as this one. The land is better too, they do it in Ostara. Perpetual spring instead of winter." He gestured to the snowcapped mountains. "Being from a place that is always hot, this test puts us at a disadvantage."

My mom was dressed for the weather though—that had to be enough. Her small frame was completely bundled, but still flexible. Her weapon of choice was the javelin. I had never seen her use it and I was glad of that; it didn't fit with my mental image of my mother. She should have a paintbrush and canvas, that was how she did the most damage. This was a side of her I'd never seen.

A small platform was set up, and Moon approached the podium. It was beginning.

"I would like to apologize to our future Guardians. Nineteen years ago, we suffered a great tragedy. In my grief, I shut down our one way to prove those of you tried and true. I offer this biannual opportunity to those of you who wish to rectify my mistake."

Moon looked like he'd said this speech in his sleep.

It took a big man to admit he was wrong. I didn't agree. If I was in Moon's situation, I would've done the same thing. Sometimes, only time can do the sorting.

"Future Guardians, please ready yourselves."

I started waving frantically to my mom a lump rising in my throat. Jett clasped my hand and gave it a squeeze. She smiled bravely and gave one firm wave. An alphorn blew once long and low, and into the fray she went. A few stray tears betrayed me.

Moon stood talking to the man I had seen at the Vetr table at the induction ceremony. These were Vetr lands—my stepmother's lands.

My father's wife was standing next to him in a floor-length fur coat and a dress I was sure I'd seen Scarlett O'Hara wear. She was as beautiful as her frosty daughter, and just as cold.

"Old man Orion and his vampiric wife Cassiopeia," Jett said to me, catching me looking at the couple on the platform.

"They're Vetrs?" I asked him.

"He's a Vetr, she's a Natt, your future aunt-in-law. That is Dahlia's sister." That explained a lot.

"Why do you call her a vampire?"

"The Vetrs choice of punishment is death by pike. They leave the remains on the pikes outside their castle to rot."

Was he joking? Maybe it was an old wives' tale.

"She bathes in their blood. She uses calling to absorb it, keeping her looking young," he said, quirking an eyebrow, daring me to disbelieve him.

"Rumors, Jett. Just rumors," Hawk said gruffly.

"I didn't say they did it to the people; they do it to the tribes to keep them under their thumb."

"The Vetr do punish the tribe members severely. I have never seen the pikes with my own eyes. I would hope they are wrong. Moon is the deciding voice on all matters concerning the law; I respect him greatly. I do not think he would let past occurrences cloud his judgement." But I knew that what he said and how he felt were two very different things. I was sure that Hawk did not believe the Prime had put away his past.

"In all fairness, Elivagar's tribes are the most volatile." Jett gestured in front of him.

Walking together were two monsters. They walked upright like men...but they were not men. They were over six feet tall and covered in fur, their faces those of grizzly bears. I fought back a scream. I knew that the tribes were all hybrids, but in my mind I had concocted cartoon versions of them; the real thing was terrifying. Their eyes showed just enough to show me they weren't all animal. That, and they had on long woolen tunics that reached the knees of billowy pants cinched at the ankle. I wondered if they had just put clothes on to fit in, as if that was possible with their bear faces.

"They are the Bjorn. Literal translation is *bear*. There are quite a few tribes in Elivagar. Minotaurs, Lycans, Jotnar...Crathode," Slate explained.

I couldn't believe he was speaking to me after what I'd said to him.

I didn't want to be prejudiced against the Crathode. Hearing their tribe was there though, it made me angry...and a little frightened.

Slate must have read my expression. "The Crathode responsible, the Red Kings, have either been executed long ago or imprisoned for life."

"We have a prison? Is it on Valla?" I asked.

It was the first time I'd heard there was a place for criminals. It made sense; I didn't know what else they would do with them. My mind deliberately skipped over the Vetr's pikes.

Jett's eyes lit excitedly. It was going to be good, I could tell.

"We do. It's underwater..." He let it trail off, wanting to dangle me along a little while. I appreciated him trying to distract me from worrying about our mom.

"Okay?"

"It's on the back on a giant crab. The prison is Leshy magic bound so you can breathe and everything, but it's impossible to escape. The crab would snap you right in half." He snapped his hands like claws.

"Aren't the Crathode a distant cousin of the prison crab or something? Why wouldn't it just let them go?"

He rolled his eyes. "No, they aren't cousins, not even distant ones." He smiled his smug smile. "Its name is Karkinos; it's not *the* Karkinos, but a descendant. There's a few giant crabs roaming around the ocean." I was baffled by his casualness.

"Big enough for a building to rest on its back?"

"Bigger." He waggled his fingers in front of my face.

"Wouldn't people be alarmed when they're scuba diving and run into a giant crab? What's to stop them from finding it? Or these islands, for that matter?"

I hadn't even thought about it until that moment—the look on someone's face when they sailed into an island with bear men who wear pants. After they were through being terrified, they would be an internet sensation.

Jett shook his head. "The lands are protected. Like the portal doors, if a regular Joe was sailing his yacht in the Atlantic and happened upon one of our islands, he would be transported to the other side of the island. Happy as you please, no one's the wiser. Same for Karkinos, except humans are naturally driven away from it. They could never swim to it, it would repel them. There's only one entrance, and that is through the Prime's office."

"So the entrance to Karkinos…is a portal?" I asked.

"Yup."

My mind was blown. I knew we were magical, but the most I could do was make some plants grow and blow around wet air with the occasional fireball.

Hawk, ever observant, smiled, just a little one. "We do not have that kind of *calling* any longer. It died out with the elementals. We up keep it as best we can but ours is restricted to the elements. Our purpose is to balance, not to create magic buildings under the sea." The little smile grew a bit.

Gypsum had finally spotted the Bjorn. His face was that of a person whose favorite comic book character had just sprung forth from the pages and started chatting him up. Afraid, but intrigued. Tawny had paled and was trying to burrow into Steel's side. He put an arm around her; it was *not* uncle-y. Gypsum saw them out of the corner of his eye. His eyes darkened. We were going to have to have a talk soon. Maybe I could cajole Jett to do it. Jett had all but adopted Gyps as his own brother; so had Slate, for that matter. Two very bad role models.

Only about twenty people had gone into the Ragnarock. Would someone take pity on her being alone and team up with her?

I started to crowd watch again. Only an hour had gone by. My family had warned me it might take all day, but the average time was around five hours. They were setting up aid tents for those who would come back beaten up. I had mixed feelings about their presence.

I was lost in my own thoughts. Our whole family silent as we waited two hours, then three, then four. Four and a half hours after the beginning of the Ragnarock, the first person broke through the forest line. My heart sank.

Not only was it not my mom, but the man was bleeding heavily from a head wound, his right arm hanging. The blood dripped off his fingers into the stark white snow. Bile rose into my throat and a whimper escaped. Jett tucked me into him.

"Don't worry, she's stronger than she looks. Stronger than you think. She'll be healed and sleep it off." Jett's voice was muffled as he talked into my hair.

The waiting began in earnest. After each person came back, most of whom bleeding to varying degrees, they were healed and they headed to the platform. Moon embraced them and welcomed them to the Guardians. They were now tried and true. They each received a gold torque bracelet. Their families led them away afterwards, and they left the stage rejoicing.

Six hours, seven hours. I was shivering, and not from the cold. My anxiety was shooting adrenaline through my body. I couldn't control my jerking movements. I could feel my *calling* lying in wait on my fingertips ready for use. I looked at the stage, taking my eyes of the forest line for the first time in an hour; eighteen of the twenty people had returned. Only our mother and one other person was left. I saw my father. He wore a long, white, fur-lined cape; his jaw was clenched, his blue eyes hard.

There was commotion at the tree line. I sprung to my feet. Two shapes trekked into the clearing, one half dragging the other over their shoulder. A trail of blood dripped behind them. My heart skipped. *Mom.*

I saw my mother limping into the clearing carrying the other Guardian. The *calling* already ready at my fingertips, I used air. It pushed me from our seats in the stands to the snow-covered ground. I rolled and broke out in a run. I met her at the line. I took the semi-conscious person from her shoulder and we both staggered. The aid healers were right behind me and carried her into the tent, taking the other woman from me.

I was huffing, my head hurt, and my heart was thumping. I'd used more *calling* than I'd even known I'd had. My vision swam as a blurry Slate lifted me.

I could hear voices talking in trenchant tones. I opened my eyes again and looked into the concerned face of my father. When my eyes came into focus he looked...*happy*.

I jackknifed up from my cot.

"Relax. You fainted."

His voice was guttural, thick with concern. He put a hand to my back. I flinched and he removed it. My dad just *touched* me.

"I fainted?" was all I said, stupidly. I sounded like I'd just woken up. Which was apt.

"You did, after you ran to your mom. Do you remember how you came off the stands?" He asked. I *felt* curiosity and relief.

"I ran," I said, knitting my brows.

"No, you...jumped from your seat."

We had been nearly thirty feet into the stands. I would have to have jumped over all those people and onto the ground—he must have been mistaken.

"No, I saw my mom and...I just remember running."

"You ran once you hit the ground. No matter. Others will want to know how you managed enough calling to propel yourself from your seat." He said it as a warning.

"Am I in trouble?" I couldn't fathom why, but I swallowed hard anyway.

"No, they will...want to know how to do it." I looked around. We were in the aid tent, white sheet walls on all four sides. "They are on the other side, and they do not know you have woken. I have guarded the room against listening." I looked at him quizzically. "Air. Anyone attempting to listen would only hear the rushing of air."

"Oh. Thanks."

He smiled, the panes of his face rising. It didn't look like he smiled often. He turned to leave.

"No, really. Thanks...*Dad*." He froze, his eyes unreadable. I *felt* his storm of emotions; they mostly left me feeling hopelessly sad.

He clenched and unclenched his jaw. "Scarlett, we will do this the right way another time. Remember, your *calling* works in any way you can imagine to use the elements." His face smoothed and he ducked under the tent sheet.

I slid off the cot and went out towards where I could hear nervous talking.

I gave a shy smile. "Sorry for stealing your thunder," I said.

My mom spun at my voice; she was perfectly healed, but looked bone weary.

"Scarlett!" she yelped, fighting back a sob. She held me with all her new muscles, crushing me.

"I'm fine, really." I shrugged, trying to smile again.

Everyone's eyes were on me.. Even the people on the platform were staring at where I stood in front of the aid tent. I cleared my throat.

"Scar, you *flew.*" Gypsum whispered with awe.

I blanched.

"Gyps, I cannot fly. I don't know, I guess I was all hyped up on adrenaline. I jumped."

Gyps shook his head; he was dead-set on me being some kind of superhero. Everyone's eyes on me was making me extremely uncomfortable—none more so then the Vetrs and my evil stepmother who stood talking to my father but with clear eyes on me.

"Can we get out of here? I feel like a freak show," I said softly, hoping none of the aid workers were listening.

My mom nodded. "Yes, I had to finish my ceremony while you were out. We can leave now. We will talk about this later."

We started to head towards the path leading down the mountain, and I felt a tap on my shoulder. Old man Vetr stood before me. I could tell he'd been very handsome once. Bitterness and the cold made him look older than he was. His blue eyes looked empty, I felt sorry for him.

"Ms. Tio?" he asked in a croaky voice.

"*Um*, yes...?" I didn't know what to call him. "Mr. Vetr."

He gave me a smiled that never touched his eyes. "Orion, please. That was quite interesting, what you did back there."

"Thanks...I don't remember much before I fainted."

I was nervous and had no idea why. Slate slid up next to me so his fingers brushed my hand. Orion's eyes regarded him for a moment and turned back to me.

"I will be keeping an eye on you. I pray you do not mind. Purely interested. I expect greatness from you. I am never wrong." He made to leave, but something caught his eye.

His empty gaze filled with something like disbelief, but more so. He was thunderstruck. Unless someone was an empath, however, I doubted they would have been able to tell; his face was still smooth.

"Sparrow."

I turned, Sparrow was at the start of the path looking back at us. She looked frightened. Orion's eyes scanned our group. Whatever he saw, I *felt* confirmation. "I will be in touch," Orion said as he turned.

When I looked back, everyone's emotions were out of control. It was suffocating, literately. I started gasping for breath.

"Scar, you okay?" Tawny asked, stepping from Steel.

"Everyone...has...to...calm...down..."

Slate was the only thing keeping me from curling into a ball and rocking.

I'd been around highly emotional people before, but all of this anger, fright, worry, displeasure, love, nervousness and million other emotions that had slammed into me was too much from our group.

Slate wouldn't leave my side; he walked around me like a bodyguard I couldn't shake. I despised that his constant presence offered me a soothing warmth I had not anticipated.

I knew something significant had happened today; I just didn't know if it was bad yet.

No one was in the mood to celebrate after my mom finished

Ragnarock. I went upstairs to change and then to the kitchen to find some food, trying not to bother the staff. I heard an argument going on inside one of the halls I passed. I couldn't help but listen.

"You must tell her. Better it comes from you than someone else." It was Steel's voice, and it was the most animated I had ever heard him speak.

"You don't have kids, you don't understand. This will be hard on her. With Valla U, and the move...I can't. I can't jeopardize it." Hawk sounded distressed.

"Do not drive her to them. Bind her to us. They *know*. It is too late for hiding." Steel was adamant.

Tawny. My hamster wheel was turning. Something Jackal had said about nineteen years ago...something Indigo had said about a son dying....something Jett had said about a son dying. Tawny was Orion Vetr's granddaughter. When it dawned on me, things clicked into place. I didn't know how it had taken me so long to see it. Her father was the only heir to Elivagar. *Tawny* would be heir to Elivagar.

"Frigga's sweet grass. Steel, you have only the first clues as to how many secrets this family holds. We open that door and who knows what skeletons come out...how many lives are ruined in the process." Hawk sounded defeated and it confused me.

No wonder Orion had acted like he'd seen a ghost.

CHAPTER 17

 Seeing dead bodies in your dreams was always a nightmare, but when they have your mother's face...I woke up crying. It had felt real. It was residual worry from my mother's Ragnarock. I felt guilty that we hadn't celebrated her finally being tried and true. It was a huge accomplishment. I made sure to tell her how proud of her I was at breakfast.

We ate in awkward silence. I hated it. Yesterday had affected everyone.

"Maybe we could do something to celebrate? You feel any different?" I teased my mom, hopeful she'd take the bait.

"Hmm? Pardon, hun?" Never mind.

Jett had gotten Moon's permission to wed Amethyst, and now my brother was officially betrothed to both Amethyst and Cerise. Jett said it was surprisingly easy. Moon asked if it was what Amethyst wanted, and when she said yes, he agreed.

Things started happening quickly after that. My mom was going back and forth to Ostara to try and reach the Aves. She was officially their ambassador. We never celebrated her success, and then suddenly she was too busy. She was away nearly all of the time.

When my mother wasn't busy with work, she was helping the girls plan their wedding. They wanted to marry at the Midsummer festival in Thrimilci. I thought it was going fast, but that was how they did things.

My life was consumed with Valla U. I loved it. Information was my drug. I trained with Fox daily. He was impressed with my burgeoning blade skills. He started me on throwing and stealth. He was making me into a knife-wielding machine and I basked in his praise.

Even Ash was busy. He took training very seriously. One of my favorite things about him was that he let me train with him. He was especially good at encouraging my... *ahem*...calling. I liked him best when he gave himself over to me for what I referred to as *practice*.

Before moving from Chicago, Ash would've been the type of guy who left me tied in knots. I wouldn't have been able to approach him. In Tidings, though, he wasn't just a hot quarterback; he was gorgeous and driven. I watched him get cornered by the pretty redhead again, his most ardent fan. I smiled as our eyes met; it was his little game. I didn't mind, he could keep his fan club.

I started seeing Slate with a petite, black-haired girl. It rankled. She was striking with her up-tilted eyes and long, straight hair. She opted for battle clothes rather than the dresses the rest of the girls wore. It wasn't exactly frowned upon, but if I'd learned anything in my time in Tidings it was that they clung to their traditions. She was just the kind of girl I could see Slate with, equal in darkness and danger.

For some reason, Ash's groupies didn't bother me, but Slate's little bad girl did.

Ash and Sage, who still hadn't warmed up to me, walked ahead of me and Tawny to our Magical Beings class. We sat in our tiered seats, the usual ones. Provost Ford Tio taught the class, another of my redheaded extended family.

Tribes and magical creatures were taught in the same class. As if hybrid humans didn't already scare me enough, I now had to take into account that some had powers of their own. Fairies, trolls, and giants fell into the in-between category. Fairies were self-explanatory, but they were more like pixies. Ash had already told me when we first met that fairies were little, twig-like people. Trolls had overly large wide faces for their teeny tiny bodies and were barely a foot high. Trolls didn't seem nearly as frightening as they were in books. They had wide round wrinkly faces and bodies that managed to be both gangly and frumpy.

Ford also used a computer for his class like Dahlia did, although he didn't act like it might turn on him at any moment. For me, it was excellent. He had slides of all the magical beings. I could actually see them in full color. It was surreal. I wouldn't have pegged Ford for a classroom type teacher, he seemed more hands-on. He assured us we would be taking a field trip in the future. The Guardians' relations with the trolls and fairies had never been in poor standing, and it would be safe.

Boa Sunna taught Focus and Nurturing. We would spend an hour and a half meditating and making plants bloom; it sounded boring, but it was the perfect balance with all the battling we were being taught. Time in the expansive green house was wonderful. Citrus and flowers blooming, mixing in the sweetest scents. It was all stained glass, meticulously kept. When I needed some quiet time alone, I lay down by the pond. There were three ponds in the green house. It was like some giant had set the glass house right on top of Utopia.

Our next class was Calling with Boa's twin sister Asp Sandr. She was an exotic beauty, and looked very much like Slate's little girlfriend. I wondered if they were related. She taught us the basics of calling and helped to expand our imagination.

My father was right: you could do anything with the elements you could imagine. Unfortunately for some, they had no imagination.

Counter Calling was taught by my other cousin, Sky Tio, who was heir of the Tio family as the oldest of the siblings. Counter calling was the only part of *calling* I had a problem with because of my inexperience with it and inadvertently killing someone. There was no healing for death.

I stood facing Tawny as she *called* some unseeable element and shot it at me. I saw a rope of air come at me, designed to tie me up. I *called* fire and formed a barrier between myself and the rope of air. I fell back, tied up with searing air instead.

"You try too hard. Think simply. What if you called *more* air at the rope? Try to reverse it instead."

That was the sucky part of counter casting: you tend to get your fanny packed kicked.

"Switch," Sky told us.

I stood facing Tawny in the large stone room—it was the only classroom without seats. If Sky had something more to say, you just sat right there on the floor. I *called* water in an attempt to douse Tawny. I didn't like using my *calling* against people, so my counter calls tended to be wimpy. She blew it away easily, reversing it back at me, but this time I was ready. I didn't want to be drenched by my own *call*. I *called* fire again and the water evaporated in the air. The entire interaction only took about five seconds.

What could I say about Languages other than the fact that I was a lost cause? I was so glad Jackal taught the course; he poked fun and told me I was lucky that A) Valla U was pass or fail, and B) the tribes and magical creatures all had at least one member who spoke English. *Thank goodness.* And my personal favorite, C) I was pretty, I needed only to smile and nod.

Battle was still the best. It was River Straumr's day. We were encouraged to do extra training for strength and speed, but River had us do a little of each to warm up every day. Out of the three brothers, he was the most level-headed. River was just sort o...normal—well, as normal as one can be when they force teenagers to run through the Gauntlet. The Gauntlet was the obstacle course that was set up on River's days. It was punishing.

I wasn't not judging, but I was sure some of those girls jumped in front of the dull blades hoping to get scratched enough to need medical assistance so they could get out of the rest of class. I thought it was poor planning on whoever put River and Fox in charge of such a physically intense class with half a hundred women and possibly some men who wouldn't have minded a bit of rough and tumble.

I jumped to the side of a giant mallet aiming for my midsection. I ran behind it on its upswing. Then, I stood there, timing the crushing wood pallets—some kid had to have his leg healed after shattering his fibula when he fell. He probably should have been glad it wasn't his head. I rolled underneath as a pathway between blades swung,, three in succession. I bounced back onto my feet. I jumped forward over the dull saw as it retracted and ducked as the spinning saw at my head cut across. I pushed through all the tyros beating me with semi padded staffs and rolled under the guillotine-like blade that came crashing down behind me.

River patted my back as I trotted past. "Good job, Tio. Next!" He marked something down on his clipboard.

After battle training, we were all heading home for the first time since my mom's graduation. I couldn't really say I was homesick—it was more like I didn't feel like I had a home. I was *family* sick. Jett was spending time was his in-laws, both sets, so was hardly ever back. My mom had been camping below the Aves's floating tree that homed them. It took her a month to find and was there for an additional month hoping the bird hybrid folk would allow her to come up or send someone down. I spent time at Valla U with Indigo; she didn't care to go home either. It was tense at home, she told me. I could get that.

I hadn't stopped thinking about my father since the day of my mom's Ragnarock. I wanted to ask Indigo about him, but I had no idea how. Like, *oh hey how's your adopted dad? He's my dad too! I'm his illegiti-mate daughter!* Nope. Not going to work. Indigo quickly became one of my best friends, so that made her and Tawny. Two. I was close with Cherry and Amethyst because they were always around, but I didn't confide in them. Tawny had been M.I.A. since she and Steel had gotten engaged. They still hadn't made any wedding plans: I thought Tawny feared the commitment it implied and didn't think it would ever happen.

I walked with Tawny and Cherry to the portal rooms where we were meeting Jett, Amethyst, and Slate. I squinted my eyes. Slate's newest little girlfriend was with him. She leaned against the wall, one hip cocked in her tight pants. I didn't think the standard issue ones were so tight. I felt my blood boil.

Slate didn't bother explaining *her* presence. Cherry ran up to Amethyst and Jett, kissing them both. Tawny was eager to get to Steel. I grumbled. I'd be the only solo on the trip.

His little girlfriend swaggered over to me, black leather pants low on her hips. "Shale Sandr. Scarlett, right? I have heard them speak of you many times." She gestured to Slate, Jett, Tawny, and the girls. *Traitors.*

I gave a small cool smirk and told myself not to be a witch with a capitol "B." It was an uphill battle.

"Sorry, they never mentioned you." I shrugged.

She moved her tongue in her mouth as if poking at her teeth. "I guess you will have to get to know me then."

She gave me her best *two can play that game* face. I wanted to punch it off. I didn't look at Slate's face; I already knew he would *love* it.

It was Tawny's twentieth birthday. Just under two months until Jett's wedding and the Midsummer Festival mid-year break. Slate was keeping to his promise that he would take whomever wanted to meet the Wemic, possibly the Faunelle. I was elated.

Pearl was so happy about having everyone home for once that we were eating in the formal dining room. Its ceiling was a huge dome of kaleidoscope mosaic art. A chandelier hung from the center over the single longest table I'd ever sat at without a bench. Its light wood was just as intricately carved as the informal room's table, with swirls of gold and silver painted in the etchings.

I had taken extra care to get ready. I did big curls in my light brown hair, threading Slate's jade fetish prominently so it lay in a thin curled braid where my neck met my collar. I lined my green eyes with thick lashes and a smoky eye.

I ate in a mint green strapless dress that made my turquoise eyes pop. I hoped Shale could see how good I looked from across the table where she sat next to Slate. I growled internally. She was being welcomed to our family. I hoped she would choke on a chicken bone. My mother sat by Slate talking to Shale over him irritatingly. Irritating to me, that was. The whole family seemed delighted Slate had brought a girl home.

Shale's straight black hair was pulled over her shoulder. She was tiny but I could see her toned muscles even in her chest as she ate. *Gods,* I hated her. My one buddy had gone over to the dark side; Gyps thought she was the coolest thing to come around since ice cubes.

I wasn't doing a very good job of blocking my emotions and Pearl kept turning her attention towards me expectantly.

Focus; the day was about Tawny. She looked every bit the woman she had transformed into. A flattering deep purple, low-cut dress, hair loose in dark waves, her wide hazel eyes shining. I could see her engagement ring nestled between her breasts. I wondered if anyone else noticed. Gypsum had finally been told after the Ragnarock about Tawny and him only being half siblings. Surprisingly, he took it well. He didn't care—she was still his sister no matter what. He didn't know about their engagement.

"What's on your necklace? Is that a ring?" Gypsum asked in total innocence.

What happened next could've played out differently: she could've said, "Oh, look at this cool ring I bought!" Instead, totally caught off-guard, she choked. Not literally, but she stammered and turned seven shades of red.

"Tawny?" asked Sparrow.

Her look said, *What the hell is that ring? What are you so obviously guilty about?*

That got Hawk's attention, as well as everyone else's at the table. I wanted to save her, but I didn't know how. Tawny made the mistake of looking at Steel. His face was just as red and his lips had gone white. They were both panicking.

Gypsum didn't know what he had just done, but he knew he had somehow gotten Tawny in trouble; he looked embarrassed and guilty. Hawk was watching Tawny and Steel closely. I'd seen Hawk angry once, *maybe* twice. Mostly he got quiet and you knew he was upset. I couldn't have predicted what happened next.

Hawk stood up, came around the table in measured steps and punched Steel so hard in the face his legs went over his head.

Tawny screamed, "Daddy! Don't hurt him! It's all my fault!"

Things were starting to sink in for everyone gathered around. You would have had to be blind and deaf not to see that Tawny had just confessed to some impropriety with her assumed uncle.

Steel picked himself up, Tawny standing between them. Steel looked angry, hurt, and guilty. The emotion was getting thick in the room and I wondered how Pearl could stand it so calmly; I felt like I was drowning. I started gasping a little, trying not to make a scene.

Steel walked in front of Tawny, hands up, trying to wave the white flag. Hawk's eyes darkened again when Steel touched Tawny.

"You have to tell her, Hawk. You *have* to. I love her."

Tawny let out a half groan, half low cry, and I sprang from my seat to comfort her.

Hawk launched himself at Steel only to come up short when my mother stepped between them with a look I had never seen on her face before.

"Hawk...*never* lay a finger on his head again," my mom said in an eerily calm voice.

"He slept with my daughter!" Hawk said helplessly, his fists still balled.

"She's not your daughter!" Steel yelled over my mom and she squeezed her eyes shut. Immediately Steel looked like he regretted his outburst.

Everyone was looking at Tawny, who was crying helplessly. I stood at her side trying to soothe her, but she shook me off.

"What did you say?" Her crying suddenly stopped.

Steel turned around to face her. "I didn't know how to tell you, it wasn't my place," he said softly.

She knitted her eyebrows. "You knew....all this time, you knew?" He nodded. "Does everyone know?" She turned to me. I couldn't meet her eyes. I felt ashamed. "Everyone knew." She looked at Gypsum who had tears welling in his big brown eyes, frozen in his seat.

Sparrow stood smoothly, trying to keep from crying. I could see her lips quivering. Even the Amethyst and Cherry were crying now.

"Tawny, Hawk is very much your father. Your birth father died less than a year after you were born," she said, reaching to put her hands on Tawny's shoulders.

Tawny took a step back, looking disgusted. "Who is my *real* father?" She might as well have punched Hawk in the gut the way he sunk into Slate's vacant seat, who had slid up alongside my mother to prevent Hawk from clobbering Steel.

"Ridge Vetr, Orion Vetr's son. You are Tawny Vetr, not Dagr. You are the last remaining heir to the Vetr name, but you are also the last Dagr."

Tawny nodded, accepting everything Sparrow told her. She turned and walked out of the dining hall. I chased after her, but Steel ran after her faster than me, reached her first in the hall.

"Stay away from me. You knew all this time and you let me think...What is *wrong* with you?!"

Steel let his hands drop to his sides. "I'm sorry, I wanted them to tell you. I thought you'd hate hearing it from me considering what we were up to," he said pleadingly.

"Don't follow me."

Then her eyes passed over me. Never in all my life had she looked at me like that. I hoped she never would again.

"And you? *You*, who are supposed to be my best friend. My sister."

"I took a blood oath. I *couldn't* tell you. I couldn't even mime it," I muttered, making odd hand movements as *if* I could actually mime adoption.

To my surprise, she laughed.

"Scarlett, you're so smart, and sometimes you're stupid." I frowned as she sighed. "I wanted to be adopted so badly these last few months," she confessed. "But now...now that I know Hawk isn't my real dad..."

I started to interrupt, but she held her hand up. "You know what I mean. I feel so lost all of a sudden, like my whole life is a lie." She looked at Steel who was trying to make himself small. She sighed and shook her head. "Nothing would ever change how I feel about you, but don't you think this information would've made my life a lot easier?" That was Tawny—more of a sprinter than one for the cross country race. A hot temper that cooled just as quickly.

"Tawny, I love you so much. I don't know what would happen if I lost you."

I was starting to feel like a third wheel. They were suddenly embracing and making out like their tongues were attached.

They separated and I saw the ruby on Tawny's finger. I started bawling. I was happy all her dreams were coming true. She and I hugged until I stopped crying. The three of us were smiling like idiots.

We walked back into the room. Steel's jaw was swollen from the blow landed by Hawk, but he was smiling nonetheless. Everyone looked incredibly somber. Their eyes jerked up when we walked in.

"Now that that is all settled, I think we shall have two weddings." Pearl pronounced.

Just like that, everyone's faces changed. Sparrow and my mom started bawling, hugging Tawny and Steel. Everyone got in on the action. Only Hawk hung back, looking hurt and confused.

Tawny walked up to Hawk holding hands with Steel.

She hugged him. "You'll always be my daddy," she said.

Hawk broke down. I couldn't imagine the emotional weight lifted off his shoulders in that moment.

The rest of the night went between everyone awkwardly ignoring the fact that Tawny had gotten engaged to a man she thought was her uncle and the girls excitedly talking about their upcoming weddings. Jett looked like he wanted to stab himself in the ears. That made me smile. Sparrow was even swept into the wedding planning. I felt bad I didn't have a wedding for my mom to plan, but she was more than compensating as she took the role as Steel's mom while Pearl hung back with a small content smile playing on her lips.

I decided to put my theory to bed. Even if my mom had been Steel's mom, it wouldn't have changed a single thing. Steel really was more our brother than our uncle. I would have to let it go.

If Ash had his way, we'd be engaged before the end of the year. We hadn't even talked about being exclusive yet. I knew he'd be more than willing to take that leap, but I was dragging my feet. I liked Ash, but it had been months and I wasn't in love with him. From all the books I'd read, shouldn't I have felt it by now?

I had been moping for weeks back at Valla U.

Tawny's engagement was heard around the world, it was a huge scandal. I even heard someone say that Hawk took her away so our family would inherit Vetr castle! *Imagine!* Some people were crazy. Tawny's true heritage had been let out of the bag with news of the engagement, for obvious reasons. As far as the Vetrs were concerned, they were remaining quiet. I didn't think it would last much longer. Tawny wanted to invite them to the wedding. No one had the heart to tell her no.

"Why so sad?" Ash pulled me to him under a strong arm as we walked the halls of Valla U.

I sighed, and he chuckled.

"Smile, my future wife."

He gave me a cocky smile with his full lips. I didn't feel like smiling.

We climbed the stairs of Valla U and headed towards Ash's room. It was the first time I'd been in there. It was one of the strict rules I had: our times together should be between us. No voyeurs. I trudged up the stairs trying not to think, my traitorous mind always betraying me with its traitorous thoughts.

He closed the door behind us and leaned against the door, watching me. I waited for him to tell me which bed was his. His room was set up the same way ours was. Four beds spanned the square yellowed stone room with a stained glass roof that cast brilliant shades of color across the room, despite the brightly lit sconces.

His bed was second from the right, and I kicked off my boots and lay down in the warm brown cherry four-poster bed. His comforter was a grayish green and downy. I lay atop it and waited for him to come to me. Ash's roommates, Sterling, Sage, and a blonde guy I didn't know well, were gone for the weekend.

He was still at the door, hand resting on the doorknob behind him.

"What's up?" I asked him.

This was unlike him. He was always eager to surrender himself to me, and I didn't mind it.

"Do you enjoy our *practice?"*

I quirked an eyebrow. "Yes." I did.

I hated that I loved it. I got to do things to him with my *calling,* rendering his usual cocky confidence into a moaning mass of caramel muscles. He *wanted* it. I didn't feel like he wanted anything else from me some days.

"Show me you enjoy it," he said quietly with hooded celadon eyes.

I hadn't meant to spend the night in Ash's room, but so much *calling* had left me drained and I'd fallen asleep. I'd missed dinner at home, and I'd never hear the end of it from my mom. Normally I'd be grounded, but that didn't do much anymore since I spent all of my time at Valla U anyway.

It was a beautiful ring. A teardrop shaped lavender amethyst ringed with diamonds in a gold setting, nestled in a white velvet box, had been presented to me as Ash had knelt between my legs, his eyes glittering with amusement at my astonished expression. Well, he had said he wanted to give me something *special* last night.

I shook my head ruefully. I had pushed my *calling* to the limit last night while pleasing Ash. He'd enjoyed every second—even now his expression was sated. I leaned down and kissed his cheek before jotting down a note letting him know I'd headed home.

CHAPTER 18

A messenger had come for Hawk and Pearl by dinnertime, requesting a formal meeting between them, Ash, and Basil for my hand.

Marriage contract was the only thing—lit like a billboard—flitting through my mind along with blood vow.

Everyone was elated. They brought out champagne.

I insisted on having more time to consider, which no one seemed too concerned about except for Pearl. I did notice the sparkle in Slate's eyes, and couldn't help but feel like he'd just taken on some personal challenge. I squirmed in my chair across from him.

"Torch."

Not Rabbit. Slate had only called me that once before when I'd challenged him.

Something trailed across my cheek and slid over my chest, tracing my neckline lightly, and I tried to pry my eyes open. I heard a moan of appreciation, low and rough, as my skin prickled.

I'd taken to wearing a light silky fabrics that Ash liked. But it was Slate that lay next to me. My blankets around my waist, I threw an arm over my chest and scowled at him. Locks could never keep Slate out.

"What time is it?" I asked, my voice extra gravelly with sleep.

He smirked. "Time to wake up, Torch. We have things to do."

I groaned and rolled over. "I'm not going anywhere with you."

Slate was so close I could feel his body heat. "Do you have any idea what your moans do to me in that sultry voice of yours?"

I kept my eyes closed for fear they might betray me. "If it's the same thing it does to Ash, then yes," I retorted.

"By the Mother! Are you wearing panties? You test a man's will, Torch," Slate said huskily and his breath tickled my back.

"Of course I'm wearing panties!" I pulled down the hem of the nightdress.

"I think I have to verify that fact," Slate said in a playful tone I barely recognized.

I felt the back of my nightdress lift and I spun around to see Slate's devilishly smiling face. A girl could have worse stalkers. I'd trapped his hand under me, but he could have easily slid it out from under my bottom; he left it there on purpose. I lifted my hips so he could remove it, but he just stared at me. Silver eyes slid over my lifted hips and I inhaled sharply as I scooted a little farther away.

"What are these things we have to do?" I asked, sitting up and straightening my clothes.

I crossed my long legs in front of me with my Mod About You pink toes.

Slate licked his lips in an involuntary way—I didn't think he knew he'd even done it. "Word has come back that another creature is loose in the river, most likely released by the same people who loosed the bauk, with the hope of finishing what they started. I was wondering if you wanted to come. This creature has taken to drowning women in the River Mani. It is called a vodyanoy. Are you up for some revenge?"

I leaned forward from my headboard and leveled my eyes at him. "You're kidding, right? Of course I'm in. Are the others coming? Last time, just the two of us didn't work out so well."

"Afraid of what you might do if you are alone with me, Torch?" he growled, his full lips curling in a delicious way.

I bit the inside of my cheek. "Even if that were true, I wouldn't tell you. I've graduated to Torch now?" I said as I shifted my legs on the bed so they folded beside me and I leaned forward on my arm towards him.

Slate nodded and shifted closer. I breathed him in. Something was wrong with me.

"Yes. You have your rabbit tendencies, but you have shown your true fiery nature. I am only disappointed that it was not I who released them." He ducked his head and breathed deep by my throat. I nearly shuddered.

"I can smell the fire on your skin, an incendiary just below the surface. I bet you are positively combustible." He had turned his face at my neck so he whispered against my cheek.

For some insane reason I smiled. "That's funny. I would've said the same thing about you, except your scent is more like fire and brimstone."

Slate laughed, tickling the hair that lay over my shoulder. His pure, unadulterated laugh, and my ability to make him do it, did undesirable things to my body, but I was still smiling. He turned his face to me, revealing the brightest smile I'd ever seen on him, his cheeks creasing the hard panes of his face, his perfect white teeth bright beneath those full lips.

That was unexpected. He noticed it too. "If I had known smiling would work better than flirting, I would have done it more often."

"You get more flies with honey than vinegar. Flirting? Is that what you call your stalking?" I scooted to the edge of the bed and started to climb over his legs.

Slate would always be too quick for me. He grabbed me around my biceps and pulled me over him as he shifted his body. When he lay back on my pillows my chest was smashed against his, and I had to hold my head back so our faces wouldn't touch. He was so warm under me, it would have been so much easier to melt into him and stop fighting.

"I would take eternal punishment for the unfaithful in exchange for one night with you," Slate breathed.

It was so hard fighting Slate and myself. I groaned as I dropped my head against his shoulder and he stiffened. I almost laughed as his hands loosened around my arms and he stroked my hair.

"What for? Am I just some itch you need to scratch and then you'll get over it? No more testing me, pushing. I really thought you'd give up after I spent the night with Ash," I murmured against his neck.

I watched his Adam's apple bob as he swallowed. "I am selfish. You are not an itch."

A sigh escaped me and I was amused to find his skin prickling as his strong jaw flexed. "We both know it would only be physical. I would have to give up everything to let you in. The future I could possibly have with Ash, just for one night with you."

"You were ready to do it before."

"He wants everything, and with me. You want...my body. I'm much more than that," I said, ignoring his comment.

He still wasn't moving so I turned to face him, my cheek on his shoulder, and brought my fingers up to his jaw. He inhaled sharply as the pads of my fingers ran up into his hair. Despite the evenness of my movements, my heart was thundering.

"I cannot marry you, Torch," he rasped in his deep voice.

I swallowed. "That is why I say no."

He turned his head towards me and held onto the hand I'd been touching him with. "You would?" he asked in disbelief.

I blinked. What had I just said? "The point is moot. You said you'd never marry. I don't want to have children with someone I'm not married to."

"Children?" Slate asked, eyes going wider.

I shook my head. I wasn't saying things right, my thoughts were a jumble. "I could be with someone if I knew I was the only one, committed to only me. A marriage would be nice, but it isn't necessary. But I do want kids one day. I bet you don't want kids." I gave him a small knowing smile.

"I could not have children," he admitted.

I sighed. "We want two very different things. You're in it for the moment; I see things for the rest of my life. I won't end up like my mom. What if I gave in to you and I got pregnant? You wouldn't want it, and I'd be on my own with a child. You don't think of these things, and that's fine, because I do. That day in the building, one of those men…"

It was a matter of my own personal beliefs. A child would be cherished no matter the father, but if I had the option I'd want him in the picture. Here, they had herbal teas to keep women's fertility in check. If I looked in any one of the girls' nightstands at Valla U, I'd be able to find their own personal stashes.

"I saw," Slate said thickly as his hands moved over my back. "I wished you did not kill him so quickly so I could have made him suffer."

My leg had slipped between his and he was holding my hand in his. I could feel the hardness of the daggers below his thin shirt under me.

"It's over. That day is over, and long behind us." I sighed as I climbed from the bed.

I dressed for the trip in tan, snug pants tucked into beige suede boots that folded over, and a taupe colored, breezy, long-sleeve shirt that laced to my collar. I wrapped a white scarf around my neck to use for later and started to the portal room.

No Slate there.

I went to the dining hall, the blue morning glories Pearl had grown blooming against the wall, a permanent fixture in the already blue and gold saturated room. I found Slate eating breakfast with the rest of the family who looked at me expectantly. I sat down next to Gyps. The seating plan had changed since Tawny and Steel had announced their engagement, so now she sat on the other side next to Steel.

Slate didn't meet my questioning gaze, but I noticed Jett was dressed for travel so I guessed he was coming with us. I also realized that the rest of the family was unaware of our agenda. I kept my mouth shut and ate my light breakfast of an egg white omelet and orange juice.

I dodged a few questions from my mom about when Ash was planning on coming over next, but she was easy to deflect with questions on planning Jett's wedding since neither Amethyst nor Cherry had mothers still with us. I was glad when the meal was over and I could finally go to the portal room to see if Slate would show.

He did. I pushed off the wall and faced him, and saw my brother enter just after him.

"Hey Jett, didn't know you were coming," I said, uncrossing my arms, but then not sure what to do with them I crossed them again, then uncrossed them and scratched my head.

"Slate asked me to come before breakfast. Were you two planning on going alone?" Jett asked, looking between the two of us.

"That did not work out well last time," Slate said, moving past me.

What did I do wrong? I didn't understand.

"Good. You two could use a chaperone since last time Slate came back trying to convince you to make the beast with two backs with him. I don't think you have anything to worry about this time though, baby sis," Jett teased.

Slate was pointedly ignoring us and he went through the portal.

We exited out in Thrimilci's town heart and started towards the river on the other side of the palace, the opposite direction we'd gone in last time.

I wasn't letting it go. "Why do you say that?"

Jett laughed. "He left before breakfast and came back smelling like sex. I am intimately familiar with the scent myself," Jett joked.

I felt like I'd been punched in the stomach.

"Your sister can take care of herself," Slate said, walking in front of us.

I scoffed before I could stop myself. "I've been known to make poor decisions, especially where men are concerned."

Slate's back went rigid as he walked, but Jett just laughed as if this was common knowledge.

Most of Jett's stories included Steel and Slate and all the mischief they'd gotten into as boys. I found myself feeling bad for poor Pearl; they must have driven her crazy. She'd raised four boys and a daughter, I couldn't imagine the patience that must have taken.

Somehow, Jett always managed to steer the conversation towards something raunchy. He told me about his first time with an older woman when he was barely a teen. I couldn't help, but feel sick to my stomach. Children shouldn't be doing adult things when they could risk having children themselves. I said this and Jett waved a dismissive hand at me. Pearl must not have known because I couldn't imagine her being okay with it and I wondered if I should speak up.

I grew quiet as I mulled over what I could do years later and didn't like it. Not that it happened and that there were no consequences.

Jett sensed my mood sinking further. "Hey, you can prevent the children thing with condoms. We're not completely barbaric here."

"No thank you." I muttered mostly to myself.

"I thought you gave him his share from the bundle you had before classes," Slate said, falling back and taking a sudden interest in our conversation.

Jett laughed. He had a great laugh. He managed to do it with his whole body as he radiated joy. Even if he was laughing at your expense, you couldn't help but smile.

"She's probably used them all already." He nudged my shoulder, which sent me ricocheting into Slate; Jett was not a small man.

"*Ew*. No. They're yours if you want them."

I sucked in a breath and held it until the moment passed.

Jett was looking at me with glittering green almond eyes. I turned away. "You let everyone think the two of you slept together. You didn't though, did you? You haven't. Even after all these months?"

I watched the ground beneath my feet. Not today, not now. Some people lied about who they slept with, some lied about how many. I hadn't told any lies; people made them up on their own. I had drawn a firm line in the sand with Ash.

"Please drop it, Jett. This isn't something siblings talk about."

"That's admission enough. May I ask why not?" Jett prodded as persistently as our mother.

I sighed. "I'm not ready." I was glad Slate was keeping his mouth shut, though I could feel those grey eyes burning the top of my scarfed head.

"It explains a lot," Jett mumbled.

"What's *that* supposed to mean?" I stopped walking and turned to him. Now he was just hurting my feelings.

"The spot is just ahead. You two can talk about this later. Now is not the time or the place," Slate finally said.

I turned on him; I knew I had hurt in my eyes. "Did you tell him something?"

Had he said how hopelessly inexperienced I was? The thought hurt so badly I thought I was going to cry.

Slate scanned my face and must have seen it. "No, Torch. Not a soul." "Tell me what?" Jett pushed.

"Nothing," Slate and I said.

I turned on my brother. "What is the rumor mill pumping out these days?"

If it was Ash saying I was inexperienced, I wouldn't believe that for a second. Ash knew where I stood and took to teaching me things as a point of pride.

Jett licked his full lips again, so much like mine. "Forget it. The girls are right,

I'm an idiot."

"Tell me, Jett. If you can't be honest with me then who can?" I guilted him.

He ran a big tan hand over his shaved, dark blonde head. "Ash still sleeps with Jonquil. Amethyst told me, she didn't feel right about telling you and betraying her cousin. Not everyone knows, he doesn't tell anyone—but Jonquil does."

Acid filled my stomach. I started walking again in the direction we were going. I could smell the river from where we stood. Some silent communication was happening behind me between the two men. They caught up quickly with their longer strides.

"You knew too," I said to Slate. It wasn't a question.

Ash and I weren't exclusive, that had been *my* choice. He had made it abundantly clear he wanted to be with me, but I was holding back for some indiscernible reason.

The terrain along this side of the river was mostly red clay with sparse vegetation, and few wild animals, it reminded me of the southwest, back in the States. Gods, how I wanted to run back to Chicago.

"It's not cheating. He can fuck who he wants," I said to no one in particular.

"Scarlett!" Jett said, amazed that I'd cussed.

"Far from it," Slate murmured under his breath.

"We're even."

"Even how? You slept with someone?" Jett shouted.

I rolled my eyes. "Jett, take it easy. It's done. The past is the past."

Jett stopped. "Did you fuck my sister?"

I stopped too and looked between the two men. "Jett! Shut up! Don't say it like that."

Slate looked like he wanted to say something unpleasant to both of us.

Jett shook his head. "Scar, I've never had a sister. Bear with me here. I love Slate like a brother, but—"

"I am well aware of all of his women and if I decided to have sex with him, that's *my* choice. You can warn me, and I appreciate your warning, but it's not like that. So you don't have anything to worry about. I think I'm just going to join the nearest nunnery and be done with all you stupid, womanizing, confusing, sexist hard-ons with legs and hope you suffocate under a mountain of vaginas!" I stomped off red-faced and left my brother gaping.

They hung back for the rest of the trek. I must have been getting my period; I never had outbursts like that. I was a cliche teenage girl. I sat down in the red dirt at the edge of the river and threw clumps of mud, watching the water splash up to swallow it.

I was upset about Ash. We were doing well, I'd thought, despite my kissing Slate, but now I was second guessing everything. I hung my head and pulled my scarf low so my face was shaded. I wished I hadn't found out in front of Slate. Jett couldn't have known what had happened between us, so it wasn't his fault.

The sun was high when I walked to where the guys were eating lunch; they'd left me on the shore to brood in my hormones alone. It was a thing only guys would do; if Tawny had been here we would've talked it out until I didn't have a word left in me.

They didn't say anything when I crossed my legs and started to make my own sandwich. I laid with my back on the ground and watched the sky. It was darker than it usually was at midday in Thrimilci.

"Looks like rain. Does it rain here?" I asked, filling the silence.

Relief rolled off my brother as if he was afraid I'd stopped speaking to him. Hadn't he ever heard of don't shoot the messenger?

"A few times a year. Yeah, it does look like a storm is coming. It still won't get bad. Rain water's warm, it'll cool things off for a day or two."

I closed my eyes and let the sun warm my cheeks as I pulled my scarf a little looser. "Scar, that was tactless. I should have told you in private. If I had known that you two were...whatever you are doing...I'm an idiot, but I'm not callous."

"It's cool, Jett. No sweat." I didn't bother correcting him.

There was no *are,* only *were,* and even that was *nada.*

Another protracted silence stretched before Jett spoke again. "A mountain of vaginas?"

I laughed and raised myself up so my forearms pressed into the grit of the clay and smiled at the two scoundrels. "It's the only thing I could think of that the two of you would willing suffocate under."

Slate fought a smile, but didn't look my way. Jett laughed loud and freely and I threw a clump of mud at him which he batted away with an easy swipe.

"I could find you a boy toy to keep on the side. I bet Solder would be more than willing," Jett teased.

"You might be the most inappropriate brother ever." I blushed at mention of the armor store employee.

Jett smiled with an arrogant jut of his square jaw. "Just looking out for your best interest."

I sighed. "Don't you guys have group of women who abstain and worship stuff? Just point me in their direction."

"The Valkyries: they worship Freya and Mother Earth. You would have to shave your head, it would be a pity," Slate said.

"Why's that?" *Say something sweet, anything,* I mentally pleaded.

He shrugged. "Although it would be easier, less time in the shower."

I slumped back down on my back and cursed myself for a fool. "I like my hair. You didn't seem to have a problem with it when you had your hands wrapped in it."

They both choked on their sandwiches and I *called* water into my mouth as the clouds turned grey and tumbled forth. I'd welcome the rain. I missed it; it *should* rain in the spring, and since it was June, it was a long time coming.

"I miss Chicago." My voice broke and I *called* more water into my mouth.

They shifted around on the red clay and I shaded my eyes to see my brother walk towards the shore. Then Slate was next to me, leaning over me, one hand on my other side, face above mine.

"Slate..." I admonished.

"I am not finished with you," he said, coming down to his elbow so his chest leaned against mine.

"No, I seem to remember you had sex with someone after you left my room. So you finished...it just wasn't with me." I lowered my hand when the sun hid behind the dark clouds.

Slate took a deep breath. "You are a vexing woman."

I laughed sarcastically, "You knew about Ash and Jonquil, but you didn't tell me. Why, Slate? You may not care about me like *that,* but I can tell you care."

"Coming from me it would have made you angry, maybe even angry with me, thinking I only told you to bed you." He had a point.

I sighed. "Okay, but that doesn't change anything. I'm still with Ash and you still sleep around. We can agree to disagree when it comes to one another. Friends?" I asked, holding out my hand.

Slate looked at my hand with no interest whatsoever until I basically watched a lightbulb go on over his head. He grabbed my wrist in his viselike grip and placed it below his belt line. I pressed my lips together as he grew under my palm.

"What? Are we going to go at it here behind my brother's back in the dirt? You sure know how to woo me, Slate Sumar," I said dryly, but he only narrowed his eyes at me.

"I will take you any way I can get you. All that matters is *you,*" Slate growled and he shifted my hand and thrust it under the fabric of his undergarments.

My body had no respect for itself. My insides clenched at the feel of him, silken, hard, and thick under my fingers. He held my hand there as he slowly moved his hips so he rubbed against my palm.

I opened my mouth and found words at the ready. "Ash is bigger."

He carefully dislodged my hand from his pants and I sat up, rubbing my palm against the grit beside me, willing the velvety feel of him off of me. I'd just touched Slate's cock. I had to say it aloud, or at least my head, for it to register.

I had lied. I'd never ever touched Ash with my hands, only my *calling.* The lie burned on my tongue. Slate couldn't go around shoving my hand down his pants whenever he felt like it though, so I'd gone right for the ego. Men were so predictable. If he'd thought about it for even a second past his pride he would've known I was a big fat liar.

"Ouch," Slate said rolling onto his back.

I stamped out the guilt that welled and looked around.

"Jett. He's gone."

Panic flared. Heat washed over me. Before Slate could move , I ran to the river, kicked my boots off, and dove.

The vodyanoy was only supposed to take women. I thought *I* was the bait, but Jett *was* a beautiful man; maybe the vodyanoy was making exceptions. I pushed deep into the waters and spotted my brother.

The vodyanoy must have grabbed him when he was looking away, which meant he had seen Slate and I on the ground. I'd cringe later. Right then, some froggy faced, kelp beard abomination was dragging my drowning brother into the dark depths of the river.

I *called* and air propelled me faster than I ever could have swam on my own. I wanted to kill the vodyanoy, but I had to count on getting my brother back to the surface and it coming after us. The creature was so intent on stealing away my brother that it didn't see me until I was ten feet away.

It smiled with its frog lips and showed me thin, yellowed, spiny teeth. I divided my *calling* paths and used a blade of air to cut the vine it was using as a rope to haul Jett away. Jett was not moving. The thing snarled and leapt at me as I rammed into Jett and grabbed him tightly around the middle. If Jett died because I was touching my first penis I'd never forgive myself.

Something snagged my foot and I lost hold of Jett. I turned around in time to see frog face bite his spiny teeth into my ankle. I fought back a scream and slashed out with my seax, catching it in its webbed hand. Its yellowed bug eyes looked murderous—right before a blur crashed into it. *Slate.*

I looked around for my brother and found him floating down towards the riverbed. I propelled myself forward and caught him again, then sped towards the surface.

We broke through and I gasped and coughed like a lunatic as I dragged Jett to the land. I used my seax to cut him free of the rope-like plant and tilted my brother's chin back to feel his pulse. *Check.* But he wasn't breathing. I prayed I'd seen enough movies to do it right.

I blew into his mouth holding his nose, waited, and blew into his mouth again. Slate came onto shore dragging a green body behind him as I blew into Jett's mouth and was rewarded with a coughing fit, followed by vomiting up water. I rolled Jett over and started that weird crying laughing thing I did.

"What were you doing?" Slate asked in an amused tone.

"He wasn't *breathing*," I stressed.

Why was he looking at me like that?

Jett looked like he'd been through the wringer so I *called* and healed him. He gave me a side eye and Slate laughed. I sat back on my heels, shivering in my soaking wet top and pants that clung uncomfortably to my legs.

"I could've gone my whole life not knowing that you *really* do carry a vanilla and spiced apples scent, and died a happy man," Jett said hoarsely as he sat up.

I gaped at him. "But...you drowned. I had to give you C.P.R..." I trailed off when it hit me.

Jett gave me his best lecherous grin as he wiped his face free of river water and gargled his own *called* water. "I know I'm a good-looking bastard, but honestly, I'm your brother."

"Something is seriously wrong with you, Jett Sumar. I didn't think of using my *calling*. I thought you were dying. I did what needed doing, how I knew how to do it. If you don't like it, go jump back in the river and this time I'll let you drown," I snapped.

Jett held his hands up in surrender, laughing. "Now I know why Slate calls you Torch."

"That is only one of the reasons," Slate stated from behind me, so suggestively that I blushed.

Jett laughed. "Scarlett, you really need to get diddled. I was willing to literally look the other way to that end."

"Did you just tell me I needed to get laid?" I asked crossly. "And I *do* have a sense of humor, and no one has been diddled!"

I limped off to go find my boots, chased by their laughter. Slate had certainly forgiven me quickly enough. He must have figured out I'd been fibbing. Well, it was *so* nice they were best of friends again, laughing about what happens in my pants. Jett had almost died and he tells *me* I need to get laid. As if I didn't already know that!

I screamed.

CHAPTER 19
JETT

Scarlett screamed and Jett leapt to his feet just in time to see a man spring up from the ground. He had been *calling* to blend in with the red clay so nobody had seen him. The man snapped a nix torque around Scarlett's neck, cutting her off from her *calling*. More men sprung up around her until Jett counted twelve.

What cowards.

Twelve men to take down a young man and a girl; they couldn't have known Jett would be with them.

The man lifted Scarlett so her bare toes skimmed the clay surface. He was nearly as big as Jett and Slate and looked filthy, an untrained mercenary. If he hadn't been pressing her firmly against his disgusting body like a shield to block the *calls* from Slate or Jett as they stalked near, he'd already be dead.

Slate and Jett stood side by side, shoulders bunched, legs apart, ready to attack. Slate had jumped in the river in everything but his boots and shirt, so his crisscrossed belts of knives showed over his bronze

375

chest. Jett's hands were raised, ready to draw the long seaxes that crossed over his back in an instant.

The hulking man who held her by the throat and waist spoke. "We just want him. If he comes with easy-like, we will let you live and let her go once we finish with her."

They gestured towards Slate and Jett glanced at him out of his periphery. He would give himself up for Scarlett in a heartbeat.

There were a number of jeers from the men around them. Jett's anger fumed inside him and he could feel Slate's body poised at the ready. How to get Scarlett away so they could end this?

Slate and Jett snarled. "Let her go, and I will come. No fight; I will swear a blood oath," Slate growled.

One of the other men shook his head. "No can do. She helped kill my brother; if I do not get to kill her for it...there are more creative ways for recompense."

Jett's jaw clenched as the man who spoke leered. That was not happening. Jett watched helplessly as the man holding her ran his tongue from her neck to her jaw. He saw the raw terror flash in her eyes and Slate's face contorted; his features darkened as his eyes—full of menace and that savage predator that dwelled within—shone silver. Jett felt panic rise in him as he watched her face search his; she would never allow herself to be taken by these men.

She licked her lips as a tear slid down her cheek and Jett looked on, helpless. She smiled reassuringly at him making Jett feel like she was saying goodbye. Her gaze swung to Slate, and Jett nearly started forth. Scarlett had never so much as said a single kind word to Slate besides that he was an attractive guy...but that look. *That* look said more than Jett had known was lurking there.

Jett looked at Slate, alarmed, and shouted, "No!"

She'd been slowly pushing against the man's hand so when she reversed and pulled it across her throat. The man cursed and dropped Scarlett onto her face against the red dirt.

Slate exploded forth, roaring. Jett *called*, slicing and dicing men left and right, not giving them a chance to pull their weapons, and turning his back on Slate. His brother was in the worst rage he'd ever seen him in, but judging from the way Hawk had described the body of the bauk

—or rather the lack of one—after their encounter, Slate had no tolerance for those who would hurt Scarlett.

Slate was making short work of the men, so Jett slid up to his sister and tore the nix torque from her throat that was spilling blood at an alarming rate. Nix was the only material that could cut off Guardians from their calling

She was gulping for air like a fish out of water so Jett wrapped his hands around the wound, flooding her system with healing. A moment later, Scarlett was healed; she'd be just fine. Jett smiled his smug smile. He wouldn't lose his sister without a fight. Her eyes fluttered closed from the healing and the stress from the situation.

Slate rushed beside him leaving the gore and carnage behind them before placing his hands on Scarlett's body.

"We have to get her out of her blood. She should not wake up caked in it as a grisly reminder," Slate said thick voice.

Jett counted to ten in his head to cool his temper. Ever since his decision to stand by Slate as this train wreck played out, he found himself doing it more frequently.

"Why don't you carry her into the river and clean her and I'll search their packs? How are you holding up?" Jett asked, cautiously eyeing his brother.

Slate heaved a sigh. "Fine. We should get back to the palace. She needs to rest."

Jett closed his eyes to count again. It took an effort to bite his tongue. It became an even bigger effort when he opened his eyes to find Slate removing her shirt. It was drenched in her blood, but still.

Jett took her shirt to the river and watched as Slate started to run his hand over her chest to wipe away the thick dark blood on her skin. Jett counted in his head again.

CHAPTER 20

I floated in the water.

Did I mention how much I love water?

Abruptly, I was turned upright, forcing my head out of the water. My head lolled at first until a sharp smack brought me to my senses. I wasn't dead!

"Do not hit my sister, you bastard!" Jett shouted from where he was washing something in the river.

Slate held me in the river, his eyes two reflective mirrors; I'd never seen them so intense. "Never ever do that again," he bit off in stilted words.

"They were going to kill you and rape me." I sounded detached and Slate shook me.

"Give her a minute, she nearly died!" Jett shouted at Slate.

"Do you have no faith? Did you think we could not save you and defeat those degenerates?" Slate was shouting at me and still shaking me.

"They were using me as a pawn against you. I will not be a liability."

I wished I had more spirit in me, but I was still groggy and trying to put things together.

We weren't very far from the shore and the water was only up to our chests where we stood—well, my chest. Slate was looking rapidly between my eyes with his brow drawn down.

"Why am I in the river? Where's my shirt?"

"To wash all your blood off you. We could not take you home to our mother drenched in your own blood, could we? Jett is washing your shirt. What did I tell you about putting me before your own wellbeing?"

I put my hand over his mouth, but he slapped it away *hard*.

"Not just you, my brother. I've had a lifetime with my mother, but she just got Jett. I couldn't let them take him away from her." The last worded sounded strangled as it came out.

Slate wrapped his arms around me and held me close as I collected myself.

"Scar... I don't know what to say, but that was foolish. Trust us more." Jett must have been standing at the water's edge to have heard me and for me to hear him so near.

I nodded against Slate's warm chest and realized finally that it was raining. Its cool drizzle washed over my heated skin as I clung to Slate, clasping my wrists behind his back. I let myself be held by him as I closed my eyes, indulging in a few quiet moments.

"Did you mean what you said?" Slate rumbled.

I swallowed. I thought I was going to *die*. Jett had seen what my eyes said too.

"I didn't say anything."

Just hold me a little longer, I wanted to tell him.

Slate lifted my chin up with his knuckle and rivers of rain ran down his soaked shirt over his sculpted body. His dark waves had a little curl to them, his thick dark lashes held drops from his intense grey eyes, no longer silver.

No objection rose to my throat when he slanted his lips over mine. He didn't deepen the kiss, he simply cupped my face, breathing me in as I allowed myself to indulge in a brief moment of insanity. The charge of his skin on mine made my body thrum, and it radiated through my nerves with the promise of becoming stronger if I'd will it. The sound of rain hitting the river blocked out all other noises other than the low growl that Slate was making from somewhere deep in his chest. Certainly that wasn't a purr. Did men purr?

I melted against him. It was more than sweet. It managed to be full of emotion that wasn't lust, though there was plenty of that as well. I could get lost in his kiss. I could lose myself in it. I couldn't help but feel like Slate was showing me a different side of himself. The way he could be with *me*.

"I don't know how I'm supposed to ignore this!" Jett shouted over the now pouring rain. "Have a little consideration, I'm getting drenched over here."

I broke from Slate with a shy smile and started towards the shore. Slate hung back, and when I shot him a questioning glance, Jett laughed and said something under his breath about sleeping with sisters.

It was pointless to dry my clothes with the downpour so I tugged on my shirt and soaked boots and hung my scarf strategically over my chest.

Jett said the only evidence of who'd hired the men was a single name he'd found in the pack of one of the attackers.

It had been scribbled on a scrap of paper one of the men had. It didn't ring any bells to any of us. We made it home by early evening, the only evidence of who was trying to capture Slate was a little slip of paper, if that was even evidence at all.

I was feeling sour and irritable when we made it back to the town portal. We were soaked to the bone and Jett was trying to ignore, with great effort, everything I had put him through. I felt miserable. I'd kissed

Slate again. I needed to stay far away from him; he tested my willpower habitually and I hadn't put up a fight at all this time.

It had been more than nice...it felt like it could lead to...more.

We came in through the portal room and trudged our way to the informal dining room. Slate looked back at me with fury in his eyes when I came in through the doorway. After the intensely promising kiss we shared, I couldn't fathom why he would give me such a hard look.

I gave him a questioning look as I raised my hand to brush his arm, but let it drop when he nodded towards the table.

Basil and Ash were eating dinner with my family at the long, intricately carved, lightwood table. My stomach hit the floor. The day could not get any worse.

Jett had taken Slate out to drown in his cups so neither was at dinner. They had told the family of our adventure before leaving, since my family had had a million questions for me when I sat down.

Basil and Ash had been over to get friendly with my family and to probably bend Hawk's ear to try to persuade me to agree to the marriage sooner. Ash had found the ring on my necklace and smiled that I was already wearing it on a visible part of me, if not where he would like it.

My mother watched nervously after I downed goblet after goblet of chilled champagne. She didn't say anything, but she could tell I was upset. I wasn't sure why I was. I had kissed Slate, but it wasn't the first time. It wasn't even the second. Nothing had changed, so why did I feel like I was being smothered all of a sudden?

Ash was nettled with my drinking, but he kept it to himself since I was as friendly as ever to Basil. I genuinely enjoyed talking to him and picking his mind. His knowledge of Guardians' history was endless.

We said goodnight and I waved off Hawk and my mother before heading to my room.

"Rabbit."

Back to Rabbit. I kind of liked Torch.

I was vaguely aware of someone crawling into bed with me. The events of the day had left me exhausted, and after peeling off my dress I'd crawled right into bed without even brushing my teeth. It hadn't helped that I'd drank so much and was still half in my cups.

"Oh, Rabbit. Tell me you did not sleep with him tonight." Slate's voice came from right next to my ear and I felt his big hand slide over my bare stomach.

I felt the rough callouses on his palms scratch over my skin.

"Hmm?" I murmured, unable to open my eyes, much less articulate a full sentence.

"Did Ash spread these supple thighs tonight, Rabbit?" he rumbled against my ear as his fingers moved down my stomach, over my hip, to slide over my thigh. He moaned as he pressed his hips against my back.

Something shot through me then, waking me enough to be somewhat concerned.

"What are you doing?" I asked in a numb tone.

Slate's hand had moved back up to my stomach so his big palm was flat against my navel. "I want you Scarlett; I *need* you."

His kiss seared against my skin just below my ear and I dumbly shook my head.

"Uh-uh. Go to bed."

"Here?" he asked, and I could *feel* him trying to restrain himself from pawing at my skin.

I was starting to fall back to sleep again, so I hummed an unintelligible sound before Slate shifted to press a kiss to my cheek and pulled me to him. His body was warm and hard and I fit snugly inside his arms along the curve of his body. It was dangerously comfortable and I faded away before my mind could raise any flags.

He was gone before I awoke.

I came back every weekend until the Midsummer Festival. I helped the girls make their decorations, *calling* assisted, of course. We grew flowers and sliced lemons. They had gone with hot pink and sunny yellow centerpieces, with pink and yellow globe lanterns in the hall.

Jett, normally Mr. Cool himself, was going through a *thing*. I wouldn't call it cold feet—he wanted to be with the girls. It was the wedding part that scared him, the implication of that commitment.

Ash was my date. He had been surprisingly accommodating when I'd seen him at the university. He didn't often want to visit Thrimilci where I spent every weekend.

The big day had arrived. I was finally on my Midsummer break and it was the wedding day. I wore a hot pink, floor-length gown that the girls had picked out.

Gyps, Steel, Slate, Ash, and Amethyst's three brother's, Crag, River, and Fox, were standing up for the guys. The girls had contemplated asking Indigo, but decided against it. She was there, all the greater families were, everyone had been invited. I did mean everyone, even my father and his evil wife.

The hall was beautiful. I patted myself on the back. My mom, Sparrow, and I had worked our fanny packs off while Pearl had ordered around the staff. Bronze, Cricket, and Katydid had worked their magic on the girls. It was going to be a wonderful day.

Ash was in prime Ash mode. Charming and cocky, no one stood a chance. He had all the older ladies swooning before the ceremony started.

They had hired a band and were doing the ceremony on the balcony overlooking the waterfall at the back of the Sumar palace. They had garlands of pink and yellow flowers wrapped around the enormous stone pillars. Staffers floated yellow lanterns just above the guests' heads. It was the most beautiful scene I had ever witnessed.

The band started playing. Everyone sat in their chairs looking back to see who was coming through the doors. Pearl walked out with Steel, my mom with Jett, and Sparrow with Gypsum. I walked next with Ash down the aisle scattered with pink flower petals. Slate followed with Diamond, and then Steel and Tawny. Fox, River, and Crag came walking up next and stood off to the side.

Cerise walked down the aisle first, escorted by Viper Enox. Cherry looked gorgeous. Her blue eyes sparkled and her lips shone red against her lace wedding dress. Viper lifted Cherry's veil and kissed her cheek, then shook Jett's hand. Moon and Amethyst were next. Moon looked ancient walking down the aisle. He actually looked like he was losing a daughter as he said goodbye to her. He shook Jett's hand stiffly and I thought Jett's smile looked forced.

The ring exchange was a real sight. They had worked it out so Jett put a ring on Cherry, Cherry put a ring on Amethyst, and Amethyst on Jett. It looked complicated. Cherry was crying tears of joy. They held hands and said the blood oath.

If the rings looked strange, the kiss was even more interesting. Jett kissed both girls, then the girls kissed. Jett stood in the center and turned to the crowd. Everyone cheered.

Jett yelled, "Let us feast!"

The happy married people ran down the aisle smiling throwing flower petals as they went. My eyes met Slate's over the crowd and the falling petals.

I walked down the aisle with Ash and headed to the dining hall. "Beautiful ceremony," I said, trying to break the tension between us.

"We should join in the festivities," Ash said.

I hadn't been spending much time with him and he was getting testy.

Old man Vetr had shown up. He sat at a table with Moon and my father. Apparently the wives were all busy. I was sure it was considered an insult for the most powerful women in Tidings not to show. At least in the eyes of the parents and grandparents, but you'd never know it at the moment because they hadn't stopped smiling. Two older men that I didn't recognize also sat at the table with Moon.

One man had dark blonde hair with white at the temples; his eyes were blue, his jaw was square. He didn't smile much and had a similar look of lassitude Moon sometimes got. The other man had close cut white hair. His eyes were deep set with heavy lids, and when he spoke his lips barely moved.

"Canis and Cygnus," Ash said, keeping his voice low. "They are Vars." My great uncle and grandfather.

I saw the resemblance between the blond man and my father. My father caught me staring and gave me a nod. I averted my eyes. He'd promised a meeting, an official meeting, but it had never happened.

"Look at the lovebirds. Enjoying the Midsummer break?" It was Jackal, pretty full on wassail already.

Jackal was not Ash's favorite person, and he rolled his eyes. A momentary lapse in his carefully executed facade. Jackal just laughed; he didn't care what anyone thought of him.

"It's going well. And yours?" I asked.

"Come, let us not bore young Ash with our gossip. I feel like dancing!"

I laughed, Jackal acted more like a big brother than anything.

"Your future husband does not like me," he said as he led me around the dance floor.

"He doesn't like many people. Though he usually does a better job of hiding it. And he's not technically my future husband." I smirked.

Jackal raised an eyebrow at my correction. "He will be if he has his way. His dislike could be because I cohabitate with his cousin." Jackal laughed, full of mirth.

I had worked out that factoid out for myself. Jackal spun me around and caught me in his long-fingered hands.

"Jackal, may we speak candidly?" I asked.

He flashed perfect white teeth and we danced in a circle. "Why, of course, Ms.

Tio. If this is about me being your uncle, I already know."

"Yes, there is that. I actually wanted to know about Orion." I whispered it as if invoking his name might make he appear behind me. He was still sitting at the table with my father.

Jackal nodded as he dipped me, "Not much to tell. He has two evil daughters with an equally evil wife, and he is old and bitter. End of story. Or do you mean what will he do about your friend Tawny?"

I tapped my nose and he smiled.

"I suspect he will take an interest in her. If his wife allows it. Who knows what her plans are for the Vetr lands."

Cassiopeia Natt was Orion Vetr's wife and a complete stranger. She looked none too pleasant.

"What about your dad? What is he like?" I glanced at the table they sat at. They were watching us on the dance floor, faces unreadable, even my father's.

Jackal scoffed. "How one man can be influenced by other men...I would not worry about your grandfather. He does not lift a finger without Canis's say. I do not know why we keep up the illusion that my father runs Ostara. He never has. Your mother would do well to remember that," he said seriously.

"You think my mother might be in trouble?" I asked.

Mom was spending all her time on Ostara. She had to search the lands every time she went to the Aves because their tree was never in the same place. That meant she was alone and wandering the lands of Alder's family.

"Only one person knows for sure." His eyes went to Canis. "I know one thing for certain: if Delta finds out Alder's missions to the Jorogumo include your lovely mother and her very long stays at a certain cottage, she would consider her every breath a personal offense. Natts never forget a slight."

My mouth was suddenly very dry. I knew my mom was at risk from the tribes, but I didn't know the threat could also be from people who found out about her affair with Alder. Apparently their affair was alive and very well.

"Maybe I am a sucker for a good conspiracy theory. I am sorry for upsetting you, Ms. Scarlett." Jackal gave a much smaller smile than usual.

"Jackal, have you heard of someone named Styg?" I asked, carefully watching his expression.

In my experience, adults think lying to you saves you from knowing horrible truths or being afraid, but what it really does is leave you in the dark. I asked Jackal because he's one of the few adults I knew that might have a clue what or who a Styg was, and he'd always treated me as an adult.

His step faltered as we danced and thought I may have imagined it, but then I noticed a tightening around his big blue eyes. "Styg...you are sure that is what you heard?"

"Not heard, saw." I gave him the gist of the attacks and creatures that had been turned loose. "We'd thought it'd make good training, but each time men have shown up and tried to cart Slate off."

Jackal appeared to mull it over. The slow, trance-like music played in the background of our thoughts. "Styg," he repeated. "Are you sure it was not Stygian?"

"It had started raining, so I suppose the ink could have bled and erased the other letters. Why? What's Stygian?"

I couldn't tell you why, but I felt like I had to whisper it. Even then, Jackal glanced about to see if anyone had heard.

"Talk to me after class when university is in session again. Stay away from where the creatures are being released, and keep your dark and dangerous friend away from them too." Jackal gave me a forced smile. "Getting a lot more than you bargained for here, I imagine." He quirked an eyebrow and stopped dancing while looking past me.

I turned to look; my father was standing there. "Can I cut in?" he asked Jackal.

Alder was a mountain of a man. It wasn't hard to see what my mother had seen in him. His face looked like he used to be incredibly handsome, in a time when he had less worries. He was *still* handsome, but he lacked something in his eyes that softened his hard planes. Although, he did look better than the last time I had seen him.

"Be my guest," Jackal said, handing me over to my father. He placed my hand in his. His hands were dry and calloused. I wondered what he did to make them so.

"Your brother looks very happy," he said.

"He is."

I smiled as I looked at Jett. He was definitely drunk now, smiling and laughing with Cherry on one knee and Amethyst on the other. They were blissful.

I could feel my father's eyes boring into me. "Are *you*?"

"I am," I said. I couldn't bring myself to look at his face, into his eyes. I kept them averted.

"Powerful marriages are not the only kind," he said cryptically.

He spun me around so I faced Tawny and Steel, holding hands and drinking with each other while laughing and chatting with Hawk, Sparrow, and my mother.

"You do not have to get married, ever. You can live free." I knew what he meant. Free of the responsibility of it. Free from the obligations.

"I have seen what being alone can do." I thought of my mother and her profound sadness that I had grown used to, so much so that I thought it was her personality, until we came here and I understood that that wasn't her at all.

"I suppose I deserve that," he said gruffly. Whoops. This was starting to go badly in a hurry. I needed to fix it.

"Did you help my mother get the job on Ostara?" I knew the answer.

I had been self-involved since coming to Tidings, but I knew he had been seeing my mother. It was all over their faces. The way they avoided all contact in public, and not because there was pain there. Sure there was plenty of that, but there was also a heat that only an empath could *feel*.

"I did." He tone was careful, not sure where I was going with this line of questioning.

I nodded. "Just don't break her heart again."

He didn't respond to that, only looked down at me as we danced. "You may be wiser than I was at your age," he said quietly.

I guffawed, then whipped my hand to my mouth. "Funny, I frequently hear how I don't know much of anything." I smiled timidly.

He gave a knowing smile. I wondered what my mom had told him about me. My mood lightened, imagining my parents together in the warm spring weather of Ostara.

"What do you think about Ash Straumr courting me?" I asked him.

"It is a mistake. It is more beneficial for him; you are ignorant of your true potential," he said.

I was more than a little stunned. I hadn't regretted my decision to let Ash court me until that moment...or perhaps I had been in denial.

"You think he would keep me ignorant?" I asked. I didn't know what he meant.

"I think that what you did at the Ragnarock was just the beginning. If, say, you marry and have children with Ash, you would never go against him. He would be able to manipulate you into doing...things you would not have done otherwise. Children are the ultimate incentive." His words sent a chill down my spine.

"You make it sound like Ash is a criminal mastermind or evil or something," I said, trying to smile.

"No one thinks what they do is *evil*. Necessary. A means to an end. Ash is a very driven young man. He hopes to be Prime one day."

Necessary evils...for some reason that resonated with me. I couldn't see Ash doing anything other than being Prime or an ambassador. I hadn't thought of how our marriage would benefit him, only that I wouldn't be alone.

"I have to ask. It has been bothering me since I arrived. Do you know Steel well?" I asked, licking my lips, feeling like a fool for asking.

"Well enough. When he showed up at the masquerade three years past, I thought he was Jett," Alder noted.

I thought I already had my answer with his comment. "He looks so much like me and Jett...my mom never introduced me as his niece. He usually says he's like a brother. He's not? My mom and you never had a son before Jett?"

I caught his expression of surprise and then he knit his brows. "I met your mother when she was sixteen. We were together for a short time before she went a different direction three years later." The corner of his mouth quirked. "It would explain a great deal, but I am afraid she has only told me of Jett. As far as I have been told, Steel is Pearl's son." Mystery solved.

We danced for quite some time. I caught my mom's expression when she saw us, bittersweet. I wish I could lecture my mom on what a bad idea my father was, but if she hadn't learned her lesson yet, she never would. She was approaching the dance floor.

"May I?" she asked, her voice silvery.

I stepped away.

"Thank you for the dance, Scarlett," my father said as he took my mother into his arms.

I stood unmoving for a moment, people twirling past. Skirts shimmering under the lantern lights, men, handsome in their cravats and waistcoats.

I felt him take my hand. *Slate.* He pulled me into his arms and started leading me around the dance floor, stepping and spinning to the band's tunes. It was pretty gutsy of him since Ash would probably pitch a fit. I swore I was only a little amused by the idea.

"To what do I owe the pleasure?" I asked him with a sarcastic smile.

His glossy locks were braided with his usual fetishes minus the white ones, and the front was pulled back in a leather strap.

"You were in need of a rescue."

"How *noble.* I was fine. Just distracted."

"Learn everything you wanted?" he asked. I was hyper aware of my hand in his and the charge between us.

"As much as he was willing to say. Looks like you aren't the only one to disapprove of Ash and me." I wasn't going to tell him about Jackal until I had more information; if it turned out to be nothing, I didn't want it to spoil our trip tomorrow.

His face was smooth; I wondered idly at what age boys started shaving. Slate had probably had to shave since he was five. I smiled at the thought of a five-year-old Slate, wild black curls and a face full of stubble.

His eyes were grey. He pulled me against him as we danced, and *oh* he smelled divine. Cloves, earth, and all man. Too much man. Too much pull and testosterone and that sensual charge to him that caused every pore on my body to prickle.

No one else existed outside of us. I felt his breath heavy on my hair. I wanted to melt into him, but happiness with Slate never lasted long. It was like being dunked into ice water while asleep when it was over. That's how it would be if I ever gave myself to him fully: it'd be hot one moment and icy the next. I could indulge in a moment though. I didn't even have to say anything mean to chase him away.

"Your betrothed beckons."

I turned to look and I felt the rush of cold at the absence of Slate's body. He'd left me, like he always would.

Ash was watching me from the table he sat at with Moon and Basil. Orion, Canis, and Cygnus were still there with them. I had two choices: 1) Walk away after we had made contact and risk upsetting him, or 2) Deal with it now.

I chose door number two. I was intimidated by every person at the table. I could feel their power before I had even reached them. I wasn't looking forward to seeing Orion again. The one time we interacted was enough for a lifetime. The men's eyes rested on me as I approached the table, reflecting back at me varying degrees of interest.

"Good evening," I said, standing in front of the table, waiting to be invited to sit. I could've sat, but it didn't feel right to do so uninvited, at least not with these men. I looked to Ash who was regarding me coolly. He was rightfully upset; I didn't blame him.

To my surprise Orion was the one to save me. "Scarlett Tio, good to see you again. Do not think I have forgotten about you."

It felt like it was supposed to be a joke, but he had forgotten how to joke a long time ago. It sounded like a promise of destruction. I swallowed hard and mustered up some charm.

"I look forward to it, Patriarch Vetr," I said, and gave him my most pleasant smile.

Ash's after class lessons, aside from our practice, included familiarizing me with the common phrases and pleasantries of Tidings. I liked to think it wasn't because I embarrassed him when I'd called an older gentleman a "mister."

"Please, Orion. Have you had the pleasure of meeting Canis Var, and Cygnus Var, Patriarch Var, Ambassador Var to the Anguillan?"

I shook my head and directed my smile towards the older gentlemen.

"I have not. Very pleased to meet you." I nodded to Moon, who nodded back, and Basil who beamed at me.

At least one of them liked me. Canis was weighing me, but inclined his head. Cygnus was very calm on the outside, but I felt a hurricane of emotions at his core.

Ash was still giving me the silent treatment.

"Please join us," Orion said in his croaky voice, gesturing to the vacant seat next to Basil.

"Thank you, Orion." I slid into the seat.

"How are you, my girl? You look absolutely lovely." Basil kissed my cheek.

A shy smile crept over my mouth.

"Yes, how are you? Any other unexpected events?" Orion was clearly referencing the Ragnarock flying incident.

I shook my head and joked. "No, nothing like that." "What unexpected events?" Cygnus asked.

I didn't know how his insides could be in turmoil while keeping his face so unreadable.

"This young lady *called* enough air to propel her from her seat three stories high to the arena floor in a single bound." Orion said it without any exaggeration.

The men at the table were suddenly looking at me in a different light. There was renewed interest on Canis and Ash's faces. Moon was hardly paying attention, lost in his undoubtedly sad thoughts. You would think the wedding of his only daughter would deliver some relief. Instead he drowned in the depths of his loss.

I bit my lip. "I didn't know what I was doing. I was having an emotional day," I tried to explain to them.

Ash looked angry again, probably because I hadn't told him about the incident. I didn't want it to be a big deal. I sighed internally; I just couldn't win.

"That is quite the feat. You must have expert teachers." It was Canis. He spoke in bursts, his breath rushing out with his words, his lips barely moving.

"Ash was actually the first person to teach me to *call*. Otherwise, there has only been Valla U, unless you count my home battle trainer. He's here somewhere."

I looked around for Slate, grateful for some reprieve from their hard eyes. I couldn't stop what Pearl had said from popping into my head while sitting with them. She believed Alder had been threatened into not running away with my mom. I wondered which of the men at the table had done it.

I saw Pearl approach, her eyes intense. I knit my eyebrows; she looked concerned. The men stood when she got to the table. No one had stood for me.

"Scarlett, darling, I have been looking for you. Gentlemen, how nice of you to join us for this union." When she said *gentlemen* it sounded like *vermin*. Still, her eyes sparkled.

"Pearl, we are getting to know your granddaughter here. Shame she has only arrived in Tidings this year, she could be much further along," Canis said, eyes hooded.

She gave a knowing smile. "Canis. Yes, it is unfortunate she is only just being introduced to her heritage. I trust you are all enjoying yourselves. How wonderful it was to see you all." She didn't wait for them to respond before turning.

"Your son Hawk. For a moment, I thought he was Flint. He resembles him. Strong genes. The Hausts have strong genes as well. Your granddaughter looks nothing like Lark," Canis said after her.

Cygnus's emotions spiked, while Orion seemed resigned. I didn't know the history between Pearl and Canis, but their hate for each other was palpable.

She pursed her lips in exaggerated fashion. "Canis, how right you are." She looked to Hawk at the head tables. "Handsome and brave, like my Flint. May he rest in peace. Gentlemen." She ignored his comment about my appearance.

The Hausts were there. They took up a whole table to themselves. Neither daughter brought a date, though I had seen Nova and Fox dancing on more than one occasion. Sterling had joined Indigo at the Var table since Delta went to sit with her sister at the Hausts.

CHAPTER 21

 Slate had organized our packs. He wanted to keep them as lightweight as possible since Tawny, Gyps, and I had never set foot in a desert, much less hiked through one. The good thing about deserts in Thrimilci was that they didn't have much of a tempera-ture drop in the evenings. Apparently, this one could get down to the mid-seventies, but not cooler.

I wore a pair of tan pants tucked into a pair of soft suede boots I had bought earlier in the week, with a tan, fitted, lightweight shirt that covered my arms. I knew I could use my *calling* to cool off, but I wanted to rough it.

"You think there will be lion people?" Gypsum asked, trying to be cool and not act as excited as he was.

"I'd believe anything at this point." I gave him a lopsided smile and nudged his shoulder.

He was taller than Hawk now. I stood behind him, braiding copper beads into his long raven hair like a certain someone he'd come to revere.

"I know. I'm sort of bummed out there aren't any dragons," he said seriously.

I startled him with my burst of laughter.

"Sorry. *Oh*, I needed that."

My laughing tapered off. His dimples popped when he smiled shyly. *Ugh*, the little heart breaker. My little chief.

Slate came into the informal dining hall. He was similarly dressed in tans; I thought it was the only time he I'd seen him not wearing something black. A thick wavy lock fell free with a silver bead as he checked through his pack adding a few things, mostly weapons.

"You think there'll be trouble?" Gypsum asked.

One look at his face would tell you what he'd prefer. *Yes*, he wanted to test out his new body. And it *was* a new body. He'd always been toned the way athletic boys were, but now he had real muscle. He had gained weight since January and his chest was broader. I made a pouty face.

"We have before, better to prepare. We will take the safest route just in case," Slate told him. He caught me looking. I didn't have the grace to look away. "What is it?" he asked, looking slightly irritated.

He quirked an eyebrow. *Are you going to answer me or am I going to have to strangle it out of you?*

"I've never seen you in anything, but dark colors. You look surprisingly bright," I said resentfully.

How dare he make me confess my thoughts.

"Where are your weapons?" he asked me, eyes roaming around my body.

Whoops. I had taken the idea that it was a vacation a little too lightly; this could be potentially dangerous.

He glowered. *You should know better*, his look said.

Sheesh.

Gypsum backed away slowly and put on his seax, not wanting to get chastised either. I dug through the pack Slate had prepared; I wasn't sure where he'd put them. Slate grumbled something and grabbed the pack from me. He pulled out my boot blades, short seax, then my dagger belt, and left my wrist blades in the pack.

He kneeled in front of me and slipped the holsters for the boots blades onto my boots, buckled my short seax to my right thigh, and snapped the belt out like a whip and circled it around my waist. He grabbed the other end as it swung around pulled it through the Daymark buckle extra tight. His eyes lifted to mine before looking back down to pull it through.

"I've put on belts before," I mumbled, aware of Gypsums's confused look.

Slate just grunted.

"We are ready." Steel walked in with Tawny, both in khaki.

They had scarves hanging loose around their necks. *Where's my scarf?* Slate passed a white one to me as I thought it, wrapping his own around his neck. Gypsum got one from Tawny, who was smirking as usual.

"Grab a pack. We need to get on the road, it will take a full day to get there," Slate said. "Last chance to change your mind." Slate looked from Gypsum to me to Tawny. We three shook our heads. "Move out."

We came out through the portal in town and headed into the desert.

When I thought of a desert I thought of sand. There was a lot of sand but there was clay and red dirt too. What I didn't anticipate was that it would be completely flat stretch of land and that I would eventually have to use the bathroom. Word to the wise: popping a squat twenty feet away from four other people, completely sober, in the middle of the day so there's not even a shadow to hide in, is embarrassing. I waited till I was fit to burst before going again.

There were random trees around small oases once we were out of the flats, there was some various kinds of cacti, but over all not much for vegetation and few and far between. I was thankful for all the training I'd done. Even with the heat, I managed to keep up with the group. I was impressed with Gypsum: he'd had less intense training than I had, but didn't fall behind. We rotated who we walked with constantly, the scarves protecting our heads from the harsh sunlight.

It was early evening when we came to some red and orange striped hills.

"Sandstone," Slate said. "We will camp where this ends for the night."

CHAPTER 22

Formations that seemed to roll and swell with red and orange earth WERE ON either side of us. The sun was going down, and the hills cast long shadows over us, so I took off my scarf. The temperature was starting to drop and the breeze that flowed through the hills felt *marvelous*.

We came to the end of the undulating forms and Slate decided it was safe to have a fire as long as we stayed inside the hills. While he got it started, Tawny and I got a meal of cured meats and breads together for everyone. After our little meal, we set up our rolls and lay down in front of the fire. Steel set his roll down at the side facing the path we were headed, and Slate put his directly across from where we had come. Tawny set up next to Steel. Gypsum, taking the hint, set up beside me, while Slate was on my other side.

I lay down on my stomach facing Slate's profile. The flames flickered across his strong jaw and high cheekbones, looking severe in the light. Poor Gyps had passed out the moment he hit the roll. I could hear murmuring from Tawny and Steel. Steel chuckled deeply and doused the fire.

Slate turned over onto his side to face me. I could just make out his face in the moonlight.

"I can't sleep," I confided.

"What do you want me to do?" Such a loaded reply; I could *feel* his evil grin. I was glad it was dark so he couldn't see me blush. "Just talk to me."

"About what?" he grunted.

I thought for a minute; his response could spoil my trip, but I had to know.

"Did you and Shale break up? She wasn't at the wedding," I asked, trying to control my voice.

He stretched out an arm and grabbed my roll and pulled it across the red dirt until it touched his.

"Why do you care, Rabbit?" he asked, his tone dangerous.

"Just making smalltalk."

"Wrong answer."

He rolled onto his back. I grabbed his shirt and pulled him back.

"I want to know."

"Why?"

"Why won't you just tell me?"

"I want to hear you say it."

"Say what?" My voice had started to get high so I quieted back down. "You're impossible," I huffed, now turning onto my back.

He grabbed my belt and pulled my hips toward him; my body had no choice but to follow.

"Tell me." His voice was low and deep. I felt a sharp pleasure shoot through me.

My arms felt numb, but I pushed back so I was completely on my own roll again. "I wanted to know if you were sleeping with her still. There. Are you happy? It's just a question." I pouted.

"If I was?"

My heart sank.

"Never mind."

Terrible question. It was none of my business. I turned back to him.

"Why do Pearl and Reed have the same last name? Every other woman has a different last name than her brother."

This would be a lot easier if I could read his expressions, he had blocked his emotions from me. I thought I could *feel* disappointment.

"Pearl's parents were brother and sister," he said simply.

I could only see the moonlight shine off his silver eyes, but I knew he was looking at me.

"Don't you think that requires a little backstory?" I said irritatedly.

You couldn't drop a bomb like that and not explain!

He chuckled. "Many people do not like that your male line kept the Tio name. The only Tio girl was lost; she was in Valla when she was separated from her family. They had a son after she disappeared and named her brother a Tio. They will do that for Tawny. She was found fifteen years later, and she and her brother fell in love. They married. Reed and Pearl are their children."

I was stunned. "So they let them get married? Why? It would be against all the rules, and like...science. I'm sorry. I'm trying to wrap my head around the fact that I'm inbred."

Slate's lips curled. "Pearl's grandfather was Prime; he couldn't say no to his own children. The Tios have been twice as strong as any of the greater families since."

No wonder they all hated us. "Isn't there a council? Someone who could have stopped them? Not that I don't want to exist, but..."

"Yes; the only ones who sided against him were Vetr, Var, and Natt. Guess which families hold the most influence now? Haust and Geol have been reduced to almost nothing. Dagr? Sparrow and Tawny are the last, and Tawny is taking the Vetr name. Tio fell out of favor and Vetr and Var rose."

I was starting to get tired. "Do they know who your parents were?" I asked hesitantly.

"No." He said it without a hint of emotion. It broke my heart.

I reached out and placed my hand on his. He looked at it suspiciously. Things on the other side of the fire were reaching their pinnacle. I pulled my hand away, feeling things below my belt start to awaken.

Slate grabbed my belt and pulled me to him so I was tucked into him. I felt him *call* and I fell asleep in his arms before I could feel guilty about it.

Slate's muscled arm was around my waist and pulled tight to my chest. I could've died there and been happy forever, but...I really had to pee. I carefully lifted his arm and rolled out from under it. I kneeled in front of him, just able to make out his sleeping face in the moonlight that was quickly becoming dawn. His full lips rested feather light together, his silvery eyes were closed; he looked like a young man instead of the dark and dangerous womanizer I had come to know. I pushed a stray hair away from his face.

I shook myself mentally and half ran past Steel and Tawny, who thankfully were dressed. I didn't want to risk someone waking up to see my bare fanny pack squatting in the dawn light, so I went behind one of the low hills a little ways away.

I pulled down my pants and started to go in the red clay. I heard something that sounded like rattling over my stream. I spun, trying to pull my pants up and pull out my short seax simultaneously. And then I saw it. A six-foot-tall...*well*, it was a spider.

A giant grey spider.

It had six legs and two-foot-long pinchers below a human-shaped head. Its back was a big black sack. The rattling noise was coming from its mouth as its six legs scrambled at a speed I would have thought impossible. I couldn't think to *call*. I pulled the seax free and held it out as the creature ran into it, face first. It toppled onto me, its dead weight pinning my arms underneath it. That sack weighed a ton...and my pants were still around my ankles. The entire interaction lasted less than ten seconds.

I didn't have time to get my wits about me before three more giant spider people came running down one of the hills. I had to think fast. I used air to push the spider I'd killed off of me, and the others were on me. One looked identical to the one I had killed, one had only four legs and a man's upper body with pinchers protruding from his jaw, the other looked even more like a man with four crouched legs and a man's chest and hands. The man-looking spider had six black eyes and deep ridges going across its forehead, and a fan of long, wild, inky hair. Its pinchers were as thick as an arm, but it also had a mouth like a man.

They attacked all at once. A spider man got close enough for me to push a dagger into one of its eyes while it tried to pinch me. I started *calling* fire, attempting to keep them at bay. My leg movements were restricted by my pants on my ankles, but my boots prevented them from coming off. The spiders kept snapping their pinchers and jumping out at me before pulling back. I threw modesty to the wind and used my seax to sever my pant legs at both calves.

As I looked back up from my shredded pants, I saw the six-legged one jump over my flames and land on top of me. Its body knocked me off my feet, and its pinchers dug into both of my shoulders simultaneously. I wanted to scream, but I was afraid that someone might come running and they'd be killed, or worse, I'd lead the spiders to camp and my friends would all die. I took the pain. I felt something else snap down around my neck, shutting off my wild flames. I had burnt the spider that fell on me to a crisp but not before they cut off my *calling*.

Just what were these things? The man at the river had used the same thing to cut me off from my *calling*.

I tried not to panic; I could still fight. I tried to push myself out from under the crispy spider, but its pinchers had torn the muscles in my arms and I could barely lift them. *Please don't let this be how I die*, I thought piteously.

The one I'd stabbed in the eye shoved off Crispy's carcass and rattled down at me. White, thick fluid oozed out of its eye. It must have thought I was beaten, lying there like I was, but I had curled my legs up as soon as the weight was lifted. I had my boot knife now, and I threw it straight into the spider man's rattling mouth. It screamed and thrashed at its throat.

My legs were free and I rolled away. I couldn't see where the human spider was. He kicked me with two of its four legs as I rolled. I stopped and curled into a ball; I tried to *call* but it was still blocked. It grabbed my dagger belt and ripped it off with its too human hands.

It rattled from its throat, *"Little Guardian taste delicious."*

My jaw was clenched, and I was praying a scream didn't tear free. That was when its face split up its jaw, and a gaping maw full of tiny, thin, razor-like teeth rattled down at me.

Surely the camp could take on this *one*. I was ready to loose a scream to end all screams. It must have sensed it, though, and its pinchers clamped down on my throat. The spider's venom burned as my muscles cramped, my rapid heartbeat pushing the venom quickly through me. My breathing grew harsh, my tongue felt thick and useless.

I blinked and the spider was off me. I could hear its ear-bleeding shrieking like someone was torturing it.

Less than five minutes ago, I had left camp to pee. I tried to turn my head carefully towards the sliver of red on the horizon. At least in the daylight they would find my body. I closed my eyes.

"Torch!"

Someone slapped me. I blinked my eyes open. It was Slate. My thoughts were sluggish.

"Ow," I tried to say, but my tongue wouldn't make the motions. Slate's pained face broke into a sad smile.

"Do not move, it punctured your throat. I am going to heal you." I felt him touching my body. It was dull, like he touched me through a thick blanket. He was cursing as he went.

I tried to swallow. "I think I've been poisoned," I tried to rasp.

"Lie still. One thing at a time."

Poisoning seemed pretty serious to me, but whatever, I guess I'd just *die* if this didn't work. He was moving my limbs again.

He ripped off the thing wrapped around my throat and a warmth fell over me.

I felt myself knitting back together slowly. The poison seeped out onto the ground. I could breathe again.

Bone weary, I had phantom soreness everywhere. Slate curled an arm around my neck, putting his other on my back.

"Slowly; you are healed, but you are going to be tired."

Tired wasn't the half of it; I would've fallen asleep right there if he wasn't forcing me up. My clothes had been torn to shreds and completely singed off. My boots and bra were the only two things that had survived. Even my sheath had been ripped off at some point.

He was still holding my back up watching my face. "I'm alright, I think. Just tired beyond belief."

The relief on his face made me want to cry. And then I did. I sobbed, pants-less in the desert after almost dying, for about five minutes, the most sensual man I had ever laid eyes on cradling me like a baby until I finished.

"You are safe now."

Slate stroked my head. My breathing slowed to a normal pace, my tears dried up.

"You must be so sick of saving me."

He held a finger to my lips. He wiped the tears that lingered on my face with a calloused thumb.

"Quiet, Rabbit."

I flung myself around his neck like a child. I was so grateful. He pulled me away slowly. Suddenly aware of my state of undress, I covered my bikini area with a hand.

He gave me a small smile. He picked up his shirt off the ground and pulled it over my head—it hung to my knees. His shirt smelled like him, like the wind, fallen leaves and trees mingled with sweat and spicy man. I breathed in deeply. My head spun and I almost fell.

Slate caught me.

His pants were frayed, but his boots and weapons belts were still on. It was how he looked after the fight at the river too. The spider man must have really done a number on him.

"I am going to carry you back to camp."

Long shadows danced over the red and orange hills. Steel and Tawny stood cautiously. Gypsum sat at a fresh fire munching on breakfast.

Steel noticed my lack of pants, and then the singed scraps hanging off my ankles. "What happened?" he nearly shouted.

Steel and Hawk were similar men, intelligent and kind, but when driven to anger they were just as violent as any other man.

Tawny put a hand on his arm. "She's obviously healed; let me clean her up and you can talk to Slate," she said, trying to calm him, but with obvious alarm written all over her face.

Slate set me down on my roll. Steel didn't want us to go anywhere in case there were more monsters, so they stood facing the hill exit while Tawny stripped me, *calling* water onto a scrap of my shirt to clean off all the dried blood—the spider's and my own. What was left of my shirt was black and red by the time she finished. She had to help me pull on my change of clothes because I didn't have the energy to sit up any longer.

"I don't know how you keep getting your fanny pack kicked, Scar."

Six months ago I was in college, a semi-normal teenage girl living a hectic, teenage girl's life.

The men came back to camp to talk with Tawny. I was still awake, but too tired to move.

"She has had a lot of healing. We cannot stay. I doubt they are the only ones. We need to move onto Wemic territory. They had nix torques." It was Slate; he sounded proud and frustrated at the same time.

Steel cursed. "Another one? That's the fourth one we've found outside of Karkinos. Why now? Are the tribes that unhappy?"

"We should go. Slate, are you strong enough to carry her while she sleeps?" Tawny asked.

Steel interrupted. "I'll carry her."

"No, if there are more out there, I won't be able to fight well, I am weaker right now. I used all of my energy to pull the poison from her. I will carry her until we reach the Wemic," Slate told him.

I was aware of constant movement as I slept. I opened my eyes a few times during the six hours from the red hills to the Wemic village. I would stare up at Slate's clenched jaw as he walked. At one point he was looking down at me when I opened my eyes. He said something my fog-stuffed brain couldn't comprehend and I ran a hand from his ear to his chin and he smiled. A *real,* cheek-creasing smile. Then I fell back to sleep.

I finally woke up right before we arrived—good thing too, since we had to hike through canyons. Red dirt canyons cracked open deep into the earth.

"Wemic lands. Not long now, we will start to see their lookouts soon," Steel told us.

Gypsum was carrying my pack filled with what they had salvaged from the spider people. The straps of my sheath were completely singed off, but at least the sheath and seax were okay. I had back all of my knives and my belt.

"What happened?" Slate asked as we traversed through the cracks.

"I went to pee," I told them, embarrassed. "I literally got caught with my pants down."

Tawny laughed and Gyps gave a nervous chuckle. Slate was stone-faced; he did not think I was amusing.

"It was my fault, if I wasn't being so weird about peeing in front of you guys I wouldn't have wandered so far away."

I ran a hand through my golden tresses pulling out tangles. I'd deal with the mess of emotions later—for now, I was just thankful to be alive.

"Why didn't you call for help?" Gypsum asked.

"I didn't know how many there were. If you guys ran to save me and they killed you, or if there were more and it led them to the camp while you were sleeping?" I shook my head. I would've died anyway, no need to get everyone else killed.

Slate looked at me incredulously, "Rabbits scamper. Why is it whenever faced with death you run into its arms? Why not trust me to help? *Us* to help," he corrected.

"I don't go looking for dangerous situations, they find me and I do what I think is best. I'm usually the most expendable person. I just didn't want anyone else to get hurt."

Slate's eyes narrowed at me and I realized I'd stopped walking. I turned to catch up with the others.

"You are not expendable."

Slate walked at my shoulder looking ready to curl up and sleep. I shook my head. "That's not what I meant. Just that, the first time, you were outnumbered, I didn't feel like I was doing anything foolish. The second time, okay, you've got me there, but I'd rather be dead than touched by those men. This time was different; if it had been Gyps or Tawny who heard my cries for help and ran into those things..." I couldn't finish my sentence, I'd never do anything to put my family at risk if I could help it.

Slate's big chest rose and fell, but he kept his exasperated comments to himself as we finished our trek.

We came across the first lookout. I'd always thought Slate moved like a big cat, but this lookout person was *actually* was a big cat...man. He had the same shape as a man except his hands ended in claws and his feet were paws. His ears ended in points and he had the muzzle of a cat, but it was somehow flatter, not protruding at all.

He trotted up from the canyon and smiled with his catlike mouth and sharp teeth. "Steel! We expected you weeks ago."

The cat man clasped Steel's neck and brought his forehead to his own. He was bare-chested with a loincloth on and a beaded belt. Short black fur covered his body.

"Rikke, I promised to bring some guests along, and we had to wait.

This is my niece and nephew, Scarlett and Gypsum. And my mate, Tawny," Steel said with a hint of pride.

I saw Gypsum wince. "Mate" implied many things Gyps did not want to think about when it came to his sister. Slate greeted the cat man in the same manner as Steel had; the two appeared to be friends.

Rikke walked up to Gypsum and pulled his head against his as he did with Gypsum. "Family of Slate and Steel are family of ours."

He turned to me and greeted me in the same way. He gave Tawny an appreciative look and smiled at Steel as he greeted her as well, leaving her fair skin flushed.

Rikke's eyes were lime green with vertical slotted pupils; his black hair was pulled back into a ponytail with feather fetishes adorned through it. The fur on his clawed hand was soft. Even with his thin layer of fur, you could see how powerfully built he was. He smiled and it was terrifying. Smiling must be something he reserved for humans—all those sharp teeth were petrifying.

"Rikke, have there been any unusual happenings around the lands?" Slate asked as we started our descent into the canyons below.

He thought for a moment, scratching his furry chin. "What happened?" He obviously knew something, but was deciding what he should say.

"We were attacked by the Jorogumo in the red hills," Slate told him.

Rikke nodded. "There have been some occurrences. Best if you speak to Reski." At that the sable furred man cat started at a jog into the canyons.

We saw more Wemic as we came near their village center. Little, round-topped mud brick homes were made right along the canyon walls. The canyon had opened up to reveal a small river and some vegetation in the heart of the canyon. Little cat children ran around us, naked and laughing. I fought the urge to pet them; they were adorable.

Most of the Wemic had white, red, and blue designs painted onto their arms, faces, and chests. Female Wemic often wore loincloths or long skirts with bra-like tops made of the same material. Leopard-, lion-, and tiger-furred Wemic watched us walk into their village. Some greeted Steel warmly, but most went about their own business.

"The Guardians return," came a snide voice.

Slate's eyes narrowed. "Nirrin, not on watch today?"

Slate did not like this Nirrin, and I could see why. Nirrin spoke to Slate with unabashed disdain, and circled him like the cheetah-printed animal he resembled.

He watched Slate with his gold eyes. "Not today, Slate. Steel, always a pleasure." Nirrin narrowed his eyes at Slate and glanced to Gypsum, Tawny, and me.

"Your mate?"

Nirrin started making a staccato purring noise at me as he circled me, sniffing me. I tried not to let him walk behind me. Slate growled viciously like an animal; I did a double take to be sure he hadn't developed a muzzle.

"She has a mate, Nirrin, and the other is *my* mate. Where are your brothers?" Steel said in a warning tone.

Rikke stood leaning on his spear as if this was perfectly acceptable. Tawny held her chin a little higher; Steel had just claimed her to these people and she was preening. And there I was, all mat*eless*.

Nirrin leered at me, taunting Slate, the black mohawk of fur on his back stiffening. "Leave it be, Nirrin," Rikke said as if he frequently grew annoyed by Nirrin.

"Too bad. She is in season." He purred. He turned to Steel. "My brothers are hunting. I was going to join them...but I think I will stay instead." He gave me a cat smile, his golden cat eyes wide, the black lines from his eyes to his mouth looking sinister.

Well, that was embarrassing. It was made worse by the fact that Gypsum was blushing for me.

"Slate!" A muscular lion man greeted Slate warmly, smiling.

He had gold fur covering his body that grew lighter under his chin and down his chest and stomach. Red paint swirled around his arms and shoulders. He had golden eyes and long golden hair pulled back with feather fetishes and leather. His muzzle was white with a black nose. I was struck by how his features were attractive even by human standards, even by *my* standards.

Steel introduced us to Keen, the golden lion man. His smile was more practiced. "Slate's family? You are not a lone wolf after all?" He laughed and came to greet us. "She is in season," Keen said, the nostrils flaring in his catlike nose, his big golden eyes regarding me with dilated vertical pupils.

Slate laughed. "So we have been told. You know it is not polite to point such things out with humans."

I wanted to die.

"Oh." His cat brow furrowed. "Would you not want to know your mate is in season?" he said talking to Slate.

"I did not mention it," Rikke said proudly with a feline smile.

Slate liked Keen, I noticed right away. Slate met his forehead to Keen's.

"She is not my mate. Keen. Where is your brother? We had trouble getting here. We were attacked by Jorogumo."

Keen nodded, unsurprised. "Yes, come let us speak in private." Keen spared me a side glance, and I noted the interest in his eye. So did Slate.

We entered the largest adobe. Three Wemic that had been sitting on cushions stood when they saw us.

Another lion man with a great mane of golden hair and golden skin was obviously the leader. Wooden beads hung from his mane of hair, and scars crossed one of his golden eyes, underlined with white fur. He too had a white chin under his muzzle and a lighter stomach. Red paint covered his cheekbones down to his jaws and on his forehead into his hairline.

"Guardians," he said, greeting us.

He paused for a brief moment, looking at me. I hoped he wouldn't say anything about my *season*. I had never kept track of that sort of thing; it was embarrassing that they could smell it on me.

There was a lynx looking man, whose fur the longest of all of the Wemic I'd seen. His ears were long and high on his head, with reddish brown and spotted fur sticking straight out.

He was also the burliest, tall and wide. "We have guests. Good timing. We must speak."

The other Wemic looked like he could Keen's brother. His hair had been dipped in red and plaited. Red paint covered his jaw down to his collarbones. He was silent and greeted us all with nods.

"Scarlett, Gypsum, Tawny...this is Tikee," Steel said, gesturing towards the lynx man. "Nekee," He continued, pointing to the quiet lion man. "And the chief of the Wemic, Reski."

Reski was impressive. He was heavily muscled beneath his golden fur, and had penetrating golden eyes. I wondered how he had earned the massive scratch over his eye.

"Steel, we have been expecting you. Please stay, Rikke," Reski told the black panther man.

"Reski, we were attacked in the red hills. Scarlett, if you would please tell them what happened?" Steel asked.

I hadn't expected to do any talking; staring and nodding, most definitely.

I told them the story of how I was caught with my pants down. Keen, Rikke, and Nekee were looking at me differently as I spoke; their cat eyes looked impressed. Maybe they were realizing I wasn't as weak as I looked.

"Rikke is our farthest lookout. He has seen them a few times," Tikee told us.

Rikke nodded, his lime green eyes on Steel. "I have tracked them into red hills. We go out with hunting parties, but cannot find where they have nested." The panther man made a face of disgust.

"You should have sent an emissary. We would send reinforcements," Slate told them.

The silent lion, Nekee, looked amused.

Steel noted his amusement. "At the very least we should alert the Faunelle in case they have infiltrated their lands as well."

Reski spoke, his voice a rumbling roar. "Yes, we thought as much. It has only been within the last two months. After your last visit."

Steel nodded. "I will report this to the Prime and will visit the Faunelle when we leave to inform them. We will most likely return within a week to flush out the rogue Jorogumo. My only issue is how they are getting here."

Reski nodded. "I fear the Merfolk may be involved."

Steel had told us that the Merfolk lived in the waters all around the island. Steel bristled; he spent most of his time dealing with the Merfolk, and they were the touchiest tribe in Thrimilci. He would see it as a personal betrayal if it were true.

"If not involved, then letting another of the tribes cross through their waters," Tikee said, long ears twitching as he spoke.

"The Jorogumo have not attacked until now. We will double our watch and ready our warriors in the event of an attack." The silent brother Nekee had finally spoken.

Reski agreed.

"We are glad to see your family is safe, Steel," Reski told him in earnest.

"We should celebrate. When Slate and Steel come to visit we have a feast. Since he brought family, and defended against the Jorogumo, we have more need of merriment," Keen said gaily, his eyes flitting to me.

Tikee jumped on the idea—the big furry cat looked like he would love a good feast. "Indeed. Much honor, Guardians."

Reski eyed his brother Keen for a moment with an indulgent smile only eldest siblings gave their youngest when he and Nekee agreed.

Tawny and Steel were ushered into an adobe to prepare them. It was tradition to paint before a feast. Gypsum, Slate, and I were led into a separate adobe. They made us change into their customary clothing and if the trip had ended then, that would have made it worth it.

Watching Gypsum fight with twin cheetah girls trying to strip him of his pants while they giggled...I was still laughing. He gave in eventually and put on a loincloth grudgingly.

I should have felt exposed, but I didn't. We looked like everyone else in the tribe. A lioness with plaited brown hair painted blue swirls down my chest and arms. They drew blue lines on my face imitating the lines under the big cats' eyes.

I watched Slate sit in his loincloth as two cat women drew lines on his chest, back, and arms. I fought back jealous surges as they slid fingers over his rippling muscles. When they were done, the three of us were artistically covered in blue paints and the girls who had drawn them were giggling as they steered us out of the adobe and into the feast.

There weren't any chairs; stuffed animal skin cushions were scattered and platters of food rested on rock tables. Jugs were being passed around with some kind of alcohol in them.

"All I need is a strong breeze and you're going to see *the goods*," Gypsum said in a pissy tone.

I chuckled. I was so glad Gypsum was there. A cheetah twin stalked in front of Gypsum purring, lifting her tail as she passed to caress Gypsum's face. He froze. I laughed harder. Even Slate was smiling.

Steel and Tawny strolled up in white paints.

Steel's tanned face was pulled down in a frown but his eyes looked but amused. I could only guess he had an internal chuckle at Gypsum who had clasped his hands in front of his loincloth. I wondered why they were white and we were blue. I saw then that there was another color, black.

White were couples, as it turned out. I thought that must mean they were married or whatever their equivalent was.

"What do you think?" Steel asked as we sat down on some cushions eating our feast and drinking something so strong it burned the nostrils.

"I love it. They're so nice, and most speak English!" I told him.

Tawny smirked. "Did they explain your markings?" Steel had given her beads that weighed down the cloths, so she was in less danger of exposing herself.

Slate was smirking too now. Gypsum looked nervous. Steel frowned again.

"Uh...no. Why?"

I was suddenly self-conscious of my exposed stomach and legs. My seax needed new straps so I'd tied it to my skirt loincloth and left my knife belt in the adobe. Funny that I would feel better with blades on me.

Tawny pointed to herself. "White is for mates; a lot of the older married couples switch to red after they've worn the white for a time. Black," she said, pointing to a lioness with a grey muzzle in a long skirt and longer top than I'd seen the other women wearing, "is for widows or those in mourning, and blue is for singles or those unmarried or *in season.*" She laughed.

Gypsum gaped like a fish. "But..."

Steel handed him the weighed belt off his own waist, probably hoping Gypsum would stop the attack he launched on his loincloth front attempting to stretch it longer.

"Just say no." Slate laughed harder.

Gypsum paled. Tawny glowered.

I wasn't too surprised. I has remembered something that popped into my head once I saw the other colors in tribal relations class with Butterfly.

"It might be *fun*," Tawny told me.

Slate no longer smirked, which just made Tawny laugh all the harder.

"Do you always wear blue?" I asked Slate.

"I am always single," Slate retorted without glancing from the dancing Wemic.

He must have still been angry with me from the morning's attack. Like I had instigated it or something.

The Wemic were beating drums and singing in their language while a group of them danced. It was mesmerizing. It only got better as the sun went down, the fire casting shadows on their bodies, their eyes gleaming in the lights.

The only thing that may have been a little awkward were the blue painted females around Slate and Gypsum. I could tell who favored Slate's strong build, and who liked how poor Gypsum squirmed at their attention. I would have been laughing the entire time, except Slate seemed to enjoy it a little *too* much. He smiled as they hand fed him and laughed at what were undoubtedly stupid jokes.

I tried not to be offended by my lack of suitors. Tawny and Steel had moved to drink with the chief Reski. His tigress wife was beautiful; long black plaited hair hung down her back nearly to her waist. She looked every bit the chief's wife—I bet even human men found her attractive. I was starting to understand why some humans did a little interspecies dating.

Keen sat down next to me, his sleek golden furred knee touching mine. "Are you enjoying the feast?"

He handed me a clay jug of the nostril-burning alcohol. He had blue paint instead of the red now. I would've thought the Wemic women would snatch up the chief's handsome brother. Several of the blue-painted women started doing that low staccato purring and *chirping*. I felt myself blush next to the good looking cat man.

"The single females are jealous." Keen said, bumping my shoulder, his whiskers tickling my ear.

I ducked and giggled moronically. He looked upset to have offended me.

"Your whiskers tickled me." I blushed.

He gave a cat smile, showing his sharp teeth.

"I did not know human skin was so sensitive. I have never come into contact with human woman before. I have gone into Thrimilci's town several times, but only spoken casually with them." His voice was soothing; there was something in his throat that thrummed as he spoke.

"Well, consider yourself having made a new female human friend," I told him, smiling my best smile.

He purred a little. "I think your features translate well."

"What do you mean?" I feigned ignorance, taking a sip of the fiery liquid. It burned going down.

Keen made a noise that I recognized as the Wemic's laughter. "It is very strong. I only meant you would be the most beautiful Wemic woman."

He said it so blatantly as if it was an obvious fact. I blushed.

He looked upset again. "I did not mean to offend. Do not be angry."

He must have thought I was red with anger. Of course they didn't blush, they had fur. Pointing out my blush only made my red face deepen.

"Keen, I'm not angry. It's called blushing. The blood rushes to our face and it turns red. I'm...embarrassed."

Keen's forehead furrowed. "Because I said you are beautiful? It is a fact."

He was forward and candid, with no concept of personal space, but I honestly didn't mind in the least.

"Thank you. Men don't usually tell women they're beautiful just because it's true," I explained.

"They should. Especially with beauty like yours." He said it low and close to my ear again, tickling my neck with his whiskers.

I giggled again and he smiled.

The blue-painted ladies chatted furiously.

"Why would the women be jealous?" I asked.

I *called* water into my jug; hopefully I could drink it now. My stomach was burning.

"As the chief's brother and a warrior, I am considered a desirable mate."

He wasn't bragging, it was a fact. I liked his honesty, it was refreshing. With all the secrets, half truths, and politics in Valla, I could see why Steel and Slate spent so much time with the tribes.

Gypsum was being pulled into the dancing crowd by the twin cheetah girls, completely helpless. He fit in there too; I wondered if maybe one day he could take over for Steel with the Wemic. I hoped I looked half as comfortable as Slate being fawned over by the Wemic women. I scowled; he'd find a woman anywhere.

"Do they always treat him that way?" I asked about Slate and the women.

Keen looked over and smiled. "Slate's features translate well. He is a good looking man, yes?" I nodded grudgingly. "You are not Slate's mate?" he asked.

"No. I don't have a mate. I have a suitor, someone seeking to marry me, but I haven't given him my decision yet."

I didn't like this talk anymore; I had gone out of my way *not* to think about Ash while we were in our weird fight.

Keen shook his head. "You would be with someone you have not mated?"

"That's very common with humans, maybe not anymore, but some-times. I haven't mated..." I trailed off, I was yammering.

He looked at me like I had sprouted three extra heads.

"How long?" he asked.

I chewed my cheek. "*Um*, actually never," I squeaked.

"You have never mated!" Keen shouted, drawing the attention of the others around us, and I blushed eggplant purple. "Slate's scent is all over you. He has not tried—or has he tried and failed? I would mate with you right now."

It was matter-of-fact. No beating around the bush. Oddly, I felt a small thrill at the offer. I really must have been *in season*, as they said.

I blushed and a laugh escaped me. "Thanks."

He lowered his flashing golden cat eyes at me. "It is settled then."

Keen lifted me to my feet and tossed me over his shoulder while I spluttered. My hands flew to the back of my loincloth skirt to keep my backside covered.

What had just happened? What *was* happening? The Wemic had cheered when I was lifted and the pieces fell into place.

"Wait. Keen, that wasn't an invitation," I said, mustering some dignity.

My head was upside-down over his muscled back and I held a hand to his hip to keep myself from falling. My hair left my back exposed as it nearly dragged on the ground. Something told me it wasn't the first time Keen had done this. He held me with a firm arm over my legs. I felt his lean muscles move under me as he walked to one of the adobes I'd seen close to the bonfire. They were for visiting Guardians—and apparently quickies.

He didn't drop me to my feet until we were inside and he brought me off his shoulder in one fluid move so I was cradled in his furry arms. He laid me with practiced gentleness on the stuffed mattress. I quickly sat up and swung my legs off the bed.

"Change your mind?" Keen asked thoughtfully, his clawed hands at his loincloth.

I stood up. I wouldn't be able to have a conversation with my eyes level with *that*. "No. I mean, yes. I mean...I'm sort of with someone."

Light reflected in his golden amber eyes and I saw a glimmer of the true lion. I tried not to think about what it'd be like to let my hair down for once and be subject to my whims.

Keen took a step closer, but dropped his clawed hands from his loincloth. "Tell me if you change your mind."

"I'll keep you in mind if this whole courting thing falls through." I smiled and tried not to sound so husky when I started again. "We should—"

Keen's clawed hand swept me to him at the speed of light, and his muzzled lips were over mine before my heart had a chance to complete a full heartbeat. There was something sexy and powerful about the lion man that made me want to melt against him. He released me after the brief contact with triumph in his eyes. I hadn't pushed him away.

"You're forgiven. No more of that though." I finally sounded firm.

Keen agreed and we both walked out of the adobe after I combed through my hair. I couldn't stop blushing. We were in there for only a few minutes and the Wemic were laughing and teasing us. Keen was laughing at their jests too.

Slate was watching us from his group of women trying to hand feed him like a pet, or possibly a god.

I grabbed Keen's wrist. "What do the stars look like from here? I bet this far away from town they're amazing." I was in a good mood; I didn't want it spoiled by petty jealousies.

"That was quick, Keen. Out of practice?" Slate sounded like he was teasing, but I saw the silver reflecting firelight in his eyes.

Keen laughed good-naturedly. "*Ah*. Your Norns were unkind to me this night to put such untouchable temptation in my path."

Slate's lips curled. "That one is not a temptress, she is a rabbit. Beware, she will scamper now."

I watched the interaction from Keen's side. The female Wemic were staring daggers at me. Being talked about like I wasn't there was annoying at best.

Keen turned to me and beamed his cat smile. "Come, I have a spot just for watching the stars."

We were on top of the canyon walls above the village. He took me to a spot that had a small, smooth boulder and sat down.

"Sit; I come here sometimes."

We sat with our backs against the smooth boulder. The night sky was beautiful. It was hard to believe, sitting here with this cat man, that this was the same moon I shared in Chicago. I wondered if there were nights Keen had been looking up this very moon when I had looked at my Chicago moon, the same moon.

"It's beautiful, Keen. Thank you for taking me up here." I smiled. His cat eyes reflected the moonlight. He licked my cheek, whiskers tickling my ear. "What was that for?" I asked. I figured it was the human equivalent to a kiss on the cheek.

"You are so sad. Was it the attack? I know you said nothing, but I felt there was more than you said."

Keen was incredibly observant. I wanted to tell him everything, and I mean *everything*. He was so easy to talk to.

"You're right, but trust me, you don't want to know. Being with you has made me feel much better. Thank you for that, Keen."

He smiled. "I like how you say my name."

I smiled back. "We'd better get back, people will think we were up to no good." He furrowed his furry forehead. I laughed. "Mating." Then he laughed.

"I may be able to salvage some of my reputation this way," he joked. Then he stood, helped me up, and we walked back down into the canyon.

"Would you mind giving me a moment alone? I'll be right down," I asked, hoping not to offend the lion man.

Keen looked at my face and nodded. "Take all the time you wish. I understand the need to be on one's own. Save me a dance."

"I'll only be a few minutes," I reassured him, and stood on my tiptoes to give him a kiss on the cheek.

Gosh, I liked Keen. Being with him was so effortless. Even when he stole that kiss, he had been attentive and charming, but respectful and kind. I wished I was a Wemic woman; I would've gone to Keen's bed with nothing but a smile on.

I rose to my feet after a few more minutes alone to clear my head, and dusted off my bottom before starting to descend the canyon. I was barefoot, and it was hard to walk on the red dirt floor with tiny pebbles scattering with my steps, so I was taking my time, trying not to think about which one of the Wemic women Slate would be taking to his bed.

I knew he would. The way those women treated him like some kind of deity to worship...if the men had done that to me I certainly would have given it a second, maybe a third thought.

I was deep in my own thoughts, brooding and sour, wanting to tie Slate up somewhere and leave him for something like fire ants to crawl up his loincloth.

Suddenly, I was slammed hard against the canyon wall, and bounced off of it.

My ears rang and my forehead had knocked onto the ground. I could hear the music from the village faintly, but I knew I was far enough away that they'd never hear me scream. My seax was tied to my skirt and I gingerly reached for it. Something swiped the seax from my skirt first, and I felt whatever it was clamp sharply down on my neck, its weight settling onto my body.

I stiffened. The sharp points left my neck, but only just. I started to *call*.

"You are not going to want to *call*," it rasped.

I felt the points back at my neck; it was a mouth. It bit down hard enough to flip me over, bruising my skin. A scream welled in my throat when I came face-to-face with the beast man.

It was dark and had long pointed ears that would have been in the place of human ears, with three sets of horns protruding from its head. One pair of horns looked like tusks and curved around to its jaw, another very short set curled slightly from behind its ears, and the third set curled like a ram's. Its short snout was pulled back in a snarl, revealing teeth much more frightening than Keen's. The beast man had black hair that hung from its head, held back by its series of horns.

Its eyes flashed at me and I lost all sense of my surroundings. This thing was a true predator. The Jorogumo spider hybrids had been abhorrent monsters, but not this thing. This was highly alert, and instilled a primordial fear in me, knowing it could kill me in a heartbeat. I was only alive because it allowed me to be. I didn't even know if my *calling* would work fast enough to stop the beast.

I tried to keep calm, thinking it could smell my fear and that would only incite the beast.

"What do you want?" I asked in my most calm voice; it only trembled a little.

The beast snarled and latched back onto my throat, its hot breath beating against my skin. I moved my eyes, trying to see the rest of the beast, and regretted it. The beast was nude, and what hung heavy and hard between its legs was stupefying. The beast must have been seven feet tall and three hundred pounds of bunched muscle. I was going to die. There was no way around it.

I sighed and closed my eyes. I'd been tempting fate lately; too many close calls. It was time to pay the piper. The beast's teeth left my neck again, but its clawed hands held me down. It didn't seem to be putting all its weight on me, maybe knowing it'd crush me.

"Why do you not fight?" it rasped against my ear.

Its sharp teeth tugged at my lobe almost gently as its breath fanned against my skin.

"I think you could kill me before I could make a single move," I said plainly.

I wasn't fighting to survive or to save someone. I'd resigned myself to die.

Why?

This wasn't me. I was a fighter.

"Fight me. Scream," it urged, and it lowered its weight on me. That *thing* like a third leg rested on my thighs and I tried to move it off.

"What do you want?" I asked stubbornly.

What if fighting got this thing hot and bothered? No way.

It growled and snapped its teeth in front of my face. I tried to press my head further into the ground. Alas, the ground didn't give and the beast bit into my lip. I winced at the pain, but still didn't cry out.

"Did you fuck Keen?" it asked with a rasp.

My eyes snapped open. "No!" I shouted, then gingerly prodded my lip with my tongue.

It didn't say anything else, but I knew what it wanted. It had shoved my ankles apart and I could tell it was getting aroused just by my scent and being on top of me.

"What do you want?" I asked again.

It didn't respond, but it started to lick me. It licked down my throat and between my breasts, down to my stomach where it shuddered and appeared to breathe for several seconds before returning to my face. Its dark, frightening face hovered above mine and I wondered just how far it was going to take it. I wondered if it was even a Wemic. It didn't look like any big cat I'd ever heard of; maybe one of the Faunelle, with all those horns.

"Quiet," it breathed as it licked all my exposed skin again.

Was it giving me a bath?

I shut up. It was the strangest interaction of my life and my survival instincts were kicking back in. If this thing wanted a fight and wanted to get its jollys off, it would get one. It was licking down my legs now, slow and not bath-like. Was it tasting me? Was it going to eat me? I shivered at the thought of being eaten alive.

That's what the Jorogumo had planned to do. Bile rose in my throat.

The beast hovered back up to my face, and it was...panting. My eyes widened. This was *foreplay*! I fought against it before I could stop myself. A low growl came from somewhere deep in its chest as its hips pinned me down. Then it moaned. My eyes widened further.

Its big horned head pushed against mine and it looked like it was struggling with something. I would not feel sorry for this crazy beast that accosted me and was trying to seduce me.

"I am painfully hard," it rasped, and I screamed.

I couldn't *stop* screaming.

That beast was not putting that *thing* inside me. I didn't care how painful it was, it would be ten times more painful to me. It was more like a battering ram than an appendage!

Then it did something I really didn't expect. It smiled and laughed before getting to its feet and running towards the village. I lay there for a few more minutes trying to figure out what'd just happened as my head pulsed. At least my healing would be minimal even if I was covered in beast saliva.

I sat up and put my hand to my head trying to find the places I'd been injured. My forehead had a sweet knob on it and I had a matching mark on the back of my head, but no blood. Part of me was grateful for the knobs or I would have felt like I'd imagined the peculiar interlude.

I swayed with Keen, letting him guide my hips around. There was a lot of bouncing on the pads of your feet and head swinging; when they roared I wished I could roar with them. Gypsum was trying to.

I gave Keen gestured for Keen to follow so we could sit down for a minute, and we sat back where we started and I took a gulp of my fiery drink.

"You are very good."

"Thanks, I have a good partner." I nudged him.

Gypsum walked up to us, dripping sweat, his hair damp from sweating while he danced. "Hey Keen, where are we sleeping tonight? I've got to make sure I blow this popsicle stand before the twins get any ideas." He looked at the cheetah girls dancing suggestively in Gypsum's direction.

Keen put it together after a moment and started laughing so hard he was holding his stomach. "Are you sure? You would make them very happy."

Gypsum shook his head. "I'd better not," he said, trying to avoid my eye contact.

"Very well. Our guest adobe is back there." He pointed to a small clay building with three interlocked triangles, the symbol for the Guardians, carved above the doorway. "Steel put your packs in there already. He has the one next to it. There are three available if you do not wish to share."

"Cool, yeah. If they ask, you don't know where I went."

Gypsum went around the back of the other adobes before he headed inside one of the guest adobes. He lucked out: Steel and Tawny must not have been in that one. I'd already seen more than enough of those two. I hoped I wouldn't run into them when I went to sleep.

"You will come back to visit, yes?" Keen asked, his golden cat eyes locked on mine.

I was good at reading human emotion and expressions, but the Wemics were harder. Maybe it was because they thought a *lot* about lust and I had to tune it out.

"I would really like that. This night has been so much fun. You're a very good host. Maybe I can bring a single girl with me next time," I joked.

He shook his head. "She would never be more beautiful than you."

He purred and nipped my ear. When I'd seen cats do that, it was a playful gesture like my nudges. I was going to have to brush up on my tribal relations before my next visit.

The music had stopped and people were pairing off. I could hear the result of those pairings and thought about my own possible pairing. Even Slate was gone, I tried not to think about where he could be.

"I'd better head to bed, we have to go back tomorrow." Keen looked disappointed. "Next time, maybe I can stay longer if the Jorogumo are gone."

He smiled his catlike smile. "I would like that. Come, I will walk you to the adobe." He helped me up and we walked to the guest adobe.

I stood in the doorway of the third adobe; I didn't see Steel and Tawny thankfully. I could have turned and went into the adobe, but I didn't. I got on my tiptoes and planted a kiss on Keen's mouth/muzzle. His whiskers tickled, and I giggled. He smiled and I pulled away.

"Keen, you are exactly what the doctor ordered." I giggled at his baffled expression. "Thank you for this perfect night." I kissed him again on his furry lips and went inside the adobe.

My pack was directly in front of the doorless door. I opened it, grabbed Slate's shirt I hadn't given back and a pair of boy shorts. I took off my loincloth skirt and top and pulled his shirt over my head, then pulled on the underwear. They hadn't gone very well with my loincloth skirt. I raised his shirt and took a deep breath into the fabric. I tried not to think about where Slate was, not after how good a night I'd had.

"You make a habit of kissing all the men you meet?" My face burned.

"Enjoy the show?" I asked in retort.

I turned around and saw he was in a bed against the far wall. I could just make out his figure in the dark. I couldn't stop blushing, and my stomach did a flip. I hadn't seen the third bed he was in during my first glance.

He made an appreciative noise. "Nearly as much as you like my shirt."

Just when I thought my blushing had hit an all-time high, it went even deeper; my skin was actually hot to the touch. He'd seen me sniffing his shirt like a weirdo.

"I do. Thank you. *And* I can kiss anyone I please." I crawled into the first bed.

It wasn't much of a bed, really just a stuffed mattress on a clay formed platform; but it was still better than the ground. The same material that made up the loincloths were used as sheets. My blush started to subside, my stomach settling.

"How would Ash feel about that?" he asked, dragging out his name.

"I don't want to talk about him. It was just a friendly kiss, Keen's really sweet."

I felt the bed sink as Slate climbed in. I turned to face him. His face was right there, we were nose to nose.

"Are all your kisses with men friendly?"

His voice sent a spike of pleasure to my core.

"No," I breathed. "Thank you, for saving me."

Just this morning I was attacked by the Jorogumo and almost died. It had been a long day.

"I stayed feigning sleep," he said low.

"Why?"

"Hoping you would return and lie with me."

On impulse, I pushed a lock of his hair out of his face, tucking it behind his ear. He hadn't shaved, and his jaw was stubbly, giving him a rugged look. He grabbed my hand and kissed the inside of my wrist. My heart leapt. Slate needed one of those high voltage signs to hang around his neck.

Our noses brushed. All it would take was one more inch...I licked my lips.

I jumped at a voice. "Slate, are you asleep?" I glanced to a stunning tigress with plaited black hair that stuck her head in the doorway.

"He's not," I snapped with a sigh.

Slate searched my eyes, but I turned around and pulled the rough-hewn blankets up to my chin. I felt him get out of bed and rumble something to the tigress before leaving.

Slate would not upset me enough to ruin another night.

It was hours before I fell asleep, and Slate still hadn't come back.

The sun shone in through the square window and right on my face. An arm curled around my waist and pulled me on the mattress against a warm body. What was *he* doing there?

"Good morning," Slate purred and I fumed.

"It'd be better if you'd get your paws off me," I said scornfully despite my gravelly voice.

"Tika thought I would be alone," he said, his voice thick with sleep.

"I don't care. Sleep or don't sleep with whomever you want. It's none of my business." His arm released its iron grip around me.

I sat up and realized I was still in Slate's shirt and a pair of panties while he was shirtless in bed next to me. I narrowed my eyes at him and lifted the blanket to find that he must have let the loincloth drop to the floor before climbing into bed with me because he was most assuredly not wearing a stitch.

"Scarlett."

He lifted himself up onto his elbows. His long wavy hair was disheveled like someone had their hands—or claws—in it.

I swung my legs over the side of the bed and pulled my pack to me. "Honestly, you don't owe me an explanation and I don't want to hear it." I snapped out a white tank top and a pair of snug khakis to wear with my suede boots.

After I pulled off Slate's shirt, I threw it over my shoulder at him and put my bra on before yanking on my tank top. Slate's fingers grazed my back and I tugged down the shirt roughly before sliding my feet into the pants. When I stood to slide them over my hips there was a knock at the doorway and someone stuck their head in.

It was Keen. "Good morning."

A big warm smile lit up my face as I zipped my pants. Slate folded his arms behind his head behind me and Keen arched a white brow at him.

"Keen, good morning. I was just thinking about you," I said, pulling his attention away from the big arrogant man.

"All good, I hope?"

I nodded.

Keen sat down next to me on the bed while I strapped on my dagger belt, stuck in my boot knives, and started to attach my wrist blades—I wasn't taking any chances this time. My short seax sat on the bed; I'd have to find a way to put it on. Slate watched us with an amused expression—he hadn't so much as lifted a finger to make it less awkward.

Keen held out his hands, offering to help with the wrist blades. I nodded and offered my arms, sleeves rolled up to my elbows.

"I am trying not to read into last night." He smiled his cat smile.

Slate grunted and stood for all the world—especially Keen—to see that he was not wearing any clothes. Keen chuckled.

I ignored Slate's display and gave Keen a lopsided grin. "Something to remember me by. That's all. Last night meant a lot to me."

He nodded. "I could tell you do not get out much if you thought that was good." He made a noise that sounded like laughter. I nudged him. "I can tell by her scent you were unsuccessful, my friend," Keen said over his shoulder to Slate who was pulling clothes out of his pack.

Slate chuckled deeply in his chest. "Can you also tell by her scent who she lay with all night?"

My cheeks heated and I bit back a caustic rebuke. I didn't want Keen seeing how Slate got to me.

Despite the weird licking beast and my almost-kiss with Slate, there had been

Keen. He was a breath of fresh air. I made my point clearly: he had been a great host, always honest and showering me with attention that was genuine and sincere.

Keen nodded. "You should leave this other man. I make you happier."

I laughed, always so honest. "You're right, but I can't."

That seemed to sadden him a little. "I still have you for breakfast; you will forget about him before we are through." He was smiling again.

"Great, I am famished," Slate said coolly as he pushed past us and out of the adobe.

Our heads lifted as Gypsum came out of the adobe. Two cheetahs girls watched him go from the doorway and he shot them a dimpled smile before swinging back over to us and dropping his gaze.

Slate patted him on the back and handed him a plate of food as Gypsum pointedly ignored Tawny and my glares. I wanted to scold him; he was becoming just like the rest of them.

The chief Reski, his tigress wife, his other brother Nekee, and the furry Tikee sat with our group. Nirrin the cheetah man was with two other cheetahs who must have been his brothers, giving a report near Steel and Slate. Keen and I sat off to the side sharing our breakfast, but still close enough to hear.

"The bodies were gone. Signs of a fight were still there. We checked over the hills and found no nest," Nirrin reported.

"Thank you, Nirrin. Please rest for the day, your brothers as well," Reski told him. Nirrin stalked off.

Tikee grunted. "He is mad he missed the feast."

"It is the nature of being the leader of the hunting party," said Chief Reski. His beautiful wife nodded. "Keen will accompany Steel to the Faunelle and report back to us when he leaves," he said to Slate.

Slate nodded. "Thank you. We appreciate your support and hospitality."

After breakfast, they replenished our food stores and I went to see Steel and Keen off with Tawny, who was understandably upset. I was glad Keen was leaving me instead of me having to leave him. I had enjoyed myself so much, I didn't know if I could make my feet move away.

"You promise to visit again?" Keen asked.

"A hundred Jorogumo couldn't stop me," I joked.

"For the Jorogumo's sake, let us hope they do not get in your way."

I laughed and reached up to hug him. He nipped my ear, and I planted a kiss on his furry mouth. He smiled against my lips and I fell back onto my heels.

"She kisses all her friends like that. I would know."

Slate. I hadn't heard him sneak up behind me. Fortunately Steel and Tawny were in their own world and had no clue what was happening.

Keen laughed. "I did not see you get any of those kisses. If you had, you would not let her give them away so freely."

Slate smiled, but it looked forced. "I should not let her give them away at all," he said in agreement.

"I plan to steal her away from her suitor. Then I will be the only one getting kissed. Until then..." He clasped arms with Slate.

"Until then, my friend. Journey safe."

I knew Slate liked him, I could tell. Mostly because he didn't like anyone but members of our family, but with Keen he was different; he respected him.

"Scarlett, be happy."

I bit my cheek to stop the tears. He ran a clawed finger down my face then turned to trot past Steel who waved goodbye.

"Keen would be a better choice than Ash," Slate said.

"No one asked you." I nonchalantly rubbed traitorous tears from my cheek with my palm.

"Does not change the facts."

We were still facing the way they left as they grew smaller in the distance. "It doesn't matter," I muttered.

Slate nodded and walked away. I wanted to watch Keen and Steel until I couldn't see them anymore. Tawny walked away with a heavy sigh. I stood with my arms crossed, watching their forms in the far distance. They must have been trotting to make such good time.

"Guardian girl."

I whipped around. It was Nirrin. He laughed, but his wasn't half as nice as Keen's laugh. He walked around me, watching Keen in the distance. He was purposely being menacing.

"A flower, ready for the plucking."

He was on my heels breathing in my scent. It sent shivers down my spine. Nirrin's bared teeth sneered. It was frightening with his sharp teeth.

"Nirrin, do you not have something better to do?"

Slate was back. He was trying to look casual, leaning against the canyon wall, but I could see his muscles poised to spring.

"Slate, bother someone else. The girl and I are speaking." Nirrin gave him a dangerous smile.

"We're done talking." I walked around him and headed to Slate.

"She stinks of you. You did not bed her, but you were sure to mark her. No wonder Keen failed," Nirrin called after us.

It made me angry. He was just a bad apple.

"Next time, maybe you should wait until after you are done with your *season* before coming back," Slate growled after Nirrin disappeared.

I stopped in my tracks. Now I was *really* pissed.

"You can't be serious. I have *never ever* in my life kept track of my ovulation! He didn't come on to me because I'm in *season*. He did it cause he's a huge jerk! None of the other Wemic males treated me like that! And what did he mean about *your* scent?" I stammered out.

Slate scoffed. "You do not think that the second you paid Keen attention that he did not lay his claim to you? He had you all to himself. You cannot be *that* naive. He carried you into the adobe with every intention of claiming you. It was good you had my scent on you, it gave them pause."

I was gaping. "You have no right to be jealous, you had Tika to warm your bed. Just...just stop acting like *you* have some right to me. If it wasn't Tika, it was Shale, and whoever else," I scolded him, turning to walk away.

He grabbed me and threw me against the canyon wall, *hard*. My head bounced off and left me a little dizzy, but he didn't let go. He was pressing himself against me while I pushed back at him. He wouldn't budge, so I punched him in the stomach.

If you had told me six months ago that I'd feel the need to wrestle with someone to work out my aggressions, I'd call you crazy. If you told me that I'd punch someone and welcome their own hits, I would've had you committed. But it felt *right*.

He hunched over. I felt bad for a second, and then he lifted his head and smiled; it was a delicious lip curl that I felt in my toes. Quick as a cat, he straightened back up and launched himself at me, knocking us both to the ground, his hands behind my head so I wouldn't hit it again. His body weight pressed firmly against me as he straddled me.

I gasped, and kicked into him as hard as I could, grabbing him by his shirt and body weight to roll me over him. I landed on top of him, panting.

"Enough," I breathed.

His eyes were silvery grey, his hands were roaming up my thighs, squeezing as he went. His chiseled features clenched in desire, jaw flexing. I felt how much *desire* under me.

"You can't have me whenever you want," I said before standing up. I looked down at him. "I want us to get along."

He tilted his head up, silver eyes locked on mine, unreadable. He ran his fingers through his hair and stood up. He buttoned his pants. Oh my, when did that happen?

"I would have you all the time then." He tucked his shirt into his pants as he walked away.

My head hurt. I was completely and totally confused about what just happened.

CHAPTER 23

 I had this feeling of dread when the blue and gold palace domes came into view, all my responsibilities lying in wait. Ash wasn't expecting me back until tomorrow, so there would be a small reprieve with that at least. I wasn't healed from my little scuffle with Slate or that beast thing. My head was aching and I had scrapes on my back.

I grabbed something to munch on, and a goblet to bring to my room from the palace kitchens.

Tawny was missing Steel and had decided to go to his room, so hers was empty. She'd be moving to a different room with Steel for more privacy. Amethyst and Cherry agreed to live in Thrimilci. They were moving to the floor Sparrow and Hawk lived on, with larger rooms, private bathrooms, and a nursery for future baby Jetts.

My eyes were gritty and burning; I needed sleep. Slate said I'd have to relay what had happened to the council the next day, and the sooner I got to bed, the better.

My hands were full so I used a twist of air to turn my doorknob and walked in.

Slate. He sat on my couch watching me. I could do one of three things: 1) Ignore him until he went away, 2) Get into another fight and try to throw him out, or 3) Listen to whatever he had to say so he would leave sooner.

I pursed my lips. He was wearing a towel around his waist and that was all.

I was too tired to fight, and feeling too petulant to listen freely. I decided to ignore him. I placed my food down on the table. There was plenty for both of us, my eyes had been bigger than my stomach when I'd gone to the kitchens.

I grabbed shorts and a tank top from my closet and headed into my bathroom. A hot shower would be just the ticket. He could wait if he wanted to talk.

My hair was still wet when I came out of the bathroom. He patiently waited for me in that tiny towel.

I sat down on the longer couch to my right and dug in, separating the food for us both. He was much better at the silent treatment than I was. I was suddenly mad at myself for setting his plate—I was supposed to be ignoring him!

I set his plate down and brushed the edge of the towel at his knee to heal him. . Bare chested as he was, I saw his skin tighten as it prickled.

Funnily, the loincloth had been ten times more revealing than this towel, but something about the fact that a towel is not an acceptable article of clothing made me acutely aware of what it covered. I squirmed in my seat, eating with a nearly nude Slate.

"What do you want, Slate? I'm exhausted," I asked, trying to sound more irritated than I felt.

I moved to stand behind the couch; it was much easier dealing with him when I didn't have his eyes on me.

He stood up, his towel perilously low on his hips. I bit my lip. He came behind the couch and walked towards me, *prowling.* I hadn't realized I was backing up until my legs hit the bed. His lips curled evilly. I was off-balance, and he was able to shove me back with a finger. His eyes were storming as he stood over me.

"Wait!" I squeaked.

I wrapped him up in air. *Calling* on half-naked men gave me some kind of sick rush, perhaps because it was the only time I was in complete control.

His eyes darkened as I hesitated. Then he *called*. It was only a small hole of air, but it was strong enough to cut through my own *calling*. Just enough for his hand to shoot out and grab my ankle as I moved to push farther onto the bed. I dropped my *calling* with a yelp of surprise.

He dragged me back. It was a ridiculous scene. When he flipped me over onto my back and held my arms down with his hands leaning over me on the bed, I started laughing. I had just dragged all the blankets with me, clawing them as if for my life. Even he broke out into a grin. He rolled onto the bed and fixed his towel that was now slightly lifting away from his skin. I climbed under the blankets.

"When you sort things out, let me know why you're here." I preferred being the one amused. "Not that I don't enjoy these little romps with you."

His eyes glared at me as he lay on his back. He climbed under the blankets uninvited. He pulled his towel out and dropped it onto the floor, watching me as he did it.

Don't blush, don't blush, don't blush.

I was starting to think he just liked to see me flustered. "It would fall off anyway." He shrugged. He closed his eyes with his arms behind his head.

"You can*not* spend the night in my bed!"

His evil smile sprung to his full lips. I was sitting up in bed now, trying very hard to look outraged.

"I came to heal you. Things may have gotten out of hand this morning." He wasn't smiling any longer.

I sunk back down into bed.

"How are you?"

I took a deep breath. "I had a nightmare, but I feel okay. Physically, anyway. Emotionally? I don't know. I feel wrung out lately. Have you ever heard of a horned Wemic?" I asked. If anyone knew, it'd be Slate. "I saw one. I didn't know what it was, that's all."

"Like a Minotaur? Or the Faunelle? They both have horns," he asked, intrigued.

"No. It was canine or feline. I couldn't tell, it was dark, but it definitely had horns. It cornered me in the canyon. Nothing happened, it was just weird is all." Maybe I'd imagined it. There could be some kind of drug in the Wemic drinks, a hallucinogen maybe. "Forget it."

"Did it do anything to you?" he asked.

"Not really. It licked me, but it was not a big deal. I think it wanted to...like it wanted to sleep with me, but not by force. It wanted me to let it. Does that make sense?"

"I do not recommend sleeping with strange hybrids, Torch," he said, and I gave him a look, as if I would. His hair was half-dried, waves wild.

"Could you teach me how to punch through a weave like you did?" I asked with a smile.

"Does that mean you are letting me spend the night?" he asked, grey eyes glittering.

He laughed, sliding out of my bed, and turned revealing his naked body colored by the moonlight beaming through the stained glass. I averted my eyes. He climbed back over my blankets and grabbed a fistful of my hair, enough so I had to look at him.

"Look at what you could have: all of me. Take it. Every inch, whenever you want, Rabbit. How is that for friendship?"

He crushed my lips beneath his before I could protest and was off the bed with the towel wrapped around his waist, leaving my room in an instant. I felt like I needed to fan myself. I wished he'd *called* me to sleep and stayed.

I woke up with my mouth feeling like the desert we had crossed. I felt the warmth of the body next to me and rolled my eyes. Hopefully, he wasn't naked so I could maintain a modicum of respect for myself.

"Good morning," he said. My throat clenched, my stomach flipped. It was Ash.

What are you doing here? Who let you in? A million questions passed through my mind. My face flushed.

He handed me a glass of water. I smiled as I took it. "Thanks." I drank. "Good morning."

His light green eyes were looking unusually dangerous...or was it just me?

"I wanted to be here when you came home. It is nearly lunch already," Ash said, still watching my every move, analyzing me.

I had slept through the entire morning. Our nonstop hike through the desert had taken its toll on me; I was usually an early riser. Sunlight shone through the stain glassed windows to color Ash's caramel skin in blues and reds.

"You look surprised to see me," he said, quirking a perfect eyebrow.

"I am! I didn't realize how long I slept."

He shook his head. "Surprised that it was *me*." He said it low.

Heat coursed through my veins and I found myself holding my breath.

I'd seen several of Ash's sides in the six months we'd been dating, but this calculated simmer of anger was new. Did he come suspecting I was being courted by someone else? It was only a few stolen kisses; from what Jett told me he and Jonquil were doing a lot more than that, and I had avoided the confrontation at every turn. If Slate had spent the night, this morning would have been very different—I might have been in the middle of a brawl upon waking.

"Just surprised," I told him. He looked unconvinced.

"I heard about what happened with the Jorogumo. I planned to escort you to the council meeting. You must have been *very* grateful for...reinforcements to arrive." He avoided ever saying Slate's name.

"Ash, I didn't sleep with Slate if that's what you're hinting at." My eyebrows were halfway up my forehead.

"Really? I found these in your bathroom." He gestured to the pile of dirty clothes Slate had left on the floor after he'd showered. Ash had piled them on the floor near the bed.

I was getting a headache. My brain was not completely awake yet.

Ash looked like he wanted to strangle me, quite literally. I took a breath trying to wade through the fog. He had every right to be upset. I had slept with Slate, I just didn't *sleep* with him.

"He showered here last night before we ate, and he healed me." All true.

"Why was he in your bed?" His eyes were still cruel, his lips strained as they moved as if suppressing the urge to yell at me.

Good question. He didn't look like he wanted to end things. I figured he just wasn't used to not having what he wanted. It infuriated him to think he had lost me. But...shouldn't he be *sad* if he lost me? Anger seemed normal, but there was something off about it, anger about the wrong thing.

"They say when you save a life that makes you responsible for it. I think he wanted to make sure I was alright. That I didn't have any nightmares."

I believed it was true. Slate had a funny way of doing things, but the bottom line was he cared about me in his strange way. While I didn't doubt he would have bedded me in a heartbeat, last night seemed more like he'd wanted to watch over me.

Ash's eyes changed, still angry, but curious. "I had not realized he was so adept at using *calling* on the mind."

"He didn't get a chance. I asked him to leave."

"I would not give you up so easily." His eyes were less chilling, but lit with something else now. "You are to be mine," he told me softly with a dangerous edge as he brought his mouth to mine. The kiss intensified rapidly.

I could fix this with a little openness, allow intimacy that I'd shunned before that had now driven a wedge between us. There was so much potential for Ash and me, and I didn't want it to fail because I was emotionally unavailable. Ash wanted me, to marry me, to have children with me.

I still couldn't bring myself to commit to him. Something nagged at me that I couldn't put my finger on and until that sensation went away, I couldn't go further with Ash.

I drew back from Ash's mouth. "We are giving this a try, that will have to be enough for now. I'm not ready to get married yet."

He looked at me, face unreadable. "Do you know what a challenge you are?"

"No, but I can imagine," I said, running my fingers down his beautiful face.

"Come get ready. We can go to lunch." He pulled me up from the bed and I walked past Slate's clothes and into the closet to get clothes for the day. I heard him say, "I would be greatly displeased if you should have another male guest in your bed again."

I gave my story to the council with the help of Tawny and Slate. Ash looked on passively. I wanted to tell Slate that Ash knew, to be careful with him because he could very possibly murder him. I looked into the faces of Moon, Orion, Cygnus, Pearl, and Reed. There were also three more people I didn't know well. I knew who Orion's wife Cassiopeia was, but there was a frail-looking brunette woman and a man with green eyes, dark hair, and bronze skin, around the age of my parents, sitting there.

It turned out that the brunette was Ruby Geol, Cygnus's wife and my grandmother. The other man, Peak Haust, was Nova, Quartz, and Sterling's father and patriarch of the Haust family. They sat at a horseshoe table with Moon at the head. It was less a table than a platform of judgement. They sat two feet higher the anyone else in the room, while Slate, Tawny, and I sat on comfortable chairs at a long table placed in front of them under the scrutiny of their eyes.

Slate had explained that he was escorting us to and from the Wemic lands when we were attacked.

"Where were you when the attack occurred?" Reed asked.

He looked to be crossing questions off a list as Basil sat to the side transcribing what was being said. Ash was sitting in the pews behind me with his mother. My mom, Hawk, and Sparrow sat across the aisle in a pew with Gypsum watching the proceedings. Jett and the girls were still at the cottages.

An empty Dagr chair was at the table, that might as well have had an elephant seated in it.

All of the house sigils were carved below the table space they sat at, as well as on the chairs themselves, all of them spectacular. I wondered if *calling* had helped to make them.

"Slate Sumar, what was your role in the events that transpired?" Reed asked.

Slate spoke in his deep voice. I didn't think I'd ever heard him speak so loudly. "I awoke at camp to find Scarlett Tio missing. After a few minutes, I went to search for her. I found her being attacked by a Jorogumo. I *called* lightening, struck it, and terminated it. I healed and escorted Scarlett Tio back to camp to inform the ambassador, then went to inspect where the attack had happened. When I returned we broke camp and headed to the Wemic who informed me their had been several sightings of Jorogumo. Ambassador Steel left the following day to speak with the Faunelle and we returned to alert the council."

"Thank you, Slate Sumar. Please remain in case we have further questions," Reed told him.

The council's eyes were all on me. Pearl was trying to smile to help me relax. Even Orion's eyes softened when he looked at me.

Reed gave a small smile before he started. "Scarlett Tio, what was your role in the events that transpired?"

"I was the one attacked." I tried to sound confident like Slate but my hands were trembling and my palms were clammy even though I ran them over my knees every few seconds.

"If you could please give us your account. Start at the beginning until you made it back to camp." Reed smiled encouragingly.

I nodded. I relayed the attack as best as I could without revealing that I was pants-less or what had happened with evil spider number four that tried to eat my face. When I had mentioned something cut off my *calling,* the people in the benches went nuts.

"Order! Order!" said Cygnus. The council was talking amongst themselves.

"Scarlett Tio, it says the injuries you sustained were as follows: three broken ribs, triceps punctured to the bone, throat punctured, and punctured lungs. All while being poisoned. We are thankful you are with us today."

I could hear my mom crying. There were tears in Pearl's eyes and Ruby Geol's. "How were you trapped by the Jorogumo? Was there a leash to the nix torque they had put on you?"

"It had paralyzed me with its venom," I said softly.

I heard my mom let out a big sob.

"What happened once Slate Sumar terminated the last rogue?" Reed asked in a delicate tone as if I might shatter from his questions.

They were all looking at me differently: some sadly, some with pity, and some with suspicion.

"He tried to heal me, but the torque prevented it. He took it off, healed me, then brought me back to camp."

"You were paralyzed the entire time?"

"Well, I could move my head a little, but it hurt to speak. I informed him that they had put something around my neck. My arms were too damaged to move." I bit my lip.

Sparrow was crying too now, I could hear them both.

The council deliberated.

"In light of the heroic actions of one Slate Sumar, we have decided to issue him a Mjolnir." More murmuring from the benches. "Slate Sumar, please approach the dais." Moon came around to stand in front of the horseshoe table. Slate was dressed in all black, a little shimmering brocade on his waistcoat. He kneeled before Moon as he pinned the Mjolnir on his chest.

"I do not believe we have awarded a Mjolnir to someone untried in the last two lifetimes. Your selfless feat has not gone unnoticed," Moon told him.

Slate turned stone-faced and sat back down next to me. A tiny Norse hammer, head side down, was pinned to his waistcoat. Pearl was beaming with pride. The councillors spoke amongst themselves for less than five minutes as I squirmed in my chair, eager to leave.

"In light of your testimony, we fear we must send a contingent of Guardians to the red hills. Guardians will be sent to the Jorogumo in Ostara and to the Wemic. Further investigation will be had on how a Jorogumo obtained a nix torque," Reed said to the crowd.

"Meeting adjourned," said Orion. "Ms. Tio, if you would not mind waiting a moment."

I nodded.

"Slate?" His eyes were far away. I rested my hand lightly on his arm. It brought him to the now. "Slate, are you okay?"

He gave me a smirk that asked, *You're worried about me?* Ash was getting off the bench: it was now or never.

"Ash knows you showered in my room. He found your clothes." I spoke low and fast, hoping to get it all out. Ash was quickly approaching.

Slate smile evilly. "Good."

I rolled my eyes. "He knows nothing happened."

Slate let his smile drop and gave *too bad* face. Then, it seemed his mind made a drastic assumption as he guessed *how* Ash would've known nothing happened between us. Slate looked like he wanted to rip Ash's head off.

"Slate, please don't. *Please.* We didn't sleep together." I didn't know why I was reassuring him, but I was afraid he'd attack the Prime's nephew right there in front of everyone.

Ash suddenly appeared beside us, looking particularly satisfied. "I wish you had told me all the details beforehand." He kissed my neck and hung an arm around my waist.

"Sorry," I told him. The tension was palpable.

"Thank you for saving my wife," Ash told Slate as the two men squared off.

"Not your wife," Slate growled through clenched teeth.

"*Yet.* She is mine," Ash whispered.

Slate closed the inches between them, ready to pummel him. The men stood nose to nose.

"Enough! Ash, he's my brother. Please don't antagonize him." *Brother* caught in my throat but I forced it out.

Ash scoffed. "Scarlett, I love that you are so innocent. You are a rare find. Your *brother* wants much more from you than a familial relationship. I have caught your stench in her sheets on more than one occasion." His light green eyes burned with the raw light of hatred.

My stomach burned. Ash knew Slate had been in my bed?

Slate's lips curled in that arrogant mocking smirk of his. "Her bed is very warm."

Ash returned his smirk with a cocky one of his own. "Could not be that warm for you since she still chooses me."

Slate's chest bumped up against Ash's with a growl.

Hawk walked up and clamped a hand on their shoulders. "Gentlemen. This is not the forum to work out your differences."

"There is no problem, Provost Sumar. Thank you for your concern." Ash and Slate glared venomously at one another.

Hawk looked at me for confirmation. I nodded and Slate brushed past me to leave the room. Even the small touch as his fingers slid against mine made me feel a rush of electricity.

Orion walked over to us, eyeing Ash. "Excuse me, Ash, may I speak to Ms. Tio?"

It sounded like a question, but it wasn't. I wished I was back with the Wemic, laughing easily with Keen and sunbathing, or stargazing—I wasn't picky. Today sucked.

Ash walked away politely but clearly didn't like being dismissed. "Good thing that young man showed up, hmm?" Orion croaked.

I nodded and took a deep breath to clear my head. "I think he saved my life," I told him.

"Sounded that way. You know, taking on three Jorogumo after six months of training is quite the achievement. Be sure not to sell yourself short."

I smiled. "Thanks."

He turned serious. "You may not know this, but I am not well-liked. I am a cantankerous old man that has a lot to make up for." He gave me a self-deprecating smile.

I stood there, confused, I didn't know what his confession was getting at. He glanced over at my family and back to me.

"Your grandmother has every reason not to trust me. I would like to get to know Tawny better. I would ask Hawk or Sparrow, but I would rather it be private...and I suspect they share your grandmother's opinion of me."

He wanted it to be in secret which probably meant he didn't want Hawk, Sparrow, Pearl and probably any of his frosty female family members to know.

"I think she would like that."

He showed a sliver of teeth; it was supposed to be a smile. "Do I have to warn you to be more careful?"

I shook my head and he nodded and walked back to the council. His wife watched him with all the warmth of Antarctica.

I spent the rest of Midsummer Festival with Ash. He was a permanent fixture at the Sumar palace. I was happy when they let Slate go on the reconnaissance mission even though he wasn't a Guardian. Ash's presence was a thorn in his side, and he brooded the entire time he was around.

The day of the council hearing, things had been tense. My mom didn't know how bad things had gotten and blamed herself for not coming along. Sparrow and Hawk were equally upset and wouldn't let me out of their sight until I went to bed. Ash had been spending most nights in my bed or I went to his house. It had become one of things that was assumed.

"I should have been the one to save you. I do not want you out of my sight, I will protect you."

He'd said this flashing his brilliant smile, putting my mind at ease. Ash was genuinely upset that I had been attacked and that he hadn't been there. It galled him that Slate was, and in his mind if he never left my side, it would never happen again.

The honeymooners came back the last day of midsummer break; we planned to celebrate Gypsum's birthday then too. Dahlia was having a family get-together that day that I wasn't invited to, so Ash wouldn't be over to see me at all over the break.

I trained with Slate for the first time since the hearing. Tawny and Steel had taken Gypsum out for a birthday breakfast so it was just the two of us.I was only slightly more awkward than usual as he sparred with me. I wasn't sure if his fingers were lingering at every chance or if it was my imagination.

After I rinsed off from my pool laps, I changed and walked down the aisles, and I spotted him. Shirtless, buttoning up his pants over his thin dark trail of hair that led south. He looked up at me, furrowing his brow, his head angled. Midnight waves of hair spilled over his shoulders and his lips curled.

I walked up to him and picked up the shirt he had laid over the bench—it was black.

Big surprise.

"Arms up," I told him.

He quirked an eyebrow and straightened. He humored me and raised two long, strongly-sculpted arms above his head which was feet above my own. I stepped on top of the bench, smiling down at him, and pulled his shirt over his hands and over his head. The shirt mussed up his hair so I ran my fingers through his silken waves, letting the beads rub between my knuckles.

He watched me, a small smirk playing his lips.

"Your hair was disheveled." I nearly cleared my throat; instead I gave him a playful smile. "That was much easier to do while you're conscious."

He laughed while he tucked his shirt in and put on his bracers to finish getting ready. A great thing about living in a place that was perpetual summer—sleeveless shirts on men.

"To what do I owe the pleasure?" He looked around the prep room. "I do not see your shadow."

I could deal with sarcasm. "Come with me into town to get Gyps a birthday present." I didn't want to make it sound too much like he had an option.

"You forgot the magic word." He arched a dark eyebrow at me.

"We have magic words!" He came about as close to rolling his eyes as Slate would ever get. I laughed. "*Please*."

"Done."

He pulled on his boots and followed me out, his hand warm at the small of my back.

It was a gorgeous sunny day, everyday in Thrimilci was sunny and gorgeous. I figured anything weapon-related would be a good gift for Gyps, and I had a weapon aficionado with me too.

We walked into our usual weapon shop.

"If you did not scoop her up, I would have." The salesman winked at Slate and me.

"Hopper! How's it going? I have another gift purchase to make and could use your expertise." I smiled; it may or may not have been flirtatious.

Slate's lips curled. "It appears you two know each other." He paused. "She has not kissed you too, has she?"

Hopper guffawed and I blushed.

"That was an option?" He winked again.

I rolled my eyes as Slate laughed.

"Okay, I am looking for a gift for a young man's eighteenth birthday. Any ideas? And straps for my short seax sheath." He gave me a dirty bad smile. "A woman." I gave him a flat look.

He laughed. "Come on over, sweetheart."

We walked over to the glass cases in the back where Hopper stood. The burly man pulled one of the items out and put it on the top of the display. A small etched axe with a wickedly curved blade rested there. The blade had Celtic braids etched along it and a carved handle. It was surprisingly heavy for such a small axe. I knew Gypsum would love it as soon as I saw it.

"Sold," I told Hopper.

Slate checked it out and approved. I bought it and we headed out the door.

We left with a tinkle of bells and searched for a gift for Slate to give to Gypsum.

"Come."

He reached for my hand and I stared at it for an instant, looking for a trap. Slate's eyes smoldered as he peered out at me from the waves that had fallen from the rest of his hair fastened behind his head in a leather strap.

"It is only a hand." He interlaced his fingers in mine and led me down the white shimmering streets of Thrimilci.

Slate wasn't the strolling type so he walked with purpose, and I had to trot a little to keep up with his long strides.

I stopped and his arm yanked.

I broke out into a grin. "Have you never walked with a girl before? I can hardly keep up."

He gave me an appraising look and pursed his full lips. "There are much more compelling things to do with women besides walking with them."

I took a deep breath and yanked my hand back. Who knew how many women's bottoms it had cupped? This was not the fun jaunt I'd hoped for. I thought we could mend things a bit, but we would never see eye to eye.

"Lead the way. I'll follow behind you," I said instead of saying something biting.

"I will let you lead." Slate offered his hand and acted as if he'd just made some huge, life-changing concession.

I looked at his calloused palm and back up to his grey eyes. What he hadn't said with his words, he did with those depthless silvery eyes. *Please.* Pistol Packin' pink painted fingernails found their way over bronze skin so our fingers were interlaced.

I set a leisurely pace; we strolled and I wondered how something so silly as how fast we walked could change our entire dynamic. We might have even looked like a couple out running errands.

The silence was deafening and my mind craved to fill it with my yammering. It was an effort to restrain myself, so I let a little spill forth.

"Are you seeing anyone worth mentioning?" I asked amiably.

It was a valid question since Shale was out of the picture. She was the only woman I'd seen him with in a social setting that was when he wasn't hilt deep in said social setting.

I could almost feel the eye roll he suppressed. We were both trying to be pleasant. "Not everyone feels the need to pair off; some of us enjoy our freedom." Or maybe we *weren't* playing nice.

"I imagine you are very single-minded in how you spend all that freedom. Bed-hopping and fighting is all I've ever seen you do. I use the term *bed* loosely. You'll have to excuse me if I have a bit more depth than the needs of my body."

My tone was derisive and I pulled my lips between my teeth hoping it would stop them from saying anything else rude.

His fingers clenched tighter on mine. "You have an unhealthy distaste for all things pleasurable. Why is that exactly? I do not have to finagle women to sleep with me. I am often the pursued; I merely relinquish myself to their needs." *Oh, puke.*

"Why anyone would want a man every other woman in Tidings has had already is beyond me. You give away what should only be given to those whom you love, or if failing that, at least care about. I'd settle for liking if I were you." I'd done it again. I drew in a deep breath. "Sorry."

"It seems the only thing you are passionate about is your aversion to me," he said dryly and I sighed.

"I *said* sorry. I didn't invite you out to insult your way of life. I do have passion, but I only show it those whom incite it. As far as my tastes go for the intimate, I am working on it," I admitted.

There. I could grant concessions too.

The Armored Armoire had all kinds of outer clothing for combat and travel. Cloaks, gloves, bracers, boots, and other items...it was endless. A man that was almost as pretty as he was muscled came up to greet us.

"Scarlett!" Solder said with those luscious pink lips that spread into a heart-stopping smile.

Men in Tidings should come with warnings.

I felt my blood rise and my cheeks redden as I tried to dislodge my hand, but Slate held tight. I blocked our held hands with my dress skirts and beamed a smile at Solder. The shop worker was just as handsome as I remembered.

"Good afternoon, Solder. Do you know my *brother* Slate?" I said, ignoring the sudden burn of Slate's eyes on the top of my head.

Slate let go of my hand and nodded to Solder. There was something guarded in the interaction.

"I did not know you and Steel had such a gorgeous relative, I would have visited more often. What can I help you with?" Solder's deep blue eyes skimmed over Slate and rested back on me.

They obviously knew each other, friendly enough. "She is my sister through adoption. I need a dark cloak for a man six feet tall," Slate told him, ignoring his compliment towards me.

"I have just the thing; is blue okay?" the man asked.

Slate looked at me. "Midnight blue?" I asked.

The man nodded and his plump lips parted into a beaming smile.

"Yes, that's good." I blushed at his flirtatious look as he walked away.

"Try this on." Slate moved past me and held up what I could only describe as a corset with an attached skirt like a superhero would wear.

"*Um*, I don't think so. I would look ridiculous," I said skeptically.

Had he gone insane? I would never wear anything like that.

"You *won't* know unless you try." He passed it to me stressing the contraction.

"Where's the rest of it?" I asked. It was impossibly small. "This is borderline inappropriate." I narrowed my eyes at Slate and he held his arms up to point out all the equally tiny gear.

Solder pointed to curtained room. I took off my peach flowing dress and looked at the impossible piece Slate had picked out. It was a black leather sweetheart corset with a wide golden belt. It had a skirt attached to it with triangular gold and black pieces, layered to deflect. Problem was, it was basically a miniskirt, very Wonder-Woman-gone-dominatrix.

I stepped into it and pulled it over my breasts, which it squeezed until I was nearly pouring out of the top. It actually looked pretty cool, despite the boobage. It would look better with my boots and the cloak my mom gave me. One thing could be said about Guardians: they sure loved their fashion.

The corset was soft-lined on the inside, but the outside had little black plates sewn all over it to deflect. I really liked it. I chewed my lip in the mirror, my turquoise eyes and soft golden hair in complete contrast with the look of the battle gear.

"Come out and show me," I heard Slate rumble.

I shrugged, watching my girls bounce, then opened the curtain.

"I think I'd need to be wearing my boots and my cloak to get the complete look," I said, touching the metal skirt.

I looked up expecting him to be suppressing a laugh. He wasn't.

"You should change back into your dress," he said.

His silver, mirrored eyes were positively predatory; something carnal and wild dwelled in those eyes.

"That good, huh?" I blushed.

I was not going to do my whole rabbit thing even under *that* gaze.

His lips curled and he led me by the shoulders to the full length mirror. I had never seen the two of us together. He was taller than me by whole a foot. His broad frame filled the mirror. He had more muscle definition than he'd had when I met him, as if that was even possible. His strong jaw was perfectly symmetrical with his straight nose. His narrow eyes were silvery grey, now ringed with long, thick, dark lashes.

He took a finger and made me look at myself in the mirror, *really* look. I could see most of my legs in the short armored skirt: they were tanned and toned, muscles I'd never had before. Even my arms were toned. The roundness my face had had before coming to Thrimilci was gone, and my high cheekbones were defined. I hardly recognized myself.

He leaned down close to my ear.

His lips touched it as he spoke. "Breathtaking."

Having him do it and watching him do it were two very different things. Ash was right not to trust me with him.

"I should change. I don't know where I would ever wear it," I said self-consciously.

"My bedroom," he smiled.

I blinked, thinking I couldn't have possibly have heard him correctly, as he had been restraining his usual inappropriateness...but now it was back with a vengeance.

I watched him in the mirror and unwittingly licked my lips. His eyes darkened over my shoulder and I went full rabbit mode. He bent around my shoulder and ran the pads of his fingers over his lips and pressed them to mine, lingering there to draw down my lower lip. The instinct to slide my tongue out to taste the kiss on his fingers was overwhelming.

"So full and soft. A mouth made for giving pleasure," Slate purred and my insides contracted in response.

"*Timetochange*," I breathed out in a single word as I broke myself from his spell and headed back behind the curtain.

I took the gear off and wound up buying it. Slate said I could wear it to the Wild Hunt if I wanted.

Slate left with the midnight blue cloak for Gypsum and we wandered around for a little while before we returned home. We may or may not have held hands and walked back enjoying the silence.

My little chief was being bashful at dinner with all of the attention. He had plans after dinner to hang out with friends that he was being vague about, and had a feeling I knew which betrothed friend he was going to see. I tried to give him a disapproving look.

"I have an announcement!" Sparrow called, bringing everyone's attention to her. Jett and the girls had that same glow about them as Steel and Tawny. "In addition to running the palace until Hawk decides to take over…" Hawk narrowed his eyes at this. He still didn't feel ready to run the Sumar palace. "I have been asked to take the vacant Dagr seat on the Council."

Everyone murmured their congratulations. It was a big deal to be on the council. The Dagr seat had been vacant for over twenty years. Sparrow would be the youngest person on the Council.

Gypsum booked it after dinner was over, rushing through opening his gifts, which he did very much like. The happy newlyweds went to bed to do what newlyweds did. In the morning, we would all be back at Valla U.

CHAPTER 24

On the first day back from midsummer break, the tyros asked me a million questions. Most people thought it was hilarious that I fought with my pants down—mostly those were guys, *of course*. A lot of the girls had listened to my story appalled, and then got all warm and gooey when they heard Slate had saved me. He had a gaggle of those girls giggling and following him everywhere. Then there was the last group—not many mind you—but they acted like I made it up.

Ash was not a fan of the story. Slate was an instant superstar. Shale had even started hanging out with him again.

Nightmares of what the Jorogumo could have done plagued me. The act was terrifying but my imagination took a truly horrible turn when it concocted the spider babies that burst from my stomach after my face was devoured.

"Did you hear, the Council is sending out all the ambassadors with a team to all the tribes? Well, the ones with ambassadors," Indigo told Tawny and me.

The Merfolk were being accused of aiding the Jorogumo, so Steel had to get to the bottom of it. He firmly believed it may have only been a small group breaking the laws, and he was trying to keep the Council from sending Guardians in force until I had a few days off from classes. He was stressed out, so of course that trickled into Tawny.

"What are they doing for the ones without ambassadors?"

I had found out that my father was ambassador to the Jorogumo. He was under a lot of scrutiny for the attack.

"Not sure. I overheard my dad talking about how someone should go speak to the Jotnar." She shrugged. "They're reclusive."

Jotnar were giants in Elivagar; we'd be learning about them soon enough so I kept my questions to myself.

Sterling, Ash, and Sage met us at the hall intersection where we met every day.

I'd tried to find common ground with Sage in Indigo, but I would sooner charm a rabid badger. He *had* started speaking to me; I wished he'd stop.

"I heard your uncle did not find anything in the red hills on the second search," he said smugly. Not smug like Jett. Jett's smug made his eyes twinkle with mischief, but Sage's smug had a dash of superiority to it.

They hadn't found the monster nest on the first search so they sent another one, but they still hadn't found anything.

Unfortunately, since Nirrin said the bodies were gone, we had no proof of their existence other than our word.

I opted to eat lunch in Jackal's room instead of eating with Ash and his friends with their cool attitudes towards me. They were snobs, that was the short version.

"Hey! I was wondering when you would remember me."

Jackal stood tall and lean to embrace me now that the other tyros weren't present, and kissed the top of my head.

"I've been busy. Sorry."

Jackal waved a dismissive hand and sat down behind his thick mahogany desk, gesturing to a cream upholstered seat he kept against the wall. I pulled the chair up and placed my plate of food down on his desk.

When he smiled, his blue eyes sparkled. "I imagine you are trying to dodge a wedding. It can be taxing."

I cringed inwardly; of course Jackal would know all the details. Crag still lived at the Straumr palace with Ash, I'd seen him a time or two while visiting.

I shrugged. "Did you find anything out about 'Styg'?"

Jackal looked to his open classroom door, and stood to shut the thick wood door before returning to his seat.

"How very mysterious..." I joked, but my smile dropped when I saw the serious look on my very *un*serious uncle's face.

Jackal sighed. "There is a man who goes by the name Styg. He lives in Elivagar, but frequents a pub called the Iron Maiden in Valla. I was told he is a black market dealer and that his real name is Civet. We have a mutual acquaintance. I do not know what interest he would have in your young man though. Any ideas?"

I shook my head, not bothering to correct him about Slate not being "my" anything. "What about the Stygians? You'd mentioned them as well." My uncle chewed on the corner of his lip.

"Better you know just in case, I suppose," he mumbled in a very *un*Jackal like way. "Stygians are a guild of assassins known for never giving up on a contract until it is completed."

My blood ran cold. My meal wasn't looking very palatable any longer. "They wanted to capture Slate, not kill him. So it couldn't be the Stygians, right?"

"I do not know. If I knew either way I would tell you. You best bet is to hire someone to look into Styg and work from there. I wish I had better news for you, Ms. Scarlett."

"At least we have someplace to start. It's much worse feeling helpless."

It was the day of my extra battle class. I decided to try on the battle gear I had bought with Slate over the summer—I kept it in my prep area for such an occasion.

Tawny started practicing her shot. She was ridiculously good. She could shoot arrows faster than I could keep up, and she never missed. River Straumr had her shooting targets as she ran the Gauntlet just to get her used to battle. I could see why after the fight with the Jorogumo.

Fox was there when I left the prep room. He smiled—he was always smiling.

"If my cousin was not already courting you…"

I laughed. "And my trainer."

"Right, well, some things can be overlooked." Fox winked.

He had become my unofficial trainer for my open class. Mostly we did blade combat. Sometimes he made a decent substitute for Slate, but no one could yell at me like he could. Fox was much more persuasive when he was being nice. It didn't hurt that harmlessly flirted.

"We have a guest today. Apparently, he is fluent in Wemic." Fox said it sarcastically.

There was the constant *thump* of Tawny's arrows sinking into her targets in the background. There was only one untried and true that had spent extensive time with the Wemic, but I didn't see him. He was usually hard to miss.

"Behind you," Slate whispered.

My skin prickled. I couldn't control the smile that bloomed on my face.

"Seeing how you're both specializing in blades, I will critique as you go." Fox started walking towards the combat ring.

Slate circled around in front of me, his full lips curled.

"Okay, no *calling*, three rounds. First blood wins each round. Best out of three wins. Try not to kill each other."

"All right, don't rush me. Let me stretch first."

Fox smirked and walked away.

I was hoping to break in my corset with an easy day tumbling around with Fox. There wasn't going to be anything easy with Slate.

"You like Fox." It wasn't a question.

I looked up from my stretch to Slate and smirked. "You sound jealous."

A muscle in his jaw twitched. "When I say things like that, you berate me. Can you explain this to me?"

He'd stepped so close to me that his knuckles brushed my cheek as I stretched. "That's because Fox has never tried to get into my pants. When he flirts it's because he appreciates the banter. He's also *hot*. That helps," I teased.

I was in a rare playful mood with Slate. If he played his cards right, I might favor him with one of my best smiles.

"Okay, ready as I'm going to be," I said, standing and giving Slate a light nudge with my hip. "Don't take it easy on me." I said sarcastically to Slate who followed me into the combat circle.

Slate's lips curled and took out his wicked black handled daggers as long as my forearm. He had on his wrist blades too, so I would have to be careful for those.

"Your armor fits you well," he purred, and I narrowed my eyes.

He was on me. I pulled the seax he'd bought me and parried his first series of strikes. I was going to have to spring one of my wrist blades to stand a chance. I sprung my left one and counterattacked. He thrusted, I blocked. I stabbed, he parried.

Our arms were moving so fast I saw sparks from where the blades slid against one another. I overreached and he grabbed my arm, pulling me towards him, spinning so my back hit against his chest. I knew he had me. He slid his dagger across the top of my right breast, just enough so a bead of blood dripped down. It stung. I knew it would be healed as soon as the match was over, but I was shocked that he'd actually cut me.

"Round one to Slate," Fox said as Slate let me go.

There was no remorse in his face. He looked as dangerous as the day I met him hiding in the shadows, oozing sensuality and savagery. I barely had enough time to deflect his dagger with the wrist blade he'd bought me. Funny that everything I used to slice him was bought by him.

I tried to incorporate some leg work, but I was kept on the defensive. He moved so quickly I could barely keep up. He was so much bigger than I was—I didn't want to use that as an excuse, but it was true. When he fought, all energy he had that seemed to be too much for one body, as massive as it was, seemed to spread out and consume the room. How does one fight against someone who is everywhere at once?

I saw my sliver of an opening and kicked him square in the chest. Before he had a chance to recover, I threw one of my belt daggers. It glanced his ear, blowing through his wavy midnight locks. His hand went immediately to his ear; it came back bloody.

Fox chuckled. "Round two goes to Scarlett. Careful: once I taught her to throw overhand. It's her main method of mayhem."

"No insider tips," I said breathlessly and Fox laughed again.

Slate wiped his blood off on his pant leg. I wouldn't have thrown my dagger if I'd thought it could really do some damage, but he looked angry. I didn't know, angry or maybe turned on. Possibly both.

Either way, he attacked with renewed vigor. His strikes were harder, moves faster. I was high off my last draw of blood, but even that wasn't giving me the edge I needed.

I ducked and slid my leg fast and hard, pulling his legs out from under him.

He fell back, but managed to grab my leg as he fell, dropping one of his daggers. He yanked me towards him and my blade fell when I opened my palm to catch my fall. I pushed up with an arm and brought my knee down on his throat. It barely fazed him. He pinched my thigh and calf together, keeping my leg bent, and grabbed my belt so I swung off the ground over him.

I slammed onto my back, teeth jarring. He shoved my bent leg to my chest with his body. I brought up my wrist blade, and he knocked it aside and put his knee over my arm. I started to spring the right wrist blade.

"I win."

His right hand was against my neck. He slid the knife down my throat without drawing blood until it reached the top of my left breast. He pressed the knife to it so it drew blood.

"Slate wins." Fox awkwardly cleared his throat.

It brought me back to reality. "You did. Better shove off before someone gets the wrong idea."

My tone wasn't very convincing. All velvet and throaty panting, no steel there.

Slates lips curled. "*I* have ideas," he growled.

Both my breasts were bleeding. I never knew that knife fighting could be so steamy. I pressed my lips together to prevent something stupid from coming out.

Slate finally released me.

"To the victor goes the spoils," Slate said. "What do I get?" He was talking to me, but just loud enough for Fox to hear.

"Okay, okay," Fox said. "*You* go take a cold shower. *You* go use some practice dummies. He's stronger, but you should be faster. *Be* faster."

Slate laughed. "How about I go play with the dummies too?"

Fox quirked an eyebrow. "Just stay out of trouble." His sky blue eyes looked at me.

I walked over to the dummies processing the match.

Slate was right behind me. Tawny watched from the corner of her eye.

"I am attached to my ears. I would like to keep them."

"Not if I have anything to say about it." I laughed and turned to him. "Come here, you big baby." He raised his eyebrows at me. I favored him with my very best megawatt smile. "I'll heal you. Wouldn't want you bleeding out through an ear."

I rested a hand, palm up, on the side of his face and *called* while I visualized knitting the skin back together. I rubbed off the little bit of blood left with my fingers. Why was he looking at me like *that*? He stood stock still under my palm, his face unreadable until I moved my hand. Maybe my smile was out of practice?

"Now I heal you?"

He was looking at my bloody slices, which were conveniently on my cleavage. He licked a thumb and placed it at the start of one cut, dragging it from start to finish. He licked it his thumb again and ran it along the second cut.

I looked down; both cuts were healed and the blood gone. My eyes met his.

"I think *you* might be trouble...and a vampire. Did you just lick my blood?" He chuckled and we were back to normal.

"Better get to work," he pointed out. Fox was watching us. Not that he would say anything, but he *was* Ash's cousin.

I nodded and decided to take a quick breather in the prep room. Tawny followed me.

"You can't marry Ash."

The prep room smelled of the polished wood that made up the beautiful walnut cubbies. The benches were chocolate brown padded leather that ran the length of each aisle. I stretched out along the leather to take a breather.

My fight with Slate had been *overstimulating.* "I never said I would."

Tawny sat next to my head. "I'm serious. You're so good at seeing what other people need to do, but when it comes to yourself, you're blind."

"What are you talking about?" I said, swinging my legs over the side to sit next to her.

"I mean, you are *so* into Slate."

I shook my head. "He's attractive," I said cautiously. "But there isn't any potential there. Maybe physically, but what future could we possibly have? Besides, he's back with Shale. We're good as friends."

"*Gods*, Scarlett. Okay, when you're ready, come talk to me. I can see you're in denial."

"Why would I be in denial?" I shot back. I was *not* in denial.

She looked down at me and sat back down. "Scar, I'm your sister, right? Like, no one knows you better than I do?" I nodded. "It's okay to have issues. If I grew up thinking my mom fell head over heels for a guy who left her pregnant…I would want the sure thing too."

"What's *that* supposed to mean?" I was trying very hard not to be defensive.

"Ash wants to marry you, wants the whole deal. It's guaranteed. No guesswork. Slate is, at the very least, unpredictable." She sighed.

What was she getting all emotional about?

I shook my head. "I think you're reading too much into things."

For some reason I was getting upset. It was bubbling up, threatening to spill over.

She hugged me. "No judging. It's only my opinion. I love you."

"I love you." I stood up. My stomach was in knots. "Let's get back, Fox will think I'm slacking off."

I changed into my usual gear and decided to go for a run instead of fighting alongside Slate.

"Ms. Scarlett." Fox said my name with a hint of mischief that made me smirk as Ash grumbled at his cousin's familiarity with me.

Fox crooked a finger at me and I suppressed a chuckle as I sidled from my row and walked down to where he stood in front of the first years.

Fox turned his baby blues on me and I couldn't help but smirk back. "Ms. Scarlett, how do you feel about a little sparring? You may need to work out some aggression and I do not want you getting kicked out for fighting in the hallways."

I arched an eyebrow at him. "You know me, always up for a little rolling around," I told him, keeping my voice low.

Fox was the only man I knew who I was comfortable flirting with. Life couldn't be that bad while Fox still found reasons to smile.

He wrapped an arm around my shoulder, pulling me to his side to face the class. "We will be sparring today. If you do not have a preference of who you spar with, a partner can be assigned to you. We will watch a demonstration so I can critique. Jonquil, could you please join us?"

I inhaled deeply. Fox knew Ash was still sleeping with Jonquil and was being preemptive about a blowout.

Sly Fox.

She sashayed down the tiered steps, her bleach blonde hair combed away from her face. She flashed brilliant white teeth at me with her vulpine smile.

"Do you have something so this does not get in your way?" Fox asked, tugging on a lock of my long hair.

"I can be of service." A dark-haired young man leapt to his feet from the second row and pushed between Slate and Tawny to walk to us.

He was one of the Regn brothers. He flashed me a dazzling smile and I blushed down to my toes. *Trouble.* I remembered him well; he was in my course and always sat right behind me. I suspected this was so he could look down mine and Tawny's caftans, though not ours exclusively.

Trouble was written all over his face and in the way he swaggered. Black tattoos edged up from under his collar in what hinted at a masterpiece underneath. His dark hair was just long enough to wear stylishly combed, like a modern twist on a gentlemen from the roaring twenties.

He swaggered up behind me and I tried to turn my body with him, but he grabbed my shoulders and proceeded to deftly wrap his fingers through my hair. My face was on fire as he braided it. The man was a bonafide panty dropper. He was a little shorter than Slate, but with the same powerful build that bespoke his physical prowess. Fox watched with amusement as the young man gave my braid a yank and my mouth made a perfect "O" as my eyes widened in disbelief at his brazenness.

"Thank you, Silver," Fox said with a wry smile.

"My pleasure," Silver said, giving me a wink as he walked back to the stands, flashing that dazzling, impossibly sexy smile.

I blushed again as I noticed the stern looks of disapproval on Jett and Slate's faces. Tawny had turned to Silver in the stands and he said something to her that made her fair skin turn tomato red; I was glad I wasn't the only one. I ignored the daggers Slate sent my way and turned back to Fox while touching my tight braid. He had done that far too well for it to have been his first time. "Okay ladies, no weapons, no *calling*. Submission or blood drawn, three rounds," Fox said, stepping out of the combat circle.

I let the background fade. At the moment, nothing would make me happier than pummeling Jonquil until she was a stain on the grey turf during our so-called sparring match.

The longest moment was right when you turn to face off not knowing who was going to make the first move. Jonquil thought she had a physical advantage over me since she had trained in Tidings for years longer than I had. I wouldn't let her goad me into attacking before I was ready.

Fox was right. I had so many emotions warring inside me I never knew which one would surface. Jonquil was knowingly sleeping with Ash even though we were seeing one another. It *did* bother me, even though I had my own soap opera going with Slate—but what made it punch-worthy was that she didn't know how to keep her mouth shut about it.

I wanted to make love with passion, fight with a roar, dance with abandon, and laugh in the face of everything that had been building inside me for months.

When I trained and fought I did so knowing I had something to prove, that I had years to make up for, so I had Slate to push me at every step. Jonquil, on the other hand, had grown up with fighting in her blood.

She was as fast as I was, but not as strong. She specialized in the kusarigama, a short sickle with a heavy chain used to wrap around pole arms so she could get close enough to slice and dice with the sickle. She was used to fighting close like I was. Most of the girls chose quarter-staffs or archery, some chose spears and javelins. There were even a few who had chosen long seaxes like Jett had, but I was the only girl who had specialized in blades.

I felt in control with my short seax in my hand, or when I threw one of my daggers off my belt. The spring of my wrist blades shot a thrill through me akin to how it felt when Slate whispered in my ear with his lips brushing my skin.

I felt that thrill again as Jonquil came at me. I retreated as if I was on the defensive, letting her get a kick in to my kidney. She was lithe and light on her feet. My hand snapped out, grabbing her leg as she brought it back, driving her off-balance. I hit her twice in the ribs with jabs from my right hand as I landed on top of her and locked my legs around one of hers, hooking her ankle under my arm.

"Round One, Scarlett. Classic knee bar," Fox said as he circled around us.

Jonquil was fast—really fast. Her muscles were taut and wiry with deceptive strength. I kept the smile off my lips, but I knew it was in my eyes, taunting her.

When I blocked her punches and landed a kick to her thigh, she went down on a knee, uppercutting me in the stomach. My air rushed from my lungs and I lunged at her, knocking her on her fanny pack. She grabbed a fistful of my shirt and locked her legs around my back, but I managed to get my arms between hers and wrapped them around her head, keeping my elbows close, and pulled the back of her head up so her face was pushing into my cleavage as her back curled.

"Round two, Scarlett, can opener."

Jonquil shot Fox a look of pure death. I was breathing heavily. She had got in a good hit to my gut.

Fox inhaled deeply as he looked at Jonquil. "Alright, last chance. Make it count."

It was no holds barred when she came at me, fists flying. Her reach was longer than mine, and she was putting all of her effort into her attacks now that she realized I was tougher than I looked. She landed a blow to my ribs and when I bent down on instinct, she dropped an elbow to my face. I saw stars for a moment, but I reached for her waist, tackling her down to the ground.

It ended up being a scuffle. We had given up actual combat and were now trying to tear one another apart like a couple of rabid cougars.

Fox and River pulled me and Jonquil apart as we glared at one another. "We will call that one a draw. One more to decide it even though you are both bleeding?" Fox asked.

I put my hand to my cheekbone and my fingers came away bloody. Jonquil's short hair was wild; she smoothed it back with a slim hand and licked the blood off her lower lip. We both nodded, not taking our eyes off one another. We both wanted this, needed it.

River looked at Fox and nodded. "Fourth round, first blood, or tap out," he said, stepping back out the ring.

We didn't waste a second. We were all over one another, throwing blows faster than ever before. I landed a kick to her back and she buckled. When she got close, aiming for my jaw, I blocked with my left arm and twisted at my waist, leaning forward on my right foot as I sideswiped her jaw. Her head snapped to the side and her eyes glazed over. She staggered back and I gave her a moment to collect herself, wanting to win because I was better, not because she was dazed.

I closed the distance in a heartbeat and I could tell she was wearing down. I opened my palm as I backhanded her and she lost her balance. A satisfying smack rang out and I heard the tyros behind me *ooh*. It wasn't a nice thing to do, but neither was what she'd been doing.

Jonquil's eyes widened. She couldn't believe I'd backhanded her. She spit to the side and glared at Fox.

"That does not count." There was blood in her mouth. The cheater.

Fox made no move to stop the fight; he was going to let us get it out. Better there than in the halls. I could *feel* her emotions—she was livid.

"Did he tell you he was busy this weekend? That is because he will be with me. You will smell me on him the next time you see him, *taste* me after he has kissed me here." She none-too-delicately cupped herself.

I inhaled deeply and let myself go loose; going rigid now wouldn't do me any favors. Still, she was a *bitch*. I had no cute phrase for the "B"-word because good girls didn't call other girls that, but maybe I wasn't feeling so good. I narrowed my eyes at her and set my jaw. But why was I so angry? Ash *had* told me he'd be busy, but our relationship was on my terms, and I wanted to keep things casual.

Didn't I?

I wasn't the crying out type. I attacked silently and swiftly—it was the knife fighter in me. Her eyes bulged slightly when I ran at her and dropkicked her in the chest. She flew and I chased. We were outside of the combat circle now and Fox followed us, not wanting it to get too out of hand. When I reached her, I cocked my arm back, but dropped it when I saw a knife pommel sticking out from my chest. She had held the knife up at me and I'd thrown my body weight right on top of it.

My brain was still registering it when she got to her feet and clocked me in the jaw so fast my body spun in place to face the tyros. I watched several people leap to their feet as I took a shaky step forward. Hands caught me before I fell face-first, pushing the knife deeper.

"You stabbed her!" Fox loosed a curse.

I was turned around roughly and I saw my rescuer. Olive hands, not bronze. It was Silver.

"It was an accident," Jonquil snapped.

"Jonquil. That is unacceptable." I couldn't see Ash, but I could hear him.

Slate hovered into view as Silver had pulled the knife from my chest. "I am going to heal you, okay?" Silver whispered close to my ear so his lips brushed at my earlobe.

I nodded against his shoulder, and I felt his warm healing flood through me. I breathed deep and his scent filled my nostrils. Sandalwood, cedar, patchouli, and something distinctly male mingled on Silver's skin.

"Take her to get washed up and get her to dinner," Crag said from behind me.

Slate's head snapped up to the battle trainers and then to Silver. He narrowed his eyes and Silver laughed. Jett slid next to me and gaped, sticking a finger in the bloody slice in my shirt. Jett cursed and jumped to his feet.

"Stop him!" I shouted at Slate.

Slate reluctantly stood and followed Jett, who was getting in Ash and Jonquil's faces. No good would come from that. I was relieved to see Amethyst float into view next to Jett.

"Scar, are you okay?" Tawny hovered into view as Silver scooped me up.

"Yeah, a little tired."

Jonquil nicked something serious for me to have felt so weary after the healing Silver had given me.

Indigo and Cherry looked at me and gave small smiles until Jett's shouts rose above the others and Cherry narrowed her eyes at Jonquil. Maybe I wouldn't be the only one receiving healing today. Sure enough, Silver started to walk towards the prep rooms and a fight broke out. Jonquil made the mistake of getting in Jett's face and Cherry lost it. They were cousins, but they were not close.

Silver's big arm was under my legs, and he pulled me up to his chest. I leaned against him, not caring for the moment how it looked. My family was awesome.

Fox spoke up from the fight he was breaking up with his brothers. "If Ms. Scarlett attends class with her hair braided tomorrow, I will hold you personally responsible."

Fox's voice held a warning, but I didn't see anything wrong with a braid. I rather liked braids.

Silver laughed, full and hearty; it was a delicious laugh that made his hard chest swell with mirth as I leaned against it.

"We can ask her if she *wants* her hair braided. Do you, *Ms. Scarlett?*" Silver asked, speaking loud enough for them all to hear.

I knit my brows at him. "I like braids," I said stupidly, and Silver chuckled again, but this time it was filled with promise.

"Do not worry, I will cheer her up," he said as he looked down at me and his dark eyes glittered.

Silver took me into the men's prep room and placed me on a bench which I promptly lay back on as he went to go get a towel. I closed my eyes.

Ash was going to be livid that Silver had hinted at his...creative ways at cheering me up. I had to admit, he was undeniably attractive in several ways. The way he walked, the easy way he talked, his smile— you just knew he would light your world on fire if he ever got you into bed.

I'd spent all of ten minutes with him and I had already imagined what he'd look like naked.

A warm, wet towel started to dab at my face and my eyes popped open to find Silver kneeling at my side. I had seen him here before; he was always leaving the girls' wing in the mornings. I'd seen Slate doing the same thing. Could he rival Slate's bed-hopping?

"I'm an empath, so I can feel everything you're feeling. Just so we're clear, I won't sleep with you," I said, trying to put some force behind it, but I was just too tired.

"I believe the words you are looking for are *thank* and *you,*" he said with that smile that must make women line up naked for a chance to be with him.

Not me, mind you—*other* women.

I bit my lip to stop the smile that wanted to spread. He was good.

"Thank you..."

"Quick. As in Quick Silver. Only my family and the provosts call me Silver. Do not let the name fool you, I always take my time." He gave me a wink as he dabbed at my face.

"How bad was it?" I asked sitting up.

"A few scrapes and bruises, but she nicked your heart. Any higher and she would have killed you." Quick took his finger and traced the slice of my shirt over my cleavage and back up to the hollow of my throat

I arched an eyebrow at him and he smiled that dazzling smile again. "Perfect."

"Thanks," I said warily and took the towel from his hand before he tried dabbing at the blood on my chest. "So, you're a friend of Slate's?"

Quick let out an exasperated sigh and sat down beside me. "I told him you were in love with him. This just proves it."

My cheeks heated. "Who?"

He arched a dark sculpted eyebrow at me. "You may lie to yourself, but you cannot lie to me."

I narrowed my eyes at him. What did that mean?

"Does your brother attend the university as well?" I asked changing the subject.

"You *would* notice Brass. No, he does not go here. Disappointed?"

"I don't even know him, why would I be disappointed?"

"Do you ever *not* answer a question with another question?" he asked as if he had an investment in my answers. "What I would not give to have Brass's talent."

"You didn't answer my first question," I said pointedly.

He laughed. "Torch. I see it now. Yes, I am his *friend*." Quick said it like it was a pathetic explanation to what they really were.

"I think I am all better now. Are you going to join me for dinner?" I asked.

"Do you want me to join you?" he asked.

"Will you answer more of my questions?"

"Why are you so curious?"

"Wouldn't you be?" I retorted.

Quick let out a breath. "Slate spends the night with you; I do not know how he stands it."

My cheeks heated.

"He told you?"

His lips spread into a slow smile. "*You* just did. He disappears when he should be with us, and is vague on where he sleeps. Slate does not care who knows whom he beds, until you."

Clever *and* devastatingly handsome. He was a deadly combination. He sat so close I could almost see what the black ink hinted at underneath his collar. He saw me looking and stood, putting his hands on the fabric by his trim waist.

"Want to take a peek?" Oh, that smile was trouble.

"If you're offering." I'd seen plenty of half-naked men over the last year, one more wouldn't be still my beating newly-healed heart.

He crossed his arms as he lifted his black shirt over his head and revealed the muscles upon muscles that beneath his olive skin. Over his multitude of muscles was a tattoo, or a series of black tattoos, that went across his pecs and down his left side to disappear under his waistline. Jagged Celtic tattoos that were thick and masculine, lending a certain badness to him, wrapped around him. He turned around and I saw that they also covered his back.

"How far do they go?"

I hadn't seen many people with tattoos in or outside of Tidings, and Quick was a walking talking work of art.

His lips quirked on one side. "Only one way to find out," he said, holding up his hands.

"Do you think I'm afraid of underwear?" I said dryly. I stood up on the same side of the aisle as him so we were inches apart. "I can't tell if you're daring me to see if I'll do it, or because you want me to unbuckle your pants," I said, narrowing my eyes.

"Does it matter?" he said with heavy lids as he looked down at me.

Curiosity won out in the end. "It's just a tattoo, and these are just pants. Don't get too excited," I said, but my fingers were already on his belt buckle.

I hoped he didn't notice how unskilled I was at unbuckling his belt, and how my fingers seemed clumsy over his button.

"I do believe your hands are trembling," he said in a low tone.

I raised my narrowed eyes to his. "They're not *trembling*," I spat, and he chuckled.

"Have you unbuckled a man's pants before?" he asked much too huskily and I shot him a look.

"Once or twice," I admitted, and dropped my eyes to focus and because his eyes had flared excitedly at my inexperience. Trouble.

He raised his hand to my hair. "I want to braid your hair for you again. Would you like that? I think you *should* wear it to class tomorrow. I think I could spend a few mornings braiding your hair," he said, winding his fingers through my braid that had fallen over my shoulder.

He was trouble with a capital "T." Maybe he should start going by Trouble instead of Quick. I unbuttoned the last button and felt a thrill of triumph. My eyes shot to his with smugness. I'd done it and hadn't even blushed. I didn't see why he had made this such a big deal. I tucked my thumbs into the waistline of his pants and pushed them down.

"TORCH! What the fuck are you doing?" Slate roared. Where had he come from?

My hands were still on Quick's hips. I felt with my fingers as they went lower and lower still. Nothing but smooth, silky flesh.

"You're not wearing any underwear, are you?" I asked as a wave of heat burned so hotly through me the insides of my ears burned.

Quick flashed his dazzling smile and shook his head once. His fingers were still in my hair. I closed my eyes. When I opened them, maybe I wouldn't be there. Maybe I'd be in my bed and this all would have been a mortifying dream.

"Quick! You are the world's biggest bastard!" It was Jett. *Awesome.* Now we had a party.

I opened my eyes and lifted my hands from his hips. I took a step back and my calves hit the bench, forcing me to sit, and I was eye-to-eye with his waist. I yelped and threw my hands up to cover my eyes. I ducked on reflex and my head came into contact with flesh. I heard a grunt and I yelped again. I did not just head butt his groin!

I took my hands off my face. "Oh my gods! I'm so sorry! This is your fault! You should have told me you didn't wear underwear!" I shouted, red-faced, knowing there was no way I could possibly be any more embarrassed.

It was physically impossible for me to get any redder.

Jett busted out laughing and I turned to them. Slate wasn't as angry as I'd imagined he would look in my head, and Jett was doubled over laughing. I pinched my lips together as they started walking forward. I hooked an arm under Quick's and tried to help him straighten. He pulled his pants up as he sat on the bench.

"I am sorry. I thought you'd be, *um,* covered," I said, sitting down next to him.

He leaned back, buttoning his pants, then sat back up and picked his shirt up off the floor. He arched an eyebrow at me.

"You could rub it and make it feel better." His dazzling smile bloomed on his face and I felt the overwhelming urge to slap him.

I did.

I stood up in a huff and turned to Slate. "This is the company you keep?" I pointed to Quick who was still smiling—he must have known I'd slap him.

"How do you sleep with her? In thirty minutes, I have been slapped and had my cock smashed," Quick said, shrugging into his shirt.

I turned to him indignation welling up in me. "I did not do things to his cock!"

I slapped my hands over my mouth. I didn't say that word.

"Did my baby sister just talk about your cock?" Jett asked.

"Does that mean you are not going to rub it?" Quick asked, standing so I backed up and clunked the back of my head on the cubby.

"*Oh*! You are such a fanny pack!"

Ass would have packed a bigger punch, but I had already said the "C" word and the "B" word—though those were both in my head. I used both my hands and shoved Quick as hard as I could and he fell back on the padded bench as he laughed but held onto my hands.

"Gods, you are cute, *Torch*," Quick said, holding my wrists.

Slate's big hand clasped over my arm. "Do not call her Torch. Torch is mine.

You have aggravated her enough, Quick. Thank you for taking care of her."

I nearly spluttered. "Taking care of me? He was trying to get me to...to do stuff. Are you alright?"

What did he mean by *mine*? The pet name or me?

Quick laughed. "Truth, Ms. Scarlett."

Slate looked at him and I felt like I was missing something again. I glanced to Jett who had crossed his arms and was leaning against the cubbies.

"Are you okay, Jett?" I asked.

"Yeah, *are* you okay?" Slate asked.

"I've been better. Jonquil is just jealous of you. Cherry was sent to Uncle Reed's, but she got in a few good licks before Crag pulled her off," Jett said with a note of pride.

"Yes," I told Slate and turned to my brother. "She won't get kicked out, will she?"

Slate was still holding my arm.

"Give it up. I tried questioning her earlier. She does not give straight answers," Quick said, mimicking Jett's posture on my other side.

Jett shook his head. "Amethyst is her wife, Moon's daughter. Not a chance," he said.

I let out a relived breath.

"You didn't fight, did you? Are you okay?" I asked Slate, knowing exactly who he'd *accidentally* hit.

"Are you worried about Ash or me?" Slate asked, looking down his nose at me.

"Both," I answered.

"Lie," Quick said, and I made a face at him.

"I am fine. Answer me. Are you worried about him or me? Pick one," Slate said with glittering grey eyes.

I was feeling cornered. What was with the strange question? I was acutely aware of Jett and Quick waiting for my response, and I started to fidget. Slate reached up to my braid and started to run his fingers through it, so it hung loose. "Answer me, Torch. *Please.*" Please?

How many times had Slate said *please* to me? I was missing something, and Slate was distracting me by running his deft fingers through my hair. Why was I allowing him to do that? I pushed his hand back to his own body and ran my hand through my own hair, loosening the braid the rest of the way.

"Why?" I asked, nervously shifting my feet.

I'd been stabbed in the heart; didn't that grant me some respite?

Quick laughed. "I told you."

Slate closed his eyes and appeared to be counting. "Torch," he said dangerously low.

"I don't want you to get kicked out."

"Truth."

"Were you worried about me or Ash?" Slate ground out.

"Take it easy, she just had her heart stabbed, Slate," Jett said lightly, but I could *feel* the edge of irritation in him.

"I guess if I only have one choice, I was worried that you would be kicked out—because Ash wouldn't have been," I told him and I saw the disappointment in his eyes.

"Truth," Quick said again.

"You're an interrogator!" I accused Quick and he held up his hands.

I'd heard about them. They were used when people were questioned about crimes and during trials to discern the truth—they had been feeling me out for the truth.

"Guilty," Quick said with a dazzling smile.

I cocked my head at Slate and I hoped I didn't look as hurt as I felt. Did he think I was a liar?

"Really?" I asked.

Slate turned his back to me. "You should change. Are you coming home this weekend, Torch?"

I'd been spending a lot of time at the Straumr palace, everyone knew it.

"No," I said, but I was careful not to say where I *was* going.

"The Straumr boy's?" Slate asked and his face turned enough so I could see part of his profile.

I gave him a nod and pushed passed him. "I'll be home in the morning." "Truth," Quick said without his usual hint of amusement.

CHAPTER 25

Everyone was so used to me going to Ash's on the weekends that I wasn't questioned by the girls when I hung back instead of going to Thrimilci. I'd purposely nodded to Slate instead of voicing my *yes* when he asked about going to Ash's because of Quick's lie detecting abilities. I wasn't going to spend the weekend with Ash.

I decided to go check out Styg.

The Iron Maiden didn't sound like a place I would frequent if I was the kind of person who went to bars.

There wasn't much for clothing in my closet at Valla U, so I decided to go for a different look, a very *un*Scarlett like look. Styg dealt with people who bought illegal items—criminals. When I thought of criminals, I thought of a very cloak and dagger type look. I took out my mother's cloak she'd lent me when I'd gone to the Straumr cottage, and raided Cherry's closet. She'd said I could borrow whatever I pleased, but her clothes were a bit more risqué than what I would wear so I'd never taken her up on the offer.

I chewed my lip, looking at myself in the skintight black leather

476

pants and a black leather corset with matching boots that laced all the way up to my knee. This *had* to be what duplicitous women wore. I would have the cloak to hide myself anyway so even if I was way off-base, I figured I'd still be able to blend. I did my makeup much darker than I normally wore it and glossed up my lips, so they shone. I teased my hair and wore a black headband in case I ended up fighting this guy Styg—although I seriously hoped I wouldn't. I had no delusions about the men in Tidings. They were all beautiful, and it seemed like their beauty was relative to their deadliness.

I took the portal room to Valla's town heart. I'd only been there one other time, when Ash had taken me to his family's cottage in the country before we started at Valla U.

I asked the Guardian that guarded the door where I might find the Iron Maiden and he gave me a long look that made me fidget. He sent me down the long, cobbled road that led me to the Skuld gate, and I pulled my cloak up as I walked. I'd worn all of my blades. My wrist blades were fastened tightly, my belt of knives hung low on my hips, I had my seax strapped to my thigh, and two knives in each boot that were surprisingly comfortable despite the heel.

It was chilly for a fall night so I held my cloak closed over my corset that fit so snugly I thought if I angled my chin down it would rest on top of my breasts, or at least pretty darn close. I hated to admit that I had liked the way the pants looked. The tight leather molded to my skin and left little to the imagination, but it made me feel sexy and badass. I never felt sexy or badness. Pretty or cute, that was me...apple pie. Or it *was* me before I had spent the last year doing hard physical training, learning how to kill things and defend myself. Now my body felt like a weapon.

I stood outside of what my uncle had called a pub. I had asked a woman who may or may not have been a woman of the night—but then she probably thought I was one too—where the Iron Maiden was. She gave me the same measured look the Guardian had, and I now stood in front of a filigreed metal door at a dead-end street.

Pub implied a warm beer serving corner bar, where as Iron Maiden was most definitely an exclusive club.

Would I have to know a password? It looked like a place people entered and were never heard from again. I should have told someone where I was going, but it was too late.

Some of the girls I had gone to high school with had gotten into bars with bad fake IDs, and they said as long as you were pretty it would work. I guessed I'd find out. I pushed back my cloak and touched up my hair, moving the cloak away from my chest. I walked under the recessed blue lighting and knocked on the metal door that had no outside handle. It was not a great sign.

A little door at eye level embossed with a filigree flower and swung open so a hard face appeared—or his eyes did. He angled down to look at me and his gaze settled on my cleavage; I tried not to breathe too deeply under his scrutiny. The little door closed and my heart sunk.

But then, I heard a series of locks and the door opened to a blue-lit hall and man as big as Quick stood to the side, the universal gesture for *come on in*. I put a little sway in my hips as I walked past the coffee-colored man with the shaved head and stoney face and felt the first vibrations of bass.

It was *not* a pub.

It was an underground nightclub. At the end of the hall was a metal catwalk that lined the huge room where people danced. Metal stairs led down to a platform lit from underneath that was constantly changing colors while people danced atop it. Below the platform was a bar that

478

spanned three solid walls, and tables for mingling. The fourth wall, and what I assumed must have been the V.I.P. area, held roomy booths with impeccably dressed people drinking amber drinks and others that held a hint of purple.

The club had an industrial feel, and cool air constantly blew from big fans that hung from the ceiling amidst the flashing lights. I decided to take off my cloak and get a drink.

"Anything fruity with vodka," I told the bartender.

She gave me a nod; I was glad vodka was a universal liquor. Truth be told, I'd only had it once before. The first time I ever drank, and it had been a terrible idea.

I slid a nickel Hunt to the waitress and she beamed a smile at me. I was still terrible at the local currency. I turned around and rested my elbows on the slick metal counter. I recognized the song playing. I thought Jett would love the place—maybe I could take him there if he didn't already know about it.

"I have never seen you here before."

My eyebrows jumped to my hairline when a man with up-tilted dark eyes and spiky black hair leaned over to talk to me.

I was a terrible spy. "My first time here!" I shouted back over the music.

"Have you been out of the dance floor?" he asked with a disarming smile.

I gave him a lopsided grin. "I'm not here to dance. I'm looking for someone."

"That accent. Where are you from?" he asked, changing the subject with ease.

He was average height and leanly muscled with a trim waist. He was wearing wrist blades, I noticed.

"Chicago. I'm surprised you recognized it," I said with what I hoped was an equally disarming smile.

His smile brightened, creasing the skin around his eyes. "I am Haarder. My cousin left Tidings to study at the University of Chicago. I have visited him there a few times. Who are you looking for? I might know her...him?" I shook his hand.

I mulled it over; this was probably my best chance of finding Styg, short of going around and asking each person if they were him. I didn't know if I was supposed to know about Styg though, or if just asking about him would get me into trouble.

I didn't have a choice. I'd have to ask someone.

"Scarlett, I'm looking for Civet," I said, watching for a reaction.

"Who?" he asked looking genuinely confused.

"Styg," I tried, and watched his eyebrows quirk. *Score*.

His smile faltered. "Tell you what. Join me for a couple dances, and I will tell you where you can find him."

"How about I *agree* to a few dances, you tell me where he is, and then I make good on my word?" I offered instead.

He pursed his lips in mock contemplation then broke out into a beaming smile. "Cool. See that guy up there in the white?" He faced the booths and I looked in the direction he faced, keeping careful not to point.

The man in white glowed in the blacklight above the booths. He was rail thin and towered over the women who sat around him. He looked like money. *Creepy* money. He had short brown hair combed into an undercut. I could see the hollows of his cheekbones even from across the room, and eyes that penetrated everything. Even when he smiled, it never touched those eyes. The women around him were like trophies, each one more different and unique than the ones beside her.

I hadn't the first clue of how I would get close to a man like him. Earlier tonight, I thought I'd go to a pub, buy him some beers, get him wasted, and ask him some questions. I was in way over my head.

"How about that dance?" I asked.

If I was in a club, I might as well make the most of it.

I patted the necklace around my throat, which was my quasi-engagement ring hanging from the Yggdrasil pendant against my breasts—being squished by them, more like. I noticed that my dance partner had on two torques and a necklace twin to mine. He was a tried and true Guardian.

I followed him onto the dance floor as "Bangarang" by Skrillex was remixed over the sound system. My cheeks were flushed from my single drink as we danced over a purple floor, and laser lights shot green across my face. I let Haarder guide me, but I could dance to this music on my own, no lessons needed, unlike the traditional ethereal music of Tidings.

My body bumped up against the bodies of several others as I hung my head back and let the music flow through me. I had needed a release and this was better than I could have asked for. Haarder was watching me move and matching me, but he must have spent a lot of time there because he had some serious moves. Like, backup dancer moves. I found myself smiling and shouting with the people around me as we made a circle around Haarder.

"Excuse me?" Someone tapped me on the shoulder while I danced with my partner.

I turned and furrowed my brow. I'd never seen the person before. "Yes?" I shouted into his ear.

"Styg would like to know if you wish to join him?" he said in my ear and my blood froze.

"Yes," I said with a nod.

I turned to Haarder and gave him a wave and he waved back; our dances were up.

I followed the burly man off the now red platform and to the chained-off area that led to the V.I.P. booths. The burly man removed the chain and held out his arm and I walked the thin metal catwalk that led to Styg's booth.

He was taller than Slate when he stood and couldn't have weighed much more than two hundred pounds. He took my hand as I stood in front of his purple upholstered horseshoe booth and kissed my hand. My cheeks flushed and he deepened his smile that didn't touch his grey eyes.

One of the girls grudgingly moved over so I could sit down with the other three women he had already accumulated. One of them poured a glass of champagne and handed it to me. I took it, held it up to them all in a sort of *cheers,* and downed it. A moment later I scolded myself to slow down; I'd need my wits to figure out what I'd do next.

"I do not believe I have seen you here before. I would have remembered."

Styg would have been handsome if he'd had more meat on his bones, or even if he just smiled. Instead he looked like a snake in human clothing—albeit, stylish clothing. The black market must not have been hit by the recession.

I gave him my best smile. "First time here."

His bottom lip twitched as he scanned my face and then looked down to what I was wearing. I realized he was checking for my torques.

"You are a tyro?" he asked.

"Yes," I replied. Maybe if I seemed open, he'd let something slip. "Do you know many other tyros?" I asked.

Slate was a tyro. "Some," he said cryptically and sipped amber fluid from his glass.

One of the girls started talking to me, and at first I was grateful. Then I realized she talked *a lot*. She probably did it because she was nervous, or drunk, but she was distracting me from my purpose and I could feel Styg watching me carefully. I was afraid I'd reveal something about Slate, and the jig would be up.

I'd just about given up getting anything useful that night when Styg got up and asked me to join him. At first I thought we were going to the dance floor, even though Styg didn't look like the kind of guy who danced.

The burly man who'd escorted me off the dance floor led us along the catwalk and I realized we were going deeper into the club and down another hall.

Red flags were flapping in the breeze.

He opened a side door and I entered, Styg right behind me. It was a narrow room with plush blue couches that lined the mirrored walls. The room had a sweet fragrant smell that covered up the mix of bodies and booze from the greater room of the club.

With all the other emotions floating around the club, it had been hard to get a read on Styg, but I was getting it loud and clear now.

Change of plans.

"I have to get going," I said, trying to get around him.

He smiled but it didn't touch his eyes. I shivered. It wasn't a pleasant smile. "I chose you. I could have had any of those girls. You are the lucky one tonight." His bony, long-fingered hand reached out and I reacted.

I took another step back. "*Dude*. No. No means no, not like I'm playing hard to get. I've got more men than I know what to do with in my life and I don't need any more, not even for one night."

He chuckled as if I'd just said the most hilarious joke he'd ever heard and I moved to get past him; he moved with me. I leveled my eyes at him, or rather I glared up at him.

"Are you not the least bit curious to find out if I am proportioned?" he asked with a sly smile as oily as his slicked-back hair.

"Not in the least," I said in a stringent tone.

"You look like you like to fight. How are you in your battle training, little girl?" he asked, unclasping his white jerkin.

I narrowed my eyes. "You want to find out?" I asked, trying to make it sound like a threat.

"Indeed I do." He laid his jerkin down on the blue couch carefully and revealed lean wiry arms in a white sleeveless shirt.

I had killed men before. I didn't enjoy it. I'd locked those emotions up so deep they never resurfaced. But they did now when I was facing this man who towered over me, weighed nearly a hundred pounds more than I did, and wanted me to fight him with the winner seemingly getting what they wanted.

"I'm warning you. I'm having a bad day. You don't want to test my patience now. Let me go and leave Slate alone, and I won't have to kill you," I told him.

He cocked his head at Slate's name. "The Grand Mistress's pet?" he asked, sounding surprised that I knew him.

I didn't know anything about a Grand Mistress.

"What is he to you? Are you trying to get close to me to get to her? I should warn you, she does not let anyone get close. At least, no one without a cock. Do you have one? I think I should check to be certain."

He lunged at me; his tall, spindly frame rocked me off my feet and I hit the mirrored wall behind me.

I fought him like a cornered wolverine. I gave up all pretenses of trying not to *call* and threw *call* after *call* at him. They evaporated around him like mist. I watched, dumbfounded, and he showed me a second torque around his wrist.

"A nix torque; I cannot *call* but none of yours can hit me as either," he said with a smile.

Unscrupulous black market scoundrel. He tackled me and I felt fear for the first time since being attacked by the Jorogumo. It shot adrenaline through me as he laughed in my face, pinning me down to the floor. My breathing was harsh from his weight on my ribs and the tight corset I was spilling out of.

He looked down the swell of my cleavage and I felt his grip loosen just a little as he moved south. I freed my hand and triggered my wrist blade. He bellowed.

"You bitch! You cut off my hand!" he screamed at me and back-handed me so hard my feet lifted off the ground and I hit the couch.

He was being dramatic. His hand was still mostly attached.

The burly man came in the room and saw the spurting blood of the end of his arm and me, lifting my head, holding my cheek.

Was my nose now on the side of my face? Gods! That smarted, but I didn't taste blood. I snarled.

"Throw her out and come back!" Styg shouted and I lost it.

I wouldn't stab the guy just doing his job, but I wouldn't go quietly either. He ended up putting me in a bear hug and dumped my body outside the filigree door, throwing my cloak out after me. I'd been dragged through the club like a petulant child throwing a tantrum and dumped on my fanny pack.

My prior experience in the spying field could be reduced to a single night when Tawny'd had a minor crush and we had taken my mother's car to drive past his house after we'd gone out for milkshakes. He had been hanging outside his car with his buddies and they'd recognized my mom's car and waved to us. I sped off like a lunatic, embarrassed that they'd caught us stalking past his house. We probably could have gotten out and talked and chalked it up to happy coincidence, but subterfuge has never been my strong point.

I lay outside for the next half hour. Eventually, Styg came out alone, probably having already sated his sexual appetite on one of his eager beavers in the back room. I pulled my cloak up and followed as he walked alone along the streets of Valla, a blazing beacon in white as if he was untouchable and daring anyone who might be foolish enough to attack him. I did notice his hand was reattached. Pity.

Eventually, he walked down a dead end that led to a three-story building that had no door. I stood at the mouth of the alley and watched as the wall opened up.

The stone dead end was really a door that slid into the building. He paused before the entrance and I retreated behind the wall. I thought I saw him cast a smile over his shoulder before entering the building.

Once he was in, the wall began to return to its original position. I started forward. It may have been a trap, but I didn't know if it required some kind of special key to be opened, so I had to get in before it closed. I sprinted down the dead end at breakneck speed.

I'd always been fast. I could make it. That was, until I was blind-sided by a body that emerged from the shadows like a ghost, slamming me so hard into the building beside the secret entrance that I cried out.

Big, rough hands gripped my wrists and pinned them behind my back with a knife at my throat, his body pushing mine into the wall.

"If you so much as think about *calling*, I will slit your throat," he said close to my ear.

I had expected him to have a guttural voice. Maybe an evil cackle, something that would say, "I'm a murdering maniac." Instead, his voice was deep and smooth, and it sounded like a dark promise instead of a threat. It wasn't a voice I recognized, but it was tugging on a memory like a dream. A voice like his *belonged* in my wildest dreams.

"What are you doing following Styg? Tell me the truth because I will know if you are lying," he said in his smooth, breathy voice.

"He's a jerk who tried to capture my friend," I gritted out. "I wanted to be sure he was the one who planned it." And then kill him.

"You cannot kill Styg, even if you could manage it, which I doubt. He is too valuable alive. Your friend will have to deal with it," he said as his hand started to search my body for weapons.

He felt between my legs to unbuckle my short seax, then threw it behind him and unbuckled my knife belt with one hand and threw that too. He pressed his big body harder against me, my sore cheek against the brick wall as he reached into my boot and pulled out my knives. He'd found all of my weapons. I cursed my luck. He thrust his hand down my cleavage, groping around my trussed-up bosom, and pulled it back out as I yelped. Then he felt up my back with calloused palms.

"You took them all," I ground out, cheeks heating.

"Just checking," he said, and I could hear his smile.

"Now what are you going to do with me? A disarmed girl in a dark alley?

Things aren't looking so good for me tonight."

I had done it again. How did I keep getting myself into these dangerous situations?

"I will not hurt you. I am only here to warn you. Leave Styg alone, forget where you followed him, and go home. Have babies, get fat, live life. If you do not leave well enough alone, then someone will come for you, and it will not be pretty. Understand?" he asked, his lips brushing against my ear through the cloak.

I could smell the cinnamon on his breath, and *feel* how sincere he was. He would regret having to come after me.

"*Or* you could help me so I know my friend and I are safe? What kind of man are you? Honorable or a scoundrel?" I asked.

It was gutsy considering my situation, but men had prickly honor.

I *felt* his temper flare and he whirled me around and gasped. "*You?*" he asked incredulously as he pinned me back with his body.

My hood had fallen back when he spun me. I looked at the man and something nagged at me. He was over six feet tall and broad, built like Slate or Quick with dark hair that grazed his broad shoulders, threaded with a few braids, bronze and ebony beads catching the moonlight behind his ears. Dreamy amber eyes peered out at me from long lashes under thick masculine brows. His features were strong with an anvil dark honey jaw dusted with a trimmed stubble and symmetrical nose, but not hard like Slate's. His lips, those cinnamon scented lips, were well-defined and plump like they were made for kissing.

He smiled and I melted a little. It was a warm, inviting smile that made you want to bask in its light. *Brass.* Slate's dark-haired cohort.

Most definitely Coyote and Quick's brother. I racked my brain trying to remember everything I'd gleaned about the middle Regn brother.

"Stop looking at my lips," he said, looking at mine.

I flushed. "I wasn't." I definitely was.

He smiled again and something inside me groaned. So close, and his cinnamon smell was intoxicating as he breathed inches away from my face. I was looking at his lips again. I brought my gaze back up to his eyes. Deep, knowing eyes full of welcome.

"Go on. Get out of here," he said in his deep, smooth voice.

"What's in there?" I asked, my curiosity piqued.

He arched a dark brow as his eyes searched mine. "You do not want to know. Trust me."

I scoffed. "Lately, I don't trust anyone. If you don't take me in now, I'll come back when you're not around," I promised.

A rogue strand of hair brushed against his high cheekbone that moved when I breathed. I hoped I didn't smell like the champagne I'd been drinking.

His lips quirked and he leaned in. "You smell like vanilla and...spiced apples," he said, taking a deep breath and looking down at me.

I'd tilted my chin and hadn't even realized it while I watched him lean in to smell me. He moved closer as his lips brushed mine and I inhaled deeply, sucking in his cinnamon scent, and he closed his lips over mine. He *did* taste like cinnamon, his lips *were* as soft as they looked. My lips had parted of their own volition and I felt his velvety tongue on mine.

My eyes shot open. Did I just simper?

I turned my head. That did *not* just happen. He took a step back and walked over to the door. I gave myself a mental shake. He was Slate's friend, and I'd just made out with him. I had permanently engraved my name in hell, saving myself an extra special place.

Brass looked at me expectantly and waved me over. "Are you coming or not?" he asked with a smile. His hand touched the secret door and it started to slide open.

"I'm coming," I said, and he laughed as I blushed.

Oh yes, Quick's brother.

We walked down polished wood steps and the temperature changed so I took off my cloak and hung it over my arm as I followed Brass. It was weird knowing his name without him telling me.

"Where is Silver?" he asked.

"Why would I know?" I asked.

"He is supposed to be keeping an eye on you. You know, this is a very bad idea, but I can tell you are going to find out what is here no matter what. Better now than later," Brass said smoothly.

I walked behind him and realized most of the men in my life these days had this fluidlike grace—the deadly grace of a man confident in his abilities to be one of the biggest baddest men wherever we ended up. I thought it said more about me than it did about them. When did I start hanging out with trained killers?

In high school, I'd hung out with football players and guys from the baseball team. Cocky, funny guys who doubled as surrogate brothers, before I started getting curves. In college, I didn't hang out with any guys. Like, *at all*, because I was so busy with classes. Now, I was surrounded by men whose mothers had obviously not gotten the memo about growth hormones in cows' milk.

We reached a hall and I saw low-hanging lamps from the ceiling. I smelled leather even before we reached the room, and heard the sound of pool balls cracking against one another. The large, loft-like room had spots of bright light existed between spots of darkness. It wouldn't have surprised me if there had been cigarette smoke in the air, but this was Tidings; cigarettes didn't exist here. There was a bar, complete with bottles, tender, and stools.

Two pool tables and four couches were scattered around the expansive room. There were card games going on, and the players didn't even bother to spare us a glance. A few nodded to Brass, but that was as far as their acknowledgement went. Their ages ranged from middle-aged to young teens. The walls were painted a dark purple and there was wood flooring with a few dark rugs covering the ground. There were no windows to speak of. I wondered how far underground we were.

This wasn't what I'd been expecting at all. It was so...modern. I noticed they even had arcade machines and a dart board.

"What is this place?" I asked doubtfully.

"Our rumpus room," Brass answered, eyeing the door across from us.

There were stairs at either end of the room going both to a lower floor and leading to the floor above. There were three doors along the room. One lay straight ahead. Faint music drifted from the bar; it sounded like country.

Brass turned to me and there was something in his eyes like he was apologizing for something that hadn't happened yet. "I am here if you need me."

The door directly across from us opened. Quick came out first and waited outside of the door, still speaking to whoever was in the room. He was smiling his dazzling smile and a feminine laugh sounded from within. Red flags went up and I stiffened. There was no controlling my heartbeat.

Slate came out next, his eyes on the woman still in the room. He was smiling as if a joke was made at his expense, but he recognized its hilarity.

The worst came to mind. My scenarios started with Quick secretly being a member of the group trying to kidnap Slate. Since seeing Slate unharmed, for the time being, I knew that to be false and settled on Slate having found Styg first and after deeming him not a threat, stayed for a night cap. It was plausible.

Though, He would've been at Iron Maiden and not in the super secret hideout with the sliding wall entrance.

Out came a woman just behind Slate.

She was older, with dark, wavy hair that came down to her chin. Thick, high-arched, dark eyebrows were above her equally dark eyes. Even from there, I could see her red lips. She was talking familiarly with Slate, her hand curled around his elbow. Her other hand was on his chest—her nails were bright red to match her lips. I decided to toss out my red nail polish the moment I got home.

She was much shorter than he was. Despite her small stature, her presence commanded attention and obedience. Her fingers squeezed at his bronzed elbow and he bent his head down obediently. She planted a kiss on his lips.

I had seen Slate do a great many things with women—pretty much every single sex act, now that I thought about it. This was different. More intimate, somehow. My first thought was denial: it must be like his aunt or something. Obviously, he had no family left, so yeah, denial. When his big hands rested possessively on her shoulders, I felt something inside me rage. I realized this was the raven-haired woman I saw him with the first night I met him, and again they were together at Coyote's baby's Ausa Vatni.

"I could bring you back here another day, Scarlett." Brass hovered into my line of vision, blocking out what was going on behind him.

"Who is she?" I asked, trying to collect my thoughts.

Rich amber eyes filled with sympathy. "My aunt."

I blinked rapidly and tore my eyes away from them to look at Brass. "Your aunt is Slate's lover?" I asked, incredulous.

Brass gave a curt nod. "One of them. Has been for many years."

I felt like I'd been punched in the gut. Did he mean one of his aunt's lovers or one of Slate's? Both probably. All his sugarfoot about not wanting to get married or have kids, and he had been seeing this woman. I hated liars. To add insult to injury, many years implied before what would be even legal in the States. I hadn't asked, but I assumed it wasn't allowed in Tidings either.

I closed my eyes to collect my thoughts, grateful I'd never let myself be seduced by one Slate Sumar. For a brief time, I had actually thought I might have *feelings* for him. My blurred lines were perfectly visible now and there would never be a future for Slate and me.

"What the fuck is she doing here, Brass? I thought you were supposed to chase her off?" It was Styg, and he sounded super pissed.

"She is no threat to you," Brass said in an easy, soothing tone.

"That bitch cut off my hand!" Styg said, and out of the corner of my eye, I noticed we'd drawn Slate away from the old hag's mouth.

"You're lucky that's all I cut off!" I ignored the look the old bat shot me as I marched to Styg to finish what I'd started with my bare hands.

Brass was suddenly between us; I stumbled backwards and Brass punched Styg so hard in the face he was knocked down on his fanny pack. Styg held his nose, dumbfounded, as it gushed blood.

"Never ever speak to her that way again," Brass said evenly, not even breaking his smooth tone.

I stared at him, awed. Did he just punch a guy for saying something mean to me? Ash never defended me, and Slate was usually the one *saying* inappropriate things. Brass turned back to me with an apologetic smile—and then it spread as he noticed my wonderstruck expression.

"Torch, what are you doing here?" Slate hovered into view and I was temporarily distracted from my hero.

"I was following that guy." I pointed to Styg who was rubbing his nose.

Slate looked furious, but a delicate red-nailed hand touched his forearm and he took a step back. So it was like that, was it?

She was petite like Shale; I was willing to bet she was deceptively strong like her as well. Her skin was a creamy beige, and her dark eyes almost looked devoid of an iris, they were so dark.

"We haven't met yet. I'm Scarlett Tio." Quick and Brass moved to stand next to her and Slate took another step back so we faced off.

A smile played on her lips as she visibly assessed me. I wished I wasn't wearing such a slutty outfit, but I didn't flinch under her unrelenting eyes. She brought her gaze back up to mine.

"I am Grand Mistress Cordillera." She paused and angled her body to address the men but kept her eyes on me. "Is she a khoraz?"

I knit my brows and looked to men. "No, Lera," Brass said sternly with a disapproving expression.

"She does not usually dress that way," Quick offered as he raked my body with his eyes.

"What's a khoraz?" I stumbled over the word.

Styg was back on his feet, and he scoffed. "If she was a khoraz we would be back in the Iron Maiden with those oh-so-fuckable lips wrapped around my cock."

I saw Quick hold back Slate with his *calling*, but even Brass was looking murderous. My mouth popped open with an audible pop; *no one* said things like that to me.

Pieces were clicking together in my head as I turned to Styg. "Why didn't you just tell me you didn't mean him harm? That you knew him? I would have left you alone," I said, shaking my head.

"I told you I knew the Grand Mistress's *pet*. What did you think I meant?" he shouted, stepping close, looming above me like an angry giraffe.

"I don't know, it was kind of hard to think when you were trying to tear my clothes off!" I was trying to get in his face, but he was much higher up than I was even with my heels on.

He smiled and for the first time, it touched his eyes; it was much more frightening. I wanted to tell him to go back to how he was doing it before. Suddenly, Brass was at my side.

"Stop that line of thinking right now, or I will personally gut you," Brass said low and smooth like a caress.

Styg laughed cruelly. "I knew you would be a fighter, girl. The fun we could have together. Did you fuck these boys? Is that what makes them deranged enough to threaten me? I would give one of my rarest pieces to find out what loyalty you would inspire in me."

Slate roared so loudly that I covered my ears as he lunged at Styg, knocking him to the ground. Quick and Brass were pulling Slate off Styg, and I was on my backside, but not before Slate's fists beat in the degenerate's face. I didn't know what to make of the change in events. I scampered over to where Styg lay. So the guy wasn't a murderer, but he was a pervert that would have taken advantage of me if he'd won our fight I found myself healing him on the wood floor. His face was a bloody mass of pulp.

I *called* and rinsed his face after I'd healed him, but he was still passed out. I sat back on my heels and turned to where Cordillera was speaking sternly to Slate, right in his face, as he leaned his hands against a chair with his head hung.

I hated her talking to him that way. Who did she think she was? I got to my feet and marched over there, but I was intercepted by Brass.

"If you want to be trained here, bite your tongue," Brass said.

I persisted.

He gave up and tossed me over his shoulder when I started struggling towards Slate and Cordillera. Slate's head lifted; he noticed Brass carrying me and straightened. Brass stopped walking and turned around.

"I am bringing her downstairs to cool her head," Brass said like he was trying to deal with a rabid wild animal.

"I will go with him. Do not worry, I will make sure she behaves," Quick said, and I was swung around again to face Slate and Cordillera who was glaring at me.

The brothers didn't say anything as I was brought deeper into the building. We walked down several flights of stone stairs with wrought iron balustrades until we came to a set of metal double doors. Brass pushed them open, and we were suddenly in a modern prep room with black metal cubbies and gray marble tiles skeined with white and black marble benches.

They led me through until the end, where three massage tables were set up and showers were off to the left. Quick looked back at me and smirked as we reached another set of metal double doors.

It was much warmer here, and when he opened the doors I understood why. Brass led the way up another set of stone steps until we stood along a stone wall meant for spectators that looked down upon the training area. *Area* might not have been the right word for it, though. A whole village could have fit in the expanse of land that made up the training *area*.

"This is our crash course," Quick told me.

I stood there gaping, leaning over the wrought iron balcony railing. There was a man down there running the course. Which included a simulated earthquake, complete with falling boulders, a lava pit with floating rocks on its surface, and wooden rafts that rested on crashing waves. That was just the right half. Tall trees stood in the center of the room, like a small woods dividing the room. The left half had a battle ring and something that looked similar to the Gauntlet at Valla U with all its wicked looking blades.

"Come, let us show you around," Quick said, amused at my gaping expression.

I knew my eyes must have been glittering, because I was in heaven. It was awesome. It would push me to all my limits. We walked around the room on a track that wrapped around the whole thing. I noticed an enclosed glass portion across from us.

"The Grand Mistress's seats," Brass explained. "We have competitions and people can come here and place bets on the outcomes."

"You're like gladiators?" I asked in disbelief.

Brass smiled. "No, no one dies, there are no lions. We compete."

"We get bonuses if we win. Spectators pay for the company of the victor if they should...make themselves available," Quick elaborated.

My eyes widened. "They pay you to sleep with them?" *Appalling* was the only word that came to mind.

Brass and Quick laughed. "You do not have to. It is for the privilege of your company."

I made a face. "What *are* you exactly? Obviously you work as body-guards. You guys are the good guys, right?"

"Shadow Breakers. The less you know, the better. For all intents and purposes, you can think of us as mercenaries," Quick said as I followed his retreating back.

"Mercenaries." I tried the word out on my tongue.

I balked. *Not* the good guys; muscle for hire.

Quick reached the stairs on the other side that led into the arena and began climbing down. Brass walked alongside me. "Silver is being dramatic. We are the lesser families who cannot get ambassador jobs, or who do not want them. Civilian life holds no appeal and neither does teaching or being a soldier. This is an alternative."

Quick walked to the combat circle at the back of the arena and Brass and I followed. "How are you feeling, Ms. Scarlett? Perhaps you have been knocked about the head too much tonight?" he asked.

Slate was standing in the prep room doorway and Brass and I stood side by side as he entered the room. His eyes were still fierce, but I wasn't doing my rabbit thing. Or maybe I was. I couldn't look away as he marched right up to me and grabbed my chin.

"Why has she not been healed?" he asked coldly without breaking eye contact with me.

"We showed her around, she did not seem to be in pain…but we were getting to that," Quick said, looking at Brass.

"I'm fine, Slate." I tried to jerk my chin away, but his grip was firm.

I felt warmth flood through me as he healed where I'd been back-handed, as well as all the unseen bumps and bruises I didn't even know had. My eyes were narrowed at Slate and I wished for the umpteenth time in my life that my upper lip wasn't so full so I wouldn't look like I was pouting instead a casting a proper glare.

"Why did you bring her here?" he asked Brass without looking.

"She followed Styg to the entrance and he let her see him enter. He told me someone was following him, and if they were armed, to dispatch them. Instead, I found *her* trying to dart into the entrance," Brass said with a smile in his voice.

My lips quirked for some unknown reason and Slate's eyes hardened. I turned away from Slate and faced Brass.

"Do you think someone will steal my weapons?" I asked.

He had disarmed me, so the person following Styg *wasn't* armed. Clever.

Brass smiled back at me with glittering amber eyes. "No one comes down this way. They know better."

"Is it because you tackle *them* into walls too? That'll teach them," I said, unable to fight the smile that rose to my lips.

Brass chuckled. "There is that. Though I do not think they would be as fun to disarm."

My cheeks flushed, remembering how he'd shoved his hand down my corset then spun me around and kissed me. "Hopefully, they'd all be women." My tone lifted in the end as if it could be a question.

Brass's eyes twinkled. "One can hope."

"I cannot believe what I am listening to. Are you *flirting*?" Quick asked in disbelief.

Brass shrugged. "I did not know it was her at first." "At first?" Slate asked in a deep rumble behind me.

I felt another flush of heat. "Then I realized it was her," Brass said simply; it was borderline insolent and I could *feel* Quick's incredulity.

Slate spun me around. "You know him, Torch?" he asked.

"I know he's your friend. I've seen the three of you together. I know he's Quick's brother. Brass Regn. That's it. I met him tonight in the alley after he tackled me...and frisked me." I bit my lip to keep from laughing.

Slate's face turned apoplectic. "You frisked her?"

"Standard protocol," Brass shrugged his broad shoulders.

"And then?" Slate ground out.

"Then when she was disarmed, I kissed her. She is having a bad day. She needed to be kissed," Brass said in his defense.

Slate roared again and let go of my arms, and Quick darted between Brass and Slate. Quick moved faster than I'd ever seen anyone move. He was as good as his namesake.

"Slate, you have no right to be upset because of a kiss. I walked in on you kissing Cordillera, remember?" I said, widening my eyes.

Slate whirled on me and my breath caught. "*You*, who run from me, yell at me, fight me every single step of the way. *Torch*. You push a man to his limits." I crossed my arms and his eyes shot down to my cleavage. "What are you wearing? No wonder he did not recognize you."

I tried to glower. "Clothes. I was trying to do some research at the Iron

Maiden and find out who Styg was and see why he was trying to capture you."

Slate shook his head of glossy waves. "Styg is under our protection. He would not want to capture me."

Quick snorted. "He might want to *kill* you now."

"You don't tell me anything. You could have saved me from this whole night if you just communicated a little bit," I said in frustration and then frowned.

That was such a girl thing to say.

"You did not ask," Slate said, then turned back to Brass. "You are relieved from duty; you will no longer be guarding her."

"I'm being guarded?" I asked, moving to stand between the three men so I could see them all at the same time.

"Because of a little kissing?" Brass asked.

"I told you, I have eyes on you. Our mother wanted to make sure you were protected, but how does one protect you from yourself? And *yes*, because you became intimate with the client," Slate growled.

"Well, then you have to get rid of Quick too," I said, crossing my arms again.

"WHAT! You kissed Quick?" Slate bellowed and turned on Quick.

Brass was laughing and Quick had his hands out. "Whoa!"

"No! I don't kiss *everyone*! I have seen him, *um*, naked, and stuff. That is pretty intimate if you ask me," I said, stumbling over my words.

Quick stared at me like I was a traitor, and Brass was laughing so hard he was doubled over. "She headbutted your cock?" Brass asked between laughs.

Quick adjusted himself.

"He deserved it," I huffed. "Wait, how did you—"

Brass righted himself and looked right into my eyes. "Cinnamon."

My cheeks flamed and Slate was looking between us both.

"How..." I whispered.

The corner of his lips curled and I blushed again.

"Someone had better tell me what the fuck cinnamon means," Slate said in a dangerous tone.

"She thinks I taste like cinnamon," Brass said with a curl of his lips, and I turned my gape on him. "You did not say it aloud. I can pick up images and words from your mind."

I could only gape. I was still in the dark about *so* much Guardians were capable of.

Slate closed his eyes and curled his hands into fists.

"I always thought I was the biggest scoundrel in the family, but it would appear that I was incorrect," Quick said, casting an admiring glance at his brother.

"Do not sell yourself short," Brass said with a rakish grin.

"Those are my private thoughts. All of my thoughts are private.

Sometimes I don't even know what I'm thinking before it pops out of my mouth," I said aloud, not knowing why I was explaining myself.

"It is refreshing. You can surprise even me," Brass said.

"Enough!" Slate roared with his eyes still closed. "By the Mother, Brass, if you do not get out of my sight I cannot be held responsible for my actions."

"Silver, knock it off before I tell him what you are currently thinking," Brass said with a smile.

Quick guffawed. "Do not drag me down with you. She never wears anything like this. Why could it not have been *me* in the alley? You frisked her? In that top? How did you get your hand—"

"You have until the count of one before I tear both of you apart and heal you with one another's limbs," Slate said, taking deep breaths with his eyes closed.

The brothers laughed and trotted away, but not before Brass made his way past me. "It was a pleasure to finally meet you face-to-face. If you need me, just think of me. I can pick up your thoughts," he said with a warm smile.

"The pleasure was all mine," I said with a smile and watched Slate's eyes spring open.

The brothers left through the prep room, and suddenly it was just Slate and me. "So it was Stygians all along. You should have told me. Is that why you have the Regn brothers guarding me? You should have told me about them too. What is this place? Obviously it's a headquarters of sorts. Quick said you're mercenaries. Why are you a mercenary? You don't need the money. And why were they calling you 'captain'? You spend the night here, don't you? I'd bet my short seax you spend the night with her, you *liar*."

I strangled my frustration. I would not be jealous.

Slate sat right down on the ground right where he'd been standing and looked at me with an unreadable expression. "Yes, it is the Stygians. That is why I have the men guarding you. I am their captain. I do not need the coin; I enjoy having something to do other than lazing about the palace. I spend the night here sometimes. Currently, you do not have a seax to wager."

"You spend it with *her*," I clarified.

He sighed. "I have fallen asleep next to her, but I do not wake up in the mornings next to her."

I felt like acid had been injected into my bloodstream. My body burned with an emotion I couldn't put a name to. Frustration, sadness, disappointment...feelings I had no right to have.

"Okay," I said coolly.

"Okay?" he said, looking up at me in astonishment.

"I want to be trained here. Go bring me up to your lover and get her to let one of your men train me. Not you. Someone else," I stated.

"No," Slate said simply, and I swore I could feel my nostrils flare.

"*Fine*. I'll go ask her myself."

I passed the metal cubbies and continued out the metal doors and climbed the stairs until I heard the crack of pool balls and the *bing* of a pinball machine. More than a few eyes watched me as I stalked across the room and past the bar. I gave serious thought to having a beer, but I decided against it and headed for the door I'd seen the woman come from.

It was open as if she'd been expecting me. The office held a couch and two sofa chairs that faced an ornate deep cherry wood desk and matching chair, upholstered in a dark red where the aunt/lover sat like a cat twitching her tail.

Slate stormed in after me and stood behind her chair, leaning against the wall.

If she hadn't offered me a seat I would have sat anyway, and I chose the dark red couch. Quick sat in a matching high-backed chair and Brass came in and closed the door, locked it behind him, and sat down next to me with my weapons in his hands. He set them down on the floor; I picked up my short seax and buckled it onto my thigh.

When Brass sat down, Cordillera started her onslaught. An image of Slate's naked body in explicit detail kissing hers shot through my mind. My breath caught for a moment, but that was all the outward appearance I gave at acknowledging what had happened. Her lips were turned down at the corners.

She recovered just as quickly. Her face was narrow, but grudgingly beautiful. What bothered me most was that she was at least as old as my dad. My mind raced through the themed years; Cordillera was a land formation, which meant she was the same age as Peak Haust, however old he was...but he was Sterling's dad.

"What can I help you with?" she asked in a tone that was all business, none of the woman who was laughing at Quick's jokes. She was in head-to-toe black leather just like everyone else at the Shadow Breakers' hideaway.

"I was told you train people here. I'd like you to train me...with Shadow Breakers, or by them."

I had laid my cards on the table. She could deny me outright or accept it. My guess, though, was that she wanted me under her control any way she could have me. People like that always wanted to control, she was like my evil stepmother that way. I wondered if she and Delta had been best friends at Valla U. She was certainly old enough to be in school at the same time as she was.

Another image shot across my mind. Slate's face between her legs.

"Lera, enough," Brass chastised.

"You can transmit images into people's minds," I said aloud, and Slate stiffened; he must have known they'd be about him. "Are they ones you've witnessed or can you fabricate them?" I asked smoothly.

Cordillera leaned forward. Another image burned into my mind: her mouth on him as he shuddered.

"Only ones I have seen myself," she said with a smirk. I gave a curt nod and swallowed.

"What are you going to do for me in exchange? I do not want your money. That is not why we train Breakers. If we did, it would be

SCARLET SORROW

unprecedented. The only people allowed here are those being trained to be Shadow Breakers," she said with those red lips.

"Okay. You do not need to show me those...images. I get the idea, and I don't think you understand our relationship. Brass told me you hold competitions. I could train for you and compete in exchange," I offered, willing her to stop her onslaught.

"Lera, what are you doing?" Slate asked, warily taking a step towards her.

She inhaled and leaned back in her chair. I hung my head with my eyes open, trying to erase the images from my mind. I'd never forget what she'd shown me. It was impossible.

"I am being courted by the only nephew of the Prime; he is a prospect to be a future Prime. If I married him, I'd be in a position to bend the ear of the Prime," I rasped

As horrible as she was, I'd seen Slate and Quick in battle training. They were the best of the best and I wanted to be the best. The Shadow Breakers could help me be stronger, faster, and more skilled.

"No, Scarlett," Slate said.

Her name on his lips. She shot me the image so fast, I almost gasped —Slate shouting her name as he climaxed.

"What talent do you have?" she asked in an even tone.

"I am an empath. I recently discovered I can, *um*, influence others' emotions as well," I confessed and raised my eyes to her.

She was taking my measure again. "Can you demonstrate? I know what an empath does, but how can you influence someone's emotions? Their will?" she pondered.

I nodded and averted my eyes from Slate.

"Have you used it before?"

I nodded.

"How?"

"I use it to push people away," I said in a squeak and heard the gust of air Slate let out.

"If you can prove it, I will train you. You will compete the first Friday of the new year. Do we have a deal?" she asked, pulling out a piece of vellum.

I nodded. "Demonstrate it?" I asked.

"Brass, do you mind if she uses you?" Cordillera's red lips curled.

"She can use me," Quick offered, and Slate shot him and death stare from behind Lera.

Brass let out a long exhale. "I do not mind."

I angled myself on the couch towards Brass. "Sorry," I said beforehand.

"For what?" he asked, cocking an eyebrow.

I hadn't unleashed the full extent of my abilities before, but if the old hag wanted a show, I'd give her one. I only hoped Brass would forgive me for taking away his will.

"I've only used it to see how people are feeling—*but* I can probably use their feelings to push them one way or the other. I've never tested it." I explained, and Lera made a gesture like, *okay get on with it.*

I licked my lips and raised my eyes to Brass's amber pools. I had exactly one shot to make it work and I had no clue if it would.

Desire...lust...sex...

Brass's lids grew hooded and he licked his plump sculpted lips as he looked at mine. He was fighting it, but it was an uphill battle. I pushed harder.

Passion...hunger...ache...

A low deep moan pulled from his throat before he lunged at me. His hands were everywhere. I'd dropped the manipulations as soon as I saw that it had worked. I had been trying to get him to kiss me again since I knew he wanted to.

But I was in over my head. He wrapped his hand in the hair at the nape of my neck and forced my mouth open, sliding his tongue deep. His body was pressing mine against the side of the couch, his hips pushing into me as he gripped under my thigh.

"*Brass!*" Slate barked.

I was gently trying to push him off. It was not Brass's fault in the least. I'd exploited his emotions and when he'd finally given in, they'd overwhelmed him.

"I'm sorry, Brass," I said, lifting my mouth away from his and trying to pull his hands off me.

His forehead pressed against my shoulder as he breathed heavily against my trussed-up chest. My cheeks heated. It had worked much better than I'd expected. Brass's stubble had scraped at my skin and my lips were swollen from his demanding kisses.

"By the Mother," he breathed.

"Gods. What did you do to him?" Quick whispered.

"Manipulated his emotions. He fought it," I said, hoping to offer Brass a boon.

"It is my turn, right? I bet I could fight it too. We should try and find out," Quick said, still sounding awed.

Slate growled and Brass chuckled and lifted his head to look at me. His pupils were dilated to saucers and his lips were just as swollen as mine. He looked at my lips again. Lingering effects of the manipulation, I was sure.

"You can do this in more ways than tricking men into your bed?" Cordillera asked coolly and Brass pushed away from me to shoot her a look.

"Enough. She passed your little test. You train her willingly or I will do it anyway," he snapped.

Cordillera narrowed her eyes at him then turned back to me. "Done. Brass will train you. Slate, your team may spar with her, but she is under his direction," she said, sliding the vellum over to me.

It was a blood contract. I picked up the blade and pricked my thumb, pressing it to the paper after she'd filled in some of the lines. I was sworn not to reveal them or their hideout so greater families kept their noses out of Cordillera's business. I could deal with that. There wasn't anything about following her explicit instructions, though it did oddly have a stipulation that I was not allowed to have my own room there.

"Understood," Slate said harshly through gritted teeth.

I pushed the contract back across her desk and she picked it up, pinching it between her thumb and index finger lifting it so Slate would take it. He scanned it and I thought I saw a resigned look in his eyes, but it quickly vanished so when he lifted them up to me there was only his smooth regard.

"Brass, would you please see me to the portal gate?" I asked, offering him my hand.

Brass looked at my hand and past me to Slate and Cordillera. His dark honey hand wrapped around mine and he stood, looping my arm through his.

"Of course. I will be back within the hour," he said to no one in particular, but I thought maybe he meant it for Slate.

Once we were outside I rounded on Brass. "I am so very, *very* sorry. I have never used my manipulations to do anything but push people away, not bring them in. I cannot apologize enough. You weren't reading my mind and just doing what I was trying to will you to do to placate your aunt, were you?"

I was mortified. Brass had scoured my mouth with his tongue, and I hadn't needed to look down to see the effect I'd had on the rest of his body.

"All you." His eyes slipped down my face. "I would have trained you against her wishes, but this way will be easier."

Brass was the picture of control, as if what had happened on the couch in Lera's office in front of three other people had never occurred. I told myself my ego wasn't wounded in the least bit; there was no reason for him to still harbor feelings of desire for me after I'd finished manipulating him.

An easy smile spread on his face. We stood in the dark dead end where, only an hour or so ago, he had tackled me into the building's wall. He took a measured step closer so he was inside my personal space bubble, and I struggled with the urge to take a step back so I wouldn't have to crane my neck even in Cherry's super high-heeled boots.

"It is strange to be speaking to you after having watched you for months," he said as his amber eyes roamed over my face.

Brass had followed me and Ash to the portal doors in Valla after the masquerade on my very first day. He had been watching me since then?

That was before I had found out about the Stygians...had Slate known the Stygians were after him since then and not told me?

Brass was looking at my face like he was quenching a thirst. His expression left me feeling self-conscious and I dropped my gaze. His finger lifted my chin back up.

"I am going to kiss you. Not because you want me to, or because you are thinking about it, but because I have wanted to since you danced with my brother at Copper's Ausa Vatni."

My breath caught; that was in January...it was August!

The corner of his mouth quirked scant inches from mine and cinnamon wafted from his breath as he spoke.

"You thought he was handsome," he said matter-of-factly, and I blushed.

Coyote Regn *was* handsome, and intense. Brass seemed to be a mix of Quick and Coyote, not quite the playboy, but not too intense. A better blend had never been made, I'd decided. Brass's lips brushed mine and my lids slid lower. He kissed my upper lip, then the lower and brushed my lips with his again. Butterflies were sent soaring. His kisses were sweet and warm, just like him, and my eyes closed all the way as my lips parted under his.

Somewhere inside me I knew kissing Brass was a bad idea. He was Slate's friend and had been guarding me during times I had no idea he was even about.

Brass was unabashedly caring and genuine and didn't try to hide any facet of himself. His tongue slid into my mouth to find mine like a silky caress. He didn't just kiss me; he made love to my mouth with his tongue. It hinted at the way he would worship a woman's vulnerable body if she should lie beneath him.

I didn't know how long we kissed, but when he drew back my head tried to follow his and I had to take a step forward to prevent myself from losing balance. My eyes opened dreamily to find those lips curled into a knowing smile. I pulled up and looked anywhere but at the man who had given me a detailed insight into the two very different ways he could be in the bedroom.

"Are you sure that wasn't a lingering effect from my manipulation? I wouldn't want to take advantage of you," I breathed.

He chuckled and looped my arm through his as he led me away from Shadow Breaker headquarters. "You chose to try to make me kiss you because you knew it would be simpler than trying to get me to, say, leave the room, or punch Silver." He chuckled again.

He'd read that in my mind. He'd known I was going to try to get him to kiss me and that's why he'd fought it, to see if he could. My mouth opened and closed. I had no idea what to make of my interactions with Brass.

"Try not to overthink. I wanted to kiss you. So I did," Brass said as he walked down the cobbled road.

Could he really be that uncomplicated? My only interactions with men had been endlessly complicated. The only one I'd met lately who *wasn't* was Keen, and he wasn't a human.

He told me more about the Shadow Breakers on our short walk to the portal gate. On a direct route it was only fifteen minutes from head-quarters to the gate. Cordillera had been promoted to Grand Mistress after the previous one had stepped down; she used to be a regular Breaker like Quick and Brass. Slate was one of three captains that led the Breakers under Cordillera. The brothers had met when Slate, Jett, and Steel had been training with Cordillera at Pearl's behest.

I felt my blood boil at the idea of a fourteen-year-old Slate and Cordillera who would have already been a grown woman.

"Not everything is as black and white as it seems," Brass said crypti-cally when he picked up my thoughts.

I sniffed. Seemed clear-cut to me.

"Now that you know Silver and I are guarding you, try not to search us out. We are more effective if whoever would harm you does not know you are being watched," Brass said when we reached the gate.

"Right. I won't do it on purpose. So, when I come to train, do I just look for you at headquarters?" I asked, not sure how it would work.

I didn't have a set schedule, but Ash would have to be worked in somehow. I had never had more doubts about our relationship than I was having that night. How could I commit to Ash when men like Brass were out there? We wouldn't be a power couple like Ash and I were, but I'd be happy.

I gave myself a mental shake; was I honestly thinking about Brass and me as a couple? He'd kissed me exactly three times, and like a creeper, I was mentally scribbling Mrs. Scarlett Regn on my notebooks.

Brass ducked his head and I had the distinct feeling he had muffled a laugh and was hiding a smile. I scowled.

"Yes. I am tuned to your mind now, and I can hear your thoughts at distances. Think about me and I will come to you," he said, raising his head.

The moonlight made his amber eyes glitter.

I nodded. "I can do that. Thanks for defending me tonight, with Cordillera and Styg," I told him, trying not to do anything cliche like fiddle with my keys at my front door.

"You are a good person, Scarlett, with a pure heart. They were both wrong. It is none of my business, but I do not have a choice about what I see in your mind, and if something escalates with Slate..." He paused to make sure he knew I wasn't going to deny anything had happened. I knew better already; Brass and Quick were lie detectors. "You should try to keep it from Cordillera. I do not condone lying but being discreet would be more beneficial to your cause."

"Brass, I have no intention of pursuing anything with Slate," I told him, feeling sure of my words after the night's events.

After tonight, I would start pushing a chair up against my bedroom door so he couldn't sneak into my room for impromptu sleepovers.

"I am not judging. I am only offering a word of advice. Cordillera is territorial. That extends to Slate. Goodnight, Scarlett. Tonight has been...better than I had hoped."

His stubbled jaw brushed my cheek as he planted a kiss on my cheek.

"Goodnight," I waved moronically before I crossed through the portal gate.

The night had not gone at all as I'd thought it would.

BIBLIOGRAPHY

"Among the Multitude" by Walt Whitman

"To a Stranger" by Walt Whitman

"A Woman Waits for Me" by Walt Whitman

"Now" by Robert Browning